THE
DRAGON
PROTECTOR

Book Three of The Dragon Stalker Bloodlines Saga

D.K. Drake

Dream Doers Publishing LLC
North Carolina

Cover designed by Karri Klawiter
Visit her website at www.ArtByKarri.com

Author D.K. Drake
Visit my website at www.AuthorDKDrake.com

Published in the United States of America by Dream Doers Publishing, LLC

Print ISBN-13 978-0-9907463-4-8

FOR MY SISTER MARCY

My childhood roommate and boldest friend

NOVELS BY D.K. DRAKE

The Dragon Stalker Bloodlines Saga

BOOK 1: *The Dragon Collector*
BOOK 2: *The Dragon Hunter*
BOOK 3: *The Dragon Protector*
BOOK 4: ***The Dragon Destroyer (coming soon)***

Get Exclusive Access to More {FREE} Stories Today!

When you become one of my email buddies, you get FREE access to the D.K. Drake starter library that includes the short story "Cops, Robbers...and Dragons?" (This is the story that sparked the idea for the entire Saga!)

You'll also get notified about new books and deals, have a chance to join the Advanced Reader Team, and keep up with my real-life adventures as an author, a runner, and a foster parent.

All you have to do is visit www.AuthorDKDrake.com and sign up to the Insiders mailing list for FREE today.

WHAT ARE DRAGON STALKERS?

Dragon Stalkers live in the Land of Zandador, a place where both dragons and men can live anywhere from 700-1000 years. Four types of dragons roam the Land of Zandador: Midnight Stalkers, Dawn Stalkers, Noon Stalkers, and Dusk Stalkers. They eat once a day and are named for the time of day they prefer to eat.

About three hours before their peak feeding time, their scales change from grey or white to their designated colors. If they are not fed before all their scales turn colors, their appetites become insatiable. They will go on a hunting rampage and enjoy feeding on as many humans as they can find.

The Midnight Stalker's scales change from grey to black as midnight approaches. The largest of all the Stalkers, the Midnight stalker grows up to twenty feet, breathes electric bolts, and lives in mountainous territory. This type of stalker is characterized by pointy wings, impressive strength, and high intelligence. Its weakness is loud noise.

The Noon Stalker's scales change from grey to gold as noon approaches. It can grow up to fourteen feet tall, breathes fire, and lives in the jungle. This type of stalker is characterized by round wings, invisibility, and a light-hearted, humorous nature. It's terrified by ants and ladybugs.

The Dawn Stalkers' scales change from white to rainbow colors of red, orange, pink, and purple as dawn approaches. It grows no taller than ten feet, breathes acid, and lives where waterfalls abound. It has no wings and is characterized by its vanity and ability to teleport. It is terrified of winged insects.

The Dusk Stalker's scales change from white to rainbow colors of pink, purple, blue, and green. It grows no taller than ten feet, breathes poison, and lives in the Forest of Crooked Trees. It also has no wings and is characterized by its sensitivity and speed. It is scared of water.

When man couldn't agree how to coexist with the dragons, four factions developed:

- **The Collectors** believed man should work with dragons and that dragons thrive when given a purpose: to serve and protect man.

- **The Hunters** believed dragons should be enslaved and used as tools to gain power over their fellow man.

- **The Protectors** believed dragons should be free and have no one to look after except themselves, so man should protect the dragons from harm.

- **The Destroyers** believed dragons were dangerous creatures and should be eliminated.

Since these four factions, or Bloodlines, couldn't agree how to govern, they chose to fight it out.

Whoever collected, hunted, protected, or destroyed each of the four dragons first would assume the throne for 100 years. Then, in the last year of the king's reign, another Battle for the Throne would ensue to determine who would rule for the next 100 years.

If no one won the Battle, the current ruler would keep the throne for another century. And if dragons were to become extinct while a ruler was on the throne, he would become the King of Zandador for the rest of his life, and his descendants would rule after him.

A Hunter is now on the throne. King Omri has ruled for nearly 500 years and uses his dragons to control every aspect of the people's lives. With dragons on the verge of extinction, he is set to rule for the next 500 years.

But he lives in constant fear of the Prophecy:

The war between the Bloodlines will divide the nation and cause the people to scatter. Many kings will rise to power, but one who masters the dragons and their scales will remain on the throne for centuries. He will rule with a cruel hand, suppress the will of the people, and seek to annihilate all dragons but his own. If his power remains unchecked, he will expand his rule to the world beyond the portal. Gaining control of that world and its resources will allow him to reign for a thousand more years, bringing death and destruction to those who dare defy him.

All hope is not lost. A young Collector whose eyes shine like emeralds and whose ears can hear the thoughts of any dragon will enter the competition in the final months of a Battle for the Throne year. He will be the only one capable of dethroning the king and must collect all four Stalkers by sunset on the final day of the battle year. If he succeeds, however, collecting the four Stalkers will not be enough to defeat the king.

The dethroned king will use his dragons and loyal subjects to wage a war unlike any Zandador has ever seen. The Collector must therefore unite the four opposing Bloodlines, for only the united front of the four Bloodlines led by the young Collector will be strong enough to win a war against this most powerful of men.

If such a war is fought, the outcome thereof will determine the fate of the dragons once and for all.

YOU ARE NOW ENTERING THE LAND OF ZANDADOR...

PROLOGUE

Those eyes. Those green eyes. It had been dark, and the baby had only opened his eyes for a quick second, but she couldn't stop thinking about the way those emerald eyes seemed to glow.

As Taliya dumped another handful of pebbles at the edge of the cave, she wondered how that baby was doing. She had helped her father and two other men get the baby through the portal five nights ago.

Apparently, the kid was special and would be back looking all grown up to collect dragons and overthrow the mean king. The strange part was that she was going to have to follow him. She could imagine a lot of things, but imagining that little baby as a man who would tell her what to do seemed like a stretch for her seven-year-old mind.

Taliya sat on a moss-covered rock and dangled her feet over the ledge. The sun would be setting in a few hours, but right now it made the waterfall to her left sparkle all the way to the clear lake a hundred feet beneath her. Grass and moss and bright green ferns covered the rocks all around the waterfall, except on the cliff beneath her. Because she wasn't just sitting on a wall of rocks. She was sitting on the portal in South Zandador that led to Earth.

At first, hiding out in a cave above the portal waiting for her father to return seemed like a great idea. She thought she would have a chance to explore the woods and waterfalls all around them, but the man who stayed with her wouldn't let her go anywhere or do anything except practice shooting rocks with a slingshot inside the cave.

He was a boring, serious man who made her work, work, work all day so she would be ready to fling rocks and create a distraction once the portal activated. She wanted to throw the rocks, but he said she was too little to throw them very far.

The worst part was that he was right. She didn't like being tiny and had to stand on her tip toes to pretend like she was three feet fall. Taliya was sure she had stopped growing and was doomed to be this little for the rest of her life.

A crackle broke the silence of the afternoon, and the rock she sat on began to vibrate. "Finally!" She snatched her slingshot from her waistband, scrambled back into the cave, and loaded it with a pebble.

Kneeling on one knee, she hit her first target on the other side of the lake to signal the boring man that the portal had been activated. Then she waited. The three soldiers that patrolled the area would be flying by on okties any minute.

Taliya kept her slingshot loaded and her blue eyes on the sky despite the portal flashing to life under her. No soldiers. No okties. Maybe her father and his dragons could get through before anyone noticed.

The vibrating, mossy rock she stood on began to get hot just as three figures appeared in the sky. The sight of the soldiers made her hands shake, and she suddenly realized it was a very bad idea to have a kid in charge of flinging rocks at grown men.

"Shoot, Taliya!" The boring man shouted at her from the ground. He sure did have a loud mouth for her to be able to hear him when she was up so high. "Shoot as many rocks as you can!"

"Don't rush me, mister," she shouted back. She still didn't know the man's name. He might have told her, but she refused to remember once he told her she would have to stay in the cave and couldn't explore the area. "I have to wait until they get closer."

The soldiers noticed the active portal and began flying straight down to her.

"They're close enough. Shoot!"

"Fine." The hickory handle of the slingshot felt cool in her left hand. That calmed her nerves as she loaded a jagged rock in the stretchy vine and pulled back with her right hand. She squinted and aimed through the Y of the sling at the nose of the soldier in the middle. "Bet you won't be expecting this."

She released the weapon, but her hand wobbled at the last second, and she lost the rock in the waterfall. "Oops. Better try that again."

"Jolt blasters ready," the middle soldier said, pulling a gun from his side. "Stun anything that steps through that portal."

"I'm not gonna let you stun any dragon my father brings here," Taliya mumbled. She loaded her sling, fired. Loaded. Fired. Her first few shots hit the wings of the okties, disrupting the flight pattern of the soldiers. Her barrage of shots after that added to the confusion and forced the soldiers to focus on staying alive rather than pay attention to the portal traffic.

After her sixteenth or seventeenth shot, the glow from the portal vanished, and she heard her father's voice. "Taliya, enough! Get down here. Now!"

"Coming." Taliya shot one last rock in the direction of the flailing soldiers, tucked the slingshot in her waistband, and untied the thick vine tied to a branch near the cave entrance. She'd been waiting to fly out of here since the boring man explained the escape plan.

With a big smile on her face, she wrapped the end of the vine around her waist, gave herself a short running start, and jumped.

She dropped faster than she expected, but that made the fall even more fun. She swayed across the lake, back toward the portal, across the lake, and landed when her father snagged her foot as she swayed back in his direction in front of the now dormant portal.

"Hello, father." Taliya gave him a kiss on his bearded cheek. But when she looked around, she didn't see any dragons. He had taken two eggs with him through the portal and should have brought two baby dragons back with him. "Where are the dragons?"

The boring man cut the vine with his sword. "Get her in the wagon. We have to go before the soldiers recover and can track us."

Her father carried her down the rocky hill to a leaf-covered wagon attached to a red, four-legged beast with a long, blue horn sticking out of its forehead. "That dragon got big fast," Taliya said. "And I didn't know they had horns."

"That's not a dragon," her father said. "That's a unicorn. The dragon is in here."

He pulled back the leaf cover and pointed. "That's a dragon."

A shivering white creature with a long nose and big round black eyes stared at her from the wood floor. "Ksss," it said, wrapping its tail around its small body and oversized claws.

"It's so cute," Taliya exclaimed. "But why aren't there two of them?"

"The other one didn't make it," her father said. "This is the Dawn Stalker. She's going to be your responsibility until the Collector comes back to claim her."

"My responsibility?" Taliya looked at the dragon through widened eyes. "Why? What's her name? How long will it take the Collector to come claim her?"

"Enough with the questions," the boring man said. "We need to leave."

"You'll figure everything out in due time." Taliya's father dropped Taliya in the back with the dragon, and the two men took their seats up front.

As the wagon took off over the bumpy ground, Taliya studied the dragon that was almost as tall as her. "What should I name you?"

"Ksss," the dragon said again.

"That's not much of a name. How about...Kass? Kiss? Kisa?"

The dragon's tail thumped against the floor at the last suggestion.

"Kisa it is, then." She reached out her hand, but the dragon shied away. "That's okay. I don't need to pet you to protect you."

She would keep this dragon safe. No baby with glowing green eyes was going to take her Kisa away from her. Ever.

CHAPTER 1

The Protector's Perspective
(Fifteen Years Later)

The lights from the freshly activated portal that connected the city of Nahat in Keckrick to the city of Japheth in Zandador faded as Taliya wove her way through the crowd searching for Javan. He should have returned by now, and she was hoping he had snuck his way through the portal along with the soldier who had just arrived from Zandador.

She was too short to see the soldier over the heads of the sweaty folks around her, but she could hear his haughty speech to the people of Keckrick. "King Omri is pleased with the super flowers you've been sending, but he wants more. I am here to oversee these valuable shipments and make sure none get left behind."

"Those are my flowers," she muttered between clinched jaws. She had planted them with her grandmother shortly after her arrival with Kisa in Keckrick fifteen years earlier. After her grandmother had died in a sudden volcanic eruption, those fields and fields of humminglo flowers had allowed Taliya to feel connected to her grandmother long after her passing. Now those fields had been decimated because of King Omri's greed.

The thought of her precious flowers sitting in storage shelters waiting to be dissected by his physicians made her blood boil. She wanted to stick every one of his soldiers milling around the city of Nahat with her poison-tipped darts to keep them from taking any more of her humminglos. She started to pull one from her hip pouch when she spotted Javan.

"Javan!" Taliya grabbed Javan's hand and pulled him out of the crowd to a quiet spot under the dock. "What happened in Zandador?"

"Micah hasn't told you yet?"

"No. He said he would make an announcement after he brought Mertzer back. He was looking for you, too. He won't tell us anything without you present. I was worried when I didn't see you return with Micah."

"I got hung up but found someone willing to help me return."

"So what happened? Micah said Omri was willing to negotiate. Is that true?"

"Yes, but things are more complicated than Micah realizes. I need to talk to him before he makes that announcement. Where's Varjiek?"

"I don't know. I haven't seen him."

Javan cocked his head and squinted his eyes. That's the look he got when he was listening to his dragon's thoughts. She envied that ability.

"Varjiek?" Javan ran out from under the dock and looked around. "Where are you?"

The Noon Stalker must have made himself invisible and answered because Javan glanced up to the top of the building attached to the dock they stood beside. Without a goodbye or word of explanation to her, he took off toward the building.

He didn't offer her an invitation, but she followed him anyway.

◊   ◊   ◊

Although it required serious upper body strength, Javan pulled himself onto the roof from the handrail of the dock. He lay in a heap on the hot mud roof and addressed his invisible dragon through strained breaths. "Thanks for the help, buddy."

You didn't need my help traveling to Zandador. You shouldn't need my help to climb on a roof.

"That's why you're upset? Because I went to Zandador without you?"

You are my responsibility. I cannot keep you safe if I do not know where you are.

"I thought you were my responsibility."

Nonsense. I became responsible for you the moment you landed on my back. That's what makes our relationship work. It does not work when you disappear without telling me where you are going.

"Ah. Okay." Javan stood and brushed the dirt off his clothes. Varjiek felt left out. Javan could fix that. "Sorry I took off without you. I would have told you, but you weren't back from eating. I saw an opportunity to follow Micah, and I had to take it at that moment."

Varjiek snorted.

"It's a good thing I went." Javan didn't like arguing with an invisible dragon. He couldn't tell if Varjiek was still upset. Since he wasn't responding, Javan kept talking. "I learned some things I need to tell Micah about. We need to go find him before he finds us."

Too late.

"Too late? What do you mean?"

I mean he is here.

"Javan!"

Javan turned to find Micah yelling for him atop the bridge. He was sitting on Mertzer, his Dusk Stalker, and demanded the hushed attention of everyone in the vicinity. "Javan, stay right there. I have news for you and the people of Keckrick from the King of Zandador!"

Before Javan had a chance to respond, Mertzer sped down the bridge.

◊   ◊   ◊

The speeding Mertzer stole Taliya's attention from the edge of the roof that she couldn't quite reach from her precarious perch atop the rail of the dock. The sleek white Dusk Stalker moved with ease through the parting crowd and delivered his rider to Javan by allowing Micah to jump straight from the dragon's back to the rooftop where Javan stood.

She had had a chance to ride Mertzer with Micah halfway across Keckrick and had gained a new appreciation for the word "fast." Even though the dragon didn't have wings, it felt like he flew over the land, and she was sure his claws spent more time in the air than they did touching the ground.

She just wished she had been there to protect him from Micah's sword back in Zandador. Then Mertzer wouldn't be missing half his tail, and he wouldn't have to live as a slave to Micah the Dragon Hunter for the rest of his life.

"I have spoken with King Omri on your behalf." Micah's voice interrupted her thoughts, and a hush fell over the crowd. She found her own breathing had stopped in anticipation of his next words. Had he been able to convince his father to spare the people of Keckrick?

She started to feel a bit lightheaded from the lack of breathing when he finally announced, "He is pleased with the super flowers!"

Taliya let herself breathe again and jumped down from the railing. That didn't prevent her from keeping her ears tuned to the conversation between Micah and Javan.

"Micah," Javan said, "before you say anything else, we need to talk."

"No," Micah said, keeping his voice low. "I found a way to spare Keckrick. If that is what you truly want, you need go along with whatever I say."

"You don't know the whole story. Your father--"

"My father," Micah said, raising his voice to address the crowd, "has agreed to spare the lives of all of Keckrick!"

That brought wild yells and shrieks of relief from the people in the streets of Nahat. She wanted to dance and celebrate with them until she heard Micah's next sentence spoken quietly to Javan. "He only asks for one life in return."

The sound of a steel blade sliding out of its sheath stole the joy from Taliya's soul. She had grown to trust Micah, and now he was about to kill her Javan!

"No!" Taliya screamed from the dock and climbed back onto the railing. She hadn't been able to protect Mertzer, but she could certainly protect the Dragon Collector. The only problem was that she was still an arm's length shy of the edge of the roof.

If she didn't find a way to grow in the next ten seconds, she would never be able to scramble her way onto the roof in time.

CHAPTER 2

The Bloodlines Unite

Taliya studied the gap between the tips of her fingers and the roof. If she jumped, she was sure she could grab the raised edge and pull herself up the way Javan had. He had made it look easy. Then again, he was a good five inches taller than her.

Silence settled over the crowd. What could they see that she couldn't? Had Javan drawn his stalker swords? Were the two men about to duel? She had to get up there to keep them from killing each other. But how?

"Just go for it, Taliya." At her own prompting, she bent her knees as low as she could from her perch on the railing and vaulted straight up. Her fingers latched onto the wood, but that was as far as she could get. She dangled from the corner, unable to tug herself up or swing her legs high enough to snag the roof and use them to take some of the pressure off her arms.

"Psst. Mertzer. A little help?" Her words sounded soft and strained to her own ears and failed to get Mertzer's attention. She began contemplating the best way to contort her body to cause the least amount of damage upon colliding with the ground when the dragon peeked his head around the building.

"Hey, buddy." Her muscles burned, and her sweaty fingers started to slip. "I know Micah hasn't given you an official order, but---" She lost her grip and braced herself for the inevitable impact with the ground. But the dragon's head broke her fall, and she landed flat on her belly between Mertzer's eyes.

"Good thing you can move quickly." His scales were warmer than she expected them to be. He needed to get out of the city and back under the protective canopy of the rain forest. He would be able to if he was free like all dragons should be.

"Thanks for catching me." She rubbed behind his soft ears to show her appreciation as he lifted her to the roof. She slid down his snout and landed discreetly behind Javan just as Micah was placing his sword in Javan's hands.

"If I kill you, my father wins," Micah said, dropping to his knees and putting his hands behind his back. "That is why you must kill me."

Taliya watched in disbelief as Micah lowered his head and Javan stared at him like a confused statue. When nothing happened, Micah looked up.

"Go ahead," Micah said. "Kill me. Take Mertzer. Win the throne."

Javan stuttered his reply. "I...I don't understand."

Neither did Taliya. What had happened in Zandador that made Micah want to turn on his father and die?

"It's not hard," Micah said. "You need a Dusk Stalker. Mertzer is the last Dusk Stalker alive. The only way you can collect him is if you kill me."

"I get that," Javan said. "What I don't get is why. The deal you made with Omri involved my execution in exchange for letting the people of Keckrick live."

"No one else was in that room. How did you know about that?"

"That's irrelevant. What matters is that I know the real deal. So why are you changing the terms?"

"Because I found out what my father is doing with the humminglo plants."

◊   ◊   ◊

Micah noticed Taliya take a step toward them at the mention of the humminglo plants. Taliya? What was she doing up here? How did she get on the roof, and how long had she been standing there?

"What Omri is doing with the plants changed your mind?" Javan sounded baffled. "So it had nothing to do with the Destroyer?"

"What Destroyer?" The sudden appearance of Taliya already had Micah distracted, so he wasn't sure he heard Javan right. Most of the Destroyer Bloodline had died out centuries before Micah was even born. The few who remained had abandoned Zandador and retreated to Tirza. Why would Javan be talking about a Destroyer?

"Never mind." Javan shook his head, tossed Micah's sword aside, and pulled Micah to his feet. "What's Omri using the humminglo flowers for?"

Micah took a deep breath to regain his focus and explained what he had learned. "When the liquid from inside the web of the flower is consumed, it somehow cuts off a person's ability to think for themselves. My father plans to use this substance to control the Land of Zandador. He won't need an army to enforce his laws, and he won't need dragons to inflict punishment. He'll gain complete and total power over everyone."

"Mind control?" Taliya interrupted and walked over to stand beside Javan. "Are you sure?"

"I wouldn't be willing to die if I wasn't sure," Micah said. "And I am sure my father won't bother destroying the people of Keckrick once he gets his hands on their entire supply of super humminglos. The flowers are more important to him than anything else."

"This doesn't make sense," Javan said. "You like having control over people. You should be trying to harness the power of the humminglos for yourself, not be asking me to usurp your father."

Micah cringed at Javan's assessment of his character. That is who he used to be; it wasn't who he wanted to be anymore. He would sacrifice his own life to prove it. "My father is wrong. People matter. You taught me that."

Determining that Javan would prefer to use his own weapon, Micah drew the stalker sword from the scabbard hanging on Javan's right hip, pointed the tip at his chest, and forced Javan to hold the handle by smothering Javan's hands with his own. "But my father thought I was dead and didn't care. My death should bother him. It will if you kill me and take Mertzer."

Micah could tell by the way Javan's chest heaved up and down that he was considering pushing that sword in a few inches. He needed to. It was the only way Omri could be defeated.

"Don't do it, Javan." Taliya put her hand on Javan's shoulder. "You're not a murderer."

"What other choice do I have?" Javan kept his glowing green eyes glued on Micah's for a long moment before shifting his gaze to Taliya. They seemed to speak a silent language Micah didn't understand, and he knew Javan would never act without Taliya's approval.

"Javan, stop stalling." Tears dripped down Micah's cheeks. He needed this to be over. He needed to die. "Put an end to my agony. Please."

"I will. But not by killing you." Javan yanked his hands away from Micah, put his sword away, and offered his hand to Micah to shake. "Join me. Be part of my team. Fight with me and Taliya to overthrow your father."

◊   ◊   ◊

Javan's words reminded Taliya that she had already agreed to go with him to Zandador. She was not thrilled with the arrangement. She had spent the first seven years of her life in that place and didn't want to return. The only reason she said yes was so she could continue to protect Kisa even though the Dawn Stalker now technically belonged to Javan.

"No." Micah refused Javan's suggestion. "Mertzer can never be a part of your collection as long as I am alive. You need him."

"No. I need you on my side." Javan smiled. "I know of another way to collect a Dusk Stalker."

"There is no other way. You have to--"

"You have to shut up and trust me."

Micah cocked his head and narrowed his eyes. "All right," Micah said after a long pause. "I'll trust you." He stuck out his hand, grasped Javan's, and shook.

"Fantastic." Taliya put both of her hands on top of theirs and lowered her voice as she looked at Javan. "Now that we have this team thing established, let's go somewhere with a little more privacy to discuss how you intend to collect a Dusk Stalker that doesn't exist."

CHAPTER 3

First Team Meeting

That's your plan?" Taliya's stunned words echoed off the walls of a vacant, musty house amidst the ruins in Nahat. A splintered, dusty table propped up on its final leg near the door was the only furniture in the small room. Light streamed in through two windows, one on either side of the door. A torn, motheaten blanket hung from the ceiling in the far corner, separating the kitchen and living space from the bedroom area.

She, Javan, and Micah had sequestered themselves in the abandoned house on the side of the river across from the portal to hear Javan's idea. She always embraced bold, daring adventures, but Javan's plan seemed too risky even for her. "That is ambitious, but I don't think you realize how long it will take to--"

"That's the problem," Micah said, cutting her off. "It will take time. Lots of time. Javan, you know you only have three months left to collect two more dragons, right?"

"That's plenty of time," Javan said. "It took me less than a month to collect my first two. I would already have three if you hadn't gotten in my way."

"How did you get in his way?" Taliya didn't understand the tension between the two guys and wondered about their history.

"I did what I do; I beat him in a sword fight and captured Mertzer." Micah shrugged his cockiness away. "But that doesn't matter anymore. What matters is that Javan has access to a Dusk Stalker right now, the same one I kept him from collecting before."

"No, I don't," Javan said. "Mertzer is yours."

"He doesn't have to be. My offer still stands. Kill me and take him. Then you can focus your attention on collecting a Midnight Stalker for the remainder of the year. It's your best chance at winning the throne."

"No." Javan crossed his arms over his chest and stuck his chin in the air. "That's my easiest chance. My best chance is to do what I've proposed."

"What you've 'proposed' is madness." Micah's dark skin flushed with anger. He stood more than a head above Javan and about three heads higher than her. His solid, muscular frame and long dreadlocks added to the intimidation factor when he turned his attention to her. "Taliya, talk some sense into the boy. Have you ever even activated the portal before?"

"I am perfectly capable of activating the portal." Taliya kept her voice cool, showing she wasn't going to let herself be intimidated by him. What she lacked in height, she made up for with attitude. "I am a Protector, after all. However, I have not yet had an opportunity to use those particular skills."

"That doesn't mean she couldn't do it." Javan put his hands on her shoulders and looked down into her eyes. He was shorter and leaner than Micah, but he was also younger, quicker, and more agile. "You know you want to try. Why else would you have taken that book from Tulkar?"

Javan unnerved her when he stared at her with those unusual emerald eyes. Even after traipsing all through Keckrick with him, she still had a hard time grasping the fact this grown-up guy with his wavy black hair, stubble-covered cheeks, and strong arms was the baby she had helped get through the portal. She had told him about that night, but she hadn't told him she remembered those glowing green eyes he was so sensitive about.

"Well..." Taliya stalled. She did take that book so she could learn how to activate the portal. Only it was more about fulfilling her curiosity than it was about actually putting that knowledge into practice. Many Protectors had died trying to operate the portal. "It is an intriguing idea, but your plan could use a little tweaking."

"Such as? I'm open to suggestions."

She wasn't sure what recommendations to make and was thus relieved when the door opened before she could respond. A tall man with bushy black hair, wide shoulders, and tan skin charged in and slammed the door behind him, causing the final leg of the broken table to collapse. His black uniform and long sword that draped from his hip marked him as one of King Omri's soldiers.

She didn't trust any soldiers. Taliya quietly took a step back and prepared to load her slingshot with one of her sleeping darts.

◊　　◊　　◊

"Hello, Vince." Javan hadn't expected Vince to burst in. The two met briefly for the first time earlier that day. This man was his great-grandfather. The family traitor. The reason his father was banished to the Land of No Return and his mother was imprisoned by the Dark King when she was pregnant with him.

But he was also the one who orchestrated his mother's escape eight months ago and sent her to Earth to find him. Something caused Vince to betray Omri and fight for Javan to win the throne; Javan just wasn't sure what the something was that caused his change of heart.

"What happened up there on that roof?" Vince's deep voice filled the small room, and he focused his hazel eyes on Javan. "One minute you look ready to chop Micah's head off, and the next minute you're shaking his hand and walking over the bridge together like you are best buddies."

"We're not best buddies, but--"

"Why are you befriending a Dragon Hunter?" Vince carried on as if Javan hadn't said a word. "How am I supposed to explain that to the soldiers who witnessed it all? Their crazy speculations are already flying through the ranks. What do you think they are going to tell Omri?"

"They're not going to tell Omri anything because they won't be returning to Zandador," Micah said.

"Whoa, Micah." His ominous tone made Javan nervous. "We can't kill them just because they saw us shake hands."

"I'm not talking about murder," Micah said, rolling his eyes.

"What exactly are you talking about?" Javan asked.

"I'm simply suggesting that we capture the soldiers and give them a new home here in Keckrick. All my father wants are the humminglos. He won't miss a few soldiers."

"That's where you're wrong," Vince said. "He'll order them straight to his throne room and demand to know what transpired here. I'm guessing that whatever happened on that roof between the two of you isn't what Omri expected to happen. When they don't return, he'll send one of his Justice Units to investigate."

"Or the Dragon Destroyer," Javan said.

"The what?" Micah sounded confused.

"When I was in Zandador," Javan said, "I learned that your father hired a Dragon Destroyer to discreetly execute you after you killed me."

CHAPTER 4

Keep Keckrick Safe

W hat?" Javan's words punched Micah in the gut and made the room spin. Of course his father would make sure Micah succeeded in killing Javan. Then he would make sure Micah was as dead as everyone thought he was. That also meant that everyone who saw Micah alive during his brief trip home would also soon be dead. The part that didn't make sense was that a Destroyer existed and that Omri was working with someone from another Bloodline.

"New plan," Micah said, his anger rising. He needed his father to know he no longer controlled him or the people of Keckrick. He also wanted to ensure Keckrick remained safe once Omri got all the flowers they provided. "We strand the soldiers by blowing up the portal here in Nahat as well as the one in Tulkar so that Keckrick is no longer connected to Zandador."

"That's ludicrous," Vince said. "Why would we do that? It would be an act of war, and the people of Keckrick can't defend themselves against Omri's dragons."

"He can't send his dragons if the portals are no longer operational, and he won't risk sending his dragons on land through the desert to attack Keckrick. It's too dangerous. He may send his army because he won't care how many of them die on the trip, but Keckrick can fight off people a lot easier than they can fight dragons."

"You do make some valid points, but I've known you too long to trust anything you say." Vince drew his sword and stuck the tip of it right under Micah's chin. "How do we know you're not pretending to be Javan's friend so you can betray him when the time is convenient for you?"

"I could ask you the same question." Micah fought the urge to defend himself by reaching up to grab the sword that rested in a sheath across his back. Instead, he took a deep breath and calmly carried on the conversation. "You've always demonstrated complete loyalty to my father as his top scalologist, and some of the uses you devised for dragon scales surpassed even my father's cruel imagination.

I'm inclined to believe you're going to report everything you witnessed here today to Omri."

"He wouldn't do that," Javan said, stepping between them and forcing Vince to lower his sword. "He's my great-grandfather, and he's committed to seeing a Collector win the throne."

Micah studied Vince, then Javan. The two did have an uncanny resemblance to one another. "You're telling me my father has had a spy from the Collector Bloodline working for him for centuries and never knew it?"

"He was aware of my heritage," Vince said. "That's why he kept me close, only I wasn't a spy. I was truly devoted to him and wanted to use my talents as a scalologist to serve in his army. Until about eight months ago, anyway."

Now Micah was curious. "What changed eight months ago?"

Vince shook him off. "That would take too long to explain, and my soldiers will get suspicious if I don't return soon. You're the one I'm concerned about. I have never known you to be on any side except your own."

"This time he's on mine," Javan said. "I trust him as much as I trust you, and I think we need to listen to him about the portals."

"Wrong," Taliya said, stepping out of the shadows. "Destroying the portals isn't necessary. All we need to do is handicap them, make it impossible for any other portal to link to them unless and until we want to use them."

"Handicap them?" Micah let his skepticism at such a wimpy idea drown his every word. "That is absurd. Destroying them is the best, safest option."

"It's not very strategic," Taliya said, fighting back. "What if Javan does win the throne and gains control of Zandador? If we destroy the portals, Keckrick will be cut off from Zandador and the rest of the Great Rift forever. It's too final. I won't allow it."

"You won't 'allow' it?" Why did this girl think she had any kind of power?

"I won't either," Vince said. "The feisty little lady is right. We can easily handicap the portal with an electrified scale taken off a Dawn Stalker older than seven. It will send a charge through the portal that makes the portal inoperable as long as the scale is in the slot. The hard part is taking the scale off the dragon."

"I've taken a scale from Varjiek before," Javan said. "I know he'll comply."

"No!" Taliya and Vince shouted in unison, then Taliya explained. "The Zandadorian portals only work when you put seven-year Dawn scales in the slots. If you put any scale other than a Dawn scale in one of the slots, it shuts the portal down for good. That's the reason we no longer have access to Xyies, the northernmost region of the Great Rift."

Micah took a mental note of this new information. Perhaps he could get a scale from Mertzer and shut down the portal with a Dusk scale before Javan could return with a scale from Kisa.

"Okay, then," Javan said. "I'll get scales from Kisa, and we'll use them to make the Keckrick portals unusable. Vince, we need you on the inside, though, so you'll need to return to Zandador alone while the portal still works."

"I'm not going anywhere until you tell me how you plan to go about collecting your final two dragons," Vince said. "The fate of Zandador is in your hands, and I need to know that you know what you are doing as a Collector to ensure you win the Battle of the Throne."

Micah forgot about his plot to break the portal permanently and waited for the show. He wasn't sure how Vince would react to Javan's crazy plan, but he was sure it would be entertaining.

CHAPTER 5

Javan's Grand Plan

"Right. The plan." Javan rubbed his sweaty palms on his pants. The sweat made him feel nervous, and he needed to sound confident.

"It's simple," Javan said. "We find a Dusk Stalker egg, take it through the portal to Earth, wait for it to hatch, then bring it back to Zandador. While it's growing big enough for me to ride, we head to Midnight Territory to collect the Midnight Stalker. Done and done."

"That is not simple!" Vince's shriek made Javan flinch. "To begin with, Midnight Stalkers are the toughest dragons to collect and live in the most difficult territory to get to and navigate. You can't stroll up there, snap your fingers, and ride the first dragon that appears."

"Point taken," Javan said, his mind churning. He needed a counterargument. Quickly. "So we take a Midnight egg with us as well. Baby dragons are a lot easier to collect than full grown dragons who are centuries old. At least I think so. I've never actually seen a baby dragon."

"I have," Taliya said. "They are adorable. Until they get big enough to eat you, which doesn't take long. They grow fast."

"You're overlooking the second problem," Vince said. "Dragon eggs are not easy to find. Protectors are very good at protecting their locations. Trying to locate the Dusk egg will be challenging enough. If you do happen to find it, do you think you'll be able to keep it safe while traipsing through the rough terrain in Midnight Territory and trying not to get eaten by Ayzyd, the Midnight Stalker who devours humans for fun?"

"I guess that could be problematic." Javan surrendered to Vince's logic but held his ground when it came to his original plan. "We'll just focus on the Dusk egg for now."

"Except you're forgetting the third thing: getting through the portal is impossible. It's constantly guarded by dozens of soldiers, plus you have to have a Protector to activate it for you."

"That's me," Taliya said, raising her hand. Strands of her long, dark hair had escaped from its braid and brushed the skin of her dark brown face. Her bright blue eyes sparkled with pride when she introduced herself. "I'm Taliya, Dragon Protector."

"A Protector?" Vince cocked his head. "That does make a difference. I assume then that you know where to find dragon eggs and have experience activating the portal."

"Those assumptions may not be entirely accurate," Taliya said, tucking some of those stray strands of hair behind her ear. "However, I do know where to find someone who knows where to find Dusk Stalker eggs, and I have the Protector's book to teach me about activating the portal."

"Wonderful. You know someone who knows something, and you have a book." Vince rolled his eyes, reminding Javan of his grandfather Ravier. No big surprise. Vince was Ravier's father, and the two men evidently shared the same no-nonsense, no-fun attitude. "Javan, your plan is foolish."

"Thank you for agreeing with me," Micah said. "Now we can get back to my plan."

"No, we can't." Javan wasn't about to let these guys dictate how he would go about collecting the rest of his dragons. "We're going to find a Dusk Stalker egg. We're going to take it through the portal. We're going to bring it back to Zandador after it hatches, and that is that. Since that is what we are going to do, our mission is to work together to figure out how to make it all happen. Understood?"

Micah sighed. "Fine."

Taliya smiled. "Count me in."

"Vince?"

Vince nodded, put his sword away, and slapped Javan on the back. "Decisiveness. I like it. I don't like your plan, but I like your confidence. I won't be able to help much in order to maintain my cover, but I can put you in touch with Ravier."

"You can?" Javan's eyes widened. "You know where he is? Is he safe? What about my grandmother Hannah? And my mother Esmeralda?" He hadn't had any contact with them since he left Gri weeks ago. If they were able to reconnect with his mother, she could teach Taliya how to operate the portal.

"Return to Japheth in three days to put your Dawn Stalker's scale on the column in Stalker Square. I'll make sure Ravier is there to meet you."

"You didn't answer my questions." Javan had a sick feeling in his stomach. Ravier and Esmeralda left to search for Hannah after Gri was destroyed. Vince's elusiveness made Javan think their search had not ended well. "Is my family safe?"

"Just be in Stalker Square in three days." With that, Vince spun around and marched to the door. Before he left, he turned and said, "Be ready to implement that invisibility trick you showed me in the castle. It will be hard for Omri to kill you if he can't see you."

The door closed behind him, filling the room with a heavy silence.

CHAPTER 6

Finalizing Details

Taliya watched the color drain from Javan's face. He looked like he wanted to be alone to mourn the implied loss of his mother and grandmother, but she had too many questions she needed answered. Micah, however, spoke up before she did.

"You have an invisibility trick? How is that possible?"

"That's irrelevant right now." Taliya knew Javan could make himself invisible by inserting a scale from his Noon Stalker into the triangle-shaped slot between the blade and handle of his stalker sword, but Micah wasn't aware of that ability. This was not the time to share such stories. "What's relevant is discussing this Ravier person. Why do we need him? The smaller our team, the faster we can move. We'll be fine with just the three of us."

"Being fast won't do us much good against the army of soldiers guarding the portal to Earth," Javan said, the color returning to his cheeks. "That's why we need Ravier. He knows how to get people safely through the portal and back."

"Oh." Taliya couldn't argue with Javan's logic. "I guess that would be helpful considering getting through the portal is an important part of our plan."

"Getting to him will be a problem, though," Micah said. "We have to get to Japheth, and there is a dangerous desert between us and the city."

"The desert isn't a problem," Taliya said. "We can skip right over it."

"No, we can't," Javan said, shaking his head. "We'll be disabling the portal after we send the crew of the Iria to Tulkar to disable that portal."

"Are you forgetting about Kisa? She's this Dawn Stalker you went to a lot of trouble to collect. Do I need to remind you what power Dawn Stalkers possess?"

"Right!" Javan slapped his forehead. "They can teleport to places they have been before."

"Exactly. She's been to southwest Zandador where the southern portal that leads to Earth is located. We can have her take us all there."

"That's also where half of Omri's army is stationed," Micah said. "That entire area will be infested with soldiers. Despite the fact that we have three dragons, we're not prepared to fight Omri's army."

"We better get prepared," Taliya shot back, "because that's the only way we can get to Zandador in time to meet Ravier in Japheth."

"Or," Javan said, tapping his finger on his chin, "we send you two and the dragons through to the portal near Dusk Territory. Kisa can come back for me once I disable the portal here."

"That could work." Taliya nodded her approval. "And it will get us a lot closer to both my hometown of Oer and the capital city of Japheth."

"It'll be safer, too," Micah added. "Omri has no need to station any of his soldiers on the east coast in Dusk or Noon Territory because Javan has no reason to be in those areas of Zandador."

"Sounds like a solid plan," Javan said, walking to the door. "Micah, you stay here and work with Lydia, Cyr, and the Iria crew on the best way to capture the soldiers; just don't make any moves till we get back. Taliya, you come with me. Kisa may be more willing to give up some of her scales if you can explain to her why we need them."

"Excellent." Taliya clapped her hands to break up the meeting. "Chit-chat time is over. Let's get to the action!"

Taliya skipped through the door ahead of Javan, excited about the adventure that awaited her. She wasn't elated about returning to the Land of Zandador and facing her father after fifteen years, but she did like the idea of hunting for dragon eggs and visiting Earth.

She had read much about that strange dimension beyond the portal and was eager to explore that unfamiliar territory.

CHAPTER 7

Snags in the Plan

"Do you see her?" Javan leaned to the left while holding onto Varjiek's neck as they coasted over the walls of Nahat. Exchanging the sight of battered houses and broken buildings for the colorful trees, plants, and flowers of the rain forest allowed him to relax and drink in the energizing air. The trick now was finding Kisa somewhere amidst the foliage.

"Not yet," Taliya said from behind him. "Where did you instruct her to go?"

"I told her to find a good hiding spot outside the city gates and wait for me to come get her."

"Have Varjiek fly over the river. She's bound to be near the water."

"Good point." That dragon did like to look at her reflection and keep her scales ridiculously clean. Her constant fixation with bathing had driven him nuts as he rode her across the western half of Keckrick on the way to Nahat.

I found her. That was all the warning Varjiek offered before taking a sharp dive, skimming the water of the river, and landing in a wide clearing edged by a clump of berry bushes to the right. He noticed Kisa laying in the tall grass licking her tail ahead of them, but the sight of the fist-size, violet berries stole his attention and made Javan's stomach rumble. The rumbling reminded him that he hadn't eaten a thing since dinner the previous night. He had been too nervous to eat breakfast and too busy to find food at lunchtime.

"These look delicious." Javan slid down Varjiek's leg and tugged a berry loose from the nearest plant. The sweet grape-like aroma caused his mouth to water while the soft outer shell felt squishy in his hand. He licked his lips in anticipation of taking that first delightful bite. Only Taliya knocked the berry out of his hand before he could sink his teeth into it. "Rude! What did you do that for?"

"It's going to be hard for you to collect any more dragons if you're dead."

Javan swallowed at the implication. "You mean that berry is poisonous?"

"You would have been dead before you finished chewing."

"Oh." He looked down at the splattered berry on the ground and no longer felt hungry. "Thanks for the assist."

"No problem. Now good luck getting Kisa to give up her scales. I doubt I'll be able to help much with that." Taliya patted Javan on the back, crossed her arms, and leaned against Varjiek's side.

You want me to what? Kisa jerked her head up and stared at Javan with her round, trusting dark eyes.

"Hey, Kisa." Javan figured the dragon might respond best if he started her off with a compliment. He slowly walked toward her and said, "Your scales are looking immaculately white and stunningly clean today."

Varjiek glared at Javan. *You've never said anything that nice about my scales.*

Of course he hasn't, you Noon Stalker. Yours are grey and always look dirty. Mine are as white as white can be and sparkle in the sun. They won't be this clean for long, though. She hung her proud head. *A storm is coming. The wind and rain will cover my scales with dirt and debris.*

"We can get out of here before the storm comes," Javan said. "I just need one small favor first."

Sure! Anything to stay clean.

"Well, in order to disable the portals and keep the people of Keckrick safe, we kind of need your help. You don't have to do anything, and it probably won't hurt too much. It's just a little--"

"Goodness man, just be blunt." Taliya threw her hands in the air. "Javan needs to rip three scales off of you."

Rip? My? Scales? Off? Not today. Not ever! Kisa doused the bushes behind her with an enraged stream of acid. The leaves and berries withered as Kisa vanished.

"Umm...where did she go?"

"She teleports when she gets mad. Guess we have to wait for her to calm down and return."

Dawn Stalkers, Varjiek said with a sigh as he nestled into the grass and closed his eyes. *They are unnecessarily dramatic.*

"I think Varjiek has the right idea." Taliya snuggled against Varjiek's body in the shade created by his hind leg. "This is a fabulous time for a nap."

"A nap? We can't sleep. We need to go find Kisa!"

Taliya didn't respond. Neither did Varjiek. In the silence, Javan's head began to throb. How was he supposed to follow through with any of his plans if he had a high-maintenance, uncooperative, teleporting dragon in his collection?

◊　　◊　　◊

Micah watched Varjiek fly away with Javan and Taliya, then sat down on the stone steps of the porch to think. His head had been spinning since he had learned how his father intended to use the humminglos to control the people of Zandador, and that spinning only got worse once he learned his own father wanted him dead.

Ironically, he had been ready to die, but his death would have been on his terms and for a worthy cause. Now with every breath he took, he grew more and more determined to live.

How would he live, though? Did he really want to follow orders and fight alongside the Collector? Wouldn't he be better off fighting by himself to bring his father down? He could still be *on* Javan's side; he just didn't have to be *by* Javan's side.

If Micah worked on his own, he could move with speed and precision. He wouldn't have to bother debating which plan was best and could act on his decisions immediately, decisions like destroying the portal.

Mertzer was wandering among the ruins near the house. One sharp whistle would bring the dragon to him, and one command would force the dragon to surrender one of his scales. Micah still had enough sway with the soldiers to walk by them without arousing suspicion. He could have Mertzer's scale in one of the portal slots before anyone realized what he had done.

"My way is best," Micah said, mumbling to himself. "Forget the team. I'm going to take care of the portal, then ride back to Zandador on Mertzer. I'm not waiting for any Destroyer to find me. I'll find him first."

Micah stuck his pinkies in the corners of his mouth and prepared to whistle for his dragon, but activity on the bridge caught his eye. Lydia, a Chief from Lower Keckrick, and Cyr, the Captain of the Iria, were halfway down the bridge walking towards him. Lydia pointed at him while Cyr waved.

He lifted his hand to wave back at the same moment a soldier shot both of them from behind with a Jolt Blast.

CHAPTER 8

Micah's Choice

By the time Micah reached his unconscious friends, the soldier had already tied Cyr's hands behind his back and was in the process of tying Lydia's hands. Micah wasn't sure whether he should praise the guy for his efficiency or berate him for shooting his friends.

He cleared his throat and opted for a little of both. "Nice work, soldier. What's your name?"

The man glanced up, resumed his tying, then jumped to his feet a second later holding his Jolt Blast. "You're Micah."

"Yes. I am aware of that. I want to know who you are."

"Ramsey. I'm, umm, Ramsey."

"Why did you shoot these people, Ramsey?"

"They tried to cross the bridge. People aren't allowed to cross the bridge. Unless it's you. You can do whatever you want."

"Of course I can." Micah found his characteristic cockiness comforting yet obnoxious. No wonder he never had any friends until he boarded the Iria and learned how to be part of a team. Although it irritated him to listen to himself, he remained in the cocky mode Ramsey expected. "I can also get you to do whatever I want."

"Yes, sir. What can I do for you, sir?"

"Drop your Jolt Blast, untie this man, and bring him to me."

"Right away, sir." The weapon clanged against the wooden bridge, and Ramsey quickly cut through the ropes on Cyr's wrists. "Where am I taking him? Back to the portal to the castle's dungeon?"

"No. We're not going back to Zandador just yet." Micah picked up the Jolt Blast with one hand, slung Lydia over his shoulder with the other, and used the weapon that looked like a handheld crossbow to point to the house he had come from. "Bring him to the second house on the left. I'll wait for you there."

While the man struggled to lift Cyr, Micah marched to the house, gently placed Lydia on the dusty cot, and waited for the soldier. As soon as Ramsey dragged Cyr inside, he turned to Micah for further instructions. "What now?"

"Now?" Indecision paralyzed Micah. He could jolt Ramsey and escape, or he could jolt Ramsey and stay to explain Javan's plan to Cyr and Lydia once they recovered from the electric shock of the blast. Either way, Ramsey needed to be zapped. "Now I shoot you."

Micah pulled the steel bow string back, clicked it into place, and engaged the trigger. A spark of electricity flashed through the shaft made of Midnight Stalker scales, and the string that scraped along the top helped create a lightning bolt that shot straight into Ramsey's right shoulder. He jerked and twitched his way to the floor.

Lydia began to stir. If Micah was going to go rogue, this was his only chance. He had to leave before she woke up. Why weren't his feet listening to his head?

"What did that man shoot me with?" Lydia sat up, shaking her head and rubbing her arms. "My blood feels like it's on fire beneath my skin."

"It's called a Jolt Blast," Micah said. "It stings for a bit at the setting he shot you with, but you'll be completely recovered in an hour or so."

"Fantastic." Lydia stood, wobbled, and regained her balance by leaning against the wall. "Where are Javan and Taliya?"

Micah looked at the door, then back at the short-haired warrior struggling to stand. In that instant, he made his decision. "You might want to sit down for this." He stepped over Ramsey and helped Lydia resume her seat on the cot. "They're working on a plan to keep Keckrick safe, and we're going to need your help to execute it."

CHAPTER 9

How to Negotiate with a Dawn Stalker

The gentle breeze upgraded itself to a moderate rustle, bringing with it the distinct smell of rain that was bound to pour from the darkening sky at any time. The prospect of getting wet didn't bother Javan. What bothered him was the fact that one of his dragons had disappeared while the other snoozed alongside Taliya.

How could Varjiek and Taliya rest when there was so much to do and so much on the line? He used the previous half hour of his life wearing a path in the grass while attempting to contrive a contingency plan for every aspect of his main plan that could go wrong.

What if they couldn't find a Dusk egg? What if they did find the egg but Taliya couldn't open the portal? What if the egg didn't hatch once they got it to Earth? He didn't yet have solutions to those potential problems, but he did think he could convince Kisa to give him some of her scales to set the action in motion...if she ever returned.

"I have a solution for that problem, too," Javan mumbled as he marched over to Varjiek. The dragon's head rested peacefully on the ground, and Javan stood on his tip toes to yell up into the dragon's ear. "Wake up, Varjiek. Time to fly."

The startled dragon jerked his wings up and stood, sending Taliya rolling under his tail. *Fly? Who said something about flying? Doesn't matter. I'm ready. Let's go. Where are we going? It's not the desert, is it? I can't fly over the desert.*

Javan ignored Varjiek and rushed over to Taliya. "Are you okay?"

"I'm fine." Taliya rolled her head from side to side as she took Javan's hand to help her crawl out from under the dragon's tail. "That was a brutal way to wake up."

"Sorry. I guess I should have known better than to disturb a sleeping dragon when a person was sleeping right beside him."

"I'm glad I could help you learn that lesson." Taliya flashed him a smile and looked around. "Did Kisa come back?"

"No. I decided we're going to go find her."

We won't have to go far.

◊   ◊   ◊

Taliya noticed Kisa before Javan did. The dragon was standing just upriver from them on the other side of the berry bushes staring at herself in the water. Sadness filled the dragon's eyes, and Taliya knew it was because Kisa couldn't stand the thought of losing any of her scales. How could Taliya protect the dragon's pride and get her to willingly surrender the scales they needed for the portal?

"I see her." Javan's irritated tone cut through Taliya's thoughts. "She better stay put until we can get to her." He started to stomp his way through the bushes, but Taliya grabbed his wrist before he got more than two steps in.

"Javan, wait." If he approached Kisa with that attitude, he was sure to spook her into teleporting again. "You're the one who needs to stay put. Just give me a minute. Let me talk to her alone first."

He sighed, nodded, and backtracked out of the bushes. "If that's what it will take to get her to give up her scales, go for it."

"Thank you." Taliya gave his wrist a gentle squeeze and wove her way under and around the branches, leaves, and juicy violet berries of the bushes. When she emerged from the patch of bushes five minutes and two spider kills later, she found herself freshly in awe of the white dragon in front of her. Kisa wasn't as massive as Varjiek, but she still made Taliya feel like she was an ant approaching an elephant.

Despite her insignificant size in relation to the dragon, Taliya knew she could convince Kisa to do whatever she wanted. The trick was to stroke the dragon's ego first. "Hey, girl. Looking good."

Kisa swiveled her neck and focused her gaze on Taliya.

"You know, your scales do more than look fantastic on you. They're also quite powerful." Kisa's ears perked up, and she moved her head slightly closer to Taliya. "They are the only things that can properly disable the portal and keep all of Keckrick safe from King Omri's dragons. That will make you a great heroine."

The dragon stood a little taller, and the pride in her eyes began to overtake the sadness. Confident that she had Kisa's attention, Taliya kept schmoozing.

"Think about it. A few days ago, no one knew you existed. Now you can forevermore be known as The Dragon Who Saved Keckrick. The best part is that no one will be able to see your missing scales."

Kisa looked away at the mention of missing scales. Taliya had to talk fast to keep the dragon interested. "Giving up a few scales is a tiny price to pray for the glory you'll receive. Plus, we'll make it as easy on you as possible by taking one scale from the underside of each of your legs. You'll still be a magnificent creature, and you may even gain the ability to run faster without the weight of those scales holding you back. In return, Javan will let you return to your cave for a bit so you can hide from the storm that will soon be blowing through here."

"I will?"

The sound of Javan's voice above her startled Taliya. She looked up to see him jump out of the sky and land beside her. "Javan!" she said, punching his forearm. "You can't be hovering around on your invisible dragon and dropping in to private conversations like that. It's rude!"

Instead of apologizing, he rubbed his arm and smiled. "I gave you the minute you requested."

"Just for surprising me," Taliya said, trying to think of some way to shock Javan the way he startled her, "you have to let me teleport back with Kisa."

His smile vanished. "What? Why?"

That seemed to hit a nerve. Good. Maybe he wouldn't pull anymore appearing acts on her after this. "You've asked me to leave my home and everything I know to go with you. And I'm in. I'd be a lot happier about it if I had a little bit of time to gather a few things to take with me that weren't destroyed when the white winds blew my house apart."

"Guess that makes sense." Javan turned to Kisa. "You promise you'll come back?" He must have gotten an acceptable answer because he then turned to her. "You promise you'll both come back?"

"My home no longer exists, and my dragon is with you. I have no reason to stay in Keckrick."

"Then it's settled. Kisa lets us take her scales, and you both get to take a short trip back to Fralick."

"Perfect." Having gotten what she wanted from both Javan and Kisa, she linked her arm with Javan's. Kisa may have agreed to give up her scales, but Taliya still wasn't about to get too near the acid-breathing dragon without the Collector as close to her as possible. "Let's get those precious scales."

CHAPTER 10

Home Again

"That scale right there." Taliya stood under Kisa's wide chest next to Javan and pointed to a scale just above Kisa's right front leg. "That's the one we should take first. I can reach it if you let me get on your shoulders."

"Why would we do that when we can take a scale from the bottom half of her leg without anybody having to get on anybody else's shoulders?"

Taliya rolled her eyes. Javan clearly did not understand how much appearance mattered to Dawn Stalkers. "If you want to keep Kisa happy, you have to take the scales from places she won't be able to notice. If you do anything to mar her reflection—like taking scales from her legs—she won't be able to function, and you'll have a sullen, useless dragon in your collection."

Javan leaned over and whispered in Taliya's ear. "Haven't you ever explained to her that beauty comes from within? This obsession with her looks isn't healthy."

Taliya whispered back. "My job has been to protect her, not teach her human lessons of morality. But if you think now is a good time to tell her how wrong she is to be so vain, go for it."

They locked eyes for a moment, then Javan shook his head. "Fine. We'll do this your way." He walked over to the dragon's front right leg and lowered himself into a squat. "Get on."

"Smart man." Taliya dashed to Javan and draped her legs over his shoulders. He slowly wobbled to a standing position, and she reached up to take the scale she had pointed out. Unfortunately, she couldn't quite reach it. "Hold still."

While holding on to Javan's hair, Taliya rearranged her feet, putting one at a time onto Javan's shoulders.

Javan swayed beneath her. "What are you doing?"

"Getting the scale I want." Taliya let go of his hair and walked her hands up the side of the dragon's leg as she stood. "Standing is the only way I can reach high enough."

Taliya felt Javan's wrists on her ankles as she extended her entire body to reach the designated scale. When she finally wrapped her hands around the cool, smooth scale, she began to change her mind. How could she pull it knowing it would cause Kisa pain?

"I'm not sure I can do this."

"Why not?"

"I don't want to hurt Kisa."

"She'll be okay." Javan's voice sounded strained. "It's for the good of Keckrick. Now yank it before I lose my balance and drop you!"

Taliya closed her eyes, turned her head away, and slowly began to inch the scale away from Kisa's body.

◊ ◊ ◊

Kisa stomped her front leg. *Has she gotten my scale off yet? I need this torture to be over!*

"What is taking so long?" Javan listened to Kisa as he kept his eyes locked on the third claw of the dragon's front foot to maintain his balance. His knees felt ready to buckle under Taliya's weight. He needed to speed the process along for his sake as well as for Kisa's. "You should have been able to remove a dozen scales by now."

"I'm not going to apologize for being gentle."

"You're being too gentle. Just rip it off. Kisa will be fine."

"You're being too brutal. I'm sure Kisa appreciates my approach."

"Actually, she's quite ready for you to be done."

"She is?"

"Yes. She said she wants the torture to be over."

"Why didn't you say so sooner?"

Kisa's leg flinched a second later, then Taliya said, "Quick. Walk me to the back leg."

Javan was about to tell her to get down and walk on her own two feet, but he felt her weight shift forward. To prevent a fall, he had to move with her. He barely had time to stabilize beside Kisa's back right leg when he saw the dragon's leg jerk and heard Taliya announce, "Next!"

Once again, she swung her momentum forward, this time toward Kisa's back left leg. "Whoa!" Javan tightened his grip on Taliya's ankles and sped up to prevent her from toppling forward. "Not so fast."

"You're the one who told me to speed up."

"I meant be faster about ripping the scales off, not scurrying from leg to leg."

"That's not what I heard." Taliya paused, dug her toes into Javan's shoulders, and grunted. "Got it."

"Fantastic." Javan sighed and began to bend his knees so Taliya could get off.

"What are you doing? Stand up and take me to the other front leg. We still have one more scale to get."

"Why?" Javan straightened his legs and stared at a piece of grass to help him restabilize. "We only need three scales: two for the portals and one for the column in Stalker Square."

"And one to make everything even."

"Seriously?"

Kisa snorted. *I can't walk around knowing an odd number of scales was removed from my body. I'd never be able to face the world again. Make her take the last one.*

"I bet Kisa will tell you she wants the extra one removed."

"She just did." Javan carried Taliya to the final front leg, grimaced as her right foot dug into his neck, and watched for Kisa's involuntary jerk reaction that signaled the scale had been removed. Once he saw her leg shiver, he said to Taliya, "Sit back down on my shoulders, and I'll lower you to the ground."

"No need." Taliya leapt off Javan's shoulders, spun around in the air, and landed facing Javan. "Look at these beautiful scales." She untucked them from her waistband one by one and stacked them in the palm of Javan's hand.

The bottom scale seemed to vibrate in his hand while he could see his reflection in the smooth surface of the whiter than snow top scale. "Stunning, Kisa. Your scales are stunning."

Yes, I know. I work hard to keep them that way.

"We should probably go," Taliya said. "The storm will be starting soon."

"All right. I'll wait for you here. But you need to be back in an hour whether the storm is over or not."

"Deal." Taliya nodded, checked her pocket time piece, and put her hand on Kisa's leg.

We'll be back, Kisa said. Before Javan could say another word, both Kisa and Taliya vanished as the downpour began.

Javan sprinted toward the trees to find cover when Varjiek swooped down, blocked Javan's path, and spread out his wing. *I'm not scared of a little rain. Hide here, young Collector.*

"Thanks." Javan jumped on top of Varjiek's back left foot and wiped his wet hair away from his face. Varjiek let his extended wing rest on the ground, providing a cozy shelter for Javan. He rested his head against the dragon's body, closed his eyes, and listened to the soothing pitter patter of the rain drumming on the wing above him.

With nothing to do except worry that Kisa and Taliya would never return, Javan allowed sleep to chase his worries away.

◇　◇　◇

Taliya's body tingled from head to toe. She wasn't sure if that was due to the teleportation or to exchanging the humid, stuffy air by the river for the cool, clear air of Kisa's cave. Whatever the reason, the tingling dissipated after a few deep breaths.

Kisa didn't appear to be bothered by the sudden change in location. Her focus seemed to be on her reflection in the shimmering rock walls of the cave.

"See," Taliya said, walking to the nearest wall and pointing at Kisa's image, "you look as amazing as always. Even you can't tell any of your scales are missing."

Kisa studied her reflection from all possible angles before looking at Taliya and nodding her agreement.

"Now that you see you are just fine, can you take me to my home? I want to see what's left of it and salvage what I can."

Kisa nodded and reached out her leg. As soon as Taliya touched it, her body tingled again as it teleported across the forest to the tree that once held her home.

CHAPTER 11

Javan's Discovery

A growl jerked Javan out of his sound sleep. He sat up and instinctively drew his swords. That's when he realized the rain was no longer falling and the growling was coming from his stomach. "I need food."

He put his swords away and crawled out from under Varjiek's wing. The sun had returned with a vengeance, having already dried the grass and plants and causing drops of sweat to form on Javan's forehead. He wiped the sweat off his face and tapped Varjiek's wing. "Hey, V. Thanks for the shelter."

Good. You are awake. Varjiek shook out his wing and folded it against his body. *My wing was growing stiff.*

"Have Kisa and Taliya returned yet?"

Not that I am aware.

Javan checked the time: 4:11pm. "It's been nearly an hour. They should be back soon." His stomach grumbled again, reminding him he needed to eat. "Do you see anything around here that is edible?"

No, but I did find a patch of blackberries when I was hunting for my meal earlier today. I can take you there.

"Can you go get them and bring them to me? I need to make sure I'm here when Kisa returns."

Sure. I need to stretch my wings anyway. Varjiek extended his wings and lifted himself in the air. *If they aren't back by the time I return, I'll fly you to Fralick.*

"Thanks."

Varjiek nodded his head and flew north.

Javan suddenly found himself alone in the middle of the rain forest. No Taliya. No Micah. No dragons. Just him amid the chirps and howls and hisses of the animals he couldn't see all around him. "This is rather unsettling."

He drew the stalker sword hanging on his right hip with his left hand, knowing he was now invisible thanks to Varjiek's scale in the triangular space between the handle and the steel blade that was a bright golden yellow on one side and a dark midnight black on the other side.

"Hmmm." Javan studied the scale. If it made him invisible, would Kisa's scale give him the ability to teleport? "That would be so cool!"

Javan retrieved one of Kisa's scales from between his belt and his back. He switched it with Varjiek's scale in the sword. He wrapped his fingers around the handle, closed his eyes, and pictured Taliya's house. After a few seconds, he opened his eyes.

"Oh well." He hadn't moved an inch. The river still flowed in front of him, and the poison berry bushes still dangled beside him. "That's disappointing."

He swapped the scales back and resheathed his sword. As he did so, the sun bounced off the golden side of the blade, temporarily blinding him. And giving him an idea. "I wonder..."

Javan drew both swords and studied the blades. The golden/black blade represented the Noon and Midnight Stalkers, and he became invisible when Varjiek's scale was inserted between the blade and handle of the Noon Stalker side. The blade on his other sword was a beautiful mix of colors: red, orange, pink, and purple for the Dawn Stalker on one side and pink, purple, blue, and green for the Dusk Stalker on the flip side.

He assumed they were called Stalker Swords because of the colors of the blades, but what if that wasn't the full meaning? What if they allowed him to take on the same abilities of Dragon Stalkers if he had a scale from each Stalker to insert in the triangular gap just under the blade?

"That's why I can become invisible when holding the sword with V's scale in it, and that's why Kisa's scale didn't work with that sword. I bet I'll be able to teleport if I put her scale in the Dawn side of the blade of the other sword."

He once again put the golden/black blade away and recovered one of Kisa's scales. He took in a deep breath as he inserted Kisa's scale under the swirls of the red, orange, pink, and purple blade.

He kept a tight grip on the handle with his right hand, closed his eyes, and pictured Taliya's face.

◊   ◊   ◊

Taliya spent an hour searching the perimeter of the treehouse she had called home for the last eight years. All she found was half of a book cover, a fork, and a handful of feathers from her mattress. Everything else was gone, carried away by the white winds that had taken her, Javan, and Micah to South Keckrick weeks ago. The only thing that the wall of white winds hadn't blown away was the tree itself along with remnants of the floor and roof of the treehouse that swayed from the tree like extra branches.

This treehouse had been a lonely home, the place she had retreated to after the volcano wiped out her village and killed her grandparents. But it was her safe place. Her learning space. Her laboratory.

She operated with a clear purpose when she lived here. She woke up every morning eager to protect Kisa; experimenting with plants to develop medicines and healing ointments turned out to be a nice bonus.

Now that Kisa was no longer hers to protect, she wasn't sure who she was or how she fit on Javan's team. Until she found a new purpose of her own to pursue, she would have to be content helping Javan fulfill his duty.

"I'm going to need more darts for that." She dropped to her knees at the base of the tree and opened a small door that gave her access to the hollowed-out tree. She crawled through the hole and stood inside the dimly lit space that was wide enough to let her stretch her arms and tickle the smooth bark with her fingers.

Years ago, she carved shelves in the thick walls to hold her most important treasures: her darts, the poison she tipped them with, the antidote for the poison, samples of her medicines, and a collection of the scales Kisa had shed over the years. Most of the shed scales were buried in specific spots in the area around the tree, but Taliya had kept some on hand to use in her medicinal experiments.

"I think I'll miss this place the most." She took a slow last look around the inside of the tree, then got to work stuffing darts in her dart pouch and filling a leather bag with a variety of her medicines as well as the poison and antidote for the darts. Then she carefully added five scales, knowing they would prove valuable assets in Zandador.

She flung the bag over her shoulder and was about to exit when the tree shook. The shake was followed by a grunt, and she heard someone yell, "Ouch! Where am I? This isn't good."

Taliya crawled through the door and looked up to find a man swinging by one arm from a thin branch fifteen feet above her. "Javan?"

"Hey! Umm...is Kisa around? I could really use her—" A snapping branch prevented Javan from finishing his sentence.

CHAPTER 12

Limitations

Javan's legs caught a sturdy branch on his clumsy plummet to the ground. He wrapped his legs around the scratchy bark and searched for Taliya from his upside-down position. "Taliya?"

He felt light-headed, dizzy, and confused. Why had he ended up in this tree? He intended to teleport himself to the ground in front of the treehouse where he, Micah, and Taliya were standing when the white winds whisked them away. Instead he found himself in the tree that used to hold Taliya's house. His teleportation technique obviously needed some work.

"I'm here." Taliya appeared below him. "I would suggest you let go so I can catch you, but we both know that wouldn't work out so well."

The image of Taliya attempting to catch him brought a smile to his face. "Right you are. Is Kisa around?"

"I'm sure she is since she just brought you here."

"She didn't bring me."

"Did Varjiek fly you here?" Taliya molded her face into a scowl and crossed her arms across her chest. "Did you not trust me to come back to Nahat?"

"No. I mean yes. I mean--" Javan shook his head and started over. "I figured out how to teleport on my own and somehow ended up in your tree."

Taliya's eyes grew wide. "You have the ability to teleport? On your own? Without the aid of a portal? That's unheard of."

"Not anymore." He hoped she would still be impressed once she learned he needed his Stalker Sword to teleport, a sword that was no longer in his hand. Where had it landed? Or did it vanish on the way here? Was it only good for one teleportation jump?

"Prove it. Take me back to Nahat."

"In case you haven't noticed," Javan said, scanning the ground below him for his sword, "I'm kinda stuck in a tree."

"Good point. You know, I do have a whistle that summons Kisa." Taliya tugged on a long, thin black string around her neck and held up what looked like a dragon's tooth attached to the end of the string. "I suppose I could blow it if you ask nicely."

"Are you serious right now?" The branch creaked, and Javan had a hunch it wasn't going to hold him much longer. "My life is in danger, and you're harassing me about saying please?"

"If we're going to be working together, I want to know I can expect you to be polite and respectful no matter the situation."

He could tell by the amusement underlying her words that she was simply enjoying his precarious predicament. Nevertheless, it was in his best interest to play along. "Please blow the whistle."

"Was that so hard?" Taliya smiled and blew the whistle. Javan didn't hear anything, but Kisa appeared in the clearing ten feet away from the tree seconds later. He needed to get himself one of those whistles.

"Hey, girl," Taliya said. "Your Collector wants some help getting to the ground without breaking his neck."

Kisa cocked her head and studied Javan. *Why are you hanging in the tree?*

"I'm not really sure. Can you please just get me down?"

Kisa walked over and lowered her nose underneath Javan. He walked his hands up her long snout, unhooked his legs from the branch, and plopped on the dragon's head. She dropped her nose to the ground and let Javan slide off. He planted his feet beside Taliya and wobbled slightly until the blood that had rushed to his head while hanging in the tree redistributed itself throughout his body.

If it's time to go, Kisa said, *tell Varjiek to make himself visible. I can't teleport him back if I can't see him.*

"He's not here," Javan said, kicking the long grass under the tree searching for his sword. "One of your scales enabled me to teleport myself here when I put it in my sword."

Kisa took a step back. *A human can teleport?*

"Yup. I'll show you as soon as I find my—aha. There it is." A glint of sun reflected off the rainbow-colored steel on the other side of the tree. He picked it up with his right hand, walked back to Taliya, and offered her his left hand. She didn't take it.

"I think you're forgetting I can't hear Kisa's side of the conversation. I'm not sure what you're wanting to do."

"I'm wanting to show you and Kisa I can teleport. Please take my hand, and I will return you to Nahat."

"This should be interesting." Taliya placed her hand on his palm and wrapped her fingers through his. "Let's go."

Javan liked the way her hand fit his and squeezed back. He smiled, closed his eyes, and pictured the bridge in Nahat. He waited for that whirling, swirling sensation that accompanied his first teleportation trip, but that sensation never came.

"If you wanted to hold my hand," Taliya said, breaking his concentration, "you could have just asked."

Embarrassed, Javan opened his eyes and dropped her hand. "I...I don't understand. I got myself here. Why couldn't I get us back?"

Your mind isn't strong enough yet, Kisa said. *Teleportation requires intense mental focus, and it's especially hard when you are trying to teleport someone else that has a mind of her own. It will take time and practice to learn.*

"What's she saying?" Taliya asked.

"She's saying she's going to teach me the fine art of teleportation. Since we don't have time for any lessons right now, though, she's going to take us back to Nahat herself."

I said all that?

Javan glared at Kisa.

Of course I said all that. I'm your dragon. I'll be happy to teach you how to teleport. It will be fun taking you to my favorite places by the waterfall and—

"Kisa! Nahat. We need to get back to Nahat."

As you wish. Kisa lowered her neck to the ground. Javan helped Taliya up, then let her help him climb up behind her. A heartbeat later, Kisa whisked them back to the clearing near the gate of the city.

CHAPTER 13

Liberate Nahat

With dusk approaching, Micah's mood darkened. He was forced to haul humminglo plants from the storehouses to the portal while Javan and Taliya escaped the grunt work to play with dragons.

What was taking them so long? All they needed to do was get a few scales from Kisa. During the hours they had been gone, he managed to capture a soldier, strategically place the crew from the Iria around the portal so they would be ready to capture the remaining soldiers, and carry countless numbers of plants to the portal through a torrential rainstorm.

He hadn't been required to haul any flowers. He wasn't sure why he felt compelled to fall in line and help, but it did sound like a better option than sitting around doing nothing. At least it had a few hours ago.

Now he smelled like a brutal combination of sweat, rain, and dirt, and he had so many pieces of dried humminglos stuck to his skin and clothes that he was certain he could recreate an entire flower from the debris. The worst part was knowing that the longer they waited to shut down the portal, the more flowers his father would get. Judging by the almost empty storehouse at the end of the row of empty storehouses, his father would be getting all the flowers Keckrick had to offer.

He threw one of the last bushels on his shoulder and spit out a piece of a leaf that floated onto his tongue. It left a tart taste in his mouth as he marched along the path by the river toward the portal and finally dissipated as he neared the bridge. That's where Lydia fell into step beside him carrying a few flowers under her arm to look like she was working.

"We can't wait any longer," she whispered. "My people are ready. We need to act now, before the last load is sent to Japheth."

"I agree. Tell your people to move as soon as I drop this bushel of flowers. Then we'll have to hope Javan gets back before Omri sends any more soldiers here to investigate."

"Did I hear my name?" Javan seemed to appear out of nowhere right in front of Micah. He was holding one of his swords and had a silly grin on his face.

"It's about time you got back." Micah hoped his stern response helped mask his surprise. He also wanted Javan to know it was time to be serious, not joke around. "Did you get the scales?"

"Yes." Javan nodded, put his sword away, and leaned in. "We're ready to commence with Operation Save Keckrick from the Tyranny of Omri by Disabling the Portals with Dragon Scales Plucked from Kisa."

"You need to work on your operation-naming skills," Lydia said.

Javan shrugged. "It sounded better when Taliya said it."

"I doubt it." Micah scowled and looked around. "Speaking of Taliya, where is she?"

"She'll be here soon. She's riding in on Kisa."

"We can't wait for her to get here," Lydia said. "Some of the soldiers will be returning to Zandador the next time the portal is activated."

"What concern is it of yours when we return to Zandador?" A soldier slightly taller than Micah with wide shoulders, oversized hands, and a bushy white beard interrupted their conversation from behind. "Enough with the standing and talking. Your only concern should be getting those flowers you are holding to the portal as fast as possible."

Micah dropped his bushel of humminglos and glared at the soldier. "We will stand here and talk as long as we want, soldier."

"Not on my watch. I have a job to do, and I'm not going to let anyone—even the king's son—keep me from doing it." The man reached for his Jolt Blast, but he slumped into Micah's arms before he had a chance to retrieve the weapon. Surprised by the weight of the large man, Micah fought to keep his balance and stumbled backwards a few steps. Once he stabilized himself, he lowered the unconscious man to the ground. That's when he noticed a dart stuck in the back of the man's neck.

"What is happening?" Lydia asked her question while swiveling her head in every direction rather than focusing on the fallen soldier. Micah stood, followed her gaze, and saw what she saw: every soldier on and around the portal was dropping to the ground as lifeless as the man at Micah's feet.

"Taliya made it back." Javan pointed to the roof top where he and Micah had faced off earlier that day.

Taliya stood there now with a slingshot in her hand, took a bow, and yelled over the crowd who had yet to realize what was happening. "Tie up the soldiers, boys. Nahat belongs to the people of Keckrick again!"

Over the cheers of the people, Micah mumbled to himself. "How did she do that?" She was a tiny little woman with a tiny little weapon, and she had taken out an entire squad of soldiers in less than a minute.

"I'm glad she's on our side," Lydia said as she picked up the bearded soldier's lifeless arm and dropped it on his chest. "I want no part of whatever kind of poison these darts are tipped with."

"She greeted me with one of those darts when we first met," Javan said, "and I know from experience these guys are not going to be happy when they wake up."

"Then let's get them tied up and moved to the storehouse." Micah used the string that held the bushel of humminglos together to tie the soldier's hands behind his back and tossed the man over his shoulder. As he carried the man to the storehouse, he decided he was never going to underestimate Taliya again.

◊　◊　◊

The flurry of action from shooting the soldiers, retrieving her darts, and delivering the antidote had Taliya's blood pumping and mind racing. She wanted to dance to celebrate the victory but needed to transition to a state of calm concentration as she stood on the portal she had only read about and studied endlessly in books.

She felt smaller than usual in the middle of the giant white portal made entirely of Dawn Stalker scales. She also felt a sense of awe knowing this circle had the power to take her anywhere in the Great Rift she wanted to go. The trick was figuring out where the openings were hidden while Javan, Micah, and the entire crew of the Iria stood all around the portal staring at her.

Lydia must have noticed that Taliya wasn't sure she knew what she was doing because she crossed her arms and asked, "Are you certain this portal connects to Tulkar? We've never been able to transport to anywhere except Zandador as long as I've been alive."

"I'm sure," Taliya said. Maybe talking through her book knowledge would help her come up with a solution. "Every portal in the Zandadorian system is interconnected. The first king of Zandador built the portals so that anyone could go anywhere in the Great Rift whenever they wanted to travel. Most of the population lived in Zandador, so four portals exist in Zandador, two here in Keckrick, and only one in the remaining regions because fewer people wanted to live in those places."

"Nice history lesson," Lydia said, "but can we get to Tulkar already? We're want to go home."

"Right. Of course. And to do that, we have to find the slot that will take you there." Taliya closed her eyes and pictured a fully-operational portal she had seen in one of her books. She could envision ten outer links but knew that the link for Xyies at the very top of the circle was a dead link. The other two links on the top half led to Gibbet and Tirza, two of the regions north of the Land of Zandador.

The two links to the left and right of the middle slot where she stood led to west and east Zandador. That left five links on the bottom half of the circle. The two on the left side connected to Upper and Lower Keckrick, the one furthest south connected to the Land of No Return, and the two on the right side connected to a town in the middle of South Zandador as well as a city in the middle of the region of Varzack.

She opened her eyes, faced the bottom half of the portal, and studied the circle. The one visible link on the outer edge of the portal coincided with the Nahat slot in Upper Keckrick. Somewhere between it and the bottom half of the circle was the slot for Tulkar.

"I know what to do." Taliya walked to the southern end of the portal, dropped to her knees, and felt the scales. She talked as she let her fingers search. "The portal is constructed of seven-year dawn scales that feel cool and smooth to the touch. The way Omri blocked access to the other portals was by filling the open slots with slish, a white substance that hardens over time and resembles a dragon scale. But it has a slight roughness to it and no sense of coolness."

"Okay." Javan followed her and dropped to his hands and knees beside Taliya. "We're feeling for a rough patch somewhere in this vicinity?"

"Exactly."

Less than a minute later, Javan declared, "I found it!"

"Really? Let me feel." Taliya bumped Javan out of the way and put her hand where Javan's had been. Sure enough, the surface looked exactly like the scales around it but felt bumpy. "That's it. Now all we have to do is find the Tulkar link."

"I thought I just did."

"Not quite. This is the link to the Land of No Return. I wanted to find this one first because the link to Tulkar is halfway between here and the already open slot for Nahat." She pulled Javan to his feet and positioned him on top of the slish-filled slot. "You stay put to help me figure out where the halfway point is located."

She stepped back toward the middle of the circle, approximated the midpoint between Javan and the Nahat slot, and skipped to it. "This has to be it." She squatted and let her fingers dance all over the area. Sure enough, they encountered a slightly rough patch among the otherwise smooth scales. "Ha! I found it!"

When Javan didn't say anything, she looked up to see his face contorted into a strange, pensive look as he kept his eyes locked on the slot that would lead to the Land of No Return. Why would he care about that place? No one did. That's why it was called the Land of No Return. "What's the matter?"

"Nothing." Javan shook his head. "Let's just find the slot for Tulkar and get on with the day."

"Umm...I just said I found it. It's right here."

"Oh. Right. Good." Javan had clearly jumped to a different place in his head and was in no mood to share his secrets.

To keep herself from asking questions to discover what had Javan preoccupied, she turned her attention to the newest problem—the slish. How was she supposed to get the slish out of the slot without damaging the portal?

CHAPTER 14

Portal Travels

Javan stared at the slot at his foot. It led to the Land of No Return, the region Omri had banned his father to before Javan was born. What if his father was still alive? This portal could take him to find out, and the sword on his hip could help them both return.

"Javan." Taliya waved her hand in front of his face and snapped her fingers a few times. "Javan, did you hear me?"

"What?" Javan shook himself out of his self-induced trance and noticed in the dim light of the setting sun that everyone except Micah had shifted to the right side of the portal, leaving Micah as the only one standing in the city square on the left side of the portal. Why the shift, and how had he missed all the commotion that must have accompanied the brief migration? "What's going on?"

"You seriously didn't hear anything I just said?"

"No." Javan scratched his head. "Nothing. My mind was elsewhere."

"That I believe." Taliya led him off the portal to where Micah stood. "We have to get the slish out of the slot to make the portal work."

"Yeah. We have to get that slish out of the slot." Javan suppressed a smile. Something about that phrase was funny, but he didn't dare laugh when Taliya sounded so serious. "What are we going to do about that?"

"We don't have time to chip away at it with a chisel," Micah said, "but a drop of Kisa's acid will eat through it in seconds."

"Say what?" Javan's eyes widened. "You want to play with a dragon's acid? Won't it destroy the whole portal if we try that?"

"No." Taliya shook her head. "The slish is a hardened rock that won't be able to resist the acid, but the acid shouldn't affect the scales surrounding the slish."

"Shouldn't? Are you sure?"

"Sure enough to try." Taliya blew her Kisa-summoning whistle. A moment later, the boards of the bridge rattled as Kisa and Mertzer stampeded over it, charged across the open square, and stopped side by side in front of the trio.

Finally, Kisa said. Javan had to concentrate to hear her thoughts over the gasps and whispers of the crowd. *I am ready to get out of this dirty place. Whom shall I teleport to Zandador first?*

Relax, Varjiek said, making his appearance known as he landed beside Kisa. *Nobody is leaving yet. The humans need something from you first.*

Of course. Kisa strutted to the center of the portal and held her head and tail high. *They want to admire my beauty.*

"What is she doing?" Taliya whispered to Javan.

"She thinks you called her here to let everyone admire her beauty."

That's not why I'm here? Kisa turned and lowered her head so her eyes stared into Javan's. *People don't want to admire me?*

"Yes, they do. And they are." Javan gulped as he felt the heat emanating from the flared nostrils of the dragon. "We also called you here because we need a touch of your acid to make the portal work."

Kisa cocked her head. *Now you want to make the portal work? I thought you took my scales so you could break the portal?*

"That's true, but before we break it, we need to open some of the closed slots. That way we can send our friends back to Tulkar and us to a strategic place in Zandador that you haven't been to before."

"Kisa," Taliya said, leaning down and sprinkling dirt on the Tulkar slot, "think of this as your very first opportunity to show off in front of hundreds of humans. If you put one little drop of your spit right here, I can guarantee this crowd will clap and cheer for you when your acid dissolves the slish."

It would be nice to be recognized for both my beauty and my power.

You won't be recognized for anything if you don't act soon, Mertzer said. *I'm sure I can claw out whatever is closing up those slots just as well as your acid can dissolve it.*

"Interesting proposal," Javan said, looking at Kisa. "Are you going to let Mertzer be the hero here?"

Kisa snorted. *Out of my way.*

"Gladly." Javan backed off the portal along with Taliya.

Kisa wiggled her body, cleared her throat, and hovered her snout over the Tulkar slot. She then let a large dollop of acidy spit drop off the pointed end of her long, pink tongue.

The acid made no sound as it spread itself over the slish, eating away at it layer by layer. In a matter of seconds, a perfectly shaped triangle slot appeared amidst the scales of the portal.

"Oh good," Taliya said, breathing an obvious sigh of relief. "It only ate the slish and not the scales."

"I thought you were sure it wouldn't."

"I said I was sure enough to try, which meant I was only about ten percent sure the plan would work." Taliya shrugged and smiled. "Sometimes risks pay off."

Javan shook his head at Taliya's bravery. He preferred to be at least ninety percent sure his plans would work before taking action. What had he missed out on or not accomplished because he had been too uncertain of the results to even try?

My cheers, Kisa said, her nose once again stuck high in the air. *Where are my cheers?*

"They're coming," Javan said, thankful for a reason to not dwell on the answers to the question he had just asked himself. He walked across the portal and encouraged the crowd to cheer for his acid-spitting Dawn Stalker.

◊   ◊   ◊

While Kisa strutted through the crowd and let the people gawk at her imposing figure, Taliya took one of Kisa's scales from Javan and handed it to Lydia. "As soon as you return to Tulkar, put this scale in one of the open slots on the portal. Keep that scale in the slot until Javan returns. Don't reopen the portal unless you are prepared to contend with Omri's dragons."

"Understood." Lydia nodded and focused on Javan. "You realize this will cut us off from the rest of the world. We're depending on you to win the throne and re-establish trade between all the regions of the Great Rift. Otherwise we will become a forgotten society with no hope for progress."

"Then I guess I'll just have to win."

"Good answer." Lydia offered Javan a nod and hugged Taliya. "It has been a privilege traveling with you. We will forever be in your debt for the humminglo flowers you sacrificed to keep Keckrick safe."

"Thank you." To keep herself from crying at the prospect of saying farewell, Taliya stepped back. "You better go. The longer we delay, the less likely we are to succeed."

"Right." Lydia held up Kisa's scale and drew her sword. "Crew, let's say our goodbyes and head home. A fight with some unwelcome soldiers awaits!"

In a flurry of handshakes and hugs, the crew of the Iria bid farewell to Taliya, Javan, and Micah and wished them well in their endeavor to defeat Omri. As the trio watched from the grass, Cyr put an activation scale in the Nahat slot, and Andre put one in the newly uncovered Tulkar slot.

After a slight delay, the portal burst to life and whisked the crew away. Once the whirling flurry of colors dissipated, Taliya immediately began searching for the Dusk slot by starting in the center of the portal and walking directly east. It only took her a few moments to locate the slish-filled slot, and when she did, she whistled for Kisa.

The dragon seemed to sulk her way back to the portal and did not look happy about being taken away from her walk of fame. "Sorry to cut the party short," Taliya said, "but we need one more drop of that acid, girl. This time it's our turn to travel."

◇　◇　◇

Micah stood transfixed by the events he had just witnessed and taken part in. How did Javan and Taliya get Kisa to do exactly what they wanted her to do without demanding she obey their every word? Reasoning with dragons rather than ordering them around like slaves was still a curious concept for him to grasp.

Then came the goodbyes. Real handshakes from genuine friends he would actually miss made his heart hurt. This, too, was a new concept. Never before had he parted from people he wanted to be around who wanted to be around him. He was used to being treated harshly by his mentors or feared by everyone else. As a result, he knew how to keep his distance from people, not live as a friend among them.

As he watched his friends disappear in the cloud of colors produced by the portal, he found himself questioning the sanity of letting himself experience the human emotions involved in friendship he had been trained his whole life to ignore. Watching the people he had come to care about leave was much too painful.

Not everyone left, though. Javan and Taliya remained. Were they his friends, or were they just three people working together toward a common goal? Could a Hunter really be friends with a Collector and a Protector?

Friends or not, they were going to be stuck together for a while, so he might as well make the best of the situation. It sure beat being alone. "How much longer, Taliya?" He approached her on the portal while she studied the acid eating away at the slish. "Every minute we wait brings us one minute closer to an attack by Omri, especially after he realizes the Tulkar portal no longer works. These people are not prepared to defend themselves."

"It's hard to tell now that it's getting darker, but I think the slish is gone. Micah, you, Kisa, and I better go."

"Wait," Micah said. "Just me, you, and Kisa? What about Mertzer? I'm not leaving without him."

"The portal is only big enough to send one dragon through at a time, and we only have one more set of activation scales that we took from the soldiers. We can send Kisa back for Mertzer once we get there."

"Correction. You can send Kisa back for me *and* Mertzer as soon as *you* get there." Micah marched over to his dragon and climbed on. "I'm not leaving without him."

"But that means Taliya will be left alone in Zandador," Javan said.

Micah hadn't thought of that. Was it more important for Micah to wait with his dragon or travel ahead with his friend?

"I'm a big girl," Taliya said, nudging Javan off the portal. "I can take care of myself, and you need to take care of business here. Are you sure you know what to do as soon as the portal resets?"

Javan held up one of the scales he had taken off Kisa that afternoon. "Put this in an open slot and wait for Kisa to return."

"Exactly." Taliya took two scales out of her bag and waved Kisa onto the portal. "I'll see you all in a few minutes."

She put one scale in the Nahat slot, and as she walked under Kisa's body to get to the Dusk slot, Micah found himself yelling, "Stop! Wait for me." He slid off Mertzer and ran onto the portal.

"You don't have to come with me," Taliya said. "I'll be fine."

"So will Mertzer. I'm ready to get out of this life-sucking humidity and return to Zandador." To prevent her from arguing, he took the second scale out of Taliya's hand and placed it in the Dusk slot.

The portal whirled and shook and blinded him with its brilliant colors. The last thing he remembered seeing was the look of sheer excitement on Taliya's face as the colors swallowed them up and transported them to the Land of Zandador.

CHAPTER 15

Waiting for Javan

I didn't expect Micah to leave with Taliya, Mertzer said. *Good for him. I think I'm starting to like the man who made me his slave.*

Javan ignored the dragon's observation and kept his gaze focused straight ahead. He tried to blink away the image of Taliya leaving in a flurry of colors with Micah, but it would be forever burned on his brain.

Why did he care? She was just a Dragon Protector who had agreed to help him collect two more dragons. He shouldn't be jealous of her leaving without him and being alone with Micah. Besides, he's the one who told Micah to go with her. Which in hindsight was foolish. He should have gone and let Micah stay to disable the portal.

Javan, Varjiek said, floating in a lazy circle above the city square, *wouldn't now be a good time to do something with that scale in your hand?*

Varjiek's words snapped Javan out of his stupor, and he stepped toward the portal. But it activated before he reached it.

"Oh, this isn't good."

And it wasn't. The figures of several dozen soldiers appeared as the cloud of colors faded.

Javan did the only thing he could think of in the moment. He drew his invisibility sword and charged the portal.

◊   ◊   ◊

"Amazing!" Taliya's insides felt like they had been shaken, scrambled, and rearranged, but she considered that part of the thrill of portal travel. She now found herself on the eastern coast of Zandador at the time of night when the moon had just taken over full control of the sky.

In the moonlight, she could see the dark purple hue of the ocean and hear the waterfalls behind her competing with the crashing waves in front of her. A hundred feet or more of fine bronze sand stood between the water and the combination of trees, cliffs, and boulders that marked the edge of the shoreline. "This place must look spectacular in the daylight."

"I suppose." Micah shrugged and walked off the portal. "We should be able to set up a decent campsite under some trees along the beach. You work on finding a good spot and building a fire, and I'll find something to eat."

"Sure." She watched Micah disappear into the woods, then spoke to Kisa. "I know you'll appreciate the beauty of the land. Walk with me, help me pick out a campsite, then head back to Javan. When you return, you'll be able to teleport directly to the campsite."

Kisa nodded her understanding and delicately stepped off the portal. Her front claws sank in the soft sand, and she snorted as she reared up on her back legs and shook the sand out of her claws.

"Really, Kisa? You're going to let your obsession with being clean keep you from enjoying a moonlit walk on the beach? That's a shame." To show the dragon she had nothing to fear, Taliya took off her leather boots and cotton socks and jumped into the squishy sand. She giggled as it tickled her toes and began jogging down the beach. "Come on, Kisa!"

With the ocean on her left and the forest on her right, Taliya ran past rocks and shrubs before settling on an inviting cluster of tall, skinny palm trees. She pointed to the cluster and called to Kisa. "Found a spot. You won't have to come far, and you can leave as soon as you check it out."

The dragon hesitated before leaving the solid ground of the portal. Then she quickly pranced her way to Taliya as though the sand was made of lava. She disappeared the second she laid eyes on the designated campsite.

"Bye, girl." For the first time in fifteen years, Taliya was too far away from Kisa to offer her protection. That thought made Taliya feel helpless and without purpose. "She's not yours to protect anymore." The reminder didn't take the sting out of the new reality, and Taliya wondered if she would ever get used to the idea that Kisa belonged to Javan.

"Stop your sulking, and get to work." Taliya obeyed herself. She used the large leaves from the trees to make three beds on the soft sand and began building a fire.

She finished her job before Micah returned from his hunting mission and before Javan arrived from Keckrick. Part of her enjoyed the soothing sounds of the crackling fire and crashing waves under the bright moon and starlit sky, but most of her felt out of sorts. She was in a new place that she couldn't yet explore. She was hungry but had nothing to eat. She was tired but couldn't sleep due to a growing suspicion that something had gone terribly wrong for Javan and the dragons in Nahat.

That suspicion grew worse the more time she spent alone, and she finally decided she couldn't take the solitary inaction any longer. She picked up her bag and began marching toward the portal. She didn't get far from the fire when she heard Micah yell at her from behind.

"Hey! Where are you going? I caught dinner."

Without turning around, she declared, "I'm going back."

"Back? Back to where?"

"To Nahat." She paused and looked at Micah. "Javan should have returned by now. What if Omri realized what was happening and sent half his army along with his dragons to Nahat? They could be fighting a battle while we're sitting here staring at a fire." She took the two activation scales out of her bag and held them up. "We need to go fight with them."

"Can't we eat first?"

Taliya glared at Micah until he dropped whatever animal he had caught and wanted to cook. "All right," he said. "I'm coming."

"Good decision." She waited for him to catch up to her, gave him one of the scales, and they walked to the portal together. Fortunately, none of the slots in this portal were filled with slish, making it easy to use. Micah put his scale in the Dusk slot while Taliya put hers in the Nahat slot.

The portal sputtered, threw off a few sparks, then shut down. Taliya started to panic. "It doesn't work. The portal doesn't work. That means we're stuck here. Without our dragons. Without Javan. Without any way to get back to them. I've never been separated from Kisa before. Why did I agree to this plan?"

"Whoa! Calm down," Micah said, putting his large hands on her small shoulders. "The portal isn't supposed to work if Javan did his job."

"True, but something's wrong." Taliya shook her head, ducked away from the too relaxed Micah, and picked up the scales. "What if Omri isn't the problem? What if the people of Nahat are mad because we cut them off from the rest of the Great Rift? What if they attacked Javan and did something with him before Kisa teleported back to him? We have no way of getting there to help!"

"Varjiek and Mertzer are there. Kisa will find them. I wouldn't want to be standing between a Collector, two of his dragons, and a third dragon he can communicate with. They'll be back soon enough."

"How can you not be concerned?"

"Because I'm too hungry and tired to think about anything except food and sleep." Micah started walking back to the campsite. "If Javan and the dragons aren't back by morning, then we'll decide what to do."

"You want to wait until morning? We need to figure out something now!"

Micah ignored her and kept walking. Raging with frustration, she marched back to the fire. Although the idea of eating sounded enticing, she had no intention of sleeping without first knowing how she would return to Keckrick, Kisa, and Javan.

◊   ◊   ◊

As Micah carefully turned the pheasant he had caught over the fire, he considered what to make of their current situation. Should he go find Mertzer, wait for Mertzer to find him, or travel north to Noon Territory to hunt a Noon Stalker and continue his own quest for the throne? If Javan had been harmed and couldn't complete his collection, the only way to stop Omri would be for Micah to hunt three more dragons.

That was a near impossible task to accomplish in a mere two months, and he would certainly need Taliya's help. But would a Protector be willing to help a Hunter harm three dragons for the greater good of the Land of Zandador?

He glanced over the fire at Taliya who had her nose stuck in a book. He opened his mouth to ask her what she was reading when a cacophony of animal shrieks and rustling leaves cut through the night.

Micah jumped to his feet and drew his sword, ready to fight whatever predator was responsible for the disturbance in the woods. However, the quick action caused him to drop the bird in the fire. The flames engulfed the meat, ruining the meal.

"So much for dinner," Taliya said as the shadow of two large dragon figures appeared on the sand. The wingless one disappeared, and Javan slid off the other.

"Hey, guys," Javan said, walking up to the fire. "I sure am glad to see the two of you. I didn't think we were ever going to get out of there."

"What happened?" Taliya's eyes grew wide as she looked beyond Javan. "Where are Kisa and Mertzer? Are they okay?"

"They're fine. Kisa couldn't teleport two dragons this far at the same time, so she went back for Mertzer. She's going to take him to the portal area instead of here. That way he can easily zip into the woods and get away from the ocean."

"That doesn't explain your delayed exit," Micah said, glaring at the Collector. Why did Javan seem relaxed? "Taliya was getting concerned."

"Really? Huh. Sorry about that, but it couldn't be helped. See, right after you left, dozens of soldiers arrived before I could disable the portal. They started blasting people with their Jolt Blasts, but Varjiek put an end to it. He swooped down in invisibility mode and began knocking the soldiers down with his tail.

"It was so funny watching those soldiers try to fight an invisible enemy, and I could hear Varjiek talking junk and laughing at them the whole time. In the middle of the chaos, I managed to sneak onto the portal and stick Kisa's scale in the Nahat slot."

"That happened right after we left?" Micah asked.

"Yup."

"That was hours ago," Taliya said. "We've been worried. What took you so long?"

"I haven't finished my story." Javan paused to sniff the air. "What's burning?"

"A bird that took me forever to catch." Micah put his sword away and crossed his arms. "This better be a good story."

"It is." Javan nodded and continued. "Once the people in Nahat saw the soldiers start to fall, they decided they wanted to fight. They rallied together, overpowered the confused soldiers, and tied them up in the storehouse with the other captives. I tried to leave, but they insisted on cooking me a feast first. I ate so much that I'm stuffed!"

"How nice for you," Micah said through clenched teeth. He had to hold his arms a little closer to his body to keep himself from punching Javan.

"I'm glad you had time for a feast." Taliya picked up a stick and threw it in the fire. "We haven't had a chance to eat anything yet. We were too busy finding food and wood for this fire and setting up camp so we would have a place to sleep tonight. And now that our very late dinner is ruined, we will have nothing to eat. So you can take your stuffed self and chill in the bed I made you while our stomachs rumble from hunger all night long."

Javan held up a bag. "Or you can eat the food I brought."

"Oh." Taliya cleared her throat and changed her tone. "That would be nice. Thank you."

Micah watched with amusement as Taliya held her chin high and took the food from Javan. She had said everything he had wanted to say, but because she began her rant before he could, she was the one who had to endure the embarrassment of misjudging Javan.

Micah also noticed that Javan didn't say anything more to Taliya to make her feel guilty for trying to make him feel guilty. He simply sat by the fire and let them eat in peace. Interesting. And admirable.

This Collector knew how to treat people well, and that was a skill Micah desperately wanted to learn.

CHAPTER 16

The Dreaded Trip

Taliya woke up with the sun and strolled down the beach while the guys continued to sleep. She soaked in the feelings of the sand between her toes, the cold water lapping at her ankles, and the warm breeze blowing through her hair.

The orange and red hues of the rising sun played with the deep purple ocean, and the stunning beauty of this quiet haven beckoned her to stay. Her heart and mind agreed. They knew the next stop on the journey would be Oer, and that was the one place in the Great Rift she never ever wanted to go again.

She had been gone for fifteen years, having escaped with the help of her father at the age of seven. Would her parents recognize her? Did they miss her? Had her father told her mother where she had gone?

Not that her mother would care. She had wanted to give Taliya away long before Taliya ran away to explore the jungle of Noon Stalker Territory that loomed behind the city walls. She remembered the look of disappointment rather than excitement on her mother's face when she returned from her exploits as well as the look of relief when she was sentenced to a life of slavery as her punishment for leaving the city limits.

She had often wondered if her mother had suggested that punishment to the governor just so her mother could be rid of her once and for all.

Memories of that miserable year as a slave in the governor's house made her feel queasy. She dropped to her knees in the sand to keep the food she ate last night from coming back up. O how she dreaded having to face that place and those people again!

"Are you okay?" Micah said, sprinting up to Taliya. Beads of sweat dotted his forehead, and his breathing was faster than usual. He almost seemed worried about her. "You don't look so good."

"I'm fine. Just nervous about returning to Oer." She stood, brushed the sand off her knees, and nodded in the direction of the campsite that she was too far away from to see. "Is Javan still asleep?"

"Yes. You want to wake him up while I keep running down the beach for a bit? We should probably get going once I return."

"I say we let him sleep. It's been a crazy few weeks, and we could all use a quiet morning to recover."

"A nice long run on the coast followed by a swim in the ocean does sound rather appealing." Micah slapped Taliya on the back. "Deal. Let's take the morning to ourselves and head out right after Varjiek returns from his noon meal."

"Noon?" Any color she had left drained from her face. "That soon?"

"You really don't want to return to your hometown, do you? What has you so scared?"

"Scared? Me? Nonsense." She motioned down the beach with her hand. "You enjoy your run. I'll be ready to go long before Varjiek returns."

To end the conversation, she trudged back toward the camp. She wasn't scared. Apprehensive? Sure. Nervous? Absolutely. Terrified? Most definitely.

But Taliya the Dragon Protector was not scared of anyone or anything.

◇   ◇   ◇

"No," Javan said, shaking his head. Sleeping late into the morning had him feeling renewed and ready to win the current argument about how best to get to Oer and who should make the trip. "They aren't coming."

"Then I'm not going, either." Taliya plopped down and sat crossed-legged in the sand in the spot where her bed was the night before. "We're a team. All of us. Including the dragons. Where we go, they go."

"We'll only be gone for a few days. After we talk to your dad in Oer and pick up Ravier in Japheth the day after tomorrow, we'll come right back here. Varjiek is the only one who can fly, so he is the only one we'll take."

"Mertzer can run almost as fast as Varjiek can fly," Micah said. "He won't slow us down."

"He will when we get to the river," Javan said. "He hates water and will not want to cross."

"Not a problem," Micah said. "Once we cross, send Kisa back to teleport Mertzer to the other side."

"Kisa is the problem," Javan said. "She's amazing when she can teleport, but she is much slower than Mertzer and Varjiek. Plus she's exhausted. Teleporting two dragons such a long distance zapped her energy. She was zonked out when I checked on her, and she is in no shape to travel anywhere today."

"I left Mertzer once," Micah said. "He's my dragon. I'm not leaving without him again."

"You don't have to leave without him," Javan said. He cleared his throat and stood tall, knowing Micah wouldn't like what he was going to say next. "You can stay here."

"And miss the action? I don't think so."

"I do. You need to remain hidden. We're going to have enough trouble finding the dragon eggs and getting through the portal. We certainly don't need the Destroyer knowing you're alive and back in Zandador. If that happens, we'll have the added complication of keeping you from getting killed."

Micah huffed. "Hiding is cowardly, but I'll stay. When this is over, though, you are going to help me find and eliminate the Destroyer. I won't hide forever." Micah kicked the sand and walked away.

"Now we must take Kisa," Taliya said, standing up and whispering. "We can't leave her here alone with a Dragon Hunter."

"She'll be fine. Micah knows she's my dragon, and he can't touch her. Besides, we don't have a choice." Javan took Taliya's hand and led her slightly inland to where Kisa was curled up and snoring loudly under some trees. "Look at her. What do you see?"

Taliya gasped. "She's...filthy."

"Exactly. She's so tired that she doesn't care that her body is covered with a dusting of dirt and her tail is buried beneath some leaves. We can't take her anywhere, and we have to trust Micah to look out for her."

"But that's my job."

"Not anymore." Javan tried to suck the words back into his mouth as soon as he said them, but the damage was done. Taliya bit her bottom lip, and tears filled her suddenly sad eyes. He needed to do some fast talking to keep her from crying. "I mean it's your job to look out for all dragons, not just Kisa anymore. That includes Varjiek on this trip and whatever Dusk and Midnight Stalkers I end up collecting. Please come with me and be Varjiek's Protector."

Taliya sniffled, threw her shoulders back, and uttered one word. "Fine."

"Then it's settled. You, Varjiek, and I will leave as soon as Varjiek returns from eating."

Did I hear my name? Varjiek swooped down through the trees and landed beside Kisa. The Dawn Stalker kept snoring.

"Yes," Javan said. "We need you to fly us to Oer. Do you know how to get there?"

I know the city. Its walls are high. Its factories are loud. Its people are mean.

"He says he knows where to go." Javan reported Varjiek's relevant thoughts to Taliya. "Time to get our stuff and leave."

"How exciting." Taliya turned and sauntered away, looking and sounding like the least excited person in the world.

◊   ◊   ◊

Varjiek kept to the coastline as he flew Taliya and Javan north. Once they crossed the wide river that cut Zandador in half and dumped into the ocean, he adjusted his flight to more of a north-west trajectory that sent them flying slowly over hundreds of miles of the Noon Territory jungle. They needed to wait until nightfall to approach her father and were thus in no hurry to reach Oer, located along the northwest corner of the Noon Territory border.

Taliya clung to Javan as she studied the vibrant green plants and the sparkling blue waters of the winding rivers below them. She wanted to jump off and play among the foliage and waterways. What plants and animals did they have here that weren't in the rain forests of Keckrick?

Varjiek must have read her mind because he dipped down and drifted just above the tops of the trees. She reached over and let her fingers touch the fuzzy leaves.

"Taliya, careful! You're going to fall."

"If I do," she said, her left hand hooked to Javan's belt, "head on to Oer without me. I think I would like living here."

"I'll be sure to have Varjiek bring you back here after you've helped me collect the rest of my dragons. Until then, you're stuck with me." He reached back, hooked his arm around her waist, and forced her to return to her upright sitting position.

"You're no fun." Taliya sulked long enough to let Javan feel like he won the battle for her safety. Once that small threshold passed, she stood and used Javan's head to help her maintain her balance on the dragon's wide back. "You've got to loosen up a bit and let yourself enjoy these moments. We're flying on a powerful dragon over some of the most beautiful country I've ever seen. The view is absolutely amazing!"

"I can be plenty of fun, and I am enjoying the view just fine from my seated position. The possibility of plummeting to the ground has a way of bringing out my boring side."

"But standing changes your entire perspective. You should try it. From here I can see monkeys dancing in the trees up ahead and--" She plopped down on her bottom, her brain refusing to form the words needed to finish the sentence.

"What?" Javan turned his head to look at her. "What did you see?"

"Oer. I saw the city walls that surround the city of Oer."

No more words were spoken as Varjiek maintained his trajectory toward the city.

CHAPTER 17

Retrieving Information

cannot just drop you off and leave you.

"We'll be fine," Javan said. Now that daylight was fading into night, Javan was ready to get going, but he couldn't allow Varjiek to come with them into the city. "We'll be invisible when you drop us off, I can keep us invisible for as long as we need to be, and no one except Taliya's dad will ever know we were even there."

What if you need an emergency rescue?

"Then I will teleport to this spot." Javan pointed at the stony ground by the lake Varjiek had brought them to before they reached the city. Wild strawberries the size of baseballs decorated the rolling hills around the water, and a sprinkling of massive pine trees provided enough privacy for Javan and Taliya to talk and stretch without being seen or heard by the guards on the walls. They didn't provide enough coverage to hide a dragon, though, so Varjiek had kept himself invisible while they waited for the sun to set. "Come back here after you drop us off."

I should come with you.

"You're too big and you know it. Take us into the city now and return for us at midnight. Stay in stealth mode."

Fine. Varjiek rolled his eyes and crouched to allow Javan and Taliya could climb up. Once they were settled into flying position, he pounced up and into the sky. They zoomed over a drab city with rows and rows of uniform, box-like houses and large, loud factories until they crossed the river.

On this side of the river, mansions acres apart from one another dotted the land in the northeast corner of the city while official-looking government buildings constructed in a square around a glowing fountain rounded out the northwest corner in front of the gates. A large amphitheater with its rows and rows of concrete seats facing away from the buildings separated the city square from the mansions.

People dressed in the standard Zandadorian garb of brown shirts, brown pants, and brown dresses streamed out of the buildings and made their way in single-file, obedient fashion toward the lone bridge.

Taliya leaned her chin into Javan's shoulder and spoke in his ear. "My father works in the building closest to the city gates. He hates crowds and is always the last one to leave. We'll follow him home and hope my mother has a late shift at the factory tonight."

"You don't want to see your mother?"

"No. If she finds out I'm back, she'll report my presence to the governor. If the governor catches me, she'll have me hanged."

"What? Why?"

"I'll explain later. Right now have Varjiek land in the open space at the top of the amphitheater."

"You hear that, Varjiek?"

Yes, indeed. The dragon floated down to the cobblestone street between the stadium and largest building in the square.

Javan drew his invisibility sword and was the first to slide off. Taliya followed, staying in touch with Varjiek until Javan took her hand. "See you back here at midnight," Javan whispered to the dragon.

I'll be waiting, Varjiek said and flew away.

Javan wanted to ask Taliya for an explanation about the hanging threat when a pair of guards walked by. She put her finger up to her mouth to warn him not to talk and led them quietly across the city square to wait for her father to exit his building.

◊   ◊   ◊

"That's him." Taliya's breath caught the second she spotted her father Hizel walking out of the double doors of the three-story stone building. She remembered him as a tall, muscular man with a well-trimmed black beard and wise, alert brown eyes. The man she saw before her now had a stoop to his tall, thin frame, an uneven long beard speckled with white strands, and lifeless eyes.

He walked with no zeal, making it easy to follow him as he worked his way over the bridge and through the narrow dirt streets on the other side of the river. Here the familiar stench of the housing district attacked Taliya's nose. The combination of rotten fish and decomposed garbage caused her to force back a gag.

She still felt like puking once they reached the house in the middle of the row of other identical houses and couldn't wait to get inside away from the awful smells of the streets. She watched her father open the door and go in before whispering to Javan. "Promise me you'll stay invisible no matter what when we go inside. This will go quicker if my father doesn't know you're here, and if my mom comes home in the middle of our conversation, I don't need you getting caught, too."

"But--"

She squeezed his hand. "Promise me. No matter what."

"I promise."

"Thank you." She dropped his hand, eased the door open, and stepped inside, the invisible Javan right behind her.

The dim light from the fireplace in the front right corner revealed the house looked the same as Taliya remembered it. The loft that used to be her room hung over the kitchen in the back left corner, her parents' room took up the back right back corner, and bookshelves covered the walls of the common room that spanned the width of the house.

The only furniture was a round table with three chairs near the kitchen and two rocking chairs near the fireplace, one of which was currently occupied by her father. Seeing that third chair at the table surprised Taliya. Her parents must have kept it there as a reminder of their lost daughter. Encouraged by the fact that they did miss her yet determined to keep her emotions out of the conversation, she approached Hizel.

"Good evening, father. I'm here for some information about dragon eggs." She maneuvered herself between him and the fireplace. "I need to know where the Dusk and Midnight eggs are kept and how to get them through the portal."

He father stopped rocking and calmly opened his eyes. That wasn't the startled response she expected. "Did the Collector collect the Dawn Stalker I sent you to Keckrick to protect?"

"You haven't seen me in fifteen years, and the first thing you want to know is whether or not the Collector collected his dragon?"

"You haven't seen me either, and the only thing you want is information. I didn't think we were going to do the sappy how-have-you-been stuff."

"Correct." Taliya pushed her emotions down once again and shoved her shoulders up. She desperately wanted to hug her father, sit in his lap, and tell him all about her adventures in Keckrick since her arrival there. But her mother would be home soon, and she did NOT want to see her mother. "I will answer your question if you answer mine."

"Deal."

"The Dawn Stalker Kisa is now part of Javan's collection. To finish his collection, we need to gather a Dusk egg and a Midnight egg, take them through the portal to hatch, and bring them back to Zandador so he can ride them."

The more she talked, the more eager she became to tell her father everything. "You know where the eggs are and how to decipher the codes to activate the portal.

I've read the book of codes kept in the library in Tulkar but would appreciate a summary. That's one thick book."

"You still are a fast talker, huh?" Her dad smiled and stood. "Hand me your bag."

"Why?"

"You'll see."

Taliya lifted the strap over her shoulder and handed him the bag that held her darts, potions, and scales from Kisa. She kept one eye on the door and one on her father. The door remained closed while her father moved a stone from the hearth of the fireplace and pulled out a small blue bag as well as a rolled-up parchment.

"This bag contains the four scales you'll need to activate the portal to Earth. Once you insert them, pay close attention to the flashing colors. Whatever color flashes first is the dominant color and determines the order in which you'll tap the scales." He put the small bag in her bag and held up the parchment. "This is the map that will lead you to the Dusk eggs. They are in an underground cave that serves as an incubator for the dormant eggs, and the cave is protected by several traps to ensure predators do not disturb the eggs.

"After you remove the egg from the safety of the cave, you have a maximum of forty-eight hours to get it to Earth. Otherwise the baby dragon will die before it ever has a chance to hatch in Earth's atmosphere."

"Understood. Where is the map for the Midnight eggs?" She asked the question on a whim. If the Dusk egg strategy worked, perhaps they could duplicate the process when it came time for Javan to collect a Midnight Stalker.

"I am not the keeper of that map, but it doesn't matter. No one can get to those eggs with Ayzyd roaming the land in Midnight Territory. She is the largest, fiercest, most dangerous Midnight Stalker to ever live, and all other Midnight Stalkers live in fear of her. She has been known to eat humans even when she isn't hungry, especially those who go searching for dragon eggs."

Taliya shivered at thought of encountering such a dragon when the door opened. Her mother stepped inside, followed by a boy who resembled her and looked to be about ten years old.

She stared at the boy in disbelief until the sharp, grating voice of her mother broke her concentration. "I thought I was rid of you."

◇　◇　◇

Standing behind the rocking chair within arm's reach of everyone in the room, Javan forced himself to remain invisible despite his immediate distaste for Taliya's mother. She wasn't much taller than Taliya and had the same brown skin, black hair, and strikingly beautiful face. However, she had an evil edge to her eyes and harshness to her voice Javan wasn't prepared for. Taliya apparently wasn't prepared either because she stood with her mouth gaping open while staring at her mother. Or was she looking at the boy beside her mother?

"What? The talkative Taliya has no response?" The woman cocked her head as she continued her speech. "Perhaps you've learned some manners wherever you have been hiding, but that won't do you much good when I return you to the governor."

"You can't turn her in, Lily," Taliya's dad said, putting the bag on the mantle and stepping between her and Taliya. "She's here on important business and was just leaving. There is no need to mention this little visit to Emilia."

Lily smiled. "As a loyal citizen of the Land of Zandador, I must obey the law. That includes turning in wanted criminals."

A wanted criminal? Javan held back a gasp. What had Taliya done to warrant that title?

"You know as well as I do that she is not a criminal," Taliya's dad said. "All she did was explore the land outside of the city. Even as a child, she had the courage to do what none of the rest of us dared. You can't punish her for that."

"The law says we can, Hizel." Lily grabbed Taliya's arm and spoke to the boy. "Samson, hold on to her other arm. We're going to collect our reward from Governor Emilia when we turn your sister in."

Javan lifted his sword but froze when a pale Taliya looked in his direction and shook her head. She mouthed the words "take the map" and eyed the bag that her father had put down.

He didn't want to take the map. He wanted to help her. Why had he made such a dumb promise to Taliya? Did she really want him to choose the map over her?

Taliya attempted to jerk free from her mother's arm. "I'll go," she said, "but you don't get to touch me."

"You are in no position to give me orders." Her mother put one hand on the back of Taliya's neck, the other on her arm, and shoved her through the doorway.

Javan rushed to the door, but the boy closed it before he could make it through. He put his hand on the handle, ready to charge after Taliya. But he couldn't chase her yet. First he needed that map and those scales. He thus turned and sheathed his sword.

His sudden appearance caused a high-pitched yelp from Taliya's father as he tripped over the hearth.

Javan didn't bother trying to calm the surprised man. "What kind of a man are you? How can you let her take Taliya away like that?"

"Where did you come from? Who...who are you?"

"The name's Javan, and right after I take that bag, you're coming with me to get Taliya back before they take her to the governor." He reached for the man's arm, but Hizel's hand touched Javan's cheek first.

"Incredible." He rubbed his thumb under Javan's left eye. "I didn't notice those eyes the night you were born, but now I see the prophecy is true. You are the boy whose eyes shine like emeralds who has entered the Battle of the Throne. You are the Collector."

Javan brushed the man's hand away. He hated it when people commented about his weird eyes. "Yes. I am. And I need your daughter to help me find a Dusk egg and get me through the portal. Without that dragon, I can't complete my collection."

"Correction. You need a Protector. I am a Protector. I can help you find the egg and open the portal."

"No. I need Taliya. We need to go get her now."

"It's too late. My wife is right. Taliya broke the law and must pay the consequences. She'll be hanged by noon tomorrow."

"Tomorrow?" Javan choked on the word. "We can't let that happen! Where are they taking her? How can we help her escape?"

"Nothing short of a pardon from the king himself can save her."

"I've got two swords and a dragon that say otherwise."

"Listen, boy." Hizel's voice lowered and took on a threatening tone. "The throne is more important than one person. Taliya has done her duty by keeping Kisa safe for you. Her purpose has been served. My purpose remains: help you win the throne. I got you to Earth when you were a baby; I can get you and a dragon egg to Earth again."

"Unbelievable." Javan shook his head in disgust. "No wonder Taliya didn't want to come home." He snatched the bag with the map and scales in it. "First, I'm going to save your daughter. Then I'm going to win the throne. When I do, I will find some sort of fitting punishment for parents who betray their own blood."

With that said, he gripped his Dawn sword and teleported to the rendezvous point by the lake.

CHAPTER 18

Imprisoned

Taliya pounded on the door for the hundredth time. "I demand to speak to the governor. I have a right to be heard."

The problem was that no one heard her, not even the guards. She had been led to the lowest level of the prison to the smallest room at the end of the longest hall. One door. One cot. One stinky bucket. No windows. No light. All she had for company was complete darkness and complete silence.

How had she let herself get caught? She should have shoved her mother, grabbed the bag, and ran. That stupid boy shocked her. She had never even considered the possibility that her parents would have another child. For one, her mother hated children. For another, she didn't think her parents would be granted the right to have a second child after Taliya had caused so much trouble.

The fact that her brother existed made Taliya wonder what kind of favor her mother or father owed the governor. The further fact that she was currently sitting in a prison cell made her believe she was the favor.

Taliya beat the door again, ignoring her sore hand. When no one came, she crossed the room in two steps and collapsed on the creaky cot. Hopefully Javan had taken the bag with the map and scales and was already on his way back to Dusk Territory. He had been with her when she hid the book of codes under some rocks. Surely he would be able to read the book on his own, decipher the codes, and get himself through the portal with an egg.

She threw her arm over her eyes and tried to force sleep upon her. "Useless." She grunted and returned to the door. "I'm thirsty! Bring me something to drink. How would it look to the Grand Governor if you found me dead of dehydration before she had a chance to hang me?"

"Maybe you wouldn't be as thirsty if you didn't talk as much."

A response. She wasn't expecting that. And she certainly wasn't expecting that response to come from a familiar voice. She put her ear against the heavy wooden door. "Javan?"

"Yup. Sorry it took me so long. I've been wandering this maze of dark hallways for hours trying to find you. I'd let you out, but I don't know where the key is."

"The head guard wears it around his neck. You'll never be able to get it off him." She sank to the floor, sadness filling her next words. "You can't risk getting caught. You must leave me and get out of here. Go find the egg. Take it to Earth. Finish your collection."

"I'm not leaving without you."

"Don't be ridiculous. I'm stuck here until they walk me to the gallows."

"Then I'll wait until they come to get you. I'm invisible at the moment, so it's not like anyone can see me. When they open the door, I'll sneak in, grab your hand, and make you invisible, too. We can run out of here together."

"These halls are too narrow, and there will be too many soldiers in the way. We'll never be able to pull off that kind of escape." She sat up a little straighter. "But if you brought Micah--"

"We don't need Micah. He needs to stay hidden. We have Varjiek. I can have him set fire to the gallows as a distraction, then take you and run."

"That's one way." She imagined the fire missing the mark and burning the people standing around the stage instead. She shook the image out of her head and proposed a less destructive plan. "Micah has the power to override the governor's decree. He can set me free with one word, and the governor has to comply. I would be able to live in Zandador as a free woman without worrying about the governor's guards hunting me down."

After a pause, Javan finally said, "That's not nearly as fun, but I'll get Micah. In the meantime, swallow your spit."

"Swallow my spit?"

"You said you were thirsty. Drink your spit so you don't die of dehydration before we have a chance to rescue you."

Taliya chuckled. "That's not the kind of refreshing drink I had in mind." Nevertheless, she leaned her head back, closed her eyes, and swallowed a mouthful of saliva. Somehow that simple act made her not feel quite so thirsty or quite so alone in the overwhelming darkness.

◊　◊　◊

Specks of sand tickled his face. Micah brushed them off, turned over, and kept snoozing. But when a wall of sand smacked his entire body, he immediately sat up, snatched the sword lying beside him, and tried to locate the source of the commotion. Was it an animal? The wind? A person?

Two large, round eyes glaring at him under the early glow of the pre-dawn sky confirmed the first option: an animal. More specifically, a dragon. "Varjiek." Micah blinked the sleepiness out of his eyes and stood, looking around for Javan and Taliya. "Javan, there are better ways to wake a man up than to have your dragon throw sand in his face."

Varjiek moved his snout so close that Micah could feel the breath from the dragon's nostrils on his chest. "Javan," Micah said slowly, "what's with your dragon staring at me like he wants to eat me?"

Varjiek gave a slight shake of his head back and forth while keeping his eyes locked on Micah's. This time he addressed the dragon. "You're not trying to eat me?"

He shook his head again and seemed to want Micah to ask him another question. "Where's Javan?"

The dragon snorted and sat down, keeping his head locked in place.

"Ah," he said, understanding the dragon's frustration. "That's not a question you can easily answer with a flick of your head."

"Okay. Only questions with a yes or no answer." Micah smiled, intrigued by the concept of having a conversation with a dragon that was not his slave. "Are Javan and Taliya here?"

A shake of the head no.

"Did they make it to Oer?"

A quick nod yes.

"Did they make it out of Oer?"

A nod and a shake.

"Yes and no? You're confusing me. Which is it?"

Varjiek lowered his body to the ground, touched Micah with his nose, and swiveled his neck around to touch his back.

"You want me to come with you?"

A nod.

"Are they in trouble?"

A short, quick nod.

"Then let's go." Eager for action, he gathered what few things he had and hopped on Varjiek's back. As they zipped away, Micah wondered what kind of trouble Javan and Taliya could have possibly gotten into in the insignificant factory town of Oer.

◊   ◊   ◊

Javan's head hurt from the teleporting back and forth between the prison and the lake. He had been tracking the head guard looking for an opportunity to take the key from him while making sure he didn't miss Micah's arrival. He didn't need Micah charging into the city on Varjiek without knowing what was going on.

If they didn't arrive soon, though, Javan would have to stay in the city and somehow rescue Taliya on his own. Noon was less than two hours away, and the crowd had already started to gather in the amphitheater to watch the show.

He sat down on a large stone by the shore and held his tired, hurting head in his hands. "God," Javan prayed, "help me find a way to save Taliya. She would still be safe if I hadn't made her come back here. Please don't let her die because of me."

"Why is Taliya in danger of death?"

Javan looked up to see Micah standing over him. Javan jumped to his feet, a sense of relief filling his anxious heart. He wasn't going to have to face this challenge alone after all. He murmured a quick thanks to God, then said to Micah, "I'll explain on the way."

Let me guess, Varjiek said, keeping himself invisible, *you need a ride into the city.*

"Good guess," Javan said.

Let's go. Now. Varjiek appeared long enough for Javan to see where he was standing. Half of his scales had already turned golden. *All this flying has made me extra hungry, and soon I will not trust myself to keep from snacking on the people in the city.*

"What did Varjiek guess?" Micah asked.

"It's not important. What's important is that we get to Oer before the governor executes Taliya and before Varjiek wants to eat every person he sees."

"Executes Taliya? What kind of trouble did she get herself into in less than a day?"

"The kind of trouble only the king's son can get her out of. Like I said, I'll explain on the way." The two men hopped on the hungry dragon and flew towards Oer.

CHAPTER 19

The Ghost

The door creaked open, wakening Taliya from a fitful sleep. How much time had passed since she had talked to Javan? Had it been long enough for him to get Micah, and had Micah ordered the governor to release her? Is that why the door was opening?

Two soldiers carrying lanterns burst in, hung the lights on hooks on either side of the door, and retreated. The tall, slender figure of Governor Emilia decked out in a purple shirt and black skirt replaced the soldiers, and she waited until the door eased shut before speaking.

"Today is a day of grand celebration." The light danced off Emilia's shiny black hair that she wore slicked back into a bun, and her dark skin glowed with delight. "I've ordered the closure of all the factories, and every citizen will be in attendance to watch you hang from the gallows on the stage in the amphitheater. You will be a fantastic demonstration of what happens to those who break the law."

Taliya remained impassive on the cot. Micah obviously had not had a chance to chat with Emilia yet, and she needed to stall to give the guys time to get to her. "If you had been sentenced at the age of six to a lifetime of slavery, you would have been inspired to break the unjustly harsh law as well."

"You are to be on your feet when speaking to me." The governor reached over, yanked Taliya's hair, and pulled her off the bed. "Nothing will give me greater pleasure than watching you swing from that rope, but you don't have to die today. We can instead make this the day we restore you to your place of slavery in my home. All you have to do is tell me how you escaped and where you have been hiding for the last fifteen years."

"That bothers you, doesn't it?" Taliya straightened her hair and teased the tyrant. "You can't stand not knowing how a little girl got out of your big, fortified city." She paused for effect and held up two fingers. "Twice."

"You are of no significance to me." Emilia's eyes narrowed, showing Taliya she didn't believe her own words. "As the leader of this city, I simply need to know where the security lapses are. If you can provide me with that information, I will allow you to live."

"Nah." Taliya shrugged. "I think you need to learn you don't always get what you want in life. I'll take my methods of escape with me to the grave."

The governor slapped Taliya's cheek and pounded on the door. "Guards! Come get the prisoner and take her to the gallows immediately!"

So much for stalling. Taliya bit her bottom lip, wishing she had kept her mouth shut. Now she had made Emilia so mad that even a pardon from Micah may not have the power to save her.

◊　　◊　　◊

Micah sensed the tension in Varjiek's muscles beneath his golden scales as he slowly circled the city center of Oer with Micah and Javan on his back. Men, women, and children dressed alike in the drab brown uniforms Omri required all Zandadorian citizens to wear filled the streets around the amphitheater, leaving the dragon no space to land but an abundance of food to eat as his feeding time approached.

Eager to get off the dragon and send him away to eat, Micah leaned forward and spoke in Javan's ear. "Have him drop us off on the roof of the tallest building." He pointed to a stone building that stood two stories higher than the rest of those around the square. Its flat roof overlooked both the amphitheater on one side and the fountain in the middle of the square on the other. "That's where the governor conducts her business."

Javan nodded and relayed the instructions to Varjiek. Without hesitation, Varjiek zoomed to the roof and darted away as soon as Micah and Javan jumped off him. At least Micah assumed he darted away. He had made himself invisible as they approached the city, and Micah could no longer see him once he lost contact with the dragon.

"What if we didn't get here in time?" Javan's voice sounded strained as he peered over the side of the building.

"We did," Micah said. "People are still streaming into the stadium looking for seats, and only a rope is hanging from the gallows. If they had killed her already, her body would be hanging there until sundown."

"We can't let her get to the gallows." Javan turned his attention from the crowd to Micah. "You've met the governor before, right? She'll listen to you?"

"Yes. And she should. She's my father's cousin and follows his laws to the letter. I've been here a few times to conduct standard inspections, and she's always treated me with the same reverence she treats my father. Whatever I tell her to do, she'll do."

"Good." Javan nodded, walked to the steel hatch door in the middle of the flat stone roof, and crouched to put his hand on the latch of the door. "Ready?"

"Yes." Micah expected Javan to open the door. Instead, he drew his sword. And disappeared. "Javan? Where'd you go?"

Javan clamped his hand over Micah's mouth, suddenly reappearing. "Shh. Not so loud. Just hold on to my shirt and don't let go until we find the governor. As long as you are in contact with me, we'll both be invisible and can go wherever we want without being noticed." Javan dropped his hand and once again vanished.

"Whoa." Micah reached out to what appeared to be thin air and touched Javan's ear, making him visible to Micah. "How is this possible?"

"I don't know how. I just know that when I put Varjiek's scale above the hilt of this sword, I can become invisible. Anyone I touch can also become invisible when I'm holding this sword, so stay close and don't touch anyone else."

"Definitely not." Micah kept his excitement in check as they slipped into the stuffy attic. He recalled Vince mentioning Javan's invisibility trick when they were in Nahat, but Micah didn't think Javan could actually become invisible. This ability gave the Collector incredible power, power he was currently sharing with Micah. What kinds of things could they do as invisible men?

"Where do we go from here?"

Javan's question brought Micah back to the present. "Emilia's office encompasses most of the first floor. A stairway at the end of the hall will take us to the front entrance, and we can get to her office from there."

Javan nodded and led them through the empty hallway and down the spiral stairwell to the front entrance. It, too, was empty.

"That was way too easy," Javan said. "Where is everyone?"

"Outside." A glance out the windows revealed soldiers prodding the crowds toward the amphitheater. "The governor will wait for the crowd to settle and will be the last one to arrive. The gongs will sound right before she addresses the people and orders the execution."

"Then you better intercept her before she can even get down there."

"Her office is through those doors." Micah pointed across the lobby to a pair of cedar doors with a bust of Omri on one side and Emilia on the other. "I can handle her on my own." He broke contact with Javan and crossed the lobby.

Without bothering to knock, he flung the doors open. "Emilia, I demand that you drop all charges against Taliya and release her into my custody straightaway."

An empty room greeted him, and the sound of a booming gong reverberating in the distance answered his demands.

◊ ◊ ◊

Taliya's breaths became faster and more shallow as a guard lifted her onto a box and slipped a scratchy rope around her neck. Yet she refused to let herself cry. She kept her head held high, determined to die with as much dignity as she could muster while the hem of the brown dress she'd been forced to put on tickled her knees.

Javan and Micah were nowhere to be seen. Neither were her parents.

The last faces she would see before dying belonged to scared, heartless strangers. That wouldn't be entirely awful if she could at least impart some final words to them, but since her mouth was stuffed with a sock and the sock was tied tightly in with a cloth wrapped around her face, she couldn't say a word.

Perhaps if she had gagged herself from childhood and learned how to obey the laws that made no sense to her, she wouldn't be in this predicament. Her mother would have loved a quiet, obedient child, and Taliya wouldn't have felt the need to run away.

She also never would have truly lived. She would have been a shell of a human being forced to follow oppressive instructions and never allowed the freedom to learn, to explore, to discover her strengths. Although her life was being cut short at the age of twenty-two, she preferred death to the hundreds of years of lifeless living the people watching her die would inevitably endure.

Once Taliya was in place and the guard secured her hands behind her back with a rope, the gongs sounded again, and the governor stepped onto the stage in front of Taliya. After the echoes of the gongs faded, Emilia spoke.

"I want each of you to take a good look at this girl." Her words sounded more obnoxious than the gongs, but they were infused with a sense of authority that even caused Taliya to pay attention. "She chose to break the law and go beyond the city gates. For that she was sentenced to a life of slavery, an act of mercy on my part because she was so young.

"How did she repay me for not banning her to the Land of No Return for her crime? She escaped again! Yet she found the world outside of these walls so harsh and unforgiving that she chose to return more than a decade later, knowing she would be facing the death penalty for her second crime."

Taliya tried to rub the gag off her mouth with her shoulder. The people needed to know that the Land of Zandador was a spectacular place that they should be allowed to explore. She wanted to encourage them to fight for the right to come and go as they pleased, not believe the governor's lies that the world beyond the gates should terrify them.

"Let this be a warning to all of you. You're safe here in the city. Dangers you can't even imagine lurk outside the gates. And if you break the law, you *will* be punished." The governor turned to Taliya with a smirk that revealed her wicked heart. "Kill her."

The guard tightened the noose. The coarse material dug into her throat.

What a terrible way to die. Alone. Unable to speak. Unable to defend herself. She closed her eyes, suddenly fearful of what would happen to her soul when she took her last breath.

Only death didn't come. Shrieks of shock and wails of surprise pierced her ears. When she opened her eyes, she saw no reason for the confusion, but everyone on the stage and in the stadium looked like they had seen a ghost.

"There he is again!"

Taliya's eyes followed the pointed finger of an old woman to what appeared to be Micah standing on the far left end of the stage.

"Amazing," the governor said. "Micah is so concerned about seeing justice served that he has come back from the grave to witness this girl's death!"

The governor kicked the box out from under Taliya's feet, sending her swinging and gasping for air.

◊   ◊   ◊

Javan stiffened at the sight of Taliya's body dangling from the gallows. Seeing the "ghost" of Micah was supposed to paralyze the governor, not prompt her to speed up the execution. He left Micah's side and ran toward Taliya.

"Wrong!" Micah crossed the stage alongside the invisible Javan, talking as he walked. His booming voice vibrated through air. "I came to take her with me."

Javan wasn't sure what Micah meant by that until he saw Micah wrap his arm around Taliya's waist. Javan immediately touched Micah, making all three of them disappear. Then using the sword he already held, he jumped up and sliced the rope that had been strangling Taliya.

She slumped forward, and Micah adjusted his hold so that he cradled her in his arms. They dodged out of the way right before the governor swiped the air under the gallows.

"Where did she go?" Emilia sounded spooked. "Why would he take her before she died?"

"Is he going to come back for any other lawbreakers?" That question by one of the guards created sheer mayhem. People flooded the aisles of the stadium. Those that couldn't reach the aisles began climbing over each other up the concrete seats, and the panicked yells and screams became a deafening roar courtesy of the amazing acoustics.

"Guards," Emilia said, "get control of these people and send them back to work. Anyone who misses their shifts will be fined three days of food." She snapped her fingers and waved the guards toward the fleeing crowd. She shivered as she studied the space under the gallows again, then exited the stage.

"Stay still and stay quiet," Javan ordered Micah and Taliya. Their best option was to hide in plain sight until the area cleared completely. Or until he could teleport them out of there.

He closed his eyes and pictured the stones by the lake outside of the city. But with the noise that surrounded them, he found it hard to concentrate, and his teleportation attempt failed.

Need a ride? Varjiek's question connected with Javan's mind above the commotion.

Javan didn't know how to answer without giving away their position. Fortunately, he didn't need to. The dragon swept the stage with his front legs, gathering the trio in one claw and smashing the gallows with his other one. Before Javan could catch his breath from the sudden jolt, Varjiek had them in the air and flying away from the city at a speed that made Javan's teeth rattle and ears pop.

CHAPTER 20

Friend or Foe?

"How far away did you say Japheth is from here?" Taliya looked out the window of the secluded cabin while Micah sharpened his sword on the other side of the spacious room. She could see a giant barn to her left, rolling hills in front of her, and a gently flowing river to her right.

"A half a day's journey by foot," Micah said, "but only a handful of minutes by Noon Stalker."

"Then why isn't Javan back yet? He's been gone nearly half a day."

"He's probably still waiting for Ravier. Vince never said what time to meet him there. Getting into Japheth is not an easy task. I wouldn't be surprised if Ravier waited until dark to show up."

"I hate not knowing what's happening." First Javan had sent her ahead to Dusk Territory. Now he had left her behind while he went to put his Dawn Stalker scale in the column at Stalker Square. Some team they made. She wanted to play an active part in this mission, not be left out of all the action. On the plus side, she did enjoy sleeping in an actual bed last night and eating fresh fruit and vegetables from the garden on the property.

"I understand the feeling. Have you forgotten that you and Javan left me behind while you got yourself captured and almost killed?"

"Nobody in Japheth wants to hang me. Javan should have let me go with him."

Movement near the river caught her eye. She opened the door and stepped on the porch to get a better look. Sure enough, a she could see a woman securing her canoe to the dock. "Micah, didn't you say this training camp belonged to you and that no one else ever came here?"

"Yes. My father had this place built just for me. Only myself and those who trained me even know this place exists."

"You might want to add that woman to the list."

"What woman?" Micah popped out of his seat and joined Taliya on the porch. "Who is she, and what is she doing here?" He propped his sword against the wall. "I'm going to send her away."

"Not so fast." Taliya grabbed Micah's arm. "You're dead, remember? You need to stay inside and out of sight. I'll go."

"If she's wandering these hills, she's probably in hiding herself and hasn't heard about my untimely passing." He jerked his arm free from her grip. "Besides, it's just a woman. She looks perfectly harmless, and I doubt one conversation with her will somehow get back to my father or the Destroyer who wants to kill me."

"Fine. Go." She watched him walk away, then went back inside for her slingshot and darts. She had a strange feeling that the woman wasn't as harmless as Micah suspected.

◊   ◊   ◊

Javan pushed the sleeves of his light weight green shirt up past his elbows, letting the warm Zandadorian sun kiss his tan arms. He probably should have worn the one brown shirt he owned that matched a normal civilian's clothes for this trip into the capital city, but this shirt Esara had given him in Keckrick with its sweat-resistant, cooling material was his favorite. It also happened to be stylish and made him feel like a dashing warrior even though it desperately needed to be washed.

I cannot wait quietly here much longer, Varjiek said as a streak of scales on his tail turned golden. *The peak of my feeding time may still be hours away, but my stomach wants food now.*

"Give me five more minutes." Javan clamped his hand over his mouth and pressed his back firmly against Varjiek's side as if that would make him more invisible. Every word had been magnified from his position on the stage in Stalker Square, and he hoped no one would investigate the noise in the otherwise empty amphitheater that made the one in Oer look shabby.

It had ten times as many rows of concrete seats. The seats wrapped three quarters of the way around a square half the size of a football field paved with Stalker scales. A wall with arched openings near the top that separated the square from Omri's castle rose higher than the rows of seats, and four fountains with life-size statues of Dragon Stalkers as centerpieces decorated the four corners of the square.

The rainbow-colored Dawn and Dusk Stalkers in the front two corners and the golden Noon Stalker and black Midnight Stalker in the back two corners were Javan's favorite part of the arena. He could enjoy the magnificence of all four fountains from his place on the theatre-sized stage in the middle of the square.

He had managed to stay still and quiet since they landed on the stage at sunrise, but that stillness was mostly the result of a very long nap he had taken curled up beside his dragon. Both of them had needed the rest, but now Javan felt anxious to meet Ravier and get on with the day.

Where was his grandfather? Had Vince been able to get word to him? If so, had he been able to sneak Ravier into the city? Javan assumed the answers to those last two questions were yes and that Ravier was watching and waiting for him to put Kisa's scale in the Collector's column.

Ravier would have no way of knowing Javan had arrived if he continued to remain invisible. With that in mind, he untucked the scale from his belt and stepped away from his cloaked dragon.

What are you doing? You are fully exposed! The stage shook, indicating Varjiek had risen to his feet. *Draw your invisibility sword.*

He shook his head and exited the stage by way of the front spiral staircase. Nerves wracked his body as he made his way to the front left column. Being in plain view of whoever happened to pass by made him feel vulnerable, but he forgot all about his surroundings when he reached the column.

The handprints he had made in the soft, malleable surface on his first trip here remained. Forming those handprints had officially entered him in the Battle of the Throne and brought him face to face with the Dark King at the same time. He traced his handprints as he recalled that terrifying meeting, then brushed his hand down the vertical line of four triangle-shaped holes above his handprints.

Varjiek's scale filled the top slot and retained its intense, golden glow despite having been placed there on his second trip to Stalker Square almost a month ago. On this third trip, he would give Kisa's scale a chance to shine.

He rubbed Kisa's white scale one final time, gave it a kiss, and inserted it in the slot just below Varjiek's. Javan jumped back as the column hissed and sparked while the scale intensified to a blinding white. Then with one loud pop, the scale began to display four bright, distinct streaks of red, orange, pink, and purple.

"So cool," Javan whispered. "Kisa would be proud."

"Are you going to stand there staring at your dragons' scales all day," said a gruff but quiet voice in his ear, "or should we get out of here before you're arrested for violating the dress code?"

He turned to find the familiar green eyes of Ravier, but nothing else about him looked the same. He wore the black uniform of one of Omri's soldiers. As if that wasn't surprising enough, his slicked-back, shoulder length brown hair and wild, bushy beard were gone, leaving his head bald and his cheeks bare.

Although he was still tall, his wide shoulders and once thick chest had lost most of their muscle mass. Had the man eaten anything since Javan had last seen him a few weeks ago?

"Grandfather?" Javan had to work to keep his voice low to prevent it from the magnifying effects of the amphitheater. "What has happened to you? And where did you come from? How did you sneak up on me like that?"

The gate opened before Ravier could respond, and nine soldiers carrying a combination of Jolt Blasts and swords entered the square. One of them yelled at Ravier. "Why are you in Stalker Square, soldier? This isn't your area to patrol."

"It's a good thing I passed by," Ravier said casually, directing his gaze to the stage rather than the small army. "I've just caught the Collector adding a scale to his column. I was going to arrest him for his blatant disregard of the civilian uniform law, but I don't think his dragon will let that happen."

"What dragon?" the soldier asked.

"That one." Javan pointed to Varjiek, who immediately uncloaked himself and roared a streak of fire through the air. "Nice, V! Grab Ravier and take him back to the camp. I'll meet you there." He drew his Dawn sword, confusing Ravier.

"What are you doing? You don't need to stay and fight. Fly away with your dragon."

"You can go with Varjiek. I don't like traveling by claw."

"Huh?"

Varjiek swooped down, scooped Ravier up in his back claw, and flew away. That left Javan alone with the soldiers, one of whom had his Jolt Blast aimed right at Javan's heart. Javan smiled and waved as the soldier pulled the trigger. He vanished a split second before the lightning bolt reached his position.

◊   ◊   ◊

When Micah stepped off the porch, he planned to shoo the woman away. But the graceful way she moved as she eased out of her canoe onto the dock captivated him. With her honey-colored skin, wavy auburn hair that brushed past her shoulders, and standard brown dress that somehow perfectly fit her tall, slender figure, she looked unlike any woman he had ever come across. What was such a vision doing wandering in the valley between the Land of Zandador and Midnight Territory?

"Are you going to stand there and stare at me all day," the vision said in a silky sweet voice, "or do you intend to say hello?"

"Hello." That wasn't the word he wanted to say. He wanted to say something witty to impress her, but watching her saunter down the dock towards him apparently dislodged the wit center of his brain.

Her brown eyes twinkled as she stopped right in front of him. "You're still staring."

"And you are intruding." He finally made his brain form words while the wonky feeling traveled to his knees. He usually towered over women, but she was only a mere two inches shorter than him and smelled like roses. "No one is allowed here without my permission. How did you even know about this place?"

"I have my ways. Besides, I was told you were dead." She shrugged. "I didn't think you would be using this place anymore, and it would be a shame to let all that food in your garden go to waste."

"Ah. You know who I am." This brought a smile to his face and helped him relax. Now he could use his status to impress her. "I could have you arrested for trespassing, but I'm willing to overlook it if you cook me lunch."

"There's one problem with that." She locked eyes with him and placed her hand on his cheek. "I'm not really the cooking type."

"Oh? What type are you?"

She slid her hand down to his neck and flipped it over so that the sharp edge of a ring he hadn't even noticed she was wearing pricked his neck. "The kind who follows orders."

"Orders? What orders?"

"The king's!" Javan yelled the answer to Micah's question from somewhere behind him. When had he returned, and why would he choose this moment to make an annoyance of himself? "Get away from her now, Micah! She's the Destroyer!"

The Destroyer? Not a chance. Javan had to be mistaken.

"How did he know that?" The woman backed away on her own. A combination of shock and anger filled her once-inviting eyes, indicating Javan was right. "I guess we'll have to finish this later." Without another word, she sprinted down the dock, leapt in her canoe, and rowed away with a speed Micah admired.

Too bad she wanted to kill him. He kind of wanted to marry her.

"She almost slit your throat," Javan said, spinning Micah around. "Are you okay? How did she know you were here?"

The jerk from Javan plus the warm trickle of blood down his neck brought Micah out of his trance. He should have thanked Javan, but the realization that he just avoided an embarrassing death brought a defensive question out of his mouth instead. "How could you not tell me that the Destroyer was a woman?"

"Why would you assume the Destroyer was a man? You should have stayed out of sight and let Taliya deal with any visitors."

"To be fair," Taliya said, approaching them from the cabin carrying her slingshot, "it is Micah's land, and I told him to go talk to her. When I saw her put her hand on his neck, I had a dart ready to shoot her with. Then you teleported yourself into my line of sight and ruined my shot."

"Um...Taliya? Javan can't teleport. He needs Kisa for that."

A strong breeze followed by a thump swallowed Taliya's response. A bald soldier appeared in the grass a few feet away, and a suddenly visible, partially golden dragon turned a somersault in the sky as if to say hello, then vanished.

"Don't you ever tell that dragon to carry me in his claw again," the soldier said, shaking his finger at Javan. "I ride on his back or not at all."

"Sorry, Grandfather," Javan said. He shrugged and tried unsuccessfully to hide a smile. "We needed to get out of there quickly, and that was the fastest way."

"No. The way you left was the fastest way. How did you get from there to here without riding on your dragon?"

"Yeah, Javan," Micah said, wondering the same thing. Surely he couldn't actually teleport himself. "How did you get here without riding Varjiek?"

One look at the Collector's sly smile answered Micah's question.

CHAPTER 21

The Fourth Team Member

"You can teleport?" The voice of Javan's grandfather sounded oddly familiar, but the soldier didn't look like anyone Taliya had met. Where had she heard that voice before?

"Yes," Javan said. Taliya noticed a shift in Javan's body language as he addressed his grandfather. He forced his shoulders up and his chest out, yet his words seemed to lose a dose of confidence. "A lot has changed since the last time I saw you."

"Apparently. You can teleport. You have a tiny little sidekick. And you befriended your enemy." The man drew the sword at his hip and stuck it under Micah's chin. "Javan may trust you, Micah, but I don't."

"Here we go again." Taliya rolled her eyes. Why was it that everyone who encountered Micah immediately wanted to kill him? He could be a tad selfish, but that was no reason to murder the man. "First of all, I may be tiny, but I am no one's sidekick. Second, put your sword away. This Protector-Collector-Hunter combination may be the strangest alliance Zandador has ever seen, but for once, we're all on the same side."

The man didn't move his sword but glared down at Taliya. "Who are you?"

"Taliya. Who are you?"

"Did you say Taliya?"

"Yes. We've covered that. That means it's your turn to answer my question. I'm assuming you're Ravier since Varjiek dropped you off, but the soldier's uniform makes me suspicious."

He lowered his sword and forced his full attention on her. "You're not supposed to be alive."

"Were you in Oer when you saw me disappear from the hangman's noose?" Taliya jumped back, loaded her slingshot with a dart, and aimed it at Ravier's chest.

"I will shoot you and destroy the antidote to the poison on this dart before I let you take me back there."

"He's my grandfather, Taliya," Javan said. "He's here to help us, not take you back to Oer."

"Impressive," Ravier said. "I see you've learned how to shoot poisoned darts rather than rocks out of the slingshot I taught you how to use."

"What are you talking about?" Taliya lowered her weapon and dug into her memory to recall the time she learned how to use a slingshot. Was that why she recognized Ravier's voice? She imagined what the man standing in front of her would look like with lots of hair and a bushy beard. "You are him! You're the boring man who stuck me in a cave and took me and Kisa to Keckrick."

"I am not boring." His penetrating gaze made her uncomfortable. "I am practical and do what's necessary to survive."

"Hold on," Javan said to Ravier. "You've met Taliya, and you knew Kisa existed? Why didn't you ever mention that fun fact when I was first trying to collect a Dawn Stalker?"

"Because I thought they were both dead. I heard that a volcano erupted about five years ago and wiped out the entire area where I left them."

"It did," Taliya said, her mind flashing back to that awful day. "My grandfather sent me across the river to care for Kisa just before the eruption. She and I survived by hiding in the maze of caves, but I lost my grandparents and the entire village of Fralick. Kisa and I have been on our own ever since."

"I'm sorry to hear that, young lady." His voice softened. "Your grandparents were good people. But what happened to the dragon? Where is she now?"

"She's part of Javan's collection and is waiting for us in Dusk Territory."

"Speaking of dragons," Micah said, "I'm ready to return to mine."

"We will as soon as Varjiek finishes eating and can fly us back," Javan said.

"Surely 'us' doesn't include him," Ravier said, raising his sword.

"Grand-fath-er," Javan said, dragging out the syllables, "put your sword away. Like Taliya said, Micah is on our side."

"That's what Vince told me, but I didn't believe him, and I don't believe you. How can you befriend a man who is competing against you in the Battle of the Throne?"

"Actually, Ravier," Micah said, crossing his arms as though the sword near his face didn't bother him, "I've dropped out of the competition. I was fighting as my father's proxy anyway, and I've decided he doesn't deserve to retain the role of king."

"Forgive me if I don't trust you."

"Then trust me." Javan put his hands on Ravier's and pushed his sword to the ground. "Micah is on our team. You don't have to like him, but you do have to let him live."

"Why? In addition to countless other atrocities, he tossed both me and your mother in a dungeon, then tried to kill my wife and everyone else in Gri with his dragon."

"'Tried' to kill?" Taliya noted that key word while putting her hand on Javan's arm. Her loved ones might be dead, but she wanted Javan's family to be alive and well. "So they are all safe?"

"I am not going to divulge any information about my family in the presence of this Hunter. If you insist on his continued presence, then I insist you keep personal matters personal and heed any warnings I present that indicate sabotage."

"Micah isn't here to sabotage anyone," Taliya said, letting go of Javan's arm and grabbing Micah's, "but he is going to help me gather food from the garden while you two chat about private family matters."

"I am?"

"You are." She tugged Micah toward the garden behind the cabin, thankful for an excuse to get away from Ravier. That man's intensity made her nervous, and she wasn't sure she liked this newest addition to the crew.

◊   ◊   ◊

"Well?" Javan questioned his grandfather the second Micah was out of earshot. "What happened to my mom and Hannah? Are they safe?"

"Walk with me." Ravier offered no indication of an answer and began strolling along the river in the opposite direction of Micah and Taliya. Irritated, Javan followed while Ravier continued talking. "Let me make sure I got this right. You tracked down a Dawn Stalker in Keckrick, brought a Protector back with you, turned Micah against his father, and gained the ability to teleport along the way."

"That sounds about right." Javan gripped his Noon sword and said, "I can also become invisible."

"You can what?" Ravier stopped. "Where did you go? How is that possible?"

Javan let go of his sword and crossed his arms over his chest. "The Stalker Swords you thought I was an idiot for choosing as my primary weapon have some added benefits when you add Stalker scales to them."

"Interesting. It appears you made a wise choice after all." He began walking again, apparently done with his limited praise. "Fill me in on some details. How did you know about the Dawn Stalker in Keckrick?"

"Varjiek. Getting across the desert with him was quite the ordeal, and I didn't know Micah was following us until he showed up with Mertzer at Taliya's house in the western part of Upper Keckrick. The three dragons got into a scuffle just before a wall of white winds blew me, Micah, and Taliya all the way to the southeastern area of Lower Keckrick.

"We were forced to work together to get back to our dragons with the help of the people of Keckrick and discovered this crazy plot of Omri to use the humminglo harvest from Keckrick to create a mind control drug. If he can control the minds of the people of Zandador, it won't matter if I win the Battle of the Throne. He'll be able to turn all the people against me."

"This is a complication we do not need." Ravier closed his eyes and rubbed his bald head. When he opened them again, he put his hands on Javan's shoulders. "Developing and distributing that drug will take time, time you must use to complete your collection. Vince said you had a plan to take a Dusk egg to Earth. That's risky, but I agree that it's your only option. Omri probably realizes that as well, and that means the portal will be heavily guarded."

"That's why I need you to help me get through and back again." Javan swallowed and decided it was time to press Ravier for information. "My mother knows how to open the portal. Where can we find her to get her help?"

"We can't. She is no longer in Zandador."

"Then where is she? Is she safe?"

"After you left us in Gri, she and I began searching the mountains for your grandmother and everyone else who had fled the town. We found them after two days and determined that the best option was to continue north and find a safe haven in the region of Gibbet."

"That means my mom and grandmother are alive and well?" Javan hugged Ravier. "That's amazing news!"

"Maybe not." Ravier unhooked Javan's arms from around his chest and eased him back. "Your mother was weak from the time she spent in the dungeon and had become quite ill by our second day in the mountains. She was alive when I left the group to return to Zandador, but I am not sure she survived the grueling trip to Gibbet."

"Oh." Javan bit his lip and choked back tears. He only had a few memories of his mother since she came into his life a mere two months ago. Surely he had hadn't saved her from execution simply to have her die in the mountains from sickness. To keep his mind from dwelling on that depressing thought, he changed the subject. "Why didn't you go to Gibbet as well?"

"I needed to be around to keep track of you. Vince helped me set up a new identity as a soldier in the small fishing town of Ziz south of Japheth."

"What about Astor and Hamilton?" He hadn't seen his old, wise mentor and big, burly fighting coach since right after he collected Varjiek. "Where are they?"

"I'm not sure. I left a message for them to go to Gibbet but had to cut off contact once I entered Ziz."

"Okay, then." Javan inhaled and let his breath out slowly before continuing. "We're going to assume Hamilton and Astor are safely in Gibbet with Hannah and my very alive mother. Once I collect these next two dragons, we'll bring them all home."

"Javan, if your mother's not--"

"Stop." He held up his hand. "I need to believe she's fine, and I will continue to believe that unless I have evidence that proves otherwise. We aren't to speak of this again until I have both a Dusk and Midnight Stalker in my collection."

"Then let's talk about where we go from here. Where's this Dusk egg you want to take through the portal?"

"It's safe...somewhere in Dusk Territory."

"Are you telling me you don't have possession of an egg yet?"

"Calm down. I may not have an egg, but I do have a map that shows where the eggs are. There's just one slight problem."

"What's that?"

"The map makes no sense." Javan had studied the map that Taliya's dad provided, but with its random pictures and odd poem, he had no idea where to begin to look for the supposed stash of Dusk eggs. "I'm hoping Taliya can figure it out, but first we need to get back to Dusk Territory."

"All right, but this time I ride on your dragon's back."

"Of course. We all will." Javan wasn't looking forward to the crowded ride back and wondered how angry he would make everyone if he teleported there ahead of them.

◊　◊　◊

Micah yanked ear after ear of corn off the tall stalks in the garden and threw them in a burlap sack. He didn't even like corn. It just happened to be the only food growing around him that wouldn't squish or splat when he pulled, squeezed, and flung it into the sack.

He had been utterly foolish! How could he have let the Destroyer get that close to him? Why couldn't he sense that she was trying to kill him? Had he gone soft and lost his edge since becoming one of the "nice" guys?

Seeing Ravier reminded him of his heartless past and the truly awful way he had treated not only Esmeralda and Ravier when they were his prisoners but also anyone who hadn't done exactly what he wanted when he wanted in the way he wanted. He could hear the cries of children as he carted their parents away to prison for some minor infraction of the law and the ear-piercing shrieks of the soldiers who had died in Fury's Pass because of his self-serving orders.

Ravier should hate him. He hated himself. He had chosen to treat people without respect or common decency. He didn't belong with people like Javan who treated people well.

A breeze whipped a stalk of corn into his face as Varjiek flew over the garden, skimmed over the river, and landed in the grass near Javan and Ravier.

What were those two talking about? Was Ravier trying to convince Javan to toss him aside? If so, where would he go? What would he do? He wouldn't be safe anywhere as long as his father wanted him dead.

If he wasn't safe, Javan and Taliya wouldn't be either. Maybe it was time to part ways. Working together had been convenient and mutually beneficial for all of them when they were in Keckrick, but that didn't make them friends or erase the fact that he was now more of a danger than a help.

He plucked one more ear of corn off the stalk and tossed it in the bag, resolving to detach himself from the group. He would return with them to Dusk Territory, meet up with Mertzer, then hide somewhere in the hills away from his past and any hope he ever had of a future.

CHAPTER 22

Deciphering the Map

Excitement coursed through Taliya's veins as the purple water and bronze sand of the Dusk shore came into view from her perch at the base of Varjiek's neck. This time she was here to hunt dragon eggs and no longer had the dread of facing her parents looming over her soul. Once she put eyes on Kisa, they could officially begin their egg-hunting adventure.

Varjiek landed on the soft sand just south of the Zandadorian portal. "Kisa," she yelled, "we're back!" She blew her Kisa-summoning whistle that fortunately had not been taken from her in Oer, unhooked Micah's arm from around her waist, kicked her feet over the saddlebags of food, and slid off the dragon ahead of the three men who had squeezed together behind her. Within seconds, the white dragon gingerly walked onto the sand from behind the trees. "Hello, girl. It's good to see you! It's okay if you want to stay in the woods. I know you don't like the sand."

Kisa nodded and retreated back onto the solid grassy surface of the woods. Satisfied that Kisa was safe, she turned to Javan. "Javan, where's the map?"

"I'll show you after I get my swords back."

"Oh. Right." She unbuckled his surprisingly light sword belt and held it out while he freed himself from his spot between Ravier and Micah. She had demanded he give it to her before they left to prevent him from teleporting ahead of them. "Aren't you glad you made the flight with us?"

"Thrilled." He walked stiff-legged over to her and snatched his belt. "I think I'm taller and thinner after being jammed between two men twice my size for nearly four hours."

"It wasn't exactly a dream ride for me, either," Micah said, stretching his arms and moving his neck from side to side. "I was trying not to crush Taliya while wondering if Ravier was going to stab me in the back."

"If I'm going to stab you," Ravier said, "I'll do it when you're looking. I'm no coward."

"Gentlemen, enough!" Taliya was not about to let the arguing dampen her good mood. "We made it here safely with a good chunk of the afternoon left to begin our search for the eggs. Let's focus on that rather than your mutual hatred for one another."

"Deciphering this map is definitely going to take some focus." Javan pulled the rolled up parchment out of the waistband on his back and spread it out on the sand.

"This is the map my father gave us?" Taliya expected to be looking at a layout of the Dusk Territory terrain with a clearly marked area showing the location of the dragon eggs. Instead, the "map" contained an assortment of random pictures that included an upside-down waterfall, a bird, odd-shaped trees, a mole, a tunnel, a figure eight, and stepping stones all drawn around a poem in the middle of the page. "How are we supposed to find anything using this?"

"You mean this doesn't make sense to you?" Javan asked.

"Not a bit. Should it?"

"You're the Protector. Don't you specialize in deciphering codes?"

"Portal codes, yes. Map codes?" She threw her hands in the air. "I didn't even know that was a thing!"

"Calm down," Javan said. "Maybe if we read the poem, we can all figure this out together."

"Okay," she said, letting out a deep breath. "You read. I'll listen." She sat in the sand, closed her eyes, and waited to hear the words written on the map.

◊   ◊   ◊

Javan's hands trembled as he picked up the poor excuse for a map, but he refused to let his voice falter. He needed to sound confident that they could make sense of the poem. He cleared his throat and began reading the words written on the page:

"*Start where water falls up.*
Follow the twisting trees.
Travel down through the ground.
Yell where you cannot hear.
Push when the stone yells back.
Duck to enter the cave.
Leave through the one-way door."

"Nope," Taliya said, getting to her feet. "That didn't help. All I have are questions. For instance, where are we supposed to follow these twisting trees to? How do we know when to travel through the ground? For how long? Why won't we be able to hear anything? How will a stone yell back? What are we supposed to push when it does? Where is this 'one-way' door? Why would we need to leave through that? Why can't we go back out the way we came?"

"You overlooked the most obvious question," Micah said. "Where does water fall up?"

I know the answer to that.

Javan turned to see Mertzer inching his way toward the group. "Oh? Where?"

The hilly terrain in the middle of the Territory is home to dangerous waters.

"What's he saying?" Taliya asked.

"I'm not sure yet. Go on, Mertzer," Javan urged. "Tell me about these dangerous waters."

They seem to be perfectly peaceful lakes, but you never know when the water will explode up. I have seen animals drinking from these lakes die from the explosions. It is why I only drink from small streams and am terrified of large bodies of water.

"Can you take us there?"

Only if my Master allows me.

"Of course." Javan turned to the team. "Mertzer knows where water falls up, but Micah, he needs your permission to lead us there."

"Water really does fall up? That's a thing?"

"Sounds like you're stalling, Micah," Ravier said. "Are you not wanting your dragon to assist us?"

Micah shot Ravier an irritated look, marched over to Mertzer, and climbed on his dragon. "Mertzer will take us there, and we leave now."

"Great!" Javan clapped his hands together. "Taliya, you ride on Kisa. Ravier, you and I will take Varjiek. Let's go!"

With the mystery of where to start solved, he began pondering the second problem: *follow the twisting trees.*

The last time he had entered a forest of twisting trees when he was exploring the area with Astor, the trees had won the battle. With that experience in mind, he wasn't sure how they were supposed to follow the twisting trees without setting off a maddening series of tree tremors.

◊   ◊   ◊

"Micah, slow down!" Taliya's throat hurt from yelling those words for the hundredth time. Kisa struggled to keep up with the speedy Mertzer, and Taliya once again lost sight of the dragon in front of her. If it hadn't been for Javan constantly reeling Mertzer back from his spot on Varjiek in the sky, they would have been lost long ago. "This terrain is tough on Kisa."

They had already weaved their way through a forest of huge, colorful trees, zipped across a narrow valley between two daunting mountains, traversed a long stretch of rolling hills, crossed countless streams, and wandered through flat plains covered with gorgeous flowers, pausing only briefly along the way to give the Dusk

Stalker a chance to eat. Now they were headed up a rocky mountainside in the fading light of day.

"Everything okay?" Javan asked from the hovering Varjiek above her.

"No. Kisa is tired. I'm hungry and cranky. We should be setting up camp, not trudging up a mountain this time of day."

"We can camp on the wide ridgeline on the other side of this mountain. You're gonna want to see why we shouldn't stop here."

He flew away, and Taliya mumbled to Kisa, "I'd rather have you teleport us back to the flowery meadow for the night, but let's go find out what campsite Javan has picked for us." She bent closer to Kisa's ear. "If you get me to the top of this mountain in the next three minutes, I'll personally make sure Javan cleans your scales before he gets any sleep tonight."

Kisa nodded and picked up her pace. They made it to the peak while a few rays of sun still lit the sky. That provided just enough light to show a vast valley filled patches of silver sand, sparkling lakes, and giant, ragged rocks.

"Beautiful, isn't it?" Javan asked, walking up to them. Varjiek was floating lazily in the sky while Ravier and Micah each sorted through a sack of food with their backs to each other. Mertzer curled himself in a ball away from everyone with his head facing away from the valley of lakes. "Mertzer says this is the place, but this ridgeline is as close as he'll get to it."

"Is he sure? That water appears to be perfectly normal. None of it is falling up."

"It will. At least it should. Apparently it's not a constant thing." Javan shrugged. "I figure we can get some sleep, then begin looking for twisting trees in the morning."

"Whatever you say." Taliya tapped Kisa's neck. The dragon lowered her front legs, allowing Taliya to easily slide off. "By the way," she said, putting her hand on Javan's shoulder, "you owe Kisa a bath."

"What?"

But she didn't have a chance to explain. A loud BOOM followed by a series of echoing pops from the explosion caused her to latch on to the closest thing to her: Javan's neck.

CHAPTER 23

The Trouble with Twisting Trees

The blast shook Micah's nerves, causing him to drop the bag of food, lose his footing, and stumble backwards into Ravier. As water spewed upward from one of the lakes down below, Ravier said, "Aww. Do you need a hug, too?"

"I don't do hugs." Micah quickly pushed away from Ravier and retrieved the bag. "I tripped. That's all." From the corner of his eye, Micah observed that Taliya wasn't as quick to push away from Javan. Once she did, though, the four of them stood alongside one another atop the mountain staring at the stream of water shooting towards the sky. After a few moments, it vanished, restoring the peaceful surface of the lake.

"Looks like we're in the right place," Taliya said.

"Of course we are." Pride filled Micah's words, and he was glad he didn't run away as planned. He wanted his dragon to get the credit for making the finding of the Dusk eggs possible. Then they would make their exit from the group. "We were led here by *my* dragon, and tomorrow he will lead us through the twisting trees."

"I don't think he's going to want to do that," Javan said.

"Why wouldn't he? He loves to run, and he can 'follow the twisting trees' faster than any other dragon here. Varjiek can't fly through trees, and Kisa certainly can't match Mertzer's speed."

"Those twisting trees make up what are known as slanted acres, dangerous patches of woods found in various places throughout this territory. Animals don't like entering these areas because of the tree tremors that are likely to occur if they make too much noise."

"Dangerous woods? Don't tell me you believe that tree tremors are real," Micah said.

"I'm with Micah on this one," Ravier said. "Trees are trees, regardless of their shape. They don't shake and tremor and seemingly come to life when their precious area is disturbed. It's an absurd myth."

"It is no myth." Javan shook his head from side to side. "I've been caught in one before. The only reason I made it out was because I wasn't very far in to begin with."

"My father did say that the cave is protected by traps to keep predators from disturbing the eggs," Taliya said. "The slanted acres could be one such giant trap."

"There could be traps," Micah said, making a mental note of that interesting bit of information, "but I don't think trees are one of them. If they were, the Protectors wouldn't want to carry the eggs through the slanted acres to hide them in the cave in the first place."

"It's too dark to prove anything one way or the other right now," Javan said. "Let's eat, sleep, and continue in the morning."

"Fine by me." He picked a handful of fruit from the bag and wandered over to his dragon to settle in for the night, amused by the fact that Javan believed tree tremors were real.

◊   ◊   ◊

Javan had never been so happy to see the sun rise. The steady stream of water bursts throughout the night combined with the unforgiving surface of the mountain top made sleep impossible. As soon as the sun provided enough light for him to see, he sat up from his uncomfortable bed and scanned the valley. He smiled when he saw what he expected to see on the other side of the geyser-spewing lakes: an unmistakable patch of slanted acres.

"What's that smile for?" Taliya asked from her sleeping position across the fire pit from him. Long strands of her black hair had escaped from her braided bun, and the whites of her blue eyes were red. She must not have gotten any sleep, either.

"Let me show you." He waved her over and pulled out the map. "Check out these trees." He pointed to the five oddly-shaped trees pictured in a row above the first line of the poem. "See how a different number marks each tree? The spiral starts with one, then the tree that looks like a sideways W is marked with seventeen."

"Then thirty-seven, fifty-four, and seventy-seven. So what?"

"So to follow the twisting trees, we look for these shapes in that forest over there." This time he pointed to the slanted acres across the valley. "We can fly around the edge on Varjiek until we find the spirally tree and walk in from there to find the W tree like on the map."

"Sounds logical, but what do the numbers mean? Is seventeen the number of steps we have to take to get to the second tree, or is it the number of trees between the first and second tree?"

"Whether it's steps or trees," Ravier said, joining them, "we don't know which direction to head from tree to tree."

"That's not the only problem." Micah stood and stretched. "We also don't know if the number of steps or trees between each tree increases as we get farther into the woods or if seventy-seven is the total between tree one and tree five."

"We'll just have to test each theory." Javan rolled the map up and stuck it between his back and belt buckle. "Once we find the starting point, we all walk in different directions, counting our steps. If no one finds the second tree, we start over and count trees instead of steps."

"That's too tedious," Micah said. "Let me have the map, and Mertzer and I will have the trail of trees figured out before Kisa's done eating her morning meal."

"Absolutely not." Javan locked eyes with a terrified Mertzer. The first time they crossed paths was when Javan freed Mertzer from a tree that had attacked him during a tree tremor. He wasn't going to put the Dusk Stalker in harm's way by making him run through the slanted acres. "He remains here."

"He's my dragon. I say he goes."

I must obey my master, Mertzer said. *I will cause a tremor, a vicious one if he orders me to run. You just keep everyone else outside the acres until the tremor is over.*

"He may be your master," Javan replied, "but I am the leader of this mission. You wait here."

"Are you talking to my dragon?" Micah blocked Javan's view of Mertzer. "He doesn't belong to you. He's mine. Stay out of his head."

"He basically just told me that you and he will die if you force him to run through the slanted acres. I know he's your dragon, but I will not let you take him on a double suicide mission through those woods. For the last time, he stays. We go."

"If he stays, I stay."

"Convenient," Ravier said. "The Hunter wants to separate himself from us. He could easily reach Japheth by noon on the back of Mertzer and have an army out here by nightfall to capture us all."

"If I wanted to run away," Micah said, "I wouldn't go to Japheth. *That* would be a suicide mission. My father wants me dead, remember?"

"Maybe you're thinking turning the Collector over would be a good way for you to get back in your father's good graces."

"You have no idea what I'm thinking."

"Here's what I'm thinking," Javan said, putting an end to the argument. "I'm thinking we need all four of us to figure out the trail of twisting trees. The dragons can't help us with that, so both Kisa and Mertzer will remain here, and Varjiek will join them once he flies us down there. That way we'll both be without our dragons until we find the eggs."

Micah gave him one deliberate nod. "Fair enough."

"Glad we agree. Now pack up. We leave in ten minutes."

The day had gotten off to a sour start, but he hoped it would end with a dragon egg in his hands.

◊   ◊   ◊

"So strange." Taliya's fingers stroked the smooth, light-brown bark of the tree whose trunk grew in a tight spiral a hundred feet high just like the tree on the map marked with a number one. A myriad of long, thin branches with tiny circular leaves topped the tree like a wide green hat. The other trees along the unmistakable perimeter of the slanted acres each boasted their own unique shape, angle, or design, almost as if they were competing against each other for style points. The only thing they had in common was the cluster of branches at the top.

"Gawking is getting us nowhere," Ravier said. "This is definitely our starting point. I'll head straight in. Javan, you go to the left. Taliya, you take the right. Micah, I don't care where you go as long as it's not near me. Everyone, yell if you find the tree that looks like a sideways W."

"Before we start, beware--" Water erupted from the lake behind them, drowning out Javan's words.

Taliya felt the power of the water from her toes to her nose as she turned to see it shoot up into the air twice as high as the trees. Its shiny glean beckoned her, and she wandered through the spikey grass toward it, noticing that the water did indeed appear to be falling up. Rather than drop once it reached the top, it simply faded away.

Fascinating. She needed a closer look. She needed to know what would happen to her if she let herself get caught in the rush of the upward water. Would she vanish as well if she made it to the top?

"Taliya!" Javan jumped in front of her and put his arms on her shoulders. "Stop!"

Javan's green eyes broke her concentration, and she realized she was standing on the silver sand of the lake's shore a stone's throw away from the wall of water. Once it sputtered out, she shuddered. "Let's get out of here before that happens again."

"What exactly happened?"

"You mean you didn't feel compelled to walk into the water?"

"Nope."

"Oh. Well then, thanks for stopping me." Taliya pursed her lips and strutted back to the spirally tree. She didn't like having her mind hijacked or being the only one affected in such a way. To prove she could think for herself again, she needed a practical task to accomplish. Such a task awaited her in the slanted acres. "I'll look for the W tree this way."

She veered to the right of the scowling Ravier with a scowl of her own fixed on her face. But her scowl turned to surprise when her feet hit the soft surface of the slanted acres, causing her to sink several inches. "Whoa." She kicked a layer of leaves out of her way and realized she was standing on white fluff. "This ground is made of cotton!"

"Shh," Javan whispered, "and don't kick the leaves. The trees don't like noise or sudden movements. Walk slowly and stay quiet, or we'll set off a tremor."

"Okay." Taliya disregarded Javan's warning as soon as she progressed into the woods.

"In my experience," Micah muttered from behind her, "trees don't care about noise or movement."

"Same here," she whispered back. "They don't even care when I cut them down for firewood or shelter." Nevertheless, she counted to herself as she walked.

She made it nine paces when she heard Ravier yell, "I found it! It's right here, seventeen trees in."

"Coming." As she sprinted to her left, a root from the ground shot up and smacked her in the leg. "Ouch!" Another root beat her in the back while the trees around her began twisting and trembling and shaking.

"Tree tremor!" Javan announced. "Get out! Get out now!"

Taliya squeezed between two trees right before they slammed into each other, jumped over a series of roots striking up from the ground, and fought her way through the storm of leaves showering down from above. She and Micah dove onto solid ground at the same time. She rolled once, bounced to her feet, and held her breath until Ravier and Javan joined them.

Blood flowed down Ravier's face from a cut above his eye, but Javan appeared unscathed. He immediately turned to Ravier. "What part of 'stay quiet' did you not understand?"

"How else were you supposed to know I found the tree?"

"Apparently not by yelling," Taliya said. "At least we know what direction to take now. Next time we can all go in together. How long do these tremors usually last?"

Javan shrugged. "I have no idea."

As the trees continued to shake, another blast of water erupted behind them. This time Taliya refused to look at it, but the swaying trees in front of her made her dizzy. She closed her eyes and covered her ears, feeling helpless and trapped even though she stood in an open field under the warmth of the bright morning sun.

CHAPTER 24

The Eetzy Bird

"I think it's been calm long enough." Javan stared at the spirally tree he had grown to despise. They had tried walking in a slow, single file line past that tree, entering the woods at staggered times, and climbing the tall trees to get to the branches based on Taliya's theory that swinging from tree to tree using the branches wouldn't cause a tremor. It did.

The tremors had become more violent and lasted longer with each attempt. He wiped a leaf off his sweaty forehead and reached for his teleportation sword. "I haven't tried this yet."

"If it works," Taliya said, "you'll be on your own the rest of the way."

"I have to give it a shot. We've exhausted our other options."

"You're right." Ravier clapped Javan on the back and plopped to the ground. "Good luck."

"I have dodged enough trees today." Micah joined Ravier. "I'll be happy to hang here until you get back with a dragon egg."

"I won't." Taliya was the only one that seemed to have any spunk left after a day of getting beat up by trees. "How about just you and I go in? I'm small. I won't make much noise."

"I can get a head start by teleporting myself just past the second tree since we made it that far in once." He would take her if he could. He certainly didn't want to try to figure out the rest of the journey on his own. When he returned, the first thing he would do was have Kisa teach him how to teleport people with him. "Wait here. Please."

"Guess I don't have a choice." She sighed and stepped back.

He fought the urge to hug her goodbye and gave her a nod instead. "See you soon." Closing his eyes, he brought the image of the W tree into his mind. When he opened them, he found himself standing beside it. "I do love doing that. Now to find the tree that looks like it swallowed a staircase."

As he picked up his foot to take his first step, a root swirled up his leg and slammed him into the sharp edges of the W tree. The thud knocked his breath away and set off yet another tremor. "AH!" He gripped his sword tighter, willing himself out of the woods.

But teleporting didn't work. Instead, the root tightened its hold. This time, the tree slammed into Javan. The collision knocked him to the angry ground where more roots jerked up and peppered his body with punches. He curled up, used his sword to cut himself free from the imprisoning root, and teleported himself back to safety.

"Scratch that idea." Javan winced as he forced himself to stand. Taliya, Ravier, and Micah were exactly where he had left them moments before. "The trees did notice when I teleported in, and they didn't take too kindly to my sudden appearance."

"We figured." Ravier waved at the trembling trees.

"Let's call it a day. I say we get some food and sleep, then try again in the morning."

"I'm not going back to that ridgeline." Taliya crossed her arms over her chest. "It is a horribly uncomfortable place to sleep, and hearing the constant water explosions throughout the night doesn't help."

"We can't sleep here," Micah said. "The explosions are even louder, and I don't trust those trees not to attack us in the middle of the night."

"We don't have to stay anywhere near here," Taliya said. "Kisa can teleport us back to the coast. I liked sleeping there. That was calm and peaceful."

Javan nodded. "I like the way you think. I'll teleport up to the ridgeline and send Varjiek back for you all. Once he flies you up to me, Kisa can take us to the coast."

When no one argued, Javan took one last look at the slanted acres. How did any Protector ever get through there carrying a dragon egg? There had to be some trick, something they were missing. But what?

◊   ◊   ◊

Taliya opened her eyes and saw the stars staring back at her from her bed on the beach. She had chosen to sleep in the sand rather than under trees. After spending the day running in and out of the slanted acres, she no longer trusted trees to remain still.

The strange-shaped trees had invaded her dreams, solidifying her distrust. Her dreams were only fuzzy memories now that she had awakened, but one image remained clear: the eetzy bird. With its red tail and white body, it fluttered through her dreams whistling its soft, soothing melody.

Where else had she seen that rare bird? Why did she have the feeling that she had come across it recently? That feeling made no sense. The last time she saw that bird was over a decade ago when she and her grandmother were tending to the humminglo flowers in Keckrick.

The map. The map had a picture of that bird on it.

Her sore muscles warned her not to move, but she needed to see the map. She rolled onto the sand from the leaves she had piled together to sleep on and crawled over to Javan. He, Micah, and Ravier were spread out along the edge of the woods, and he had left the map with his swords near his head. She carefully picked it up and unrolled it.

She strained her eyes to make out the picture of the bird in the dull moonlight, but it was there between the upside-down waterfall and spirally tree. It had its wings spread wide and tail feathers fanned out. It only fanned its feathers like that when it sang.

That was it. That was the secret to getting through the slanted acres. "Wake up, people." She stood and clapped her hands. "Wake up. We must get back to the slanted acres. I know how to keep the trees from trembling."

She smiled. She did have the Protector decoder in her after all...if she was right.

◊   ◊   ◊

"You can't be serious." With the sun establishing its presence in the sky behind him, Micah stared at the spirally tree and stiffened at the thought of prancing through the woods whistling for the twisted trees. He wasn't even sure he knew how to whistle. Frivolous fun had never been a part of his upbringing. "You think mimicking the music of a bird is going to prevent the trees from trembling?"

"Yes, I do." Taliya glared up at him. "Why else would the eetzy bird be pictured on the map?"

"I'm not sure, but you saw how violent these trees were yesterday. I don't understand how something as simple as whistling is going to tame them."

"Do you have a better idea?" Javan asked.

Micah shook his head. "I exhausted all my ideas yesterday."

"They we try this approach."

"Not me," Ravier said. "I'll take the lead and count the trees while you three whistle along."

Micah clenched his fists, irritated with himself for not thinking of Ravier's practical approach first. "I'll bring up the rear and signal the warning if the trees start to tremble."

"Let's do this." Javan handed Ravier the map. "Taliya, you're the one who knows what this bird sounds like. Micah and I will copy your tune."

"Excellent," she said. "If we keep the tune light and cheery, we should be fine."

"Light and cheery. Got it." Micah offered an unenthusiastic thumbs up and took his position in the back of the line. He expected to get about three steps into the acres before a tremor started, which meant no one would have time to notice whether he whistled or not.

As Ravier entered the woods, Taliya pursed her lips and let out a series of quick, high-pitched notes. She drew the notes out when she walked by the spirally tree, then repeated the quick notes. Javan joined her this time through the whistling chorus, and Micah realized his head was bobbing to the tune as his turn came to enter the acres.

He tried creating the tune himself, but all he managed to do was blow air through his lips. How were they making those musical notes? He gave up trying to duplicate the noise as they passed the W tree and followed the tune with a low hum.

That's when the trees started shaking. No. Not shaking. Swaying. And the roots began thumping to the beat. Encouraged by the response, Micah hummed louder, and the trees danced to the speed of the wordless song.

The musical trio followed Ravier deeper and deeper into the acres. The humming tapped into a part of Micah he didn't know existed. He felt, well, light and cheery instead of dark and depressed. So when Ravier held up his hand and pointed at a squiggly tree, a strange sort of sadness washed over Micah. He was going to have to stop humming and lose his newfound joy.

"We're here." Ravier pointed at the map, showing that the squiggly tree matched the drawing of the fifth tree. "Now what?"

They all looked around. At the trees. And only the trees. Following the twisting trees had gotten them nowhere except in the middle of twisting trees.

CHAPTER 25

Tunnel of Darkness

Javan wasn't sure what he expected to find, but he did expect to find *something*. However, this area of the slanted acres looked like every other area they had passed through while whistling and counting a path that ended up being seventy-seven trees long. "The next phrase on the map tells us to travel down through the ground." Javan licked his sore, dry lips. "I guess we should look for some sort of tunnel."

"The ground is covered in leaves and cotton." Ravier spoke in a soft voice as the four of them huddled around the map in front of the squiggly tree. "No amount of humming or whistling will stop a tremor if we start kicking things around searching for an underground tunnel."

"If we set off a tremor this deep into the woods," Micah added, "there's no way we're getting out alive."

"Then we better not cause any tremors." Taliya nudged Javan. "Check out the map. What is that a picture of beside the fifth tree?"

"It's a mole. Think it's another clue?"

"Why else would it be there? The top of a mole hole is signified by a mound. If we find a piece of ground rounded up like a mole hole, we should find our tunnel."

"The problem with that theory," Ravier said, "is that every part of the ground is flat."

Javan studied the ground. Sure enough, it appeared to be flat. "Maybe it's not flat underneath all these leaves. Everyone, get on your hands and knees, spread out, and search for a slightly rounded section of ground. That must be what we're looking for. Just be slow and deliberate about your movements."

Ravier remained standing while Javan, Taliya, and Micah eased to their knees. He crossed his arms and whispered, "I don't crawl."

"You do today." Javan spit out the words through gritted teeth. "Get down here."

Ravier huffed, lowered himself his knees, and slapped the ground. "Happy?"

The forest reacted. A wave of trembles knocked Javan off balance, and a root under his stomach shot up and tossed him into Taliya. He grunted, but she whistled. A slow, high note. A fast, low note. Slow. Fast.

He joined the rhythm as the tremor jostled their bodies. Micah added his harmonizing hum, and the trees downgraded to dancing once Ravier's deep hum joined the chorus.

While continuing to whistle and hum, they resumed their search. The cottony ground beneath the leafy surface reached almost to Javan's shoulders. He crawled through the fluff easily, yet he noticed it only reached his elbows the closer he got to the back side of the tree.

He changed his whistling tune to alert everyone and waved them over. Ravier and Micah continued to hum while Javan and Taliya worked together to clear the area. Underneath the cotton, they discovered a small mound of dirt. Javan furiously dug through the dirt until his fingertips touched a piece of steel. "Found a door."

"Better open it fast," Ravier said. "The trees aren't responding well to the humming without the whistling."

"Here's the handle." Taliya threw a clump of dirt out of the way and lifted the round door. She peered into the hole. "That is one dark tunnel."

An angry root slapped Javan's face. "We can deal with the dark tunnel or the trembling trees."

Taliya pointed down. "The tunnel." She threw her legs into the hole, found what appeared to be stairs dug into the side, and climbed down.

"Micah, you're next."

Micah dodged a tree lunging toward him and followed Taliya down the hole.

"Grandfather."

"No. I'll go last."

Javan couldn't think of a good reason to argue and launched himself into the darkness. The narrow chamber shook from the tremors around them, but the stairs were well-carved and easy to hold on to. He was a body length into the hole when Ravier entered above him.

"Brace yourselves," Ravier said. "I'm closing the door."

A second later, the door clanged shut, plunging them into total darkness.

◊   ◊   ◊

"People check." Taliya inched forward, irritated with her eyes for not adjusting to the oppressive darkness. It forced her to walk with her right arm testing the air in front of her for obstructions and her left hand dragging along the cold dirt wall to keep her on track. "Everyone still with me?"

"Micah."

"Javan."

"Ravier."

"Thanks, guys. I just like to make sure I'm not alone from time to time."

"Tell us another story, Taliya," Javan said. "Listening to you talk is the only thing keeping me sane."

"I've been talking for hours. Javan, why don't you tell me something fun about Earth?"

Micah laughed. "What would he know about Earth?"

"Enough with the story time." Ravier abruptly changed the subject. Why? Did he not want Javan to answer? Did Micah not know Javan had grown up on Earth? "I need some peace and quiet for a little while."

Taliya wanted to point out that if no one talked, they wouldn't know when they reached the spot where they couldn't hear and thus wouldn't know when to yell, but she judged by Ravier's tone that keeping her mouth shut was the wisest course of action. He was in the back of the line and could easily run away if he reached his mental breaking point. Javan was convinced they needed him to get through the portal, so she chose not say or do anything to drive him away.

Not talking did allow her to walk a bit faster. She pushed forward, anxious to get to the end of the miserable tunnel. She worried that she had gone too fast when she could no longer hear footsteps behind her. "People check?"

She knew the words came out of her mouth, but the sound didn't register in her ears. "Javan? Micah? Ravier? You still with me?"

Nothing. No sound. No response.

She thought she had experienced loneliness when living by herself in the treehouse far from any village, but this was worse. Standing in unbearable darkness alone unable to see or hear sucked the life from her soul.

"Pull yourself together, Taliya. You can still think and speak and feel. Now yell. Yell louder than you have ever yelled before."

She put her hands on the dirt wall to remind her she wasn't standing in a void, drew in a deep breath, and screamed. She screamed until her throat felt raw. As she cleared her throat to scream again, a skin-tingling scream answered her.

◊ ◊ ◊

Javan covered his ears, but he could still hear the eerie scream that seemed to be coming from the tunnel itself. What if it wasn't the tunnel? What if it was Taliya? Why was she screaming? He had to get to her.

He ran forward but crashed into Micah. "Let me by," he said. "I need to get to Taliya." But his words did no good. The darkness ate them, allowing no sound through except that awful screech.

Yell where you cannot hear. Push when the stone yells back.

The words from the map penetrated his mind. That screech wasn't Taliya. It was the stone yelling back, presumably at Taliya. She had reached the sound vacuum first and must have figured it out. He didn't know where or why or how the stone yelled, but he did know he could push. He thus reached for the dirt wall and put all his effort into pushing against it.

"Why is nothing happening?" Perhaps he had to find the stone and push against it. Following the noise, he squeezed past Micah and let his fingers drag along both walls as he moved blindly through the tunnel.

The noise grew painfully louder and the cool darkness pressed against his skin, urging him to turn and run. He needed silence. He needed light. But he needed Taliya more. She was here somewhere, and he wasn't going anywhere without her.

He turned to his left and began frantically racing his hands along the wall until it curved to the right. That's when his hand landed on a hot, vibrating stone. He jerked his hand away, and it connected with flesh. "Ooh. Sorry. Taliya? Is that you?"

He felt her hands on his shoulders and her breath on his cheek as she yelled into his ear. "How are we supposed to push the stone without it burning our hands?"

"Like this." He took his shirt off, bunched it up, and pressed it against the stone. With a deep breath and a prayer for help, he pushed. The deafening noise stopped as the stone wall gave way, and light spilled into the dark tunnel. Javan closed his eyes and covered them with his hand. He began blinking and slowly lowered his hand until his eyes adjusted to the light from the luminous rocks inside the cave. Scattered among the glowing, jagged rocks were hundreds of smooth, colorful dragon eggs as far as his eyes could see. "We found them," he whispered. "We found the eggs."

Mesmerized by the discovery, Javan put his foot through the door, but Taliya pulled him down by his belt before he could step all the way through. He landed on his rear end and quickly picked himself up. "What was that for? Did you want to be first or something?"

"Nothing of the sort. I just thought it would be wise to duck to enter the cave like the map said." She drew his Noon sword and tapped the top half of the doorway with the blade. It pinged against a wire Javan couldn't see. "This wire is sharp enough to cut through skin and bone. It would have taken your head off."

"Oh." Javan rubbed his throat and scratched out the words he had uttered when Taliya kept him from eating the poisonous berry. "Thanks for the assist."

"This saving-your-life thing is starting to become a habit. So you know what? I think I do want to go first." She returned his sword and ducked through the doorway as Micah and Ravier approached.

"Every time I need a reason to smile," Micah said, slapping Javan on his bare back, "I will remember how ungraceful you looked when you got dragged to the ground by a girl." He laughed and slipped through the door.

"Are you going to tease me, too?" Javan asked Ravier.

"Not right now, but I am going to tell you to put your shirt back on. This is not the time to try to impress the girl with your battle scars." He nodded toward the long scar on Javan's chest formed by the tip of Micah's sword when they were fighting over Mertzer. "Stay focused. Win the throne. Grow up. Then you can woo the girl."

"That's not why I took my shirt off." But Ravier wasn't interested in Javan's response. He entered the cave with a chuckle, leaving Javan alone in the tunnel. He put his shirt back on, bent down, and joined everyone else in the warm, humid cave.

"Pick an egg so we can go," Ravier said.

"I can't just pick an egg and go." Javan balked at the idea. "I have to walk through the whole cavern and get a feel for which egg will hatch the dragon that is the right fit for me."

"Whatever egg you pick will hatch a Dusk Stalker," Micah said. "Dusk Stalkers are all the same. It doesn't matter which one you choose."

"Nonsense!" Taliya moved to stand beside Javan. "That's like saying all humans are the same. We share similar characteristics, but we're all unique. So are dragons."

Javan pointed to Taliya. "What she said."

"You have ten minutes," Ravier said. "The day is already half gone, and we'll never be able to find our way through the slanted acres in the dark."

"Understood. I'll be as quick as possible." He took a deep breath and scanned the rows and rows of dragon eggs. How was he going to pick just one? "Taliya, will you help me--"

A thunderous roar cut off his question.

The door had slammed shut. On its own.

CHAPTER 26

Choosing a Dragon

"Why did that door close?" Micah stepped to the door and slid his hands along the wall that had been open two seconds before. "Better question. Why is there no handle? I can't open it if it doesn't have a handle."

"I'm sure it will open." Ravier shoved Micah out of the way. "It probably needs a strong push."

"We pushed it from the outside. Pushing it from the inside will do no good. We need to pull it but can't because it has nothing to pull." Micah wiped beads of sweat from his forehead. "We can't be stuck in here. We can't be stuck in an underground cave with nothing to eat or drink and no way out."

"Chill, Micah." Javan tapped his Stalker sword. "All I have to do is teleport to the tunnel, do the screaming thing, and push the door back open. Let me choose an egg, and then I'll get us out of here."

"Another idea," Taliya said. "The final phrase on the map said to leave through the inside door. I bet that means there is a door somewhere in this cave that we can easily open and escape through. It probably also means we don't have to go back through that awful tunnel."

Micah snapped. "I like Taliya's idea. Javan, you find your egg, and I'll go find whatever door will get us out of here."

"Take Ravier with you," Javan said.

"What?" Micah and Ravier asked the same question at the same time.

"It's a safety thing. We don't know what else is lurking in this cave, and I don't need you getting hurt or lost. Plus I don't want my grandfather judging me while I choose what egg to take."

"I won't judge," Ravier said.

"He won't judge." Micah agreed, desperately working to change Javan's mind. "He's the one who suggested you grab any egg."

"True, but watch this." Javan pointed to a dull blue and pink egg at his feet. "What if I want that egg right there?"

"That one?" Ravier shook his head. "That shell doesn't appear to be brilliant or strong. I doubt it would survive for ten minutes outside of this environment. You should look for a shell that is thick and streaked with strong colors."

"Micah." Javan stared at him. "Please take my grandfather with you to find the door."

"All right." Micah rolled his eyes, understanding that Ravier would attempt to control Javan's choice but not wanting to have to deal with Ravier in a one-on-one situation. "Let's go find this door, Ravier."

"Fine. I will go, but I am going because I need to be doing something useful, and watching Javan pick an egg is not useful."

As Ravier stomped away, Micah pointed at Javan. "You owe me for this."

"I know."

Micah took his time catching up to Ravier with all his senses on full alert. While his eyes searched for the door, the rest of him had to be ready to fight if Ravier chose to attack him once they were out of earshot of Javan and Taliya.

◊   ◊   ◊

"Are you sure that was a good idea?" Taliya cocked her head in the direction of the fading footsteps. "As much as those two hate each other, it's likely only one of them will return."

"I'm sure they will work out their differences in constructive ways." Javan focused on the eggs to his right while he spoke. "I just needed my grandfather gone so I can pick the egg I want, not the one he wants."

"I get that." To give him the space he desired to make his choice, she wandered a little further into the cave and touched the cool shell of an egg with one streak of pink around the middle. "Who are you?" she whispered. "What kind of dragon will you become if we let you hatch?"

She looked around and wondered the same thing about all the unhatched dragons she could see. She wanted to give each of them a chance to live. Maybe she could, with Javan's help. "Javan, do you realize that the Dusk Stalker is no longer on the verge of being extinct?"

"Huh?"

"Once you become king, you can teleport yourself in here every year, get an egg or two, and teleport to the portal. I'll take them to Earth and bring them back as dragons after they hatch. It'll be a cinch, and the Dusk Stalkers can once again have a prominent presence in Zandador."

"Why don't we start now?"

ACTUAL:

START

"Start what now?"

"I like the idea of taking two eggs. I pick one for my collection, and you pick one to bring back to live here, as a free dragon, in Dusk Territory. It can be your dragon to protect and care for when needed."

"Really?" Taliya squealed and clapped. "That's so exciting." Her smile vanished. "And intimidating. How am I supposed to pick just one? What will I name him? Or her? What if she doesn't like me? What if--"

"Let's forget the what ifs and just start by perusing the cave to see if any particular egg grabs our attention."

Taliya took a deep breath and nodded. "Okay. I hear you. Stay in the moment. Take care of the task at hand without worrying about future problems. Got it." With that in mind, she meandered along the left side of the cave, touching every egg she could reach.

The varying colors of pink, purple, blue, and green blended into one blur the more she walked. She wanted to give every egg a fair chance, but she had no idea how to determine which egg to choose. They all shared the same general shape and size with the only difference being the color of the shell.

Except that one.

A vibrant pink shell stuck in a corner on the ground level caught her eye. She ducked under a ledge to get to it, stretched her arms as far as they could go to reach it, and used her fingers to roll it close enough to her to grab it. "Gotcha!"

Once she could stand again, she turned the bright egg around in her hands. It was half the size of the other eggs and had one tiny blue dot on the top of its otherwise pure pink shell. And on the bottom, one word was sketched into it: Reiah. "Is that your name?"

Cradling the egg in her arm, she checked out the bottom of another egg. It also had Reiah sketched on it. "Why does this dragon have the same name? Unless..."

She called over to Javan. "Check the bottom of that egg."

"Which one?"

"It doesn't matter. Just pick an egg and tell me what name is scratched on the bottom of it."

"The eggs have names?" Javan moved an egg with streaks of purple and green. "Huh. Look at that. The eggs have names."

"What name does it have?"

"Brizek."

"Check one next to it."

"Why?"

"Please just do it."

"Fine." He looked at a pale green egg. "It also says Brizek."

Taliya smiled. "These eggs weren't placed in here randomly. I think they are grouped together by the names of their moms. We'll be able to trace the heritage of whatever dragon we take out of here."

"Nice." He nodded toward her pink egg. "Is that the one you're taking?"

"Yes." She held the egg in front of her with both hands. "Isn't it pretty? It's so pink that it has to be a girl, and I think the two of us will get along very well."

"But...it's tiny. Don't you want a regular-sized egg? What if it's not fully developed and was put in here by mistake?"

"I may be the only hope this egg has of hatching. No one else is ever gonna take this small little thing through the portal, and us small things have to stick together."

"All right. You just have to promise me you won't cry if it doesn't hatch."

"She'll hatch." Taliya cradled the small shell between her forearm and stomach. "This dragon is special. I know it."

Pleased with her choice, she sat and stroked the shell, imagining what the baby dragon inside would look like when it poked through its pink exterior.

◊   ◊   ◊

Watching Taliya bond with her egg urged Javan to find his special egg as well. He didn't much care for the pink, but he did envy the bright, bold color of the shell. He needed to find an egg whose bold color palette matched or surpassed Taliya's egg. That criteria helped him sort through the eggs much faster.

Many of the shells had streaks of bright colors. That wasn't good enough. He needed an entire shell bathed in color. Waltzing down the center of the cave, he scanned the eggs on both sides looking for an egg that would rival Taliya's. The dragon inside such an egg would be bold, daring, and ready to live.

The cave gradually narrowed and veered to the right at the bottom of a slope. He stumbled his way down the hill, made the turn, and tripped on a step. "Ouch." He rubbed his shin and looked up to find a stone staircase with uneven steps. They ranged in height from a few inches to a few feet tall and probably led to the inside door. That meant he had made it through the entire selection of eggs without choosing one to take with him.

Ravier and Micah would be back soon and would be irritated with him if he delayed their exit. If he didn't want the pressure of their unhappy stares to contend with, he needed to make his choice fast.

"All right." He turned back around to face the cave. "Which one of you dragons wants to let me ride you after you hatch?" He began making his way up the hill when a streak of green caught his attention. He bent down to study a shell with dark green stripes and noticed another shell laying on the stone behind it.

This shell had no color on it and appeared to have been shoved out of the way. "What's your story?" From his knees, Javan leaned over the striped egg, wrapped his hands around the white egg, and pulled it into his lap. A U and a partial Z were the extent of the name carved on the egg. "What happened? Why didn't the Protector finish writing your mom's name?"

Javan studied the plain egg with a lost heritage that had been hidden away. That reminded him of him. "You know, sometimes the things that appear to be the most ordinary turn out to be the most spectacular. So I choose you."

Proud of his choice, he rose to his feet and turned to take his egg back to Taliya, but a commotion on the stairs ahead of him grabbed his attention. He poked his head around the corner and saw Micah sprinting down the steps with blood on his shirt and no Ravier in sight.

"We found the door," Micah said, "but we have another problem."

CHAPTER 27

Grizzlets

"I knew we shouldn't have sent you two away by yourselves." Cradling her egg in her arms, Taliya approached Micah and Javan. "All you had to do was find a door. How could you end up fighting over that?"

"We fought about how to open the door," Micah said, "but only with words. This isn't my blood or Ravier's."

"That's concerning," Taliya said. She took a step back and drew her egg closer to her chest. "Who else is in this cave?"

"It's more like a what, but I can't explain here. Leave the eggs and come with me."

Taliya and Javan shared a troubled look, left their eggs together in a corner by the stairs, and fell into step behind Micah. The uneven steps spun to the right and left and up and down before ending in a dully lit oval room filled with shrieks. Loud, maddening shrieks.

Ravier stood with his back against a door. "It's about time." The door behind him kept trying to open, and he continually threw his body against it as he spoke. "I don't know how much longer I can hold this thing off."

"Hold what off?" Taliya had to yell to make herself heard.

"A grizzlet." Ravier grunted.

"Really?" She smiled. "I've never seen one of those giant birds before."

"I hope you won't get to see one now." Ravier shifted his feet and gave the moving stone door behind him a full-body shove. "One tried to get through when we opened the door, and we hurt it when we shoved it back it the tunnel with our swords. Now it's mad and keeps banging against the not-quite-closed door."

"Javan, help us out." Micah pulled Javan over to the door, leaving Taliya by herself near the stairs. "We need to get this door shut and exit the way we came in." Even with all three of them pushing on the stone door, though, they couldn't beat the animal fighting them on the other side.

"This isn't working, but I know what will." She reached for her slingshot and loaded it with a dart. "Open the door. Let him in."

"No way!" Micah shook his head. "After it attacks us, he'll feast on all those eggs in the cave. I thought you wanted to protect the eggs, not let a known predator eat them."

"I'm an excellent shot. No grizzlet will get past me."

"These things are fast and strong with thin bodies," Ravier said. "Shooting them is next to impossible. They're basically bones with wings and teeth."

"Just open the door and let him through. He'll be slightly disoriented when the resistance you're giving him goes away, and that will give me a chance to shoot him."

"That's a very small chance to work with," Ravier said.

"Just do it," Javan said. "She's a good shot, and we have to do something. This thing is stronger than the three of us, and we won't be able to hold this door much longer."

Taliya narrowed her sights on the side of the door. "I'm ready in three...two...one." In unison, the men let go of the door and stumbled forward in a hunched position.

A huge, bat-like animal with a long, wiry tail, two muscular legs, a thin, hairy body, a massive round head, and bulging orange eyes filled the entire space of the doorway and toppled into the room. It spread its wings and screeched through its pointy teeth.

"You don't scare me." Taliya chose a spot between its eyes and released her dart. The dart found its mark, and the creature crashed to the floor in front of her. "Got it!" she shouted. But she wasn't prepared for the second or third bird that swooped into the room after their friend.

◊　　◊　　◊

"Another one! And another!" Micah drew his sword. "We must have disturbed a nest!"

The birds circled the room and dove for flesh. Micah deflected a bite from one of the birds with his blade, but Ravier didn't raise his sword in time to protect himself from the second bird. His sword clanked to the ground as the grizzlet tore into his right shoulder.

Micah winced at the sound of Ravier's painful scream and noticed the biting bird's tail waving wildly through the air. "That tail is mine." Micah swung his sword over his head to keep the other bird from getting to him and sliced the biting bird's tail clean off.

The bird yelped, let go of Ravier, and spun toward Micah. "That's what you get for biting a person. You can either go back through that door or eat a dart from my friend over there." Keeping his eyes on the hovering bird and his sword at the ready, Micah asked, "Taliya, got another dart ready yet?"

"Yes, but it's aimed at the bird that's trying to get down the stairs."

"I'd help you if I could." Javan's words sounded strained over his swords swishing through the air. "But I have to provide cover for Taliya."

"Wonderful." Micah held his sword steady and locked eyes with his attacker. "Guess it's just you and me, you ugly thing. Bring it."

The bird hissed and bolted for Micah's head. It moved faster than Micah expected. It sank its teeth into his dreadlocks, lifted Micah off his feet, and slammed him into the wall. The force of the collision caused him to drop his sword. Left with only his fists to fight with, he began pounding the grizzlet's head. "Put me down!"

The grizzlet threw Micah into the wall several more times before finally releasing his hair. He landed on his back and lost his breath. Unable to move, a sense of impending doom washed over him as he saw teeth flying toward his face.

Then a flash of steel blocked his view, and a headless grizzlet landed beside him. Micah looked up to see Ravier holding his sword in his left hand; blood oozed down his right arm through his tattered shirt. "That makes us even." He tossed his sword to the ground and offered Micah his good hand.

Micah took it and let Ravier help him to his feet. "Thanks."

"Same." Ravier gave Micah a respectful nod, but the bonding moment ended a second later when the third grizzlet flew between them, knocked Javan down with a powerful kick to the back, and flew down the stairs toward the cave.

◊   ◊   ◊

Javan lost track of the speedy bird flying in circles around the room, so the kick to the back came as a complete surprise. His chin hit the cold, hard stone floor, rattling his jaw and splitting his skin. Warm blood gushed down his throat as he jumped to his feet. The quick movement stupefied him, and he fought a sudden bout of dizziness.

Taliya inspected his cut and patted him on the cheek. "Looks like you'll survive. I'll patch that up for you after I kill that bird. He better not touch my egg." She disappeared down the staircase before Javan remembered how to form words to tell her to wait for him.

He shook his head to clear the dizziness and gripped his swords for comfort. "Come on, guys." He urged Micah and Ravier to join him. "We can't let Taliya deal with that beast on her own."

"Coming." Micah picked up the two swords that were on the ground and handed one to Ravier. "Are you going to be able to fight with your shoulder torn up like that?"

"Of course. I'm almost as good left-handed as I am right-handed."

"Then let's go." Javan didn't wait to make sure the men were behind him and raced through the awkward staircase. He almost bumped into Taliya at the bottom but halted just in time.

"I was wondering if you were going to make it down sometime today." Taliya stood with a dart loaded in her slingshot tracking the grizzlet zooming in and out of the eggs. "I need you to run through the middle of the cave and let the grizzlet attack you."

"That's insane! You want me to get attacked?"

"No. I want you to be live bait so he'll leave the still eggs alone. I'll try to shoot him before he bites you."

"What if he bites me first? Those teeth are no joke."

"Just do it. Please. I'm pretty sure I can get him if you lure him into the middle."

"Pretty sure?"

"Yes. Now go."

"Okay, but I'm keeping my swords out and going invisible if I feel its breath on my skin."

"Whatever." Her slingshot continued to move in line with the grizzlet. "Go. Now."

He took a deep breath and sprinted forward. "Is it following me?"

"Keep running!"

Javan complied. He heard screeching above him but couldn't see anything except rocks and eggs. "Where is it?"

His eyes answered his question as saw the grizzlet diving for his face with its jaws open, ready to swallow his head.

"Javan, get down!"

He ducked, and a dart shot through the grizzlet's open mouth. Its wings locked in place, and it tumbled ungracefully to the ground. Javan stepped around it, sheathed his swords, and worked to catch his breath as he walked back toward the group.

Ravier was leaning against the wall with his good shoulder. With all color drained from his face, he seemed to be on the verge of passing out. Half of Micah's dreadlocks were sticking up, and he was holding his ribs, looking defeated. Taliya's eyes, however, danced with excitement, and her face wore a grin from ear to ear.

"That was a fun little challenge," she said. "I've never had to deal with an animal quite like that before."

"Maybe we should all learn how to fight with a slingshot." Ravier nodded towards Taliya. "She killed two of those nasty birds, and she's the only one who doesn't have a scratch on her."

"At least she's the one that killed them," Micah said, "and we don't have to hear you brag about how much better you are than us with a sword."

"I don't need to brag about that," Ravier said, smiling through his obvious pain. "I already know I'm better. After all, my sword is the one that killed the other grizzlet. All yours did was chop its tail off."

"I'm a Dragon Hunter. Chopping tails is my expertise, but I still bet I can outduel you in a sword fight."

"Once my shoulder heals, we'll see about that."

"I'd pay money to see that fight," Javan said, but he certainly wouldn't bet on it. He'd seen them both in action and wasn't sure who he'd put his money on to win.

"You won't be using that shoulder anytime soon," Taliya said, sifting through the bag she wore across her shoulder. "I'll put some ointment on it now to stop the bleeding, but I'll need to wash it out and properly treat it once we get back to camp. Same with your chin, Javan."

At that reminder, he put his hand on his chin and noticed the front of his shirt was soaked with his own blood. But his cut couldn't be that bad if he had forgotten all about it. "My chin can wait. Just take care of Ravier. Then we'll go. I'm ready to get out of this cave and breathe in fresh air again."

He walked to his egg and picked it up. It looked like an oversized chicken egg on steroids and weighed as much as a cement block. "You ready to get out of here, buddy?" He wasn't sure, but he was almost certain he felt and heard the baby dragon tap a response.

CHAPTER 28

Disoriented Babbling

"Wait." Clasping her pink egg in her left arm, Taliya stopped Javan before he crawled into the tunnel the grizzlets had flown out of less than fifteen minutes ago. She picked up a handful of rocks, nudged Javan out of the way, and threw the rocks into the darkness. When all she heard was the clink of the rocks on stone, she said, "We can go."

Javan gave her a sideways look. "What was that all about?"

"Once we leave this cave with these eggs, we only have forty-eight hours to get through the portal. I don't want to waste any of that time fighting more crazy birds that might be hiding in this tunnel."

"The little lady is smart." Ravier slapped Javan on the back, but that simple action caused him to lose his balance, and he dropped to his knees. "Whoa. What happened to my legs?"

Taliya studied the puss-filled gashes of torn flesh on Ravier's shoulder from the grizzlet bite. "That was scary fast. These wounds are already becoming infected. We have to get him out of here and back to the ocean as soon as possible."

Micah helped Ravier to his feet. "Why the ocean?"

"The combination of salt and other minerals in that purple water are the best chance he has to fight this infection."

"No ocean." Ravier shook his head. "I don't know how ta sthwim."

"He's slurring his words." Taliya jumped in the tunnel. She reached for Ravier's good hand with her free hand. "We need to move. Now."

He responded to her command by grabbing her hand and stepping into the tunnel behind her. "Stay with me," she said, wrapping his fingers on the handle of her bag. "Keep holding onto my bag and focus on putting one foot in front of the other."

"Othay."

"We better hurry." Taliya marched forward through the uphill tunnel, keeping her eyes on the slightest hint of light in the distance.

◊   ◊   ◊

They burned four of their precious forty-eight hours getting back to camp. Javan teleported back to Varjiek as soon as they emerged from the tunnel, but that was right in the middle of Varjiek's feeding time. Javan had to wait for the dragon to eat, then lead him back to the others, then force an uncooperative Ravier to get on and stay on Varjiek while they flew halfway across Dusk Territory carrying large yet fragile dragon eggs to the shore.

Treating Ravier by keeping his shoulder submerged in the warm ocean water took another two hours, and now the man who was supposed to devise a strategy to get them through the portal was zonked out from a fever induced coma. Fabulous.

Micah didn't seem too concerned about the prospect of getting through the portal, either. After the long dip in the ocean, he had devoured a chunk of the food they brought with them from the cabin and passed out on a makeshift bed of his own near Ravier.

Javan was still too wound up to sleep, so he made a cozy sand bed for the dragon eggs under a palm tree. He used Varjiek's breath to start a fire about twenty feet away from the sleeping men while Taliya finished wrapping Ravier's shoulder with plantain leaves. He took two carrots from the food sack and offered Taliya one when she joined him by the fire. "How's he doing?"

"Hard to say." She chomped a bite off the carrot and chewed it up before continuing. "The dip in the ocean did wonders for his cuts, but he won't be in any shape to travel for at least a day. Maybe longer." She traded her carrot for some kind of goo she pulled out of her bag. She rubbed it on her finger and reached for Javan's chin. "This might sting."

Javan turned his head away. "You mean stink. What are you trying to put on my face?"

"Just a little mixture I developed. It's good for you. Trust me."

His nose didn't want to trust her, but he lifted his chin anyway. As soon as the goo touched his cut, his skin burned with a searing intensity. He bit his lip to keep from yelping in pain, and breathed a sigh of relief when the burning subsided a moment later.

"There," she said. "All better. Until the morning, anyway. I'll need to put on a few more doses until it heals."

"Wonderful." He carefully bit into his carrot and chomped in slow motion, testing the effect of the goo on his cut. It made his skin feel like it was glued together but caused no pain when chewing. That allowed him to turn his attention to their present dilemma. "I guess we have to figure out how to get through the portal without Ravier's help. Are you ready to open it?"

"Honestly? No. But if I can have one focused day tomorrow to study the book, I'll be ready."

"Then that gives me and Micah one day to come up with a strategy for distracting the soldiers guarding the portal so you can get to it and enter the code to get it open."

"Micah's not the only other one on the team."

"I know that." Had he made her think he didn't value her input? "It's just that I thought you wanted to focus on studying the book."

"You're right. I do." She shook her head. "I'm not talking about me."

"Oh. Good." Sometimes she confused him. "But Ravier's asleep. We don't know when he's going to wake up or if he'll be in his right mind when he does."

"I'm not talking about Ravier, either." Taliya rolled her eyes at him. "I'm talking about Kisa and Varjiek. One can teleport to the exact place we need to go. The other can keep them both invisible. Why don't you send them to the portal to scout things out? It will be easier to devise a strategy if you know exactly what we're dealing with."

"Of course!" Javan rolled his eyes at himself. "I'll send them both now while it's dark and have them return before we even wake up in the morning. Thanks, Taliya. You're brilliant." Without thinking, he kissed her cheek. Then he realized what he had done, and his entire face glowed from embarrassment.

To escape the awkwardness of the moment, he ran away in search of his dragons.

◊   ◊   ◊

Micah shifted to his side, vaguely aware of the mumbled conversation between Taliya and Javan. He didn't care what they were saying. All he wanted to do was sleep now that he had a full stomach and relaxed muscles thanks to the massaging work of the ocean's gentle waves.

He breathed a deep sigh of relaxation when the voices finally subsided and the sounds of the night took over. The whooshing of the waves. The chirping of the crickets. The crackling of the fire. The perfect symphony of sounds to fall asleep to.

He took one more deep breath of the cool salty air and gave his whole body over to sleep. But that's the precise moment Ravier sat up and began shouting.

"Javan! Where's Javan?"

Without opening his eyes, Micah waved his arm in the direction of the fire. "Over there."

"Decoy. At dawn."

"What?" Micah glanced over to see Ravier staring straight ahead. Talking to no one. Javan wasn't around. Neither was Taliya. Where did they go? And what was Ravier babbling about?

"My uniform. Stalker. Eat. Chaos. Portal. Earth. Eggs. Safe." With that final word, Ravier collapsed. He resumed sleeping as though he had never said anything at all.

Micah laughed. "That made no sense, but don't worry. I'll keep your crazy babblings to myself."

He turned onto his back and mulled Ravier's words over in his mind as he stared at the stars.

A decoy at dawn. With the uniform of a soldier. To create chaos and get through the portal. "Hmm. Interesting." He rolled back over so he could face Ravier. "You know, old man, that crazy plan just might work."

CHAPTER 29

Decoy at Dawn

From the time Taliya snuck away from the sleeping Ravier and Micah to retrieve her hidden book until she ate the stew Micah had concocted for dinner the following night, Taliya trained her eyes on the pages of the book and forced her mind to memorize the patterns required to open the portal. Other than taking a few breaks to tend to the wounds of Ravier and Javan, she had dedicated herself completely to the task of learning how to open the portal.

However, the lack of sleep combined with the constant reading had turned her mind to mush. It struggled to handle the simplest of tasks—like chewing—and it made the early evening darkness of the world around her appear foggy. All she really wanted to do was sleep. But she couldn't. Not yet. She needed to read the book one more time before they teleported to the portal in the middle of the night.

Leaving her coconut bowl of soup mostly untouched, she stretched out by the fire and opened the book once again.

"Nope." Javan jerked the book away from her.

"Hey. Give that back."

"I will. After you get some sleep."

"I'll sleep after I open the portal."

"You won't be able to open the portal unless you get some sleep."

"I'm fine. Not tired at all." She yawned, and Javan smirked. "Maybe I'm a little bit tired, but I have to get through that book one more time before we go."

"Get some sleep first. Then you can read the book with fresh eyes."

"You do look exhausted, Taliya." Micah tossed a log on the fire. Sparks hissed upward and disappeared into the night. "Those eggs are never going to hatch if you are too tired to make sense of the flickering lights of the portal."

She looked at the eggs, snug in their bed of sand. They needed her at her best. Otherwise they would never have a chance to hatch. "Fine." She laid down on her own bed of leaves and closed her eyes. "I'll rest my eyes for a few minutes."

If Javan or Micah said anything else, she didn't hear them. She did feel Javan nudge her shoulder mere moments later.

"Taliya," he said, "wake up. It's time to go,"

"Go where?"

"Earth."

"What? No. I'm not ready. I need to read through the book once more. I just closed my eyes for a minute."

"Your minute was more like six hours."

"Why did you let me sleep that long?" Taliya jumped up, aware that the fire was no longer burning. "What if I can't get the portal open because I didn't have that last chance to read the book?"

"How many times have you read the book?"

"Four."

"Do you have it memorized?"

"Mostly. But not completely. That's why I needed to read it again."

"You're ready." Ravier put his hand under her chin. In the moonlight, she could see that he was wearing a new shirt and pair of pants he must have gotten from Micah. "Reading can only take you so far. It's time to put your knowledge into action."

"When did you wake up and start making sense?"

"Shortly after you fell asleep."

"We're ready." Micah approached on the back of Mertzer. He appeared to have a man slung over Mertzer's neck in front of him, but the man had no head or feet. That's when she realized it was actually Ravier's tattered shirt and uniform pants stuffed with grass. "Why is Ravier's uniform stuffed to make it look like a person?"

"Excellent question." Javan beamed at her, and she could tell by the playful look in his emerald eyes that she wasn't going to like the answer. "We're going to need you to do one thing before entering the portal code."

All three men now smiled at her, and she suddenly wished she had paid attention to their strategy sessions instead of spending the entire day reading.

◊   ◊   ◊

Javan's nerves tingled as he sat perched on his invisible dragon surveying the portal area in the dim glow of the sun that had yet to rise over the horizon. Kisa and Mertzer stood invisible under Varjiek's wings on either side of him, and Taliya had her head sleepily draped on his back and her arms around his waist. Ravier and Micah both sat on Varjiek's front paws. All remained silent. They had nothing to do except wait.

The longer they waited, the more details of the landscape Javan noticed. A tall, wide waterfall in the middle of two spectacular cliffs crashed into a shimmering lake. Vines, moss, and ferns covered the rocks to the right of the waterfall, but a twenty-foot high octagon on the cliff to the left was free from any sort of woodsy growth.

Having been to the portal in North Zandador with his mother, he recognized the smooth surface of that tall, wide octagon. He knew it was made of thousands of pieces of dragon scales, and those scales formed the portal that led to Earth. Somewhere beside the octagon was a spot to insert four Stalker scales that would activate the portal. He would leave that task to Taliya. His task was providing cover so she could get to the portal.

Standing in their way was the lake and an army of soldiers. One patrolled from the top of the cliff. Two more patrolled the shore of the lake, and another pair covered the wide area to the left and in front of the portal. And stationed like statues directly in front of the portal was a line of seven muscular soldiers.

Countless tents populated the grounds beyond the range of the patrolling soldiers while the trees were filled with sleeping okties that would soon be used for air patrol. According to Kisa's report, they didn't patrol the air by night, and she was also right about the fact that none of the soldiers on the ground seemed particularly alert this early in the morning.

Unlike Kisa. This was her prime feeding time, and her colorful scales indicated she was ready to eat. They had been waiting for her to get hungry, and judging by her restlessness, she had reached that point.

"It's time." Turning to the Dawn Stalker under the protection of Varjiek's left wing, Javan spoke, hoping the roar of the waterfall would keep his words from reaching the soldiers across the lake. "Kisa, take Mertzer and Micah to the far end of the camp, then come back here for Taliya and Ravier."

Kisa nodded and began slinking around Varjiek toward Mertzer.

"I'll take good care of Kisa while you're gone," Micah said, moving towards Mertzer as well. "We'll find a good place to hide in the mountains north of here."

"I'll remain with them," Ravier said. "We will all rendezvous at the Zandadorian portal located near Gri every day at noon until you return."

"Thank you both," Javan said.

"Dragon eggs always hatch within three days." Taliya lifted her head off his back and let go of Javan's waist in order to stretch and talk to Ravier. "They also can't survive Earth's atmosphere for more than seven days without scales, so we'll be returning as soon after they hatch as possible."

Javan tapped the food sacks draped over Varjiek's neck that now held the two dragon eggs. "Hopefully these dragons are so eager to hatch that we will be returning tonight."

"Until then." Micah climbed on Mertzer's back, nodded his goodbye, and Kisa whisked them away.

"We're next." Draping the stuffed uniform over his weakened right arm, Ravier reached his good hand up for Taliya.

Varjiek lowered his stomach to the ground, but before Taliya could slide off, Javan turned to her. "You have the scales, right?"

"In my bag." She patted the leather pouch slung over her shoulder.

"You know what to do as soon as Kisa teleports you to the other side?"

"That part I can handle. It's the opening of the portal that has me worried."

"I'm not worried." Actually he was. A little. After all, if she didn't succeed, his chances at winning the throne were dead. But he needed to instill her with confidence, not more pressure. "Remember what your father told you, and trust your instincts. You focus on the portal, and I'll protect you from the sky. Ravier and Micah will have your back on the ground with the help of Kisa and Mertzer. You let us handle the soldiers, and you get that portal open. You can do this."

"If you say so."

Kisa returned, ending the conversation. Taliya slid silently off Varjiek and moved alongside Ravier to touch Kisa's leg. In the next instant, they were gone.

You seem nervous, young Collector.

"You picked up on that, huh?"

Taliya is smart. She will figure out how to open the portal and get us to Earth.

"You just want to get to Earth so you can see Skylark."

She is the reason I let you ride me. She's been hiding on Earth long enough. It's time to bring her home.

"Agreed." Javan smiled, remembering how Varjiek's demeanor changed when he mentioned Skylark's name that day he met Varjiek. Had it not been for that cute little dragon crush, Javan may never have collected his Noon Stalker. "The first step to getting to Skylark is getting Taliya to that portal, so let's fly."

Yes, sir!

Varjiek vaulted into the air, and Javan immediately began scanning the ground for Kisa, Taliya, and Ravier. His eyes found them within seconds. They were hugging the base of the cliff, right around the corner from the portal. "You can do it, Taliya," he whispered. "You can make this crazy plan work."

◊   ◊   ◊

Taliya pointed to the stuffed uniform Ravier was about to put in Kisa's mouth. Careful not to raise her voice and garner the attention of the nearby soldiers, she said, "I'm still not sure anyone will believe that's an actual person."

"That's why we're doing this before the sun has a chance to rise." Ravier matched her quiet tone. "But I guarantee the one thing they will believe is that this dragon is hungry. I don't care how groggy they are or how dark it is, no one will miss Kisa's colorful scales. It all starts with you being convincingly scared."

"That shouldn't be a problem. I've never been this scared about anything, and I've lived through a volcano eruption."

"And you'll live through this. Just run straight ahead, yelling as you go." Ravier pulled out his sword. "Once the chaos begins, head back to the portal. I'll handle any of the guards that don't fall for the distraction."

Taliya nodded and turned to Kisa. "You ready, girl?"

The hungry glint in her eyes was answer enough. "Okay, then. Let's do this."

Ravier threw the uniform in Kisa's mouth, and Taliya began yelling and running. "Get away! Get away from here now! A hungry Dawn Stalker is on the loose. She's already feasting on one soldier and won't stop until she's eaten everyone she can catch!"

Kisa's deafening roar shook the early morning air. Taliya stumbled and turned to see Kisa standing on her hind legs chomping the last shreds of the grass-stuffed uniform. She did look pretty terrifying, and the soldiers around her seemed to agree. The ones closest to the lake dove in and began swimming to the other side. The others ran behind and around her, screaming like unashamed babies.

That woke the okties woke up. Their screeching outdid Kisa's roars. They knew they would be the dragon's breakfast if they didn't get away and flew in confused circles around their tied perches in the trees. Kisa stomped toward the camp, trampling everything in her path.

The soldiers in the tents began to emerge. And run. The blur of Micah and Mertzer slashing through the trees and tents added to the chaos. A stampede of life-saving insanity shook the ground, a stampede that took everyone away from the portal.

Leaving the people to the dragons, Taliya dashed across the rocky ground to the cliff. Ravier was the only one standing in front of it.

"You get the portal open," he said. "I'm going to make sure the soldier on top of the cliff doesn't give you any trouble."

"I appreciate that." Now alone with the intimidating wall made from pieces of dragon scales that glowed softly, Taliya took out the four full-sized scales from her bag and stepped up to the left of the massive colorful octagon. She found what she was looking for at eye level: a small circle with four open triangular slots. The four points of the triangles touched in the middle, resembling a giant four-leaf clover.

"Here we go." With trembling hands, she started to place the Dawn and Dusk scales in the right and left slots. "Whoa. That's not right. This is the southern portal. I have to put the scales in one at a time two seconds apart, not simultaneously like in the northern portal." Correcting herself, she placed the Midnight scale in the top spot, the Dawn scale in the right slot, the Noon scale in the bottom slot, and the final Dusk scale in the left spot. Then she drew in a giant breath that she didn't dare exhale and pushed.

The octagon on the wall beside her blinked to life with a brilliant flash of blue. A blurry rainbow of colors followed, and the four scales in front of her blinked off and on.

"Blue," she mumbled, studying the pattern of the flashes. "Blue is the dominant color. Now to figure out how long to hold the scales down and how many times to tap each scale."

She stepped back, forcing her eyes to focus on the pattern of the flashing colors of the portal and willing her ears to ignore the commotion behind her.

"Hey!" A voice from above interrupted her focus. "No one is authorized to touch the portal. Cease! Cease your actions immediately!"

"Cease my actions?" She craned her head upwards to see a uniformed figure staring down at her. She didn't feel the need to respond with similarly flowery language and simply yelled, "Not gonna happen."

"I said cease!" He aimed his Jolt Blast at her and fired.

She dodged the lightning bolt and looked to the sky. "Javan, where's my cover?"

"Right here." Flames appeared in mid-air, and the soldier scrambled away from the ledge to escape Varjiek's fiery breath. That scramble must have chased him right to Ravier because Taliya could hear swords clashing above her.

Hoping Ravier could indeed fight left-handed, she realized the pattern was repeating and knew she needed to enter the code before it cut off.

She stepped back to the four scales and tapped the Dusk scale. Then she pressed the Dawn scale three times, Noon seven, Midnight four, and Dusk five. "No, no, no. Six. I need to hit it six times." But it was too late. The portal went dark. The activation scales spun round and round. Then fell out.

She caught them as they fell, knowing she only had two more chances to get it right.

CHAPTER 30

Swift Action

"**S**top!" Sensing that something was wrong, Micah commanded the speeding Mertzer to halt his tirade. It took the dragon a few steps to slow down, and they finally skidded to a stop in the middle of the crazed camp.

Something was wrong. The portal had stopped glowing.

Not that anyone else seemed to notice. Their plan to create chaos couldn't have worked any better. No one whose sole job was to ensure that portal didn't activate ignored they portal that was being activated. They were instead running in the opposite direction to steer clear of Kisa as well as the random bursts of fire Varjiek blew down from the sky.

Except one soldier with an axe strapped across her back moved against the crowd. She walked quickly. Calmly. Confidently. Unfazed by the craziness around her. Toward the portal. Toward Taliya.

"Mertzer, you keep creating terror. I need to take care of the rogue soldier." The dragon nodded and dashed off as soon as Micah's feet hit the ground.

Micah zig zagged against the flow of people as Taliya restarted the activation process. With the burst of light came a burst of recognition. He wasn't following just any soldier. He was following the Destroyer, the same woman who had almost killed him in his own backyard.

He broke into a jog, determined to reach her before she reached Taliya.

◊   ◊   ◊

"Haha!" Taliya clapped her hands, proud of herself. This time, she recognized the code instantly. "Get ready, Javan! I'll have the portal open in less than a minute."

She rubbed her hands together and skipped to the four scales. Noon three. Dusk two. Dawn five. Noon one. Midnight six. Noon four. Then Noon and Midnight together and—

A hand that did not belong to her pressed the Dusk scale. Once again, the portal darkened and the activation scales spun out. Taliya caught the scales in disbelief and turned to find the Destroyer staring down at her with her arms crossed and no expression on her face smooth, flawless face.

"How dare you!" Taliya shoved the taller, stronger woman. The woman didn't flinch. "You need to back off right now or Javan will have his dragon incinerate you!"

"That won't be necessary, Taliya." Micah stepped between them with his sword drawn. "You get the portal open. I'll make sure she doesn't bother you again."

"Finally." The Destroyer flipped her axe over her shoulder and squared off with Micah. "You're the real reason I'm here, anyway. Glad you decided to come play."

She slashed at Micah's throat, but he blocked her attack with his sword. "Hurry, Taliya." He pushed the Destroyer back and lunged after her.

With the clash of Micah's steel sword against the Destroyer's iron axe handle ringing in her ears, Taliya began her third and final attempt at opening the portal. If she got the code wrong this time, she'd be greeted with a shower of acid rather than darkened scales. But if she got it right, she would be headed to Earth.

Choosing to focus on the positive, Taliya stepped back to watch the new pattern emerge. "Is that three-two-two or two-three-two?" She wasn't sure! The pattern wasn't clear. She watched it again. And the third and final time. "Two-three-two. It has to be two-three-two."

At least she hoped so. Still not certain but certain she had to make a decision, she began. Dawn two. Dusk three. Dawn two. Noon one. Midnight four. Dawn two. She bit her lip, closed her eyes, and winced as she then pressed all four scales at once.

Expecting acid to burn her skin, she found herself surprised when the once solid wall turned soft. Almost watery. "It's open," she mumbled. "The portal to Earth is open."

"I knew you could do it, Taliya!" Javan yelled from above and let Varjiek show himself as they flew through the portal.

"Stop gaping and go," Micah said, blocking another of the Destroyer's blows.

The ping of the axe striking sword drew Taliya's attention away from the portal. Micah was holding his sword in front of his neck while the axe blade almost touched his nose. He didn't look like he would be able to hold his defensive position much longer. Taliya had to help. She reached for her slingshot. "Give me ten seconds and I'll have a dart in that pretty little neck of hers."

"I got this. Just go!"

"I can't--"

"Go!"

She jumped at his order and plunged face first into the watery wall.

◊   ◊   ◊

"You got this?" The Destroyer laughed in Micah's face. "The only thing you've got is an axe about to take your head off."

"Not likely." Micah's arms ached, and his sword shook against the relentless pressure of the Destroyer's axe. He'd been in plenty of swordfights and won every single one. Once he figured out how to defeat an opponent wielding an axe instead of a sword, he would win this one as well.

"Aren't you cocky." She pushed harder. The edge of the axe grazed his nose. Blood began to drip over his lips and onto his chin. "So am I. For good reason. With you out of the way and Javan in another dimension, my job of killing the rest of the dragons will be easy. I have all the backing of Omri and no resistance from anyone."

He couldn't die here. He refused to die here at the hand of an assassin with the light from the open portal warming his skin.

The open portal.

That was it. That was his way out. He steadied his hands and smiled. "Are you ready?"

"Ready for what?"

Micah took advantage of that tiny flicker of confusion. He swiped her ankles with his foot and pushed out with his arms. Maintaining control of his sword with his left hand, he caught the off-balance Destroyer with his right arm. He wrapped his around her waist, picked her up, and carried her through the portal to the only place where he was certain the dragons of Zandador would remain safe from her bloodthirsty axe: Earth.

CHAPTER 31

Earth

Sticky water. Gooey mud. Squishy soup. Bolstered by an icy wind, Taliya felt like she was walking through a combination of all three of those things as she made her way from Zandador to Earth through the portal. She savored every sensation and let her curiosity surge her onward.

What was she going to see first when she made it to the other side? Mountains? Oceans? Deserts? Forests? Glaciers? What would the air feel like? Would it smell different than the air in the Great Rift? What about animals? If dragons were unique to her dimension, what kind of animals would she encounter that were unique to Earth?

So many questions that demanded answers, answers she would discover when she stepped through the colorful wall up ahead. Earth stood on the other side of that wall.

A spine-contorting shiver shot through her when she finally emerged from the sticky, gooey, squishy portal. The shivers continued as she took in the unimpressive scenery of a cave. Varjiek's large body took up more than half of the space. His claws rapidly tapped the stone floor, and Javan sat atop the dragon's twitching body. Laughing. Uncontrollably.

The sounds of the tapping and the laughing bounced off the high ceiling and ragged walls. "What's so funny?" Taliya managed to ask between echoes and bodily shivers. She also wanted to ask if the eggs were okay, but she couldn't get the words out.

"Nothing." Javan cackled. "Absolutely nothing. I just...haha...react this way...haha...when I travel...haha...through the portal."

"Oh. Right. The portal effect." Taliya vaguely remembered reading about how no one could get through the portal without experiencing some sort of physical reaction from the interdimensional travel. Apparently her body responded by shivering. She told her toes and her knees and her hips and her hands to be still, but they weren't listening. The noise from Javan and Varjiek didn't help. "Think you can tone it down a little? Your laughing and Varjiek's twitching make it really loud in here."

"I'm sorry." Javan covered his mouth. His body shook from the muffled laughter, and Taliya found herself starting to laugh at the sight of the silently hysterical Javan.

"Just let it out, man."

He did. His ear-splitting laugh tore through Taliya's ears at the precise moment two more people burst through the watery wall. The wall solidified, and the four scales appeared in the activation wheel on this side of the portal. Taliya couldn't stop shivering long enough to grab them and instead watched Micah wipe at the tears streaming down his face.

"What's with all the laughing?" Micah looked at his wet hands. "Why am I crying? This is ridiculous. I don't cry. Ever. I'm not even sad."

"I've got a better question," Taliya said between shivers. She nodded at the Destroyer dangling over Micah's shoulder. The woman held on to her axe so tightly her knuckles turned white. The only part of her that moved was her eyes. She was blinking as fast as a hummingbird flaps its wings. "Why did you bring the trained dragon killer to Earth?"

Micah responded by sobbing. While he cried and Javan laughed, she forced her shivering hands to take the scales from the activation circle. They had also made the trip from Zandador, and she would need to use them to return. As she put them in her bag, she noticed a piece of paper sticking out of a small crevice in the wall to her left.

◊   ◊   ◊

The sight of Micah carrying the Destroyer cured Javan of his desire to laugh. After checking to make sure the eggs had survived the trip without cracking, he slid off Varjiek and marched over to the tearful Micah. "What are you doing here? You were supposed to stay in Zandador and care for Mertzer and Kisa, not bring the woman who wants you and all dragons dead to Earth. What if she tries to kill our dragons as soon as they hatch?"

"We were fighting. I was losing. The portal was open." Micah spoke in short sentences between sobs. He took a deep breath, dropped the Destroyer on the floor, and continued with more control of his emotions. "I figured it would be easier to keep an eye on her in unfamiliar territory than it would be to chase her around Zandador trying to stop her from killing all the Midnight Stalkers before you got back. I really don't want to have to hunt for more eggs and do this trip to Earth thing again. I'm not sure how many times the army will fall for the hungry dragon trick."

"At least take her weapon away from her." Javan snatched the axe from the blinking Destroyer. "What's your name?"

Her eyes slowed to normal blinking range. She narrowed them at him but didn't say anything.

"Javan asked you a question." Micah pulled the woman to her feet and turned her to face Javan. "Tell the man your name. While you're at it, why don't you tell me what my father promised you if you killed me."

She slowly crossed her arms over her chest and pursed her lips. She cocked her head slightly to one side as if to say she wasn't about to say anything. Javan fought to keep his composure under the cold stare of the silent woman.

"What is this thing?"

Taliya's question gave Javan a good reason to turn around. She was holding a Ziplock baggie with an iPhone trapped inside it. "A phone!" He snatched the bag from her hand, took it out of the plastic bag, and turned it on. While he waited for it to power up, he asked, "Where did you find this?"

"In the wall over there. This was with it."

He took a folded piece of torn notebook paper from her and opened it. It had only two words scribbled on the middle of the page above a series of numbers: *Call me.*

"What's a call?" Taliya asked. "What are the numbers for? Who do you think left the note? Was it meant for you or someone else?"

"That's too many questions at once, Taliya." A picture of Kenton's smiling face popped up on the phone. His silver hair draped onto his shoulders from beneath his leather hat, and he had a red bandana wrapped around his neck under a collared shirt. In the background of his great-great-great grandfather's selfie were two grey dragons floating in the air above the Grand Canyon.

"I know that man." Taliya took the phone from him. "He's the one who went with my father to Earth the night they took you through the portal as a baby. Has he been living on Earth this whole time? With his dragons? They've been able to survive in this atmosphere?"

"I know him, too." Now Micah took the phone. "That's Kenton, my father's greatest rival. What's this about him bringing you to Earth? Is that how you remained undetected your whole life? You were hiding on Earth?"

Kenton has Skylark, Varjiek chimed in. *Does that thing you are holding say she's okay? Do you think she'll remember who I am?*

"Enough!" Javan's scream echoed off the walls and silenced everyone. The bombardment of questions were giving him a headache. He retrieved the phone and continued in a softer voice. "Let me make this call, and then we can play question and answer time."

He pushed the round button at the bottom of the phone twice to bring up the passcode screen. Using the numbers on the sheet of paper, he accessed the phone. The battery life was at eighty-three percent, and he had one service bar. Hopefully that would be a strong enough signal to make the call.

The only contact listed in the phone's directory was for Kenton, so Javan touched the call button. It rang three times before a voice answered and said, "Who's this?"

"Javan."

"Javan! I wasn't expecting you to come back for me yourself. That's a mighty humble act for a king. I feel honored. Let me put my house in order and gather my dragons. Skylark will be happy to hear she'll be able to eat her noon meal in the Land of Zandador today!"

"Whoa, whoa, whoa. Hold on." Javan had to close his eyes to stop his head from spinning. "I'm not here because I won the throne."

"You gave up? Unbelievable! Don't you understand how important you are to the Land of Zandador?"

"Please stop jumping to conclusions and let me explain." Javan switched the phone to his other ear. "I've collected a Noon Stalker and a Dawn Stalker. I have a Dusk Stalker with me. Kinda. It hasn't hatched yet."

"You brought an egg with you? Fascinating. Why didn't you say so, my boy? I'll get the incubator ready, and Skylark and I will be there in a few hours. Don't wander out of that cave until we get there."

Kenton hung up before Javan had a chance to say goodbye. That's when he noticed that Taliya and Micah were both staring at him like he had grown a second head.

◊   ◊   ◊

"This is a communication device?" Keeping a hold of the Destroyer's arm with one hand, Micah took the thin, rectangular object Javan had been speaking into with his free hand. Rows of tiny squares with colorful pictures covered the top part. He touched one with a grey circle inside a black object, and the device suddenly became transparent. He could see everything he pointed the device at, but the back of it remained one solid block of black. "Javan, I can see your face *inside* this thing."

"That's the camera. Watch." Javan leaned over, put his finger on some arrows in the bottom corner, and Micah could suddenly see his own face. "Now press the white circle."

"Why?"

"Just do it. Don't forget to smile."

Micah didn't bother to smile, but he did press the white circle. The device flashed, and his image appeared in a small square in the bottom left corner. "What just happened?"

"You took your first selfie." Javan touched the image in the corner, and Micah's frozen face filled the entire length of the device.

"This is madness!" Afraid of what the device would do now that his image was stamped on it, Micah dropped it and let go of his prisoner's arm. He stepped backwards as the device clanked to the floor.

Javan scrambled to pick it up. "Careful, Micah. This is an expensive phone, and the screen is fragile. We don't need it cracking after only one phone call."

"Explain that phone call thing," Taliya said. "How did you use that to talk to someone who wasn't with us?"

"I can't explain all the sciency stuff behind it," Javan said. "I can tell you that most people have one of these things, and they are all assigned a unique number. When I punched the numbers that connected to Kenton's phone, his phone made a ringing noise. He could see the number from this phone on his screen, so he knew who was calling. Once he answered, we could talk."

"Amazing," Taliya said. "We sure could use these in the Great Rift. What else do they have here that we don't have?"

"That list is too long to even start," Javan said, "but I can show you what else this phone can do besides make calls and take pictures."

"It does other things?" Taliya's eyes widened. "Show me."

"Sure. We need something to do while we wait for Kenton anyway." Javan led Taliya over to a smooth section of the cave's floor and sat down. The light from the device lit both of their faces as they stared at it, mesmerized.

"While they are occupied," Micah said, turning his attention to the Destroyer, "let's get back to those questions you never answered. We'll start with the easy one. What is your name?"

Rather than answer, she sat down, leaned against the wall, and closed her eyes.

Micah resisted the urge to kick her and instead took his belt off. "No name, no freedom." He knelt, pulled her arms behind her back, and tied them together with his belt. But something about the cocky look she gave him made him believe one little belt wasn't going to keep her contained if she didn't want to be contained.

CHAPTER 32

Up from the Cave

Taliya drummed her fingers on the cold stone floor. Her mind told her it would be wise to take advantage of the opportunity to sleep like Javan and Micah were doing, but she wasn't about to close her eyes while the Destroyer sat ten feet away with her eyes wide open, her back straighter than the softly glowing portal behind her. The way the alert eyes of the Destroyer stared at the dragon eggs made Taliya wary.

She checked the nest she had made for the eggs. Her small pink egg and Javan's larger white egg nestled comfortably on top of the burlap sacks that had been used to carry them. In case they hatched, she didn't want the babies to have to fight their way through the rough cloth after working to bust through their shells.

With nothing else to do, she inspected the eggs for cracks. Finding none, she sighed. "I wouldn't want to hatch in a cave either," she whispered to them. "Don't worry. We shouldn't be down here much longer."

At least she hoped they wouldn't. The longer they stayed, the smaller the large room felt. The fact that Varjiek was lying on his side and taking up as much space as was dragonly possible didn't help. Every few minutes, he would shift his body and spread out a little bit more. He had inadvertently confined the four humans along the portal wall with his legs while his back almost touched the solid rock of the far wall.

Hmm. That wall had no door. Neither did the wall to her left or her right. How were they going to get out of here? Were they stuck? Was this as far as they would ever get on Earth?

Varjiek shifted and scooted his body. This time the tip of his tail brushed the wall to Taliya's left. And the wall opened. Briefly. It closed back up once the dragon's tail stopped touching it.

"That's bizarre." Taliya checked the eggs again. Certain they were safe, she climbed over and around Varjiek's legs, careful not to touch the legs of Javan or Micah along the way. The Destroyer remained silent and still and watchful.

Ignoring the feel of the Destroyer's eyes on her, Taliya touched the wall she had seen open moments before. An electric charge forced her to jerk her hand back. She shook the sting of the shock away and mumbled to herself. "An invisibility shield. It's not over the portal like in Zandador but shielding the entire room."

Taliya tickled Varjiek's tail. The end of it flopped up and down, breaking through the shield. "Good job, boy." Taliya took advantage of her small size and jumped through the opening. She found herself in a corridor, and she followed it all the way up to another room. This room had a hole in the ceiling, and through the hole she could see the sky. "Earth!"

Taliya found footholds in the rock wall that led through the opening. She hoisted herself through it and scrambled onto the rough surface. She could see water. Across the water were buildings. Lots and lots of buildings of all different shapes and sizes.

They were near a city. Interesting.

"Don't move." A rough voice sounded behind her, and cold steel touched the back of her neck.

Maybe wandering in a strange dimension on her own wasn't such a great idea after all.

◊   ◊   ◊

She's here.

The two words broke into Javan's mind and disturbed his restless sleep. "Who?" he muttered, refusing to open his eyes.

Skylark.

"Where?" That name was worth opening his eyes for. He scanned the room, but the only dragon he saw was Varjiek.

I can sense her approaching. His tail wrapped around his legs, and his back arched in a rigid line. *Will she recognize me? How do my scales look? Should I go to meet her? Should I wait for her to come to me?*

The barrage of fifth-grade level questions coming from his dragon made him chuckle. "Varjiek. Buddy. Chill."

"What's going on?" Micah appeared by Javan's side. "And where's Taliya?"

"Taliya's gone?" How did he overlook that obvious fact? "How did she get out? The only way to leave the room is to use stalker dust to break through the invisibility shield protecting this place."

Scales attached to Noon Stalkers work, too. She used my tail to get through the shield.

135

"When?"

Not too long ago.

"Why didn't you wake me up then?"

"I'm not following the sense of this conversation," Micah said.

She's getting closer! I must go to her. Varjiek stuck his head through what looked like a wall.

"Wait!" Javan's echoing scream brought the dragon's head back into the room. His large eyes glared at Javan. "The second you leave this room, you are to remain invisible at all times. Dragons aren't supposed to exist in this dimension. If you're spotted, you'll be killed or captured. Don't let yourself be spotted. Understood."

Understood.

"Good. Now go meet your girlfriend."

Varjiek vanished, and a whoosh of cold air swept over the cave.

"Javan," Micah said, "you are not making sense."

"I saw my first glimpse of Earth!" Taliya burst through an opening in the other side of the cave followed by a man in a brown leather jacket and matching leather cowboy hat. "The buildings were far away, but I can tell they are different than what we have in the Great Rift. I so can't wait to explore. They also have different weapons here. Kenton has this thing called a gun. Check it out."

She pulled a pistol out of Kenton's shoulder holster and waved it around. "Kenton used it to scare me when he didn't know who I was, but I'm not really sure what it does."

Javan held his hands up. "This is not a good place to find out."

"Whoa, little lady." Kenton reached for his gun. "I'll take that—"

Two loud explosions ended Kenton's sentence. He tackled Taliya as a bullet ricocheted off the ceiling and another bounced off the wall.

"Take cover!" Javan threw his body over the dragon eggs, and Micah covered the Destroyer as the bullets pinged around the stone cave.

◇   ◇   ◇

Micah didn't move until the pinging stopped and a little metal case smaller than his pinky rolled to a stop at his foot. He picked the object up and studied it. "Why were we scared of this?"

"That, my boy, is a bullet." Kenton pointed his weapon at Micah, and the two locked eyes. "On its own, it's harmless. When it is filled with a charged powder and shot through this gun, it can cause some serious damage."

"The eggs!" Taliya didn't seem to notice Kenton's underlying threat and rushed across the room to Javan.

While those two were distracted, Kenton stepped so close to Micah that his gun touched Micah's hip. "The little lady tells me you're on our side. If I find out otherwise, I won't hesitate to put one of these bullets right through your skull."

"That won't be necessary, but you might want to keep one of those bullets ready for this Wordless Wonder." Micah pulled the Destroyer to her feet. "She's the real enemy."

"Doubtful. I've spent the better part of your father's reign hiding from the special unit he commissioned to capture me and kill my dragons. That unit is the reason my Dawn Stalker is dead. How do I know you are not part of that unit here to finish the job?"

"I no longer take orders from my father. I think for myself these days and want to see him deposed." Micah smiled. "As a matter of fact, I can't wait to see the look on his face when he finds out you are alive and have been hiding on Earth this whole time."

"I haven't been here the whole time." Kenton lowered his gun but kept his eyes narrowed on Micah. Those blue eyes radiated a cunning intelligence and seemed to be assessing the risk Micah posed. When he spoke again, his words were edged with caution and a hint of trust. "The lifespan of humans is insignificant in this dimension compared to the Great Rift; I would have died centuries ago had I come when your father began hunting me."

"But my father has had the portal locked down for centuries. I don't recall hearing of any breaches in security apart from the time I caught Esmeralda trying to get through."

"The soldiers who fail to guard the portal don't always report their failures to their king."

"Oh." Micah took a moment to consider that. If Omri didn't know of any portal activations, he couldn't punish those who allowed it to happen. "So how long have you been here?"

"I brought Javan through the night he was born. As the fulfillment of the prophecy, this was the safest place for him to live while we waited for the Battle of the Throne year to approach. When I discovered grown dragons can survive in this atmosphere, we stayed, planning to return once Javan won the throne."

"You and your dragons have been able to survive on Earth for 150 years?"

Kenton laughed. "What has Javan been telling you about his age?"

"Nothing." Micah scowled. "I just assumed he was at least 150. He certainly looks that old."

"Maybe he does look that old in Zandador, but he's only been alive for a little over fifteen years."

Micah's eyes went wide and his mouth went dry as he looked at Javan. A child was leading this expedition in an effort to overthrow a 700-year-old king? They were doomed. The entire Land of Zandador was doomed.

CHAPTER 33

Farm Life

Thrilled to be out of the cave, Taliya fed off Skylark's intoxicating energy as the invisible Noon Stalker flew fast and low over the ocean. Since everything below her was a blue blur anyway, Taliya kept her eyes closed and her arms wrapped tightly around the dragon's neck. She loved the smell of the salty air as well as the way the wind burned her skin and blew through her braided hair.

She focused on that rather than the things she wasn't happy with at the moment. She didn't like being separated from her dragon egg that Varjiek was carrying along with Javan and Micah. And she certainly didn't like the fact that the Destroyer—who couldn't even be polite enough to tell them her name—was sitting between her and Kenton.

Skylark banked to the left. The movement prompted Taliya to open her eyes. They were now racing over brown and green patches of land broken up by the occasional lake or sprawling city. Part of her wanted Skylark to slow down to allow her to take in the details of the landscape. The other part wanted Skylark to speed up and fly forever.

Then again, her bottom and legs were growing numb from the long flight. She was thus glad when the dragon slowed her speed and coasted down to a grassy meadow. Hills and trees and the glint of a lake in the distance were the only other things she could see. She was expecting this dimension to look different than Zandador, but it looked eerily similar.

"We'll hike up to the house from here," Kenton said, sliding off Skylark once Varjiek landed beside them. "It's about a half mile away, but this is the best landing spot for the dragons. It's close to the barn where they live and eat. Plus it's secluded enough for the dragons to wander around without fear of being spotted."

"I think it's sad that dragons have to be kept a secret from the people of Earth." Taliya patted Skylark. "I hate to imagine how dull my life would be without dragons."

The Destroyer behind Taliya grunted and joined Kenton on the ground. That was the first sound the woman had made since coming through the portal. It may have been a sound of derision, but at least it proved the woman was listening to the conversations happening around her.

A wave of fatigue washed over Taliya as her feet hit the soft grass. She fought it back by inhaling deeply. Oxygen from Earth's air filled her lungs. She didn't have time to be tired. She needed to see and do as much as possible before returning to her own dimension. First, though, she needed to care for her dragon.

She took her egg from Javan and cradled it in her arms. "We need to get these eggs into a warm, moist environment in order to hatch."

"Of course," Kenton said. "I have a place prepared. Follow me."

Kenton led the way up a gradual hill. They stopped at a large steel building that had two dragon-size doors, three large doors, and one human-size door. The Noon Stalkers entered one of the dragon doors, and the five humans carried on. Further ahead, Taliya noticed four more buildings. The one on the far right had two levels and windows marking each level. The other three had only those large doors that matched the ones in the dragon building. No windows were built into the walls.

"In here." Kenton led them into the windowless building closest to the house. "I used to have chickens, but they were too scared to lay eggs with the dragons roaming around. I finally sold them, but I kept the incubator. It hasn't been used in a while, but it should do the trick until the eggs hatch."

Kenton took a rope and stuck it into a wall. A warm light filled the box with the open top. He fluffed some straw in the bottom of the box and placed the Dusk eggs inside.

"Let's go up to the house. I'll make everyone breakfast, and we can get acquainted."

"I'll eat later," Taliya said. "If these eggs hatch, someone needs to be here to welcome the dragons to the world."

"You go ahead." Javan yawned. "Eat some food. Take a shower. Get some rest. I had a little nap back in the cave and can take the first watch here."

"I'm more awake than you. I'll be fine here. Please. Go. I need some quiet time after the morning we've had."

"If you're sure."

"I am. Go."

As soon as Javan left, she peered over the edge of the glowing box. "All right, you two. It's time to bust out of those shells and show me your faces."

◊　◊　◊

From his seat at the bar in the kitchen, Javan kept everyone in his eyesight. To his left, he could see the Destroyer and Micah. She sat on the floor in the corner of the living room with her hands tied behind her back. Micah utilized the only furniture in the room. He sat in the recliner mesmerized by the sixty-inch color television mounted on the wall. The murmur of the voices as Micah surfed through channels indicated Javan was clearly back in his familiar, modern-day world.

To his right, Javan could see out the window over the sink to the barn where Taliya waited with the eggs. In front of him, Kenton—who had a bizarre resemblance to Indiana Jones—whistled while he cracked eggs, fried bacon, and flipped pancakes. He looked like he had everything under control, but Javan felt obliged to ask, "Are you sure I can't help you?"

"You'll just get in my way." Bacon sizzled. Sparks of grease jumped onto the stovetop. "What you can do is explain why a Hunter and a Destroyer are in my house. They could be working together to make sure you never return to Zandador."

"That might be the Destroyer's plan, but I trust Micah."

"Why?"

"He's proven his loyalty. He was willing to sacrifice himself so I could collect his Dusk Stalker."

"What?" Kenton flipped a pancake over his shoulder. The half-cooked pancake splatted on the floor. "You mean to tell me you could have avoided this entire trip? You should be in Midnight Territory looking for a Midnight Stalker right now, not waiting for a dragon to hatch."

"I couldn't kill to gain a dragon. Human life is more valuable than that."

"A man with a conscience." Kenton beat a bowl full of raw eggs and dumped them in a frying pan. "The Land of Zandador hasn't seen that from its king in a very long time."

Booming voices from the living room interrupted the quiet conversation. Micah threw the remote on the floor and covered his ears. "What is happening?" he yelled.

"You turned the volume up too high," Javan yelled back.

"I did what?"

Javan hopped off his stool and recovered the remote. He pressed the volume button until the voices on the television became whispers. He tried handing the remote back to Micah, but Micah wouldn't take it.

"That thing has powers I do not understand."

Javan suppressed a smile and nodded solemnly. "It is a powerful wand that can make pictures change and volume increase. It must be handled with great care, but I believe you are worthy."

Micah hesitated before accepting the offered remote. "Thank you for believing in me."

"Always." Javan caught a glimpse of the Destroyer as he turned to go. Her expression remained blank but her eyes locked on him. He felt like she could see into his soul. She was searching for his fears and weaknesses, and he worried that she just might find everything she was looking for.

◊　◊　◊

Taliya chased Javan away after he brought her a plate of food. She expected the dragon eggs to hatch soon, and she wanted all three men guarding the Destroyer when that happened. That's when the dragons would be the most vulnerable, and Taliya wanted to make sure the Destroyer couldn't get near them.

But guarding eggs proved to be a very boring job. She had been at it less than an hour and was already itching for something else to do. "You two wouldn't mind if I took a look around, right?"

The eggs didn't move.

"If you decide to hatch, I'll right be over there."

What Javan had told her was a tractor and lawnmower were the first unusual things she had seen. She couldn't resist exploring any longer and walked over to the big one. Its back wheels were almost as tall as her, and its seat was enclosed in glass with a black top. "I'll come back to you. This other one looks to be more my size."

She moved to the shiny green thing with four wheels, a yellow seat, and a yellow metal thing under the seat. She climbed up and onto the seat. "I'm not sure why Javan called this a lawnmower," she said, talking to the unhatched dragons. "It sure is the weirdest wagon I've ever seen. How does it hook up to animals, and where's the bed for storing things to carry?"

She turned the fifth wheel in front of her. As it moved, so did the tires on the front. "You are for steering. So what do you do?" She turned a key sticking out of the dash under the steering wheel. A screeching noise made her turn it back. "Interesting." She pushed some knobs to her right up and tried again. More screeching.

"Maybe I need to add this." She pushed her left foot against a pedal and turned the key. This time a rumbling came from under the green top. The lawnmower launched forward when she pressed her foot against the right pedal, but the rumbling stopped. She got it going again and tried moving the black lever down. The rumbling remained strong. She pushed against the right pedal. Forward movement. Cool.

She wasn't sure how this machine was moving without the aid of an animal, but she didn't need to know the specifics. The fact that she was on the go was enough fun for her. She rolled through the open door and onto the dirt road.

"Time to discover where this road goes." Excited to find out how much of this world she could see now that she didn't have to walk everywhere, she puttered past the house. Up ahead, she saw a row of tall trees that blocked her view of anything else. She also heard an occasional rumbling sound, the same kind of rumbling that came from under the green top of the lawnmower.

"That must be another road up there. Do a lot of people get around on these lawnmowers?" She lurched toward the noises. The closer she came to the other road, she noticed flashes of color zooming by. "How are they going that fast?"

She pressed down her pedal as far as it would go, but she couldn't get her lawnmower to zoom. It stayed plugging along at the same steady pace. She finally reached a hard, black surface and paused when she didn't see any other lawnmowers. She did see several dozen cows meandering around a wide open field on the other side of the road.

Then something that was most definitely NOT a lawnmower raced by her. It had four wheels and moved without being pulled by animals, but it was blue and much bigger than that tractor in the barn. She could see two people sitting in it through a big front window.

She followed it with her eyes as it zipped by and saw a similar red contraption coming toward her. It began making a loud blaring noise, and she frantically steered her lawnmower off the paved road. She avoided being hit by the oversized red tractor but slammed into a short pole.

Her body lurched forward. Her stomach rammed into the steering wheel, and her forehead knocked against the top of her shiny green lawnmower.

CHAPTER 34

Earth Identification

Honking. Burning rubber. Metal crunching. The sounds of a car accident cut through the walls of the house just as Javan snuggled under the covers on Kenton's bed and closed his eyes. That's when it occurred to Javan that life was much more peaceful and safer in Zandador where cars didn't exist.

He took a few calming breaths to relax himself enough to get back to sleep. It would have worked if Kenton hadn't barged into the room. "Javan, you need to come with me. Now."

The urgency in Kenton's voice told Javan something important was happening. Like maybe his dragon had busted out of his shell. "So much for sleep."

Groggily, Javan shuffled into the hall and was confused when he saw Kenton rush out the front door. If his dragon was hatching, wouldn't it be easier to go out the back door to get to the barn?

"It's Taliya," Micah said, pointing out the door toward the road. "I'd go, but I can't leave the Wordless Wonder here by herself."

"Taliya's out front?" The car accident. Had Taliya wandered into the road and caused an accident? "Oh, no."

Javan busted through the door and dashed across the front yard behind Kenton. As he caught up with Kenton, he saw Taliya slumped over the steering wheel of the lawnmower she had somehow smashed into the mailbox post. Blood from her head streamed down the green hood.

"Taliya!"

"That's me." She coughed and slowly sat up. Good. She was conscious.

"What are you doing out here?" Javan noticed a gash on her forehead and helped her sit steadily in the seat. "This cut looks painful. You're gonna need stitches."

"The cut looks worse than it is," Kenton said. "I can patch her up inside."

"What are those big colorful things on wheels?" She wiped away blood dripping into her mouth. "Why do they go so much faster than my lawnmower? I want to drive one of the big, fast lawnmowers."

"They're called cars, but you need a license to drive one of those." Javan helped Taliya off the lawnmower, and they started walking back to the house while Kenton pushed the lawnmower behind the tree line.

A car whipped by them. Taliya turned and pointed at it until they could no longer see it. "I have to drive a car. How do I get a license?"

"First you have to take a class. Then you have to pass a driving test." He nodded toward the lawnmower. "I don't think you'll be on Earth long enough to pass the test."

"Or," Kenton said, supporting Taliya from the other side, "I can print you a license, give you a quick lesson, and let you drive one of my cars."

Javan stopped walking. "Are you saying you know how to make fake ID's?"

"Certainly. How else was a guy from another dimension supposed to make a life for himself on Earth?" Kenton picked Taliya up and carried her the rest of the way to the house. As Javan followed, he wondered what other illegal things his great-great-great grandfather had gotten involved with in order to make a life for himself on Earth.

◊   ◊   ◊

"I don't understand." Micah stood behind Kenton's desk in the corner room of the house that Kenton used as an office and held the piece of plastic that had his picture on it. "What is this for?"

"It's a driver's license that also serves as your identification," Javan said. He hovered over Taliya, who was laying quietly on the couch with an ice pack over her bandaged head. The Destroyer was quiet as well, but she was sitting under the window where everyone could watch her. "Usually you have to pass a driving test to get one of these. Printing your own is kind of illegal."

"We're not using them for illegal purposes." Kenton rubbed his hands together, and moved his fingers over rows of letters on what he called the keyboard of a computer. "We're just being prepared. If we find ourselves in a situation where we need to prove our identity, we can. I don't anticipate needing to leave the farm for any reason, but if we do, we will be ready. It will also make a lovely personalized treasure to commemorate your time on Earth."

"I do like being prepared," Micah said. He mostly wanted to take Kenton's side because he could see it irritated Javan. And that amused him. He studied his ID again. "What is this number on here beside my birthday? You got the day right but not the year. According to this, I'm 2200 when I'm really only seventy-seven!"

"Actually," Kenton said, never looking away from his computer, "we track years differently on Earth. Here time is divided into before Christ lived on Earth and after Christ, but the Great Rift began tracking time from the moment God created that dimension after the flood. That was 4200 years ago, but Christ came to Earth a little over two thousand years ago."

"That was too much information." Micah waved his ID in the air. "I just want to know how old this thing says I am."

Javan looked at it and said, "Eighteen."

"What? No." Micah shook his head. "That's not even close to right. Look again."

"It still says you're eighteen, which is about right. That's how old I thought you were when I first saw you."

"Fix this." Micah slammed the plastic on the desk beside Kenton. "No one will believe I'm eighteen. I pass for at least 170 in Zandador even though I'm much younger."

"Sorry, kid," Kenton said. The printer whined as it spit out another license. "Here you look like a senior in high school. That makes you eighteen. So that's what I put on your ID." He handed the newly printed license to Javan.

"If anyone asks," Javan said, "you can tell them you play football. That will make you seem tougher if tough is what you're going for. Hey." Javan scrunched his face and showed his license to Kenton. "You made me fifteen, and this is only a permit. Why can't I be sixteen and get a license?"

"Because you're not sixteen," Kenton said. "Whether you count by Zandadorian years or Earth years, you were born fifteen years ago."

Micah wasn't sure why Javan cared about one measly little year, but he was more interested in how old the Destroyer looked in Earth years. "Your turn," Micah said, crouching in front of the Wordless Wonder. "What do you think your Earth age is, and what name should we put on your identification?"

True to form, she said nothing and stared at him with an I-don't-care attitude.

◊   ◊   ◊

"How about me?" Taliya sat up. The sudden movement made her head spin, but she was tired of being still and quiet. "What's my Earth age?"

"Hmm." Kenton used his device to take her picture. He rubbed his chin and snapped. "Sixteen. You look like you're sixteen."

"Hey," Javan whined, "why does she get to be sixteen, but I don't? You even made silent girl over there eighteen like Micah. As long as we're making up ages, I think I should get to be one year older."

"What's the big deal about being sixteen?" Taliya asked. "At twenty-two, I've already lived my sixteenth year, and it wasn't anything special."

"When you turn sixteen here," Javan said, "it means you're old enough to drive. That means you get to start going places on your own without any adult having to tote you around."

"Then I definitely want to be sixteen. What else do sixteen-year-olds get to do?"

"You get to go to high school."

"What's high school? Is it a school in the mountains? And does that mean there's a low school?"

"I guess there is a low school. We call it elementary school. You start when you are five and go through fifth grade. Then we graduate to middle school that is sixth through eighth grade. High school is the last block of our required educational system. It covers grades nine through twelve. At sixteen with your birthday in March, you would be in your junior year, or eleventh grade."

"I'd almost be done with school? That's sad. I love learning."

"The learning part of school is fine. It's the social stuff that I hated. There are so many bullies and snobs. They can make your life miserable at school and online."

"Online. I don't follow. Explain."

"By online I mean the Internet you can access on a computer or phone or tablet. There are all kinds of these social media sites where people can post countless pictures of themselves. We call them selfies. Teens these days are basically addicted to their phones and base their personal value on how many likes their pictures get or how many followers they have."

"I don't understand anything you just said."

"Me, either," said Micah. "Are there any similarities between here and Zandador?"

"I'm sure there are," Javan said. But before he could share any, an ear-piercing shriek made everyone wince.

"The baby dragons!" Taliya jumped to her feet. "I knew we shouldn't have left them unattended." She rushed out of the room, certain hers was the one that had hatched.

CHAPTER 35

Dusk Baby

The dragon cried again. Only its head and front right leg had broken free from its white shell. It wiggled and turned but couldn't seem to make any more progress. "Come on, boy," Javan said, encouraging his goo-covered dragon, "you can do it. Be strong and smash through that shell."

He wanted to reach down. It would be easy for him to move the shell and free the baby. But he knew better. He knew this was a fight the dragon had to win for himself.

"Push a little harder." Taliya took over the cheering from the other side of the incubator. "Keep trying. I believe in you."

That seemed to be all the encouragement the dragon needed. With one long, loud screech, his three stuck legs kicked through the shell. Then his tail popped through the other side. He shook, throwing pieces of his shell and sticky green goo all over the hay and sides of the incubator.

"He looks like a furless cat with a long snout," Kenton remarked beside Javan.

"You're no cat, are you pal?" Javan watched the baby waddle around the edge of the incubator. His legs were unsteady, and his sticky body had fragments of his shell casing stuck to him. Javan wasn't sure what to do. He couldn't hear the dragon's thoughts and didn't want to startle the poor thing by reaching down and picking him up.

Could babies breathe poison? Was it born with a full set of teeth? Was it naturally vicious?

It rubbed against the pink, unhatched egg. "That's right," Taliya said. "Be a good friend and tell the dragon behind the pink shell to make her appearance."

The baby cocked its head at Taliya and steadily walked over to her. He then raised himself up on his back legs and reached for Taliya with his front legs. "Oh. You're a girl. And you want out."

"He's a she?" Javan was dumbfounded. He was certain his dragon should be a boy.

"No. She's a she." Taliya picked her up. "You need a bath. Let's get you cleaned up, and then you can come back and talk my dragon into hatching."

A twinge of jealousy hit Javan. Taliya had somehow connected with his dragon, and he hadn't thought of giving her a bath. What kind of Collector was he? Or was Taliya just a better Protector than he was a Collector?

◊ ◊ ◊

Taliya marveled at the Dusk baby as it swam underwater in Kenton's big bathtub with her eyes open and her ears pinned back. Such a beautiful, perfect creature in such a tiny little body. Taliya tried to imagine what the dragon would look like covered in scales, but she liked the vulnerable, soft look of the white skin. That white skin meant she needed Taliya to protect her from harm, and Taliya wanted to feel needed even if this technically wasn't her dragon.

Her desire to protect the dragon seemed to upset Javan. He hadn't said much since showing her how to fill the tub with water and sat on the edge of the tub with a sour look on his face. The dragon must not have appreciated the sulky attitude because she broke through the surface and spit water up in the air like a fountain. The water smacked Javan in the face and soaked his shirt.

Taliya laughed. "You're going to be the first Dusk Stalker in history not to be afraid of water." She threw Javan a towel. "What are you going to name her?"

"Good question." Javan dried his face, picked up the baby, and wrapped her in a towel. "You have any ideas? I had the name Shakeer all picked out, but that doesn't seem to fit for a girl."

"No. That doesn't fit at all." Taliya slid over, and the dragon crawled onto her lap. Her breathing turned to wheezing.

"That doesn't sound good." Javan put his hand on her back as she worked hard to draw breath. "Is she okay?"

"She probably just got water in her lungs." Taliya rubbed the sides of the baby, and her breathing returned to normal. "See. She's fine. But she does need a name. Why don't you ask her if she has any suggestions?"

"It wouldn't do any good." He averted his eyes. "I can't hear her thoughts. We can't communicate."

"Maybe she needs to learn how to think. In the meantime, we'll watch over her and get a good sense of her personality. Then we can assign her a name that truly fits."

The baby curled herself into a ball and fell asleep. *Don't get attached*, Taliya told herself. *Do not get attached to this dragon.* But it was too late. This dragon had already stolen her heart.

◊   ◊   ◊

"Aren't you even a little bit curious about the dragon swimming around in that tub?" Micah questioned the Destroyer. Or what was it Kenton named her? Jane. Jane Smith.

Micah tried to think of her as Jane, and he supposed it was as good a name as any. He knew it wasn't her right name, though. He wanted to know her right name and couldn't stand the fact that she refused to speak.

It wasn't only the not talking that bothered Micah. It was her whole demeanor. How could she show no emotion? None. Not even when a baby dragon had been carried right by her.

No Hunter or Destroyer had ever seen a newly hatched dragon. They had a chance to make history, and she didn't show the slightest inclination of caring. "You must really hate dragons if you don't have any interest in that baby. Maybe that's not it. Maybe it's so adorable you're worried it will make you love dragons, and then you'll have to stop trying to kill them all."

Still nothing. No reaction. It's like her face was made of stone. What game was she playing? Why sit there and not speak? And why wouldn't she tell him her name?

CHAPTER 36

Complications

Taliya fluffed her pillow of hay and let herself relax. Micah was mesmerized by the box with the people in it, and Javan was researching something called the baseball playoffs on Kenton's computer. He had tried explaining the game to her, but she was more interested in doing her job as a Dragon Protector. That meant watching over the Dusk baby and being there for her dragon to hatch.

She had thus retired to the barn with the baby and made herself a bed of hay. The baby dragon curled up at her feet, and her egg remained motionless in the incubator. She wasn't sure how long she had been asleep when a noise startled her.

The first thing she checked was her egg. "Pinky? Are you finally hatching?" She peered over the top of the box. Her egg hadn't moved.

Ding. Ping. Ding.

The noise was coming from the other side of the barn. Near the door. Under the door. She caught a glimpse of a white tail slipping under a fresh hole dug under the big door of the barn. "Oh, no."

Taliya ran after the nameless dragon. What if she wanted to test out her speed? If she ran in the wrong direction, she would end up smashed by those cars on the road. If she ran towards the open meadows and hills, though, Taliya may never find her. Either option was bad. Really, really bad.

The sliver of a moon and thousands of glowing stars were all the light available for Taliya to find the baby. "Dragon. Where did you go?" She wanted to call out the dragon's name to bid her to return, but she had no name to call out. "Sorry we didn't give you a name earlier. If you come back, we can figure something out."

Taliya slowly made her way back and forth down the hill. She should go tell Javan that the dragon had escaped, but she didn't want to admit that she had failed at her job as a Protector. She had to find the dragon. She had to bring it safely back to the barn.

To her left, a large oak tree rose to the sky in the middle of a field of dandelions. Something white broke up the pattern of the yellow weeds. The closer she got, the more the white body of the dragon seemed to glow under the branch in the shade created by the stars. "Is that you there, in the star's shade? Hmm. Starshade." Taliya whispered the name, and it felt like a perfect fit. "That's what I'll call you, and Javan will just have to agree."

Taliya slowly approached the dragon. "You can't be running around here, sweetie. It's not safe. Once we get you back to Zandador, we'll let you run as far and as fast as you want to, and it will be up to Javan to find you. If he can't catch you, that's his problem."

The dragon wheezed in reply.

"There's that wheeze again." Perhaps Starshade hadn't stopped running. Perhaps she had collapsed because she couldn't breathe. "I might need to take a closer look at those lungs of yours."

◊   ◊   ◊

Javan leaned back in the dangerously comfortable leather recliner with a piece of cold pepperoni pizza in one hand and an even colder can of Dr. Pepper in the other watching the Cubs battle the Braves in the National League Division Series. He felt like a teen again, but this version of his teenhood was better than anything he experienced in Montana.

Here he had friends and a blood relative with him. Granted, Kenton was in his office, Taliya was out in the barn with the dragons, and Micah was in the basement standing guard over Jane. He was technically alone, but he knew he was surrounded by good people.

Here Omri couldn't touch him. Jane the Destroyer had no power to destroy any dragons. Ravier wasn't watching his every move, telling him everything he was doing wrong or needed to improve.

Here he was able to take a long nap in the middle of the day and was prepared to stay up late into the night watching baseball.

He loved being here. He hoped Taliya's egg took the full three days to hatch so he could relax a bit more before re-entering responsibility land.

He took another bite of his pizza and cheered as the Cubs scored. That put them up 2-1 in the seventh. Not enough. They needed to pad that lead and give the bullpen a little breathing room for the eighth and ninth innings.

A pounding on the sliding glass door startled Javan. He looked across the dining room and could see Taliya holding the Dusk baby and kicking the door with her foot. "Help!"

He fumbled with the footrest and spilled soda everywhere as he struggled to get out of the cushy chair. "Why won't this footrest go down?" He finally gave up and jumped over the side. In the time he wasted, Kenton beat him to the door.

When Taliya stepped inside, she crumpled to her knees and placed the wheezing dragon on the floor. In a quivering voice, she said, "Something's terribly wrong with Starshade."

◊   ◊   ◊

"This shouldn't be happening." Taliya stroked the dragon's body with her ointment, only it didn't seem to be helping. Starshade continued to wheeze. "She's having a reaction to Earth's atmosphere, but according to everything I've read, babies should be able to survive for up to seven days without scales here on Earth. She hasn't even been alive for a day!"

"Then we have to go back to Zandador," Javan said. "Right now."

Tears welled in Taliya's eyes. "My dragon hasn't hatched yet. I can't leave."

"If we don't leave, my dragon will die." Javan put his arm around her shoulders. "I'm sorry."

"You're asking me to make an impossible choice." She stood, intentionally moving away from Javan's touch. "If I leave now to save your dragon, I'm sentencing my dragon to death. But if we wait for my dragon to hatch, I would be sentencing your dragon to death."

"Those aren't you're only choices," Kenton said.

Taliya sniffled. "What do you mean?"

"I mean we have a plant here on Earth that can help Starshade. I have a contact in Costa Rica who grows it for me. I pay her well to be discreet. My dragons have been going to her for years to get treatments. The longer we stay on Earth, the more often we have to go."

"Why don't you just grow the plant here?"

"I've tried. I've imported soil and attempted to recreate the Costa Rican climate in a greenhouse here on the farm. It's a unique hybrid plant that simply will not grow here."

"Where is this Costa Rica? Can I drive one of your cars this place?"

"It's too far to drive and will take half the night for Skylark to fly you there. I'll give Luisa a call while you prepare for the trip."

The tightness in Taliya's chest loosened. She could get Starshade the help she needed without having to sacrifice her own dragon's life in the process. "Hang in there, girl," she said. "We'll get you help. You just have to keep breathing and keep fighting."

The scaleless dragon looked up at her with trusting eyes, and Taliya hoped she wasn't making the dragon an empty promise.

CHAPTER 37

Leaf of Life

Javan spent the entire flight praying and trying not to let his mind even think about the worst case scenario. His mind rebelled and cooked up the scenario anyway.

If he lost his dragon, Taliya's dragon would become his last hope for gaining the throne. She would hate him for stealing this dragon from her after he already collected Kisa. Frankly, he preferred Taliya to the throne, but should he let his personal feelings keep him from doing his duty and saving the Land of Zandador from the terror of the Dark King's reign?

The flight through the night was fast and furious. Varjiek had refused to be left behind, so Javan rode his dragon while Taliya rode Skylark. Kenton had provided backpacks. Javan wore two of them. One was on his back filled with food, the belt with his Stalker swords, and two leashes. Once Starshade revived and Taliya's dragon hatched, they would both be wearing leashes to prevent them from running away.

Javan wore the second pack on his chest. It held the precious Starshade.

Starshade. Javan liked that name. It fit. And he liked that it connected Taliya to his dragon. Since she had bonded with both Kisa and now Starshade, she was more likely to hang around even after he won the throne.

"Stick with me, girl." Javan put his left hand on the front backpack. It was barely moving. "We should be there soon. Just a little longer."

A second after the words left Javan's mouth, Varjiek dove toward the ground and landed in the middle of a garden beside a visible Skylark. The aroma of herbs and the sweet scent of flowers attacked his nose. A thin figure carrying a lantern walked toward them. Soon Javan could make out a hunched Hispanic woman with shriveled skin and white hair.

She rubbed Skylark's nose and said something to her in Spanish before turning to Varjiek. "Strong physique. Beautiful dragon." Her accent was thick.

Varjiek puffed up at the compliments. *I like this Earthling.*

"Why you still sitting there?" Her soft tone was replaced with an orderly one. "Get down. Don't want dragon to die while you dawdle."

"Yes, ma'am." Javan did as he was told and handed his precious dragon to the strange woman.

◊   ◊   ◊

"Please hurry." Tears streamed down Taliya's face. She held Starshade in her lap. The dragon had stopped wheezing and was now only taking a shallow breath once every ten seconds. "She's not going to last much longer."

"Patience." Luisa picked a pointed purple leaf that resembled a hand with seven fingers off a vine. Using a stone spoon, she crushed the leaf into a powder in a stone bowl. She added a red berry and a dollop of water. "It's ready. Open her mouth."

"Gladly." Javan gently pulled the jaws of the dragon apart.

"Berry not necessary. Helps with texture." Luisa rubbed the mixture on the length of the dragon's tongue. "Close jaw and rub throat."

"Okay." Javan followed Luisa's instructions.

Taliya noted the concern on his face and the gentle way his fingers stroked Starshade's soft neck as they sat under some vines at the edge of a garden. The same stars that had inspired the dragon's name shone here, and they sat in the shade of those stars trying to keep the dragon alive.

Starshade coughed and lifted her head. Breath after breath filled her lungs. "She's breathing normally again," Taliya said.

"She will need next dose in few hours. In meantime, we must sleep. I have extra bed. Come. I will show you."

"You take the bed, Taliya," Javan said. "I can sleep in that hammock over there."

"I can't sleep yet." Taliya took her egg out of her new backpack. "I have to find a warm, moist place for my egg."

"Ooh." Luisa's eyes went wide at the site of the egg. "May I touch?"

"Sure."

Luisa stroked the egg. "I know perfect place. Follow me."

She followed Luisa deeper into the garden with Starshade trotting right behind her.

◊   ◊   ◊

Micah clicked the television off. His eyes hurt from watching the screen, and his body felt blah. All he had done since arriving at the farm yesterday morning was watch television, eat, and sleep. He hadn't even been outside.

Kenton had left after breakfast to buy food and clothes for everyone, leaving Micah alone with the Wordless Wonder. He had decided that if she could be stubborn and not talk, he could be stubborn and ignore her.

Nevertheless, his questions about her continued to race through his mind. He had hoped that making her sleep on the carpeted floor last night would inspire her to talk. He had offered her a blanket and pillow in exchange for her name. She had refused.

Now he was using food as a bribe. She hadn't eaten anything the day before and was certainly hungry. He tied her to a chair at the kitchen table and shoved three bites of eggs in her mouth. When she opened her mouth for a fourth bite, he said, "You want this? You're still hungry? I can keep feeding you, but I need your name first."

She slammed her mouth shut and pushed away from the table.

"Okay. We'll try again at lunch. Your stomach should be growling loudly by then." He grabbed the back of her chair and drug it over to the recliner. "And since you don't want to talk anyway, some solitary confinement will be good for you."

He tied her chair to the bigger chair and stepped outside. He took in a deep breath and surveyed the land stretching out before him. His feet were itching to run through the lush green grass, and his mind wanted to dash through the trees in the distance. He looked back at Jane Smith. She sat staring at the wall in front of her, not even trying to escape his excellent knots. She would be fine while he went out for a much needed run.

He stretched as he stepped outside and smiled as the sweat began to pour down his face moments later. The further he got from the house, the faster he ran through the vast fields and batches of trees.

Life here on Earth was easy. Perhaps he should stay. Mertzer would be free again, and he could create a new life for himself without worrying about anybody trying to kill him.

A gunshot interrupted his thoughts. A bullet struck a tree inches away from his face, sending splinters in every direction.

Another bang. Another near miss. Where were these shots coming from?

Then he saw her. Jane Smith. The Destroyer. She had somehow escaped and was holding one of Kenton's guns. And it was aimed right at him.

CHAPTER 38

Bullets that Sting and Bullets that Bite

Javan swallowed the remnants of his breakfast banana and stepped through Luisa's kitchen door onto the back cement porch. Clouds covered the morning sky, and the smell of impending rain filled the air. Perhaps Taliya's egg had hatched during the night, and they could head back before the rain came pounding down. With one glance to his left, however, he saw that Taliya still sat faithfully by her unhatched egg humming away. The kicker was that Starshade was curled in her lap.

He should have taken Starshade inside with him when he went to bed. That would have given them a chance to bond after her death scare. Instead, Taliya had spent the night gaining the loyalty of *his* dragon.

"Why don't you take Starshade for a walk?" Taliya held the white, scaleless, baby Starshade out to Javan. A leather leash dangled from her neck to the ground. "She could use the exercise."

"Oh. Um. Sure." As he walked over to them, he noted that in the six hours they had been in Costa Rica, Starshade had grown from the size of a cat to that of an iguana. He reached for her, but she jumped to the ground and began prancing toward the garden.

"Well," Taliya said, shooing him toward Starshade, "go."

"I don't think she wants me to go with her."

"Did she say that?"

"No. I still can't read her thoughts."

"Then go. She's pretty quick. You're going to lose her if you don't hurry."

Javan barely caught a glimpse of her long white tail as she turned the corner through some waist-high herbs. "Yo, Starshade! Wait for me."

He caught up to her in a section of red and yellow flowers and snagged the handle of the leash. "Wanna come with me to check on the Noon Stalkers?"

She sniffed a flower and slowly turned to face him.

"I'll take that as a yes."

They walked in silence as they wove their way through tall trees and tiny shrubs until they reached a clearing. Varjiek and Skylark slept back to back in the tall grass. Two long flights in less than twenty-four hours must have wiped them both out. He let them sleep and began his way back toward the house. Starshade followed without him having to tug too hard on the leash. "Glad you decided to acknowledge my existence. I'm just the guy who gave you a chance at life by picking you out of that cave."

She grunted and shrugged.

"You know, if you're growing this fast in Costa Rica, I can't wait to see how fast you'll grow once we get you to the Land of Zandador. I'm ready to take you there now, but Taliya doesn't want to leave yet." Javan crouched down and whispered to Starshade. "What are we going to do if Taliya's egg never hatches? I'm worried she might decide to stay here if she doesn't have a dragon of her own to protect back home. I don't want to do life without her. She's kinda cool, and I like having her around."

Starshade sat and stared at him, her thoughts inaccessible to his mind. Nevertheless, he pretended she wanted to talk to him and continued the conversation. "I know. I should tell her. It just sounds too sappy. I'd rather use a dragon to lure her back. You have to promise not to tell her what I'm thinking."

Starshade nodded, zipped through Javan's legs, and pulled him along the path that led to Taliya. He sped up to keep pace with her, irritated by the fact he couldn't hear her thoughts.

◊　◊　◊

Frantic, Micah dove behind a wide tree. Too late. A bullet from the Destroyer's gun clipped his side. Fortunately it only grazed his skin, but it did send a searing jolt of pain to his brain.

Why had he come running without a weapon? He never would have made such a dumb decision in Zandador. Now he found himself hiding, bleeding, and defenseless. While he held his side and listened for his enemy, he began to wonder how the Destroyer even got herself untied. Had Kenton come home and freed her? Did he put a gun in her hands so that she could complete her mission to kill Micah?

He stood and poked his head around the tree. A bullet hit a branch above him. He swatted the branch and leaves out of his way and found himself standing face to face with the Destroyer and her gun.

"If you're going to kill me," he said, keeping his eyes locked on hers, "at least tell me your real name. Let me die an honorable death at the hand of..."

He waited for her to finish his sentence. She didn't. But she did smile. Step forward. Aim the end of the gun between his eyes.

Heat from the metal warmed his already hot skin. He didn't know how to fight against this kind of weapon. So he didn't. He remained still and watched her finger prompt the gun to shoot.

Instead of a bang, the gun...clicked.

Micah let out the breath he didn't realize he was holding. "That was unexpected."

She shook the gun and tried again. Click.

"Guess today is not my day to die." He slammed her wrist against the trunk of the tree. She shrieked and dropped the gun. He caught her leg when she tried to kick him and threw her to the ground.

◊　　◊　　◊

Taliya watched Javan and Starshade wind through the rows of the garden that stretched on for acres. She wanted to walk with them and study the variety of trees, shrubs, and herbs, but she didn't dare leave her precious pink egg. It sat cradled atop a pile of logs near the back corner of Luisa's house and wrapped in a green electric blanket to keep it warm. It needed warmth to hatch. That she could provide. What she couldn't provide was more time.

Considering they had been on Earth for twenty-seven hours, her dragon clearly was not in the eighty percent of eggs that hatched in the first twenty-four hours. Of the remaining twenty percent, thirteen percent never hatched. None of the final seven percent had ever hatched beyond the three day mark. To make sure her dragon was in that seven percentile, she had stayed awake all night singing and talking to her egg.

"You not use bed last night."

Taliya startled at Luisa's observation. "Oh, Luisa. You scared me."

"Not mean to scare. Bring coffee for tired Taliya."

"Thank you." She took a sip of the hot liquid. It felt good on her scratchy throat.

"Why you not sleep?"

"I want to be awake when this egg hatches." Taliya knelt in the dirt and rubbed the edge of the rough blanket. Besides, the last time she closed her eyes to rest, she almost lost Starshade. She learned Protectors should not sleep around baby dragons.

Luisa grunted. "I have all kinds of plants here. None help unborn dragons. Sorry." She put her wrinkled hand on Taliya's cheek. "Be patient. Forget not to take care of self."

"Sure thing. I'll rest as soon as I lay eyes on my dragon's face."

Luisa walked away, once again leaving Taliya alone with her egg. She sat on her calves, sipped her coffee, and resumed her conversation with the unborn dragon. "This garden reminds me of my home in Fralick. You would love it there. I certainly did. The problem was that I had no one to share it with. Well, I did have Kisa, but she now belongs to Javan, and I no longer have a home. A wall of white winds wiped it out.

"Going on this adventure with Javan has been exciting, but I wonder if Javan only wants me around because I know more about dragons than he does. I can also operate the portal." Once they returned, would he have any use for her? Or would he toss her aside after he collected all his dragons?

"If he does abandon me," Taliya said, stretching her legs and slightly bumping one of the logs, "at least I'll have you. Which means I'm going to need you to hatch. Now would be good."

The only reaction came from an ant the length of her fingernail marching up the log she bumped. She swept it away, but two more replaced it. "I don't need any creature, no matter how small, disturbing my dragon. I'm sorry I nudged your home, but you all have to leave."

The ants didn't see it that way. Several of them crawled on her hand. She flicked them off. Most of them. One broke through. Bit her wrist. The crippling pain intensified when several more bit her arm. Another attacked her neck.

The loudest, shrillest shriek she had ever uttered in her life erupted from her gut through her lips. She tried to rip her arm off her body to ease her pain. When it didn't work, she collapsed. She cradled her burning arm and cried, certain she was experiencing the brink of death.

CHAPTER 39

Taliya's Darkest Day

"Hit me all you want." Micah encouraged the Destroyer as she grunted and pounded on his back while he walked up the hill toward the house with her over his shoulder. Those fists had given him a bloody lip and sore ribs, but he eventually won the frustrating fistfight by tackling her when she tried to run away. "I'm happy you're finally showing some emotion and using your vocal chords for something, even if it is only for grunting."

The pounding stopped. Her body went limp.

"Giving up that easily, huh? Wise decision. The sooner you understand you'll never beat me, the sooner we can work through our differences and perhaps become friends."

She grabbed his dreadlocks and yanked.

"Ow! Don't touch the hair!" He dropped her on the ground without bothering to be gentle. "Tell you what. I'll let you walk the rest of the way. All you have to do is tell me your name."

She gave him a smug look and remained silent.

"Bad choice." He picked her up. This time, he folded her body around his neck like a scarf and held her arms and legs in check. She squirmed, but his grip was too secure. She couldn't move. "This is what you get for trying to kill me."

He continued his march uphill and saw Kenton's car pull into the driveway. So he hadn't helped her. That was good news. Or maybe not.

If Kenton hadn't helped her escape, that meant she had freed herself from her bindings. How did she do that? How dangerous was this woman he carried on his shoulders?

◇   ◇   ◇

A horrifying screech chilled Javan. Had Taliya made that sound? Starshade seemed concerned as well, and they rushed through the winding, complicated paths of the garden. When they made it back to Taliya, he found her running in circles, shrieking, and shaking her right arm. "Taliya!" He tied Starshade's leash to a branch, stopped her in mid-sprint, and noticed tears streaming down her cheeks. "What's wrong?"

"Pain!" She shook loose from his light grip and kept moving in circles. "So much pain!"

"Why are you in pain? What happened?" He could see welts growing on her arm even though she refused to stand still. "I'm going to get Luisa."

"Luisa coming." Luisa stepped onto the back porch and shuffled toward them.

How slow could the woman possibly walk? He needed her here pronto. He ran up to her and latched onto her elbow in an effort to speed her up. "I think something bit Taliya. You have to help her!"

"Must stay calm. Cannot help if I am panicked."

Javan tugged her arm. "Can you be calm and move a little faster?"

"I move as fast as necessary."

Javan held back his own scream, dropped Luisa's arm, and sprinted the fifty remaining feet to the nest area. He helplessly listened to Taliya cry as he watched Luisa meander over. When she finally reached them, she said, "Ah. I see."

"See what? Can you help her? What's the problem?"

"I see bullet ants." She pointed to some ants crawling on a log close to the egg. "They give most painful insect bite man knows. One on your shoe. You should get off."

Javan looked down and yelped. He stomped the large ant on his right foot with his left foot, crushing his own toe. "Is that what bit you, Taliya?"

She could no longer seem to form words and continued to walk in circles while shaking her arm.

Javan turned to Luisa. "You have to help her."

"She dance."

"What?"

"Dancing help take mind off pain."

Taliya's mouth gaped open. "Dancing. Won't. Help." She collapsed. "Would rather die." She curled herself into a ball and shook.

Javan dropped to her side and wrapped his arms around her trembling shoulders. "Luisa, you can't let her die. Surely there is something in this garden that can help counteract this poison."

"No poison. Venom. Not lethal. Will swell. Be pain. Excruciating pain. But she survive."

"Isn't there anything you can to do help the pain?"

"Can try extracting venom. Give antihistamine. Waves of pain still come and go for about day. Be better tomorrow."

"Morrow?" The partial word slipped out of Taliya's lips. "Can't. Take this. Pain. All day."

"Luisa, please." Javan looked up at the old lady who didn't seem at all concerned about the agony etched on Taliya's face. "Tell me what I need to do to help you extract the venom." If he couldn't bear her pain himself, he would do whatever was necessary to alleviate it.

He pulled her closer to him, certain that this one going to be one very long day.

◊   ◊   ◊

Taliya lifted her heavy head off the soft pillow. A dull pain radiated from the fingers of her swollen right arm to her neck, but the want-to-die pain was gloriously gone. Whatever Luisa had given her to help her sleep must have also worked on healing the ant bites. Then she noticed the clock. And the daylight streaming through the edges of the window of the small room.

"No!" She bolted out of bed and tugged the curtains out of the way. Sure enough, the mid-morning rays of the sun stretched through the clouds and softly kissed the plants throughout Luisa's garden. "How long have I been asleep? Why did they bring me inside? What did they do with my dragon?"

She shook her head to bring the memory of her darkest day back into focus. She recalled the relentless agony. The endless tears. The throat-scarring sobs. Then Luisa had forced her to eat some sort of sour green soup for dinner. Shortly thereafter, she had fallen asleep in Javan's arms on the back porch. She liked having him hold her, but it wasn't something she should get used to. Javan's friendship was only temporary. Soon he would be king. He wouldn't need her after he won the throne. Her dragon would need her, though. If she had hatched.

She turned her gaze to the ground right below the window. The dragon's nest was empty. "Please be alive," she muttered, bursting through the door and into the kitchen. Luisa and Javan both sat at the round table eating beans and rice, and Starshade, now the size of a fat fox, sat at Javan's feet. "Where's my dragon? I saw the nest is empty. Has she hatched? Please tell me she's hatched."

"Taliya!" Javan scooted back, causing Starshade to hiss. "You're awake. How are you feeling?"

"I'm fine. What about my dragon? Where is she?"

He shook his head. "She's still in her shell. We moved her inside to get her away from the ants and the rain."

"Take me to her."

"Sure." He led her to the cozy living room with a couch on one side and a television on the other. She ran to the couch, picked the egg off the pile of blankets it rested on, and held it in her lap. Holding the egg comforted and disappointed her. She wanted to be holding a dragon, not an egg that had less than seventeen hours left to hatch.

She drew the egg to her chest, leaned back, and froze. The picture staring at her from the wall above the television took her breath away. She slowly stood and walked over to the picture of a conical volcano. It was covered with lush green vegetation surrounded by the kinds of colorful flowers and trees that reminded her of the rain forest in Keckrick. "Where is this? Is this a real place on Earth?"

"Yes, indeed," Luisa said from the doorway. "That Arenal Volcano."

"How do we get there?"

Luisa pointed to the left. "Go that way."

"You mean it's near here?"

"Si. You can see from garden on sunny day. It past town of La Fortuna."

"Take me there."

"Taliya," Javan said, "why do you want to go near a volcano?"

"Because that's the best chance my dragon has of hatching. She wants to make her appearance in the rain forest, not in a manmade nest under a roof. I'm sure of it. We have less than a day left of viability. We have to try something different."

"You sure you want to go into the rain forest? What if more of those ants sting you?"

"I'll get bit by a hundred of those ants if it means my dragon has a chance to live."

"You're serious, aren't you?"

"Absolutely."

"Okay, then. We'll fly over there after Varjiek eats his noon meal."

"Thank you." She rubbed the egg as she stared at the volcano. Not only would she be returning to the familiar territory of the rain forest, but soon she would be meeting her very own dragon.

CHAPTER 40

Time's Up

"Time to take Jane her lunch."

Micah ignored Kenton's statement and turned the television up louder. He hadn't laid eyes on the Destroyer since he locked her in a storage room in the basement yesterday morning and didn't care to know when Kenton took her food.

She had ruined his run yesterday. His still side stung because of her today. But the most irritating thing was that he didn't know how to deal with an enemy who wouldn't speak.

"Perhaps you didn't hear me." Kenton stepped between Micah and the television and kicked the footrest of Micah's recliner into the down position. He pulled Micah out of the chair and put a plate in his hands. "It's time to take Jane her lunch."

"You do it." He pushed the plate back to Kenton. "I don't want to see her."

"Tough." Kenton put his hands up, refusing to take the plate. "She's your prisoner, and I'm done taking care of her."

"You're just mad cause she won't eat your cooking." Kenton had returned with a full plate of food every time he had taken her a meal.

"She doesn't appreciate fine cooking, which is why she's only getting a simple ham sandwich and plain potato chips today. She's got to be hungry. Maybe you can use this food to get her to talk."

Micah considered that. He did want to know who she was and why she wanted him dead. "I'll try." He needed to do something besides watch the box of pictures anyway.

He carried the plate downstairs and paused before opening the door. The light was off. Why would she have the light off in the middle of the day? The ten by ten room with its two brick walls and two grey walls made of an unpainted material Kenton called sheetrock had no windows in it. Was she asleep or waiting to attack him once he entered the dark room?

To free his hands, he put the plate on the weird table that had six holes spaced along the sides and was covered with fake green grass. Only then did he moved the chair out from under the doorknob of the room. If she wanted a fight, he would be ready for a fight.

With one swift move, he opened the door with his right hand and flicked the light switch on with his left, hoping the light would temporarily blind her and allow him to throw the first punch. However, he found her sitting cross-legged on her cot in the corner staring at him with those expressionless brown eyes.

Backing out of the room, he grabbed the food and returned. "Brought you lunch. You can have it if you tell me why it is you work for Omri."

She ignored him and the food.

"Let me ask another way. What is he using as blackmail to get you to do his bidding?"

Anger flashed in the Destroyer's eyes. His instincts were right. Omri was holding something or someone over her.

"That's how my father controls people, you know. He finds something they desperately want, takes it from them, and returns it when they complete their task. Sometimes, anyway. He's not known for his integrity in deals."

She blinked back her anger. Her emotions became neutral again.

"Tell me what he has that you want. I know how he thinks. I know how he manipulates people. I can help you. I'll keep you safe if you talk to me, but you have to talk to me."

She threw her plate of food. It whizzed past Micah and slammed against the wall behind him, then dropped onto the cement floor.

"Guess you're still not ready to talk." He stepped over the scattered food. "Think about what I said. I'll be back at dinner time. We can chat then."

He closed the door behind him and replaced the chair under the knob to keep her locked in. What was so important to her that she was willing to kill him to get it back from Omri?

◊   ◊   ◊

"No." Taliya shook her head through the falling rain at the spot by some boulders Javan suggested. "We would have a nice spot to sit, but I don't think my dragon would be comfortable there."

"We've been walking for hours in this miserable rain, and it will be dark soon," Javan said. "Either we find a place to camp for the night, or we get on Varjiek and head back to Luisa's."

"You can go back if you want." She adjusted the straps on her bookbag that held her dragon and continued to follow the path of the muddy trail. "I'm going to keep hiking until I find the perfect place for my egg to hatch."

"You know I'm not going to leave you here by yourself."

"You should. Your dragon is back at the house with a human you barely know."

"Skylark is there, too. She'll make sure Starshade remains safe. Besides, I trust Luisa. She's proven herself a friend. Starshade is alive because of her."

Up ahead, snapping branches added to the sound of the rain smacking the leaves all around them. Taliya reached for her slingshot, but Javan put his hand on hers.

"No worries," he said. "It's just Varjiek. He got tired of flying over us in the rain and needed to land."

Taliya and Javan both laughed when they saw Varjiek splayed on the ground covered in mud shaking off tangles of vines. "So much for invisibility," Taliya said. "Should we help him?"

"Nah. After losing to the rain, he needs to beat the vines by himself."

"Hey." Taliya pointed to a massive tree that stood higher and taller than any of the trees around it. It had an opening in its hollowed out trunk in the shape of a triangle big enough for them to walk through. "That looks like the perfect place for an egg to hatch."

"It also looks like the perfect home for snakes and bullet ants and spiders and all kinds of other deadly animals that are known to inhabit this place."

"True. That's where Varjiek comes in handy."

"What do you mean?"

"Ask him to smoke the animals out for us."

"Say what?"

"Just ask."

Javan shrugged and talked to his dragon. Varjiek perked up, stalked over to the tree, and stuck his snout inside. His sides filled with air. He blew a cloud of smoke into the tree and jumped back. Spiders scurried out under the smoke, and a snake slithered over Taliya's foot on its hasty departure. "Good job, Varjiek. Now we can safely enjoy this space."

Once the smoke cleared, she turned on the lantern Luisa had given her and let herself into the tree. There was enough space for her to stand, but Javan ducked slightly.

"It feels good to be out of the rain," he said. He took a blanket that he had stuffed in a plastic bag out of his pack and spread it out on the dirt. "We may be soaked, but at least this blanket is mostly dry."

Taliya sat down and leaned her egg against the trunk of the tree opposite the opening. She left her lantern on and placed it beside her egg to give it the warmth it needed to dry after being toted around in her rain-soaked pack. "There," she said, rubbing the cool shell. "You're safe, warm, and cozy. When you hatch, I promise to take you back to the Land of Zandador and let you run free for your entire life."

She held her breath and waited, but the dragon refused to hatch.

◊   ◊   ◊

Muffled sobs slowly broke through Javan's slumber and brought him back to a state of wakefulness. He felt stiff after sleeping in a sitting position against the tree trunk all night, and the morning rays of sun allowed him to see Taliya sitting with her knees pulled to her chest. She had her head buried in her arms atop her knees and was sobbing.

He crawled over to her and put his arm around her shoulders. "Are those ant bites flaring up again?"

"No. Arm's fine." She sniffled and looked at him with bloodshot eyes. "It's my dragon. She never hatched. And she won't. It's been more than three days. The viability period ended hours ago." She wiped her eyes. "It's time to focus on Starshade. We have to get her back to Zandador."

Her words sounded more hollow than the tree they were in. He had to do something, anything to bring her spirit back.

He picked up the warm, pink egg and placed it in his lap. "I know your shell is all pretty and pink and you don't want to mess it up, but enough stalling already. It's time to shatter that shell and let yourself live. Cause this is your last chance. If we walk through that tree door without you, you have no hope of surviving without us." Then he leaned closer and whispered, "I need you to hatch. I hate seeing Taliya cry, and I don't think she'll ever stop crying if you don't hatch."

Shell hard. Can't break.

Javan jerked his head back. Did the egg just talk to him?

"What's the matter, Javan?" Taliya put her hand on his. "Why do you look so startled?"

"I think your dragon just talked to me."

"Huh? Starshade won't even talk to you. I thought you determined dragons have to grow up before you can communicate with them."

"That's what I thought. Maybe I was wrong." Javan shrugged and put his ear to the shell. "If you can hear me, kick."

One kick vibrated against his ear.

"Kick again."

Another vibration.

Javan sat up and held the shell. "Keep kicking! You can do this. Fight!"

The shell shook in Javan's hands.

169

"Is she seriously trying to hatch?" Taliya put her hand on the shell and looked at him through wide blue eyes when it moved. "That's impossible."

"Might want to think of a different word to use because that looks like a crack." Javan smiled and pointed to a rugged black line rippling its way along the side of the pink shell.

CHAPTER 41

Azurrior

Taliya wiped her face dry and gaped at Javan. "Are you sure that's a crack?"

"Yup." He gave her a crooked smile and placed the egg on the blanket in front of them. "I guess all she needed was a little encouragement."

"I can't believe you're communicating with a dragon before it even hatched. You should have tried that three days ago!"

"I know, right." He squeezed her hand. "She's not out of her shell yet. Her thoughts are faint, and she is weak. Let's pray she can win this fight for her life."

Javan closed his eyes and started talking to a God she couldn't see. Why would he bother to do such a thing? Did he really believe God could hear him? Surely the God who created the universe had more important things to do than answer one guy's prayer about an unborn dragon.

A claw poked through the crack. Taliya gasped. "Look!" She elbowed Javan. "She's alive!"

"I love it when God answers prayers right away."

Another claw. A tail. An ear. A snout. Then the shell shattered, and the tiniest, cutest, bluest creature emerged. She shook. Waves of color washed over her sticky skin. When she stopped shaking, her skin returned to the color of the blue sky on a cloudless day.

"Are you sure this is a Dusk Stalker?" Javan asked. "She looks more like a skinny chameleon."

"Her features like her snout, claws, and tail are those of a Dusk Stalker, but her skin is unlike anything I've seen or read about. She is truly incredible."

Javan cupped his hands together and lowered them to the ground. "It's okay," he said. "We won't hurt you."

The dragon gingerly walked over Javan's fingers and rolled onto her back in the palms of his hands. She lifted her paws in the air as though she wanted her belly scratched. "Oh," Taliya said, scratching the dragon's blue belly and laughing, "that's why you didn't want to meet me. I've been calling you a girl, but you, sir, are most definitely a boy."

◊　◊　◊

Micah paused before moving the chair that kept Jane locked in the room.

Jane. That wasn't her name. It didn't fit. Neither did any of the names Micah tried to match her with when he delivered her dinner the previous night. Since she wouldn't talk to him about whatever Omri was blackmailing her with, figuring out her real name had become his obsession.

Kenton had shown him how to find lists of names on the Internet. Micah planned to read through the list he printed to see if she reacted to any of them. He would read names out to her all day if that's what it took. Besides, he had nothing else more interesting to do with his time until Javan and Taliya returned.

He noticed the light was already on, moved the chair, and opened the door. "I know you're expecting breakfast so you can throw it at me, but I've decided discussing your name would be a more productive use of our time together." It took him a second to realize he was talking to empty cot. She was always sitting in that bed. She never moved from that bed.

A force shoved him into the wall and kicked him in the groin with her knee. He doubled over as the papers with his lists of names flew out of his hands and floated to the floor. He tried to grab her but couldn't move.

He watched helplessly as she walked out the door. Taking a few deep breaths, he started to follow when she backpedaled into the room with her hands up.

Kenton's figure filled the doorway, and he had a gun aimed at Jane. "I don't know about the two of you, but I'm tired of being cooped up in this house. How about we go out to breakfast this morning? I'd like to introduce you to some good old-fashioned southern cooking at a diner down the street."

Micah grimaced as he forced himself to stand. "You want to take this dangerous woman out in public?"

"I don't think she's as dangerous as she wants us to believe she is. Maybe if we start treating her like a human being rather than a prisoner, she'll respond in kind and start talking."

Micah wasn't sure Kenton's theory was sound, but it was worth a shot. Nothing else had worked. Maybe being kind was the trick.

◊　◊　◊

The dragon sleeping in Javan's hands looked as perfect as a glass figurine, but Javan knew this dragon wasn't fragile. "Your dragon is a fighter, Taliya."

Taliya stroked his belly with her finger. "More like a warrior."

"A blue warrior. No. Azure. That's a better description of his skin color. He's an azure warrior." Javan shifted to his knees and exclaimed, "We should call him Azurrior!"

"Azurrior." Taliya bit her lip and nodded as though thinking the name over. She finally smiled. "I like it. That's his name. Azurrior."

"This little fighter is tired." Javan carefully placed the baby on the blanket. He curled into a ball, and his tail wrapped around his body twice. "Let's let him rest for a bit. Then we'll head home."

"Thank you."

"For what?"

"For never giving up on my dragon." Her voice sounded shaky, and her eyes began to water. "I almost did. I was ready to leave him here. Alone. With no chance of survival once he did hatch."

"Nonsense." He brushed a strand of hair out of her face and behind her ear. "You're the one who made me believe."

Their eyes locked. She leaned slightly closer to him. His heart thumped as he leaned closer to her. Their lips were inches apart. He wanted to kiss her. But did she want to kiss him? Was he reading this moment right? Only one way to find out. He closed his eyes and moved his lips toward hers.

"Noooo!" She screamed, pushed Javan aside, and crawled out of the tree. "Get back here, Azurrior!"

"Azurrior's gone?" At the sound of those scary words, Javan forgot about the missed kiss and scrambled out of the tree after Taliya.

CHAPTER 42

The Blue Blur

Micah had never worn anything like the earth uniform Kenton gave him. The denim jeans were a heavier material than he was used to wearing, and the t-shirt with a big circle in the middle that encompassed the word Cubs made him feel like he was walking around with a target on his chest.

Jane also wore jeans, but her shirt had flowers on it and had two holes over her shoulders. It made her look soft and feminine despite the sour look on her face.

When they stepped in the diner with booths along one wall and stools lining a bar on the other, Micah realized everyone in the place was wearing different clothes. How could there be no order? How could everyone be allowed to wear whatever they wanted?

Then again, the clothes were comfortable. He kind of enjoyed being in something other than his stiff Zandadorian uniform.

"How about those Cubs?" A man Micah had never met pointed at his shirt. "We have a chance to go deep in the playoffs this year, maybe even win the World Series."

"Go, Cubs, go!" Kenton pumped his fist.

Micah had no idea what was happening but he attempted to play along by patting his shirt and roaring like a baby bear. The man gave Micah a quizzical look, and Kenton pulled Micah back toward a corner booth. "What was that?" Kenton asked.

"You tell me," Micah said. "Why was a man I don't know talking to me bear cubs? Was that because of this target on my shirt? What kind of uniform did you put me in?"

"It's a t-shirt that represents my favorite baseball team, not a uniform."

"Oh. Yeah. Okay. That explains everything." Micah scratched his head. Wasn't baseball the game Javan had been watching on television? How many teams played that game, and how did one choose which team to like? Did all strangers who followed the same team always comment on each other's clothes as a bonding ritual?

As they were about to sit, Jane ran into a woman carrying a tray full of empty plates. The plates, glasses, and silverware shattered to the ground. To Micah's surprise, Jane helped the woman pick up the spilled objects. An act of kindness following an accident.

Interesting. That gave Micah hope that a real person was hiding somewhere under the shell of a killer.

◊　　◊　　◊

"Are you sure Varjiek's sure we're on the right trail?"

"He's sure." Javan wished Taliya would be quiet so he could focus on listening to the dragons. They had taken to the sky on the back of the invisible Varjiek to look for Azurrior after trying unsuccessfully to track him by foot in the forest. "Azurrior's constant thoughts make it easy for Varjiek to follow, but the little guy is so small and fast that he's hard to see."

"He's been running around for hours. All that running worries me. If he's anything like Starshade, he'll have trouble breathing soon and will need Luisa's leaf of life."

"We have another problem. He's headed toward a road, and the road leads to the town of La Fortuna up ahead. I don't even want to think about what could happen if he makes a public appearance."

"Forget the public appearance. He could get smashed by a car!"

"Don't worry. Varjiek is going to grab him as soon as he's clear of the trees. Hold on."

Javan tightened his grip on Varjiek's neck as Taliya tightened her grip on his waist. Varjiek whooshed past the tree line and dove toward the road. Only he wasn't quite fast enough. Azurrior darted away while Varjiek pulled up to avoid getting hit by an oncoming car.

They continued to fly over the road and watched as a blue blur dashed across the ground and ran into a church building at the end of a square of grass.

"Land behind that church." Javan and Taliya jumped off Varjiek as soon as he landed. "We've got him cornered now, Varjiek. You go back to Luisa's and eat, then return for us. I don't need a hungry Noon Stalker hanging around a busy town square."

I will eat quickly and meet you back in this spot. Varjiek flew away, and Javan and Taliya ran to the front of the church. The doors were propped open for tourists, and no one was filling the pews on this Friday morning.

"Azurrior? You in here, buddy?"

Hard ground. Short trees. No green. Sky gone.

"You're not in the woods anymore, pal. The sky is still there. You just can't see it because of the ceiling."

Ceiling.

"Yeah. The hard ground is called a floor, and these benches are called pews."

Floor. Pews. Benches. More!

"You come with me, and I can teach you all the words you could possibly want to know."

A blue face peeked out from a middle pew, and Azurrior crept out into the center aisle.

"That's it. Come here." Javan crouched down and lowered his hands to the floor. When the dragon was less than ten feet away, a woman behind Javan screamed.

"What is that creature?"

A man answered. "Another thing that can kill you in Costa Rica!"

Kill? Danger!

The startled Dusk Stalker zipped past Javan, Taliya, and the two tourists. As Javan feared, the dragon was now loose in a well-populated area. This was bad. This was very, very bad.

CHAPTER 43

Tiny Terror

"S he's up to something." Micah followed Kenton upstairs into the kitchen after locking the Destroyer in her basement cell upon returning from the diner. "I can see it in those eyes of hers. She's working on another way to try to kill me."

"You're being paranoid. She's stuck in a windowless room with no weapons of any kind. It's safe to say that you are safe."

"I thought I was safe when I had her tied up with ten feet of rope, but I still ended up with a bullet wound." Micah still wasn't sure how she had escaped those bindings the other day. Not knowing how she had freed herself from that seemingly impossible situation made him believe she could find a way to get out of that room they had her locked inside. "I'm certain she has something planned. We can't get complacent because she refuses to talk."

"That silence is a tactic to drive you crazy. Based on how you're acting, I'd say it's working. It's also rather impressive." Kenton grabbed a bottled water from the fridge and walked to his office. "You have to have a tremendous amount of discipline to say nothing to anyone. Ever."

"Did you just compliment a Dragon Destroyer?"

"I suppose I did." He plopped down in his swivel chair and turned his computer on. "The even stranger part is that I'm having this conversation with the son of my sworn enemy. Truth be told, I dare not get complacent around you just because you're acting friendly."

"I'm no threat. Not to you or Javan. Not anymore." Micah leaned his hands on the desk. "That's a promise."

Kenton crossed his arms and met Micah's eyes. "I believe you."

"Thank you. But you also need to believe me about that Jane or whatever her real name is." Micah had tried all kinds of names at breakfast. None seemed to resonate with the Destroyer. "She's a kind of threat neither one of us has ever faced before."

"Noted." Kenton swiveled the screen so Micah could see. "Check this out. It's the Cubs website. You need something to think about besides that woman in the basement, and learning about the greatest team in baseball is the perfect distraction."

◊   ◊   ◊

"Where did he go?" From the stoop in front of the church, Taliya surveyed the town looking for any sign of the little blue dragon. The streets on her right and left were lined with shops and restaurants, many of which had outdoor seating on the overcast morning. The square in front of her had lush green grass, beautiful patches of flowers, a fountain in the middle, and walkways weaving in and around the grassy area.

"Not sure," Javan said. "I do know he's scared and confused. He's also extremely curious."

A series of shrieks drew their attention to the right. Azurrior jumped from table to table at a nearby restaurant, drank out of a mug, wailed when the hot liquid burned his tongue, and swept the mug off the table with his tail.

"I guess he's not a coffee lover," Javan said.

They took two steps toward him when he jumped down and dashed across the street to the fountain. He splashed around and doused his tongue with water, then climbed one of the trees in the square. He perched himself on a limb, hissing and spitting at anyone who came near him.

"It's a good thing his spit isn't poisonous yet," Taliya said, slowly approaching the dragon. She could see his sides heaving in and out. She wasn't sure if he was out of breath from running or having trouble breathing due to the atmosphere. "You said he's curious, right?"

"Yes." Javan matched her step by step as a loud blaring noise sounded in the distance. "Why?"

"I have an idea, but you're going to need your swords."

"I can't take my swords out in this public place. Hear that noise? Those are sirens. Cops are on the way. I'll get arrested for having these weapons."

"Not if you're invisible."

"Look around. People are watching us. Some might even be videoing this with their phones. I can't disappear. Such a thing is not a regular occurrence on Earth."

"Neither is a dragon. Talk to the little guy. Tell him what you can do. Show him. Invite him to jump on you. When he does, teleport out of here."

"What about you? I can't leave you behind."

"Do you have a better plan?" Taliya didn't want to be left behind, but her priority was ensuring the safety of Azurrior.

"No."

"Then start talking."

◇　　◇　　◇

As Javan strapped on his sword belt, he tried to tune into Azurrior's thoughts. But the dragon's thoughts were too jumbled for Javan to make any sense out of them. He whistled to calm him down. "Azurrior. Here, boy. Check this out."

"Nothing to see here, folks," Taliya said, addressing the crowd. "That's my pet lizard. He's harmless. We'll get him out of this tree and get him home. You're making him nervous. Can we have some space, please?"

Taliya shooed the onlookers away. While she distracted them, he spoke to Azurrior. "Busy morning, huh? I know you're a bit overstimulated from all the things you've seen and experienced today. How about you come on down and let me take you home? I'll make you a nice, soft bed, and you can relax."

The dragon cocked his head. *Home. Bed. Relax.*

"Yes. Home. Bed. Relax." He reached his arms up. The dragon stepped one claw toward Javan's fingers when a drop of rain pelted the dragon in the eye.

He panicked and walked closer to the trunk. He hid under some leaves to escape the raindrops.

"It's just rain. No big deal. I can keep you dry."

Too wet. Can't jump.

"I can do something that will help you forget about the rain." He really didn't want to use his swords, but a police car pulled up and an officer got out. People were pointing him in Javan's direction. "Check this out." He touched his invisibility sword. Disappeared. Let go. Reappeared.

You gone. Came back.

"I can make you disappear, too."

"Javan, what's taking so long? That soldier is almost here."

"Come on, Azurrior. Let's disappear."

"Perdon, senor and senorita," the officer said. "¿Qué tipo de mascota estás dejando aterrorizar a nuestra ciudad"

"What did he say?" Taliya asked. "Is that some kind of weird Earth English?"

"It's Spanish," Javan said, "and I don't understand it. I do understand that we need to go. Azurrior, jump. Now!" The dragon leapt into the air but didn't clear the tree. He knocked his head on a branch, and Javan caught his limp body. His free hand hovered over his teleporting sword. If he saved the dragon, he would lose Taliya. But if he didn't save the dragon, she would hate him forever.

"Go, Javan," she urged. "Please."

"I have a better idea." With his decision made, he handed the unconscious dragon to Taliya, wrapped his fingers around her elbow, drew his invisibility sword, and led them all right past the confused officer.

CHAPTER 44

The Bite of Life

"You're telling me that people's jobs are to play this game?" Micah pulled back from the computer screen after scrolling through the names and statistics of the players on the Cubs baseball team. He had trouble believing that people played games, much less that they were assigned to play them as work.

"Not just this game," Kenton said. "Basketball. Football. Hockey. Soccer. The list goes on and on. There's an entire industry known as professional sports. Before your father took the throne, we had sports in Zandador."

"No. That can't be true. I've never learned about that in the history books."

"Your father rewrote history to take out what he didn't like and added what he wanted people to believe. Why else do you think he has made an effort to eliminate everyone in his generation and those older than him?"

"He's made no such effort. People just don't live as long anymore."

"You are naïve."

Kenton's phone rang. "It's Javan. I'll put him on speaker." He placed the phone on his desk and hit a button. "Hey, my boy. How are the dragons? The pink egg hatch?"

"Oh, he hatched. Can't really chat right now. In a bit of a bind. I need Luisa's number ASAP."

"I can send that to you. What's going on?"

"I'm sure someone has uploaded a video to YouTube by now. Do a search for 'strange animal in La Fortuna' or 'disappearing boy' and you'll get caught up pretty quick. That number please?"

"I'll text it to you. Call me back as soon as you can talk."

"Will do. Thanks."

The phone made a buzzing sound. Kenton hit a red button, moved his thumbs around on the screen, and tossed his phone back on the desk.

"What's YouTube?" asked Micah.

"This." He pounded on the keyboard and brought up a video like on the big television screen. Only this video showed a tiny blue dragon creating havoc on tables and climbing a tree. Once in the tree, Javan and Taliya appeared. They talked to each other and to the dragon. Their voices were too muffled to be heard clearly.

"This is bad," Kenton said. "Why did they allow that dragon to run rampant in a public place and get it all caught on camera?"

Then Javan vanished and reappeared. Kenton leaned forward. "Weird glitch."

A moment later, the dragon jumped out of the tree. Javan caught it, gave it to Taliya, and they all vanished. Kenton hit the side of the computer. "There's that glitch again. But the video is still rolling. Did they all just disappear?"

"Hmm," Micah said. "I wonder if Javan made them all invisible or if he teleported them away."

Kenton laughed. "That's crazy."

"No. It's not. Those swords Javan has? They give him those abilities."

"Fascinating." Kenton played the video for them again and again, laughing with delight every time Javan disappeared.

◊   ◊   ◊

Taliya cradled Azurrior in her arms while Javan talked to Luisa. They made it several blocks away from the main square before finding a dry spot to hide on the patio of a hotel room. Javan had yet to let go of her elbow, so they were still invisible. She just hoped no one walked by because their invisibility did not make their voices inaudible.

Javan knew that, so she knew he wouldn't be able to yell or put up much of an argument when she told him her plan. She stroked the back of the dragon and hummed until Javan hung up.

"Luisa's on her way. She'll be here in fifteen minutes."

"I'll wait, but you have to go."

"No. I'm not leaving without you."

"You should have left without me back in the square. Now all three of us are in danger. What's worse is that Azurrior is hurt. His breathing is slowing. I'm not sure if that's because he was knocked unconscious or if he's having a reaction to the atmosphere. If that's the case, he needs medicine, and he can have it within the next five minutes if you just teleport back to Luisa."

"Let me try teleporting you, too."

"It didn't work in Keckrick. Why would it work here?"

"Because I've had more practice since then." Javan finally released her elbow, drew his teleporting sword, and wrapped his other arm around her shoulders. "Just think about Luisa's garden."

"Fine." She closed her eyes and imagined herself standing in the garden. She saw the spot where the bullet ants bit her. She shuddered at the memory of the pain.

"You okay?"

Opening her eyes, she saw they were still on the hotel patio. "We didn't go anywhere."

"I realize that. Let me try again."

She ducked away from his arm and placed the delicate dragon in his free hand. "Try again with just you and him." She stared at him until he relented.

"Uh. Okay. Luisa will be here in her car. Just lay low and wait for her until she gets here."

"I'll wait, but don't let her leave until she gives Azurrior some of her special dragon medicine. Now go." She stepped back, and Javan teleported with the unconscious baby dragon.

Suddenly she was alone. On an empty street. In an unfamiliar dimension.

She should be nervous and terrified and upset that she couldn't be there to protect Azurrior, but what she really felt was...excitement. This was her chance to explore a little piece of Earth, and she loved exploring new places.

◊   ◊   ◊

Javan heard a car rumbling away as soon as he appeared in the midst of Luisa's garden. "Great. Missed her." Javan fumbled for his phone, called Luisa, and asked her to return. In the meantime, he walked through the garden looking for Varjiek and Skylark.

When he couldn't find them, he assumed Luisa must have sent them off to a safe place to hunt for their meal. Starshade, however, rose from her bed of hay and wandered over to him. Maybe this would be the day he could communicate with her. "Hey, girl. What's up?"

She yawned. Her tail curled and uncurled. Her eyes threw him a bored look.

"I get it," he said. He couldn't read her thoughts, but he could read her body language. "You're tired of being cooped up in this fenced garden. Well, now that this guy has hatched, we can go home to Zandador. Starshade, meet Azurrior."

He knelt and presented the dragon to Starshade. The lifeless dragon. Azurrior had stopped breathing!

"He's dead. No, no, no. He can't be dead. Breathe, little man, breathe!" Javan attempted to give the dragon mouth to mouth. He tried chest compressions next.

"It's not working. He's dead, and it's all my fault. Taliya. She's never going to forgive me for this."

In the midst of Javan's breakdown, Starshade nudged Azurrior. Her gentleness touched Javan's heart. "Maybe you can help me break the news to Taliya." Starshade looked at him. Shook her head no. And bit Azurrior's tail.

"Whoa!" Javan jumped to his feet and pulled Azurrior to his chest. "Where did that come from? Why did you do that?"

Hello again. Azurrior's wet nose brushed Javan's chin. *My head hurts. My tail stings. I'm tired.*

Starshade stuck her own wet nose in the air, swished her tail around, and walked back toward the house with a "that's how it's done" prance.

Javan gave her an approving nod and was glad he couldn't read her thoughts. She was probably berating him for being an overly emotional human.

CHAPTER 45

Damage Control

Micah leaned on the desk and lowered his chin to his chest. Kenton had been mumbling to himself for the last twenty minutes as he watched the video over and over again. Micah had every sound in the video memorized, including pieces of Javan and Taliya's conversation. "How many more times are you going to watch that thing?"

"Until I can unsee what I'm seeing. How could Javan let a dragon be captured on video? I've been here for fifteen years with two full-grown dragons and have never had any public encounters. Well, I was almost exposed once, but I made the story go away. The point is that he's been here for three days, and a video of his baby dragon is on the brink of going viral."

"Forget the dragon problem," Micah said. "No one is going to mistake that blue creature for a dragon. I'm not even sure it's a dragon. Taliya even calls it a lizard at one point."

"Huh. Good observation. But how do you solve the problem of Javan's disappearing act? If you listen to the murmurs of the people we can't see, they're more awed by the fact he vanishes. If he or Taliya ever reappear, they'll be recognized, questioned, and possibly detained."

"That wouldn't be good for the dragons." He tried not to be happy about being stuck on Earth knowing the baby dragons wouldn't survive much longer in this atmosphere, but he was in no hurry to return to Zandador.

"What if they've already gotten to him? That could be why I haven't heard from him yet."

"Doesn't that phone work both ways? Can't you call him?"

"Another good observation. You are on fire today."

A series of thumps interrupted Kenton's praise parade. Micah frowned. "You hear that?"

"Hear what?"

"I'm not sure." Micah walked down the hall and into the kitchen. A door creaked open and closed beneath him. "It can't be." But it was. Looking through the kitchen window, Micah observed the Destroyer walking away from the house.

"Is that our girl?" Kenton approached the window. "How did she get out of that locked room?"

"You can't blame my knot-tying ability this time." Micah narrowed his eyes as she traipsed down the hill. "Where is she going?"

"It looks like she's heading to the big barn. That's where I keep my fancy cars and my fancier weapons." Kenton gripped the windowsill. "And Silverspike."

"You're telling me that a Dragon Destroyer is headed toward your dragon where you keep weapons that could destroy that dragon?"

The men paused and stared at each other. They bolted for the back door at the same time.

◊　◊　◊

Taliya decided she needed to get one of the small plastic things she noticed people use when they wanted to trade for food, clothes, or a variety items on display in shops around town. She was also fascinated by the other language she heard people speaking.

Thanks to her book training, she knew other languages existed. Hearing one spoken fascinated her. She wanted to learn how to speak this Spanish language as well. Perhaps Luisa knew it and could teach her.

She wandered in and out of shops in an effort to stay dry and not bring attention to herself. Which was hard. She wanted to talk to everyone around her. She wanted to find out about their world, about them. Alas, she had to do the hardest thing in the world to her: remain quiet.

With a sigh, she put her head down and started back toward the hotel. If Luisa wasn't there yet, she would be soon.

She was about to make the turn onto the hotel's street when a uniformed woman stopped her. She spoke a string of words in Spanish. When Taliya didn't respond, she said, "English?"

"Yes."

"You're the girl who disappeared from the square." The woman's English had the same sort of accent as Luisa's, but this woman spoke with more polish. "How did you pull off that vanishing act?"

She held up her hands. "The vanishing thing wasn't me."

"It was the boy, then. Where is he? And where is that strange blue animal?"

"That I'm not going to be able to answer." Taliya waved. "Gotta go."

She turned and ran away from the street where she needed to be and into an alley that she didn't recognize.

◊　◊　◊

Micah peered in through the tiny window on the door of the barn. Shelves decorated the wall on the right. They held an assortment of guns from big to small and lots of sizes in between. The Destroyer was walking up and down the wall, studying the guns.

"How many guns do you have in there?" Micah whispered, ducking down.

"Thirty-two." Kenton shrugged. "I like to hunt and shoot."

"Can any of those guns kill a dragon?"

"No. Well, maybe. A few."

Micah peered through the window again. A row of three cars separated the Destroyer from a vast space where Silverspike lay on his side, sleeping. Jane picked up a gun that looked big enough to do some serious damage to a dragon. "I think she found one of the dragon-killing guns."

He reached for the door knob. Kenton put his hand on Micah's wrist. "Wait."

"You realize that the Destroyer is about to shoot your sleeping Midnight Stalker, right?"

"Is the door of the safe in the corner open?"

He looked. "No."

"Okay." Kenton stood to look in the window as well. "Let's watch. This should be a good show."

Confused by Kenton's nonchalance, Micah watched with building horror as the Destroyer walked past the row of cars and aimed the gun right at Silverspike's head. Without a second of hesitation, she pulled the trigger.

CHAPTER 46

Lost

"I need one of those phones." Taliya spoke to the rain as she sat in the mud between the bushes and the back of some stranger's house. If she had a phone, she could call Javan or Luisa or Kenton. As it was, she couldn't contact anyone.

She hated feeling helpless, and she was done exploring Earth. She needed to get back home. Then she remembered she didn't have a home to return to.

Home used to mean Keckrick. With Kisa. Even if she did return to Keckrick and rebuild, she wouldn't have Kisa with her. She would have Azurrior, though. Maybe he would like it there. He might, but would she? Could she ever be satisfied being alone again now that she knew what it was like to have friends and be part of a team?

She hadn't been a great teammate today. She sent Javan away and missed her pickup from Luisa. How long would Luisa wait for her? What would Javan do if Luisa returned without her? Would he come look for her? He would have to. He needed her to get back to Zandador. Without her, both the dragons would die.

She couldn't wait here for him, though. He wouldn't be looking for her here, but the soldiers might.

Through the bushes, she could see the beautiful backdrop of the conical volcano. It rose high in the sky, its cone top obscured by clouds. She smiled. That's where she had to go. If Javan knew anything about her, that's where he would go to find her.

◊　　◊　　◊

Micah expected Silverspike to flinch and go limp. He didn't. He even continued sleeping.

The Destroyer pulled the trigger again and again. No bullets came out of the gun. A furious, frustrated yell erupted from the Destroyer's otherwise silent throat as she threw the gun at Silverspike. It hit the concrete floor and slid to his nose. The noise woke him up.

"That's our cue." Kenton opened the door and strode inside. A long, low, menacing growl filled the building as Silverspike bared his oversized sharp teeth. Micah didn't need Javan there to tell him what the dragon was thinking. He made sure to stay as close to the door and as far away from the angry Midnight Stalker as possible.

"The thing with guns," Kenton said, picking the gun up off the floor, "is that they need ammunition to make them work. No bullets, no boom."

The Destroyer set her jaw and jumped into the red car that had no roof. She scooted over the seat and situated herself behind the steering wheel.

"Where do you think you're going?" Kenton laughed. "To go anywhere in that Mustang, you need a key."

She dangled a key from her finger, put it in the ignition, and started the car. The engine revved, and she tore through the unopen door in front of her.

"She's getting away!" Micah dashed to the space between the other two cars. "Which car should we take to chase her?"

"Neither." Kenton hit a button on the wall, and the large door in front of Silverspike opened. "Silverspike, don't let her get to the road. And try not to damage the car. Please."

Silverspike ran out of the building. Kenton and Micah did the same. They got outside in time to see the dragon spread his wings, zoom low over the dirt road, and chase the red car. He reached it as it neared the house and picked it up with his back claw.

He made a show of swinging it back and forth on the return trip and dropped the car beside the broken door of the dragon barn. Its sides were scrunched together.

"Silverspike." Kenton sounded exasperated. "This was my favorite car. I asked you nicely not to damage it."

The dragon huffed while Micah reached for the door handle of the car. It fell off when he attempted to open it. He then tried to pull the Destroyer out over the top of the door, but her legs caught under the steering wheel that was wedged in her lap. "Great. I think she's stuck."

"Silverspike." Kenton crossed his arms and nodded toward the car.

Silverspike huffed again. He took one pointy nail from his front claw and ripped the door opposite Micah off the car. He gave the Destroyer a nasty glare and wandered back to his building. Micah walked around the car and slid the Destroyer out across the seat. "Congratulations," he said. "You don't get to leave my sight ever again."

◊   ◊   ◊

Where was Taliya? Javan had been foolish to leave her alone without a phone in a foreign country. Foolish, foolish, foolish!

She missed the pickup point hours ago, causing Luisa to scour all the shops in the area. When she couldn't find Taliya, she returned home, and Javan set out on Varjiek to search from the air. Skylark had come as well to help. When they met over the town square for the third time, Javan said, "Let's try the side streets again."

I do not think she is here anymore, young Collector.

"She has to be here, Varjiek." Javan said the words, but he didn't believe them. A sick feeling in the pit of his stomach told him she was gone. Taken into custody by the police. Without a way to contact him. And it was his fault. "We have to keep looking."

Yes. We must keep looking, Skylark said, *but perhaps we should look in a different place.*

"Where else should we look?" Javan found it odd speaking to the air. He could hear Skylark, but because she wasn't touching Varjiek, he couldn't see her. "I left Taliya here, and she has no transportation and no way to hire transportation."

She has legs and can walk.

"Yes. But she doesn't know where she is and wouldn't know where to go."

I see a familiar place, Varjiek said.

"What are you talking about?" One look ahead at the looming Arenal volcano answered his question. "Of course! The volcano. She did get super excited when she saw that picture in Luisa's house. She is probably headed back to the tree where Azurrior hatched."

I remember the way.

Moments later, with the town behind them, Javan spotted a lone figure walking along the road in front of them. "There she is!"

I see her. Varjiek landed in an open field beside the road. Javan slid off him and ran up to her.

"Taliya!"

"You found me." A smile brightened her tired face, and she gave him a long, tight hug.

He breathed in the scent of her damp hair, and he couldn't think of any words to say. He was just glad she was safe and in his arms.

"The dragons!" She gasped and pulled back. "How are the babies? Did Azurrior recover? Is Starshade still breathing well?"

"Yeah. Yeah." He had to take a deep breath to regain his composure. "The dragons are fine. Let's get back to Luisa's so you can see them for yourself."

Sometimes he wished she cared about him half as much as she cared about the dragons.

CHAPTER 47

Stubborn Starshade

An afternoon of sound sleep revived Taliya. She showered, changed into a t-shirt with a picture of the Arenal Volcano on it that Luisa bought for her, and fed the baby Dusk Stalkers. Then it was time to say good-bye to their hostess.

"Thanks for everything, Luisa." Taliya hugged her. "Make sure you keep these dragon plants thriving. I plan to visit a lot in the future."

"Anytime, dear. I like company, especially company who brings dragons." Luisa gave Taliya a cloth bag filled with the pointed purple leaves. "Take this in case dragons need."

"Thanks again." She stuffed the leaves in the front pocket of her backpack and checked on Azurrior. He lay curled into a blue ball at the bottom of the main section of her pack. Certain he was safe and breathing, she zipped the bag, leaving a slight opening at the top. "Let's get you to Zandador."

"You, too, Starshade." Javan tugged on Starshade's leash, but she pulled against him and sat beside Taliya.

"She doesn't look like she wants to go," Taliya said. "Can you still not read her thoughts?"

"No. Not at all. She knows what I'm saying to her, though. What's her problem? Why doesn't she like me?"

"Oh, she likes you." Taliya hoped she did, anyway. Starshade would be a part of Javan's collection, and Taliya couldn't stand the thought of the dragon being miserable her entire life. She also didn't like hearing the hurt in Javan's voice. "I'm guessing she wants to ride back with the girls. Is that it, Starshade? You want to ride with me and Skylark?"

Starshade's ears perked up.

"Fine." Javan threw the leash to Taliya but spoke to Starshade as he helped them get on the back of Skylark. "Be a traitor."

"Why don't you take Azurrior." She took a deep breath and handed her pack with Azurrior in it to Javan. For the sake of the Dusk Stalkers, she didn't want to be responsible for both of the babies on the flight back. "That way he can bond with the guys on the ride home."

"You good with that, Azurrior?" Azurrior poked his head out of the bag, licked Javan, and retreated to the depths of the bag once more.

"I think that's a yes," Taliya said, a twinge of jealousy marking her words. Her dragon had never licked her face before.

"Shall we fly?"

"Of course." She and Javan hefted Starshade onto Skylark. After Javan helped her up, she leaned forward to whisper into Skylark's ear. "I know you have the bulkier load with both me and Starshade, but can you still fly faster than the boys? I want to be the first ones back."

Skylark huffed a puff of smoke in Varjiek's face and took to the air. Taliya looked down, surveyed the garden below and the volcano in the distance. She hoped she would be back soon. She liked this place on Earth best of all.

◊　　◊　　◊

"Eight ball. Corner pocket." Micah rubbed the top of his pool stick with the chalk. He was one shot away from beating Kenton for the first time all day. He leaned over the green felt table and lined up his shot. He would have to scrape the edge of the black ball with the white ball at just the right angle to make the shot work. Breathe in. Breathe out. Shoot.

The stick hit the white ball. It did exactly as he envisioned, and the black ball went into the hole. "Yes! Victory!"

"Good shot. Now can we quit?"

Micah's sense of accomplishment suddenly felt empty. They had begun playing after the Silverspike incident that morning and had only taken a short dinner break. Which the Destroyer hadn't eaten. She sulked in the corner while tied in a chair from shoulders to toes while he and Kenton played pool. "You let me win so we could quit."

"You played a good game."

"Did you let me win?"

Kenton shrugged. "I might have missed a shot or two I wouldn't normally miss."

"Rack them up." Micah started taking the balls out from the sides of the tables. "We're playing again. This time play your best."

"You asked for it." Kenton racked the balls. "You want to break?"

"Yep." Micah prepped for his shot. With this table on top of the pizza and television and clothes, he was liking this world more and more. He never knew how much fun life could be. As he was about to make his opening shot, a rap on the basement door broke his concentration. He hit the top of the ball, and it weakly rolled across the table. The triangle of balls barely broke.

"You're making this too easy."

"Just take your shot. I'll get the door." Micah stomped to the door. The sight of Javan holding a sleeping dragon signaled a return to reality. Fun was done. Probably for the rest of his long, miserable life. He growled and threw his cue stick against the wall.

And that's when the startled dragon woke up.

◊   ◊   ◊

Starshade squirmed, hissed, and jumped out of Javan's arms. Before he could say a word to calm her down, she zipped around the room, scrambled over the pool table, and up the stairs. He heard her bumping into chairs and cabinets above them. Seconds later, she leapt down the staircase and into the storage room through a ragged hole in the wall. "Quick," Javan said, finally regaining his ability to move, "block   that   hole!"

Kenton made it to the wall first and used his back to cover the hole.

"Wow!" Taliya closed the basement door behind her, cradling the sleeping Azurrior in her arms. "She sure is fast."

Javan eased the door of the storage room open wide enough to see inside. Starshade ran in confused circles around the small room. Without any way for her to get out, he closed the door and let her run. Then he asked, "Why is there a hole in the wall?"

"Talk to Jane Smith about that one," Micah said. He waved his arm in the direction of the Destroyer who was tied to a chair. "Near as we can figure, she stole a knife from the diner we went to this morning and used it to cut her way out of that room to kill Silverspike."

Javan had to grip the doorknob tighter to keep from falling. "She killed Silverspike?"

"Had I kept my guns loaded she would have," Kenton said, "but the big guy is fine. No worries. On to you. I want to know why you didn't tell me you could teleport and make yourself invisible."

"I can teleport and make myself invisible." He smiled. "Pretty cool, right?"

"Not cool. That little stunt of yours has gone viral."

"You mean I'm famous?"

"Famous is bad. Famous brings attention to the fact that there is a dragon alive in this dimension."

"Nobody thinks Azurrior is a dragon. Even if they did, it won't matter. We'll be heading back to Zandador soon."

"How soon?"

"I don't know." The wall vibrated as Starshade thumped into it. Javan resisted the temptation to open the door and check on her. "Tomorrow night? I sure could use a day of just being a teenager before I return to the overwhelming responsibility of becoming king."

"Speaking of returning," Micah said, "what exactly is our plan for getting through the portal?"

"Why do we need a plan? Taliya does her open the portal thing, and we fly through on the invisible Varjiek. Nothing to it."

"Not quite." Micah shook his head. "Once the portal opens, the soldiers on patrol—and there will be a lot of them—will be expecting someone or something to come through. The standard procedure is to block the portal with a formation of okties and shoot whoever enters Zandador without permission. Varjiek may be invisible, but he'll still slam into the airborne soldiers. Then we'll have a fight on our hands while he is carrying four humans and two baby dragons."

"I hadn't thought of that." Javan slid down the wall and plopped on the floor. Why had he assumed getting back to Zandador would be easier than getting to Earth? And why hadn't Ravier helped him devise a plan to return?

Because he didn't need Ravier when he had Kenton.

"Got it!" Javan snapped and stood. "Kenton, you and your dragons will come with us."

"What? No." Kenton shook his head. "It's too risky. I can't return as long as Omri is still the king."

"If you don't return with us, he may remain king. The only way to get through that heavily guarded portal is to hit them with three dragons instead of one." Javan put his hand on Kenton's shoulder. "You've been hiding long enough. It's time to come home."

Kenton sighed. "Fine. I'll come. But if this is going to be my last night on Earth, I'm not going to spend it standing in front of a hole in the wall. That's your dragon in there. You keep her contained." He slapped Javan on the back and marched up the stairs.

With Kenton gone, Javan peered into the room through the hole and watched Starshade run in circles, occasionally ramming into one wall or another.

If he had trouble keeping up with her when she was this small, how was he ever going to catch her and ride her when she became a full-sized dragon?

CHAPTER 48

A True Battle

Not true.

Taliya launched herself up in bed, certain she had finally deciphered the words the Destroyer mouthed to her when Javan mentioned that the only way to get through the portal was with three dragons. What did the Destroyer know that the rest of them didn't?

Azurrior stirred on the pillow beside her. His blue body looked black in Kenton's darkened bedroom against the white pillowcase, and he looked up at her with tired eyes.

"Sorry to disturb you, pal. I think that evil woman downstairs was trying to tell me something. I'm sure she was staring right at me when she mouthed those two words. The fact that she didn't speak up when everyone was present means she wants to talk to me alone. Right?"

Azurrior had ceased to care and was once again snoozing.

"I bet everyone else is sleeping, too. This may be my only chance to get the Destroyer to talk." Taliya slipped out of bed but paused at the door. "What am I doing? I can't leave you alone in here. No telling what kind of trouble you might get yourself into if you decide to wake up."

She returned to the bed, picked up the pillow Azurrior slept on, and carried him to Kenton's office where Javan was sleeping in front of the desk on what Kenton had called an air mattress. Moonlight crept into the room through the blinds on the window. Javan slept in the shadow created by the desk, but an alert Starshade approached her from the corner.

"Shhhh," she whispered. "Don't want to wake Javan." She tiptoed around Starshade and placed the pillow with Azurrior on it at the foot of Javan's bed. "Can you keep an eye on him for me?"

The dragon didn't move and kept her gaze on Taliya as she snuck back to the door. Before she closed it, she peeked into the room. Starshade wandered over to Azurrior and laid down, placing her head on the pillow.

Taliya paused to savor the beauty of that moment. Two dragon babies. Both alive. Both safe. Both happy. To keep them that way, she headed to the basement to have a conversation with the Dragon Destroyer.

◊   ◊   ◊

Javan rolled over to his back when he thought he heard the door click shut. "Hello?"

Hello! Azurrior hopped on his chest, waving his tail back and forth.

"Whoa. How did you get in here?"

Taliya brought me. He spun around several times and settled himself in a ball on Javan's chest.

"Umm, you can't sleep here." He picked the dragon up and put Azurrior back on the pillow Javan noticed at the foot of his mattress. "You have to keep your distance from me. You're Taliya's dragon."

I'm nobody's dragon. Azurrior marched back to Javan's pillow and curled himself in the middle of it. *I decide where I sleep. I want to sleep here.*

"You can't sleep there. That's where I need to put my head."

I like this spot.

"That's my spot."

Azurrior wiggled himself into a more comfortable ball. *Not anymore.*

Too groggy to argue with the dragon, Javan reached for the other pillow. He wasn't fast enough, though. Starshade walked onto it and plopped down. Her head and tail hung over either end. "Oh. I guess you're sleeping here."

She didn't respond.

"You can come onto the mattress, you know. Your whole body can fit up here."

She picked her head up. Looked at Javan. Laid her head back down.

"Or you can stay right there. That's cool, too." Why couldn't he connect with this dragon?

Taliya knew he was having trouble connecting with her. Maybe she had brought Azurrior in to help bridge the gap. How thoughtful. He would work on bridging that gap later, however. Right now he needed sleep.

Without a pillow to lay his head on but content to rest between two dragons, he snuggled under the fuzzy blanket and drifted back to sleep.

◊   ◊   ◊

Taliya walked lightly down the steps, careful not to wake Micah. He was sleeping on a cot in front of the door that led outside while the Destroyer remained tied in the chair he had tied to the pole at the bottom of the staircase. The Destroyer's active eyes followed Taliya's every step as she positioned herself in front of the Destroyer.

"I know you know how to get us back through the portal," Taliya said, keeping her voice low. "Start talking."

The Destroyer smirked but said nothing.

"We don't have to take you back with us. It would be easier to leave you here, tied up like this. Then we won't have to worry about you harming any dragons. Or Micah, for that matter. You seem to want him as dead as any dragon."

Rather than respond, the Destroyer shifted her expressionless gaze to Micah, then back to Taliya.

"If you stay here, you'll die a long, slow death. That can be avoided if you talk to me. Tell me how to get through the portal. If you prefer," Taliya said, leaning closer to the Destroyer's ear, "first tell me what you want in return for helping us."

"Ah," came the soft reply, "now you're speaking my language."

Taliya drew back, surprised at the sound of the Destroyer's silky voice. She gulped and fought to keep her composure over the speedy beating of her heart. "What do you want?"

"A battle. A true Battle of the Bloodlines. Protector versus Collector versus Hunter versus Me."

Her icy words froze Taliya's blood. It took her a minute to form a response. "Absolutely not. I am not going to put any dragon in harm's way."

"Then good luck getting through the portal safely. Without my help, all of you are as good as dead."

Taliya stumbled backwards and bumped into the green-topped table with holes along the sides. Her knuckles turned white as she held onto it and contemplated the impossible choice. Should she make a deal with the Destroyer or risk death upon reentry into the Land of Zandador?

CHAPTER 49

A World Without Dragons

The sound of clinking disturbed Micah's sleep. He shifted on his cot and squinted through the darkness. He could hear the pool balls clanking against one another and see a figure leaning against the pool table facing the Destroyer. The black blob was too small to be anyone except Taliya. Why was she down here in the middle of the night talking to Jane?

Then he remembered the Silverspike incident. Taliya was probably lecturing Jane on the value of dragon lives and was happy to have a captive audience in the silent Destroyer. Sleep was more important than hearing any part of that conversation. He stretched and rolled away from the women.

Tomorrow night he would be able to sleep in that big comfortable bed of Kenton's upstairs without anyone around to interrupt his slumber. The house would be quiet. The barns would be empty. And he would be free to start his new life on Earth.

He hadn't told anyone he decided to stay. He would save that news until right before they left. That way Javan and Taliya wouldn't have time to argue with him. Soon they would realize they were better off without him anyway. Eventually, he would be better off without them.

Across the room, the tone of the murmuring changed. That tone didn't belong to Taliya and could only be coming from Jane.

He remained still and focused his attention on deciphering the words being exchanged between the Protector and the Destroyer.

◇　◇　◇

"Your terms are absurd." Taliya had enough of listening to the Destroyer. Her plan for getting them back through the portal was solid, but her demands were too steep. She pushed away from the table and whispered into the Destroyer's ear.

"We'll have the cover of darkness and three winged dragons to get us through the portal. We won't be needing your help after all."

"Darkness and dragons won't be enough to keep you safe. My way will work, and fewer dragons will die. Think about that while you sleep."

Taliya despised the idea of dragons dying, but she needed to end this conversation before she agreed to something she would later regret. "I'll let Javan decide whether or not he wants to leave you here or take you back with us as our prisoner. *You* think about *that* while you sleep." She patted the Destroyer's head and crept back up the stairs into the kitchen.

Too tense to sleep, she turned to food for comfort. She tiptoed to the refrigerator, careful not to wake Kenton who slept in the living room. The door of the refrigerator opened with one tiny creak, and inside she discovered a piece of cheese, a cardboard box filled with half a pizza, a bottle of ketchup, and fourteen cans of Dr. Pepper. She didn't know how to heat the pizza up in the earth oven and thus opted for the cheese.

"You should go for the pizza instead. It's good right out of the fridge."

She screeched, threw the cheese in the air, and bumped her head on the inside of the open refrigerator door. "Kenton," she said, identifying the speaker of the words from the refrigerator light, "you scared me. What are you doing up?"

"I like to know what's happening in my house." He took two pieces of pizza out of the box, gave one to her, and bit into the other. He stared at her while he chewed, then asked, "What were you talking to our pal Jane about down there? It must have been good if you got her to speak."

"Not really." She closed the refrigerator and took a tentative bite of the pizza. She found the combination of the cold crust, cold sauce, and cold cheese oddly satisfying. "Mmm. This is good."

"Of course it is." Kenton led her to the table and sat her down. "What were you and Jane discussing?"

"Portal travel. Dragons. Her freedom. Boring stuff."

"Her freedom, huh?"

"Yup. She didn't earn it. That's why she's still tied to that chair." She filled her mouth with another bite of pizza and changed the subject. "What will happen to this place when you leave?"

He leaned back in his chair. She held her breath, hoping he would play along with her change of topic. It took a moment, but he finally said, "I'll have it taken care of in my absence. That way you will have a place to come when you bring more dragon eggs to Earth in the future."

"You won't be here." She relaxed now that she wouldn't have to divulge what she and Jane had been discussing. She wanted to forget that conversation ever happened, and questioning Kenton helped her do just that. "How will you take care of it?"

"I've hired a cleaning service to keep the house clean and a lawn service to keep the yard looking nice."

"You have servants?"

"No," he laughed. "No servants. Contracted employees. I use that computer in my office to pay people money, and they come work for me in exchange for the money."

"Money?" She paused with her pizza in midair. "I don't understand."

"The economy here uses money to buy things rather than dragon scales or bartering. Knowing that, I brought a hefty load of gold with me from Zandador and spent a bit of time when I first arrived learning the art of investing. I used a little bit of gold to make a lot of money. Soon that money started making me money. My accountant calls me a billionaire or something like that. I'll have him look after my accounts in my absence."

"What is money? How does gold turn into it?" She forgot about her pizza leaned forward. "You have to show me how this money thing works."

"Sure. Tomorrow." He stuffed his last bit of pizza in his mouth. "Right now it's late, and this old man needs sleep. Tomorrow is going to be a very long day." He returned to the living room, leaving Taliya alone in the darkness at the kitchen table.

Learning about Earth's money system would keep her mind occupied tomorrow, but tonight all she could think about was the danger that awaited them on the other side of the portal. Was it wise to face that danger without the assistance of the Destroyer? Probably not, but there was no way she would ever agree to the Destroyer's terms.

◊   ◊   ◊

Javan stretched but refused to open his eyes. He hated this waking up thing and intended to avoid it for as long as possible. As he rolled back on his side, though, he sensed something was wrong.

The dragons.

He couldn't hear the breathing of the dragons.

He threw his blanket off, stood, and surveyed the room. The door was closed, but the dragons were gone. Had they learned how to open and close doors? If so, they could be anywhere by now. "Don't panic," he told himself. "If you panic, everyone else will panic."

He took a deep breath in and slowly exhaled. "Who are you kidding, Javan? You lost two Dusk Stalkers who are facing certain death unless you get them back to Zandador tonight. This is the perfect time to panic!"

He rushed down the hall and tore through the open door of the other bedroom. "Taliya! We've got a problem. The dragons..." His words trailed off as he realized he was talking to an empty room. "Taliya?"

A quick tour of the vacant upstairs kicked his panic level up three notches. "Where is everyone?"

"Down here."

Javan followed Micah's voice to the basement. He stopped on the bottom step when he saw Micah sitting directly across from the Destroyer. He and Jane were the only ones there, and they seemed to be locked in some sort of staring contest. "What's going on? Where are Taliya and Kenton?" He chose to keep the missing dragons to himself for the moment.

"Out." Micah never moved his eyes from Jane's, and she never moved her eyes to look behind her at Javan.

"Out...where?" Did they know the dragons were missing? Were they searching for them? Or had Taliya talked Kenton into letting her drive one of his cars? "Details would be helpful."

"Here's a detail for you." Micah looked at Javan and pointed at Jane. "She had a conversation with Taliya last night."

"That's not possible. I'm sure Taliya had plenty of words for her about the proper treatment of dragons, but the Destroyer doesn't speak."

"She's perfectly capable of speaking. I couldn't quite make out the words, but I definitely heard her talking to Taliya. She of course won't tell me what they talked about. Taliya's being cagey as well. When I approached her about the conversation, she told me she couldn't talk because she and Kenton had to take the Dusk Stalkers for a walk."

"Oh, good." An immediate calm washed over Javan. "She has the dragons."

"She also has a secret she won't share." Micah stood and pulled Javan to the other side of the room with him. "Before you go back through that portal, you better find out what Taliya and the Destroyer were discussing. They could be plotting against you, and I won't be around to watch your back."

"First of all, Taliya is on my team. I trust her. She wouldn't be plotting against me with a Destroyer. And second, what's this about you not being around? You're on my team, too. That means we stick together."

"Those days are over." He plopped down on his cot. "I've decided to stay."

"Stay? Stay where?"

"Here. On Earth." He waved his arms around. "In this house. I'm not going back to the Land of Zandador."

"That's crazy." Javan nudged Micah's shoulder. "You belong in Zandador more than I do."

"No. I don't. Not anymore." Micah sighed. "I want to live in a world where there are no dragons, no evil father, and no people like the Destroyer over there who want to kill me. Life is easy here. Adjusting to Earth is much more appealing than being a shadow of my dominating self as a Hunter in the grand Land of Zandador."

"You have to come back, man. If not for me, for Mertzer. You're his master. He needs you." Javan shrugged. "I need you. You're the closest thing I have to a brother."

"Yo, boys." Taliya and Azurrior burst through the basement door, interrupting the Hallmark moment. "Off the cot. Starshade needs it."

Both men obeyed without a word, and Javan watched in shock as Kenton entered and placed the limp body of Starshade on the mattress.

CHAPTER 50

Worth the Risk?

Standing helplessly by the pool table with Kenton, Micah cringed at the pitiful scene before him. Taliya's eyes and cheeks were red and puffy from crying. She sat on the cot with Starshade's head in her lap begging her to eat the purple leaf of life Javan brought to her. The dragon ignored Taliya's pleas, and her sides struggled to rise and fall with each breath.

Azurrior seemed anxious as well. With his leash still attached to his neck, he alternated between lapping the bedroom and laying his blue body on Starshade's pale skin.

Javan added to the pitifulness when he dropped to his knees in front of the cot and stroked Starshade's neck. "What can I do to help?" His green eyes practically glowed from his desperation to find a way to stop Taliya's tears.

"I wish I knew." Taliya rubbed the dragon's ears. "Her breathing has slowed. She's struggling and won't take the medicine. We have to leave now, Javan. We have to get her back to Zandador."

Alarm bells sounded in Micah's head. Even though he wouldn't be accompanying them, he needed to speak before Javan had a chance to agree with Taliya's request. "You can't go in the middle of the day." He stepped forward and continued adding logic to the emotional situation. "You'll be too exposed when entering Zandador, and no one would be in any shape to defend themselves thanks to the effect portal travel has on people."

Taliya's misty eyes bore into Micah's. "What's this 'you' talk? You're coming with us."

"About that..." Why was telling Taliya he wanted to stay harder than telling Javan?

"About that nothing. You're coming with us, and so is she." Taliya pointed to the Destroyer. "She knows a way to get us safely through the portal no matter what time of day we travel."

"Really." He crossed his arms over his chest. "Is that what you were discussing with her last night?"

"Of course."

"Have you forgotten that she is a Dragon *Destroyer*?" He shook his head in disbelief over Taliya's misplaced trust and fought to find the words that would inject some sense into her. "Whatever plan she has will result in dragons dying. Guaranteed."

"This dragon is going to die if we don't. And I guarantee she will get us through safely. There's something she wants, and she can only get it if we all return to Zandador alive."

Micah turned to face the Destroyer. "What is it you want?"

Her eyes twinkled and her lips spread into a grin, but still she said nothing.

"Untie her." Javan's commanding tone startled Micah. "If she can get us through the portal, we'll give her whatever she wants in return."

"No." Micah shook his head. "You don't know what her plan is or what she wants."

"Taliya obviously does, and I trust her judgment. Starshade doesn't have enough time left to quibble over details. Let's get packed and out of here as soon as possible." He picked up Micah's sword from under the cot and offered it to him hilt first. "*All* of us."

As Micah's fingers wrapped around the leather of the handle, he knew his dream of living in a world without dragons had officially died.

◊   ◊   ◊

Taliya clung to Starshade throughout the flight on Varjiek from the farm to the portal. Part of her worried the dragon wouldn't survive; the other part shook in terror at the prospect of having to follow through with the agreement she made with the Destroyer. To keep the worry and fear from causing her a premature heart attack, she focused on Starshade's slow but steady heartrate throughout the flight. By the time they made it through the tunnels that led to the cave, though, her heart was barely beating.

"Need you to hang on just a little longer, girl," Taliya said, stroking the dragon's snout as Micah held her. "You're going to ride with Kenton and Skylark through the portal to Zandador, and I'll meet up with you shortly thereafter. By then you'll be ready to challenge Azurrior to a foot race."

Azurrior popped his head out of the pack on her back and put his snout on her shoulder at the mention of his name. "You're not allowed to race anyone anywhere yet, little guy," she said, patting his head. "But when you do, I'm sure you'll win."

He swiveled his head toward Javan, who stood beside them. "He wants to know what a race is," Javan said. "I'll explain it to him while we get ourselves into position."

"Thanks." Taliya kept her pouch that held the activation scales and handed Javan the backpack with Azurrior in it. "Take good care of him."

"I will. See you at the rendezvous point." He strapped the pack to his back and climbed on Silverspike, the first big dragon in line, while Micah lifted Starshade up to Kenton on a half-golden Skylark behind Silverspike. Varjiek, also half-covered in golden scales with noon an hour away, stood in the back of the line.

"My axe." The whispered command of the Destroyer made Taliya jump.

"Right," Taliya said, trying to disguise her nervousness. She led the Destroyer over to Micah, who met them at the activation wheel by the portal. "All right, Micah. Jane here needs her weapon."

"I think I'll hold on to it until we get to Zandador." He tapped the axe that hung over his back atop his own sword.

"She needs it now. Otherwise we can't sell our story."

"To be clear," Micah said, taking the axe off and giving it to Jane, "I don't like this plan one little bit."

"Noted." She didn't dare mention he would like it even less once he found out what they were going to have to do in return for the Destroyer's help. "Please just play along. Our lives depend on it."

"Fine." He gripped the Destroyer's left arm. "But I'm not letting go of her until this whole thing is over."

"Sounds fair." Taliya stepped forward and checked with Javan before she placed the scales in the wall. "You all set?"

Javan took out his invisibility sword, and both he and Silverspike disappeared. "Did it work? Can you see us?"

"It worked. Now to get the portal to open." She rubbed her hands together before placing the scales in the activation wheel. A whoosh of colors flashed with blinding brightness. She relaxed when she recognized the pattern immediately. "Ha. Got it. This should only take a minute."

She began pressing the scales with confidence. Until an image of the Destroyer killing Starshade flashed in her mind. That startling trick of her imagination caused her to press the wrong scale, and the portal shut down.

Strike one.

◊ ◊ ◊

At the abrupt end to the activation process, Javan bit his free fist to keep his frustrated yelp to himself. He waited until he could trust himself to speak in a calm, reassuring voice, then said, "No worries, Taliya. You'll get it on the next try."

"Uncloak yourself," she said, turning to look in his direction. "I want to ask you something, and I need to see your face when you answer."

"You sure we have time for a Q and A?"

"Javan."

"Okay, okay." He took the invisibility scale out of his sword. "What's your question?"

"How badly do you want to win the throne?"

"That's a strange question."

"Answer it anyway. How badly do you want to win the throne? It's not a desire that's been ingrained in you since birth, and I don't know how much you are willing to fight for it."

A serious urgency undergirded her words, and he had a hunch his answer would make or break their mission. "I'm no quitter, if that's what you're asking. The fact I'm here proves that. If I wasn't willing to fight, I would have teleported myself back to my Earth home in Montana and forgotten all about Zandador. Besides, the prospect of collecting dragons and becoming king is a lot more interesting than the prospect of finishing high school here."

"What if you had to face the Destroyer head on? Could you win?"

"Why would I have to fight her?" Her question worried Javan. Had Taliya agreed to let the Destroyer go if she got them through the portal? If that was true, she would probably head straight to Midnight Territory and try to kill all the Midnight Stalkers to prevent him from finishing his collection. "She's our prisoner."

"Just answer the question. Could you win?"

He glared at the Destroyer. She raised her eyebrows and glared back, daring him to answer. "Absolutely. I will do whatever it takes to keep her from killing any dragons on my watch."

"That's all I wanted to know." Taliya smiled. "Let's go home."

"Yes." Although still worried, he made himself and Silverspike invisible again. "Let's go home."

Taliya restarted the portal activation process. Once she inserted the scales, brilliant colors that flashed too fast for him to process flooded the cave. Taliya seemed to be able to pick out the pattern, however, and she started pushing the scales on the wheel in a systematic fashion. "Get ready, boy," he said to Silverspike. "That portal will be opening any second."

"Oh, no!" Taliya screamed and yanked on the top scale. "No, no, no, no!"

"What's going on? What's the problem?"

She pulled the scale out of the wall, effectively stopping the portal. "I almost made a big mistake. I almost sent us back through the South Zandadorian portal."

"Good catch," Micah said. "Our plan doesn't stand a chance of working unless we go through the portal in North Zandador. Those soldiers didn't see us leave."

"At least you deciphered the code," Javan said. "I'm sure you'll figure it out next time, too." He tried to sound encouraging, but the words sounded hollow, even to him. And he was sure everyone in the cave had the same thought at that same moment.

Strike two.

CHAPTER 51

Regretful Taliya

"Clear the cave." Taliya waved everyone away before attempting to activate the portal for the third and final time. "If I miss the code, I'll be the only one eaten by the acid. The rest of you shouldn't have to die if I make a mistake."

Javan suddenly appeared beside her. "We're not going anywhere," he said, clasping his arm around her shoulder.

"He's right." Micah squeezed her other shoulder. "We're with you no matter what."

She looked from Javan's wild green eyes to Micah's serious brown ones. In that moment, she felt something she hadn't felt since the death of her grandparents: a sense of belonging. Not daring to let herself get too emotional about it, she said, "I really hope I don't kill you guys."

"Me, too." Javan pecked her on the cheek. "I'm kinda attached to living."

Before she had a chance to process the fact that his lips touched her cheek, he teleported himself back to Silverspike. Micah also stepped away, leaving her alone again with the scales and the activation wheel. She took a deep breath and inserted the scales. "Let's go to Zandador."

A smug little grunt from the Destroyer caused Taliya to look in her direction. Her cocky expression indicated that she wanted Taliya to be nervous. She wanted the dragons to die, even if she perished in the process. Taliya wasn't going to give the Destroyer what she wanted.

With a wave of confident determination, she pressed the scales. The wheel whirled, and a colorful dash of lights once again filled the cave. Blue. Green. Black. Gold. Gold. Pink. Green. Pink. Blue. Black. Was that it, or did she miss a flash of purple?

She stepped back and watched again. No. No purple. Her original assessment was right. "This is it." She took another deep breath and returned to the wall. She pushed all doubts from her mind and began pressing one scale after another.

◊　◊　◊

Javan winced as he watched Taliya press the activation scales. He half expected to be doused in an acid bath and was pleasantly surprised when the swirling colors merged into the familiar glow of an activated portal. "You did it, Taliya! We can go home!"

"We need to hurry," Kenton said. "Starshade is fading fast."

"Let's do this, then." Javan cleared his throat and gave the orders. "Taliya and Micah, head on through with Jane. We'll be sixty seconds behind you. We'll all rendezvous at the Zandadorian portal near Gri."

"See you there." Micah nodded, adjusted his grip on the Destroyer's elbow, took a hold of Taliya's elbow with his other hand, and led them all into the watery wall.

Javan began counting, being sure to give them enough time to order the airborne soldiers out of the way. As he reached second number thirty-three in his head, Kenton interrupted.

"By the way," Kenton said, "you better zip up that bag with Azurrior in it and hang on tight. Silverspike doesn't like the portal."

"You're just now telling me this?" Javan secured Azurrior in the bag and looked back at Kenton. "What does he do?"

"He may spin in crazy circles, and there's a good chance he could tip off the soldiers to his presence by blasting the ground with his lightning breaths."

I'll try not to, Silverspike said, *but portal travel upsets me.*

"Great." Javan sighed. "On top of trying to keep us invisible, I'll have to worry about falling off and being shot at by the soldiers. Some fool-proof plan this is turning out to be." Despite the sense of dread constricting his heart, he leaned forward, gripped the dragon's neck a bit tighter with his legs, and urged Silverspike into the portal.

◊　◊　◊

As the cold clung to her skin in the gooey, sticky portal, Taliya changed her mind. She didn't want to do this! She wanted to turn back and keep the Destroyer locked away on Earth forever. But she couldn't speak. She couldn't stop. She couldn't do anything except move with the current toward the light up ahead.

Would the soldiers who waited for them there submit to the unique authority of the Destroyer? Or would the Destroyer use her authority to betray them as soon as she regained control of her own life?

Betrayal might be the better option. With the power of three dragons on their side, they at least had a fighting chance of survival and escape. If the plan worked, however, the price they had to pay would more than likely cost her Javan's friendship and respect.

Tears welled in her eyes as the light grew closer. What had she done?

What on Earth had she done?

CHAPTER 52

When Lightning Strikes Water

Stay strong. Do not cry. Fight the tears. Micah coached himself all the way through the portal. He couldn't be seen sobbing the way he had when exiting the portal the first time. He would lose all respect of the soldiers, and none of them would take him seriously.

The coaching didn't work. The second he stepped through, his body betrayed him. Tears streamed down his face, making the river to his right, the woods to the left, and the forms of the soldiers charging at them blurry. More blurry soldiers on okties were moving into position above him, Taliya, and the Destroyer as they marched away from the portal toward the charging soldiers. He let go of the shivering Taliya and used his free arm to cover his face. No way would he let anyone see him cry.

"On your knees!" A female soldier leading the charge screamed the order and halted their march. Her brown hair was pulled back into such a tight bun that her pale skin seemed to stretch beyond its natural limits. He wasn't sure how she could even move her thin lips without an excessive amount of pain.

He glanced back. Good. They had cleared enough space between them and the portal to give the dragons room to step through and get airborne.

"On your knees," the leader repeated, "or my people will blast you."

"You blast me, and I'll make sure everyone in this unit is properly punished by King Omri himself." The Destroyer jerked free from Micah's grip. Surprised at the sound of her voice, he peeked at her over his elbow. Her eyes were doing their rapid blinking thing, but she didn't seem to notice or care. "Micah and I are on a special assignment from the king and must report to him immediately along with this lawbreaker in our custody. I thus need your best three okties. Get them out of the sky now. I want to inspect them, choose the ones I want, and be on my way before the portal even shuts down."

The soldier charged her Jolt Blast. "I have an assignment as well. I am under strict orders to arrest anyone who comes through this portal. Besides, that cannot be Micah. He is dead."

Micah dropped his arm. Surprised gasps rumbled through the lines of soldiers. "I am very much alive." He managed to spit the words out through sobs. They had to get this situation under control fast. Javan would be coming through on Silverspike any second. "Put your weapons down."

"And the okties," the Destroyer said. "Get them out of the sky. Now."

"Micah I will listen to," said the soldier, signaling the men to lower their weapons while staring at the Destroyer, "but you have no right to order my okty unit to do anything."

"I have more right than anyone here." The Destroyer forced the top of her shirt over the edge of her right shoulder, revealing a tattoo in the shape of an O formed by sliced tails of the four Dragon Stalkers. "I have been branded with the Seal of the King. I take it you know what that means?"

Micah knew what that tattoo meant. It gave her the authority to act with the power of the king anywhere in Zandador at any time. Only two of the king's advisors had been branded with that Seal during the five centuries of Omri's reign, and it had been promised to him on his 100th birthday. How had this woman from another Bloodline earned that sacred mark? What secrets was she hiding? Why was she so loyal to his father?

"Yes, ma'am. Yes, of course." The leader snapped, whistled, and ordered her okty unit out of the sky. One by one, the okties began to land on the path along the river.

"Look at that," the Destroyer said, speaking low enough for only Micah and Taliya to hear as they walked toward the okties, "I got us through. I'm eager to collect my payment."

Micah matched her low tone. "What exactly is your payment?"

"We might want to discuss that later." Taliya took the reins of a green okty and pointed to the sky above the river. "Looks like Silverspike is about to reveal himself."

Bolts of lightning shot straight into the sky. Then parallel to the water. Then BOOM! A bolt struck the water near the opposite shore. High bursts of water shot into the air, dissipated into bursts of steam, and finished with unhappy waves rustling the surface of the water and crashing onto the shoreline.

More booms. More water explosions. More steam bursts. More waves. All headed closer and closer to the portal shore.

"Lighting storm!" Micah screamed over the yelps of the okties, hoping the soldiers would believe his explanation. He climbed on a yellow and black speckled okty and began herding the soldiers to the trees. "Clear the area! Take cover in the woods!"

◊   ◊   ◊

The need to laugh bubbled up inside Javan as he broke free from the cold, sticky portal into the fresh Zandadorian air. He held his breath to keep the laughter inside. If he let it out, the soldiers he could see landing their okties in front of him would hear. He thus held it in long enough for Silverspike to clear the portal, spread his wings, and soar to the right over the river.

Skylark would bank left when she came through, and Varjiek would fly straight ahead to avoid any collisions of invisible dragons.

Once they were far enough away, Javan exhaled and let himself laugh. He could feel Azurrior turning flips inside the backpack, but Silverspike coasted calmly through the air. "We did it!" Javan laughed some more and stretched out his arms. They rose higher and higher, and the figures of the people on the land grew smaller and smaller.

Seeing the portal from above triggered the memory of the last time he was here. He had been ready to give up on his Collector's quest before it begun, and his mother willingly opened the portal for him to let him return to his old life on Earth.

Micah had been on portal patrol that day and captured his mother. Had Micah not shown up and been the jerk that he used to be, Javan would have gone back to Earth without ever meeting Varjiek, Micah would still be an enemy of the Collector Bloodline, and Taliya would be waiting in vain for Javan to arrive in Keckrick to collect Kisa.

Javan stared at the little people standing by the swiftly flowing river. His life had changed a lot since he last stood down there. He had changed. Had he been braver and wiser from the beginning, he would have committed to the quest at the outset, and his mother never would have had to endure that awful imprisonment.

But would he have been as motivated to collect Varjiek if his mother's life wasn't on the line?

Now wasn't the time to consider such questions. He had a job to finish. "Nice flying, Silverspike. Let's circle around and head north."

Silverspike turned north, stalled, and sputtered. *You might want to hold on a bit tighter. I feel an eruption coming on.*

"No." Javan patted the dragon's neck. "Stay steady. Stay calm. You're okay."

I can't hold it in anymore. A bolt of lightning shot toward the clouds. *Whatever happens, keep me invisible!*

He leaned forward and latched onto the dragon's neck just as he began spinning like a pinwheel in the middle of a hurricane. Silverspike shot lightning in every direction as he spun around and around while flying closer to the portal area.

I don't like this. Azurrior's claws dug through the pack into Javan's back. *Make him stop.*

"Slow down, Silverspike." Javan's legs slipped an inch with every rotation. "I'm losing my grip!"

Can't. Lightning breath. *Control.* Lightning breath. *Anything.* Two breaths of lightning.

"Then I've got no choice." If Javan fell from this high up, he didn't stand much chance of survival. If he died, so would Azurrior. "Fly fast, Silverspike. I'll meet you at the rendezvous point." He reached his right hand between his stomach and the dragon's neck. Once his fingers touched the hilt of his teleporting sword, he closed his eyes and imagined the smooth white surface of the Zandadorian portal near Gri.

◊   ◊   ◊

Taliya used every ounce of her concentration and strength to maintain control of the reigns of the okty in the midst of the commotion. It wanted to join its friends and fly away, but she needed it to stay put until the portal shut down. She kept one eye on the portal and one on the approaching water bursts and steaming waves. "Come on, come on, come on," she mumbled when the first of the waves kissed the sand near her toes.

"Taliya, what are you doing?" Micah flew down to her after chasing the soldiers away. "You'll get covered with water if you stay there!"

"I can't leave without the activation scales."

"We'll get you another set. Use that okty to fly out of here before anyone realizes what is causing that lightning storm."

"You go ahead." Those scales were the only valuable thing her father ever gave her. She wasn't about to leave them behind. "I'll be on my way as soon as—"

BOOM!

Lightning hit the water fifty feet away. Her okty screeched, jerked free from her grip, and flew out of sight. She fell to her hands and knees in the hot, wet sand at the same instant the portal closed. "Finally." She scrambled to the portal on all fours, retrieved the scales, and stuffed them in her bag.

"Taliya, watch out!"

Micah's warning wasn't in time. A giant, hot wave smashed her into the wall. Her forehead hit the rock. Blood gushed over her left eye and down her burning skin. Another smaller wave smacked her face first into the sand.

"You Protectors do foolish things for your ridiculous dragon scales." The Destroyer appeared, lifted Taliya out of the sand, and tossed her on her okty. "If I didn't need you for the Battle, I would have left you here to die."

"Worst life-saving speech ever." Dizzy and disoriented, Taliya struggled to remain upright as they dashed into the sky. And she wasn't sure, but she thought she saw the grey figure of Silverspike spiraling over the trees. Why was he visible? What happened to Javan?

He better not have fallen. He had her dragon.

CHAPTER 53

Separated

Javan expected the spinning to stop once he teleported off Silverspike. He was wrong.

He landed on his side, dropped his invisibility sword, and rolled across the wide surface of the West Zandadorian portal. He finally stopped on his back when he hit the grass. He put his hands on his chest to calm his heart and stared at the clear blue sky. What a ride.

Can't. Breathe. Azurrior's feet kicked Javan's back.

"Oh. Sorry!" He jerked to his knees, shook the pack off, and unzipped it. Azurrior's blue face stared up at him with an angry scowl. "You okay, buddy?"

He shook his head and dangled his claws in front of his chest. *Legs got squished. Not sure they work anymore.*

"That's a bit dramatic. I'm sure they'll be fine once you stretch them out." Picking the dragon up with his left hand and grabbing the leash with his right, Javan freed Azurrior from the pack and placed him on the ground. "Welcome to the Land of Zandador."

Azurrior gulped in the air and gazed around with his round black eyes. *What's that?*

"What's what?" He followed the dragon's gaze to the open meadow to the right. "I don't see anything."

That. He darted toward whatever his eyes saw. Javan's upper body lurched forward from his kneeling position and smacked into the ground. The dragon tried to drag him forward, but his chipmunk-sized body wasn't quite strong enough to make Javan move.

"Hold on, pal. I'll let you stretch your legs and explore, but you need to let me get up first."

The dragon tapped his front paw as Javan stood. *Now?*

Javan brushed himself off and nodded. "Now."

Azurrior shot through the high grass. They zigzagged through the field, chasing some figment of the dragon's imagination. But Javan couldn't maintain Azurrior's pace. He was about to put an end to their escapade when the dragon halted, sniffed, and spit.

"What was that for?" Javan leaned on his knees to catch his breath.

I swallowed a bug.

"You're a dragon," he said, chuckling. "You should like bugs."

I wasn't hungry. Azurrior nudged his nose to the sky. *They are, though.*

He turned and saw two golden dragons flying toward the portal with the grey Silverspike leading the way in a triangle formation. He couldn't make out the figures of Kenton and Starshade, but he knew they were on one of the golden dragons. "Come on." He tugged the leash. "We have to see if Starshade is okay."

They sprinted toward the portal. This time Javan had no trouble keeping up with the Dusk Stalker.

◊   ◊   ◊

"Why are we stopping?" Taliya held her hand over her bleeding head and tried not to think about how much her stinging skin hurt. Had she lost consciousness on the trip? Is that why the ride seemed so short? "Are we there?"

"We're where we need to be." The Destroyer guided the okty to a dirt patch by the edge of the river. She dismounted, pulled Taliya down with her, and took the harness off the okty. "You need to cool off before we go any further."

"Huh?" Between the warm blood filling her hand and the burning sensation overpowering her brain, that's the only word she could think to form. Her toes dragged along the dirt under the helping hand of Jane the Destroyer. They were going toward the water, the fast-flowing blue water. If she fell in, that current would whisk her downstream in a flash.

Taliya tried to back away. Jane held her in place and tied a leather reign from the okty's harness around her chest. She tugged at it but couldn't get it off before Jane threw her into the river.

Initial pain. Immediate soothing. Crazy panic.

Water filled her lungs while the current took her away. Or it tried to. Thanks to the strap tied to her chest, she wasn't going anywhere. She kicked and splashed until her head popped through the surface. She saw Jane standing on dry land holding the other end of the harness. "What are you doing?" Taliya yelled, flailing her arms to keep her head above water. "Get me out of here!"

"Not yet." She yawned. "Those lightning charged waves made your skin look like a ripe tomato. You need to soak for a bit before we go anywhere."

The sensible explanation calmed Taliya. The water did make a difference. The more she waved her arms under the water, the less pain she felt. The only part of her that continued to burn was her face. "In that case," she said, "hold on tight. I need to submerge my head."

She took a deep breath, relaxed her muscles, and dipped under water. With the current pulling her forward and Jane holding her back, she let the water wash away the burning pain. When she couldn't stand the breathless treatment any longer, she resurfaced. "Okay," she said, gasping for air. "Let's go meet up with the guys."

"Yes. Let's." Jane reeled her in and helped her out of the water. "I'm anxious to tell them about our little deal."

Taliya considered jumping back in the river. Letting herself be washed away suddenly seemed more appealing than honoring the deal she made with the Destroyer.

◊   ◊   ◊

Micah dug his heels into the furry sides of the smelly okty, urging it to fly faster. The dragons would already be there, and he wanted to send them back out to search for the Destroyer and Taliya. He had watched Jane rescue Taliya from the waves and assumed they would be right behind him. They weren't.

After nearly thirty minutes in the air, he spotted the rendezvous point. The Noon Stalkers were nowhere to be seen. They could be invisible, but the more likely scenario had them out hunting for their meal. Silverspike walked in slow circles around the portal with Azurrior tied to his neck while Javan and Kenton huddled over the limp body of Starshade. If she wasn't breathing yet, she probably wouldn't ever breathe again.

Good thing they brought two Dusk Stalkers back with them.

Micah touched down by the trees, tied his okty to a branch, and waved Kenton over to him. "Mind if I borrow Silverspike? I need to go look for the Destroyer and Taliya."

"No can do." Kenton shook his head. "Silverspike is still too hyped up from his trip through the portal to do any flying."

"Why do you need to go look for them?" Javan entered the conversation from fifty feet away and marched toward Micah as he spoke. "What happened? Why aren't they with you? I need Taliya here. She's the only one who knows what to do to help Starshade."

The desperation in Javan's voice made Micah cringe. Taliya or no Taliya, Starshade didn't stand much of a chance. He didn't know how to tell Javan that, though. "You know what?" Micah shrugged and waved off his concern. "I'm sure Jane and Taliya will be along shortly. The okty they are on must be flying slower cause it's carrying two people rather than one."

"That wasn't the plan," Javan said. "You were each supposed to get your own okty. If she needed a ride, why didn't you pick her up? How could you let Jane take her? What if she plans to turn Taliya in for a reward?"

Javan's words brought life to Micah's fears, but he wasn't going to take the blame for something that was out of his control. "We were ready to ride out of there free and clear until Silverspike decided to put on a lightning show."

"I see what you're doing," Kenton said. "You're implying it's my dragon's fault that you couldn't protect the Protector."

"I wasn't implying anything. I was stating a fact. It is Silverspike's fault!"

"Yo!" A familiar voice interrupted the growing yell fest. "Why are you shouting at each other over there when this baby dragon over here clearly needs help?"

Micah looked between Javan and Kenton. The first thing he noticed was Kisa standing on the portal. Then his eyes looked over to see Ravier kneeling by Starshade. Thankful for the distraction and suddenly anxious about Mertzer, he pushed through the two men in front of him and ran to kneel by Ravier. "Since you're here and safe, am I correct to assume that Mertzer is also safe?"

"That's all you're worried about?" Javan asked, approaching them. "Your dragon? What about my dragon who is almost dead and Taliya who might already be dead?"

"Taliya's dead?" Ravier stood, alarm sounding in his voice. "I saw three people and assumed one was Taliya." His eyes stuck on Kenton as the man strolled over. "Grandfather? What are you doing back in Zandador? It's not safe for you yet."

"Calm down," Kenton said. "This place will be safe for me soon enough. As for Taliya, she is most certainly alive. It wouldn't be in the Destroyer's best interest to kill her at this point."

"Agreed." Micah nodded and rose to his feet. "We have something she wants, and she won't do anything to harm Taliya until she gets it." He wanted his words to be true. That didn't mean they were. If something had happened to her, he would forever regret letting her and the Destroyer out of his sight.

"I'm not following," Ravier said. "Who's this Destroyer you speak of, and what deal did you make with her?"

"We don't know her name or what she wants," Micah said. Movement in the sky caught his eye. At first, he thought it was one of the Noon Stalkers returning, but the blip was too small. That could only be an okty. He pointed to the sky, hoping that okty had two riders. "I have a feeling we're about to find out together."

CHAPTER 54

The Destroyer's Deal

"Starshade!" Taliya forgot all about her headache, water-logged clothes, and tingling skin the second she saw the white dragon laying on the ground struggling to breathe. She jumped off the okty before they even landed and rushed to Starshade's side, ignoring the inquiries of the four men surrounding the dragon. "Come on, girl. Breathe."

The dragon took in a shallow breath, released it, and waited for another eleven seconds before breathing again.

"No. You have to do better than that. I need you to survive." Taliya lay her head on the dragon's side, willing herself to hear a steady heartbeat. When she thought she would never hear what she wanted to hear, the dragon took in a big gulp of air and lifted her head.

"Thata girl!" Taliya hugged her and rubbed her side. "Now keep breathing. Deeper and more often."

"How did you do that?" Javan stared at her with wide eyes. So did everyone else. Except the Destroyer. She stood at a distance from the crowd with her arms crossed and looking bored.

"All I did was talk to her." Content with the dragon's stronger breathing pattern, she stood and changed the subject. Otherwise Javan might realize that Starshade was acting more like her dragon than his. "Ravier, it's good to see you and Kisa. How is Mertzer? What have you been doing while we were gone? Is there any news we should know about? Did you find your wife? Did you bring any food with you?"

"He can answer those questions later," Micah said. "Except the Mertzer one. That I want answered. But it's your turn first. What did you promise the Wordless Wonder over there in return for her help in getting us through the portal?"

Taliya rubbed her throat as all eyes—dragon and human—trained themselves on her. "Is anyone else thirsty?" Eventually she would have to divulge the deal, but she wanted to stall. She preferred to talk to Javan on his own before sharing the deal with the entire group. "That trip through the portal has me parched. Perhaps we should find a source of water before we continue this conversation."

"Talk." Micah issued the word through a growl. He looked ready to turn her upside down and shake the words out of her.

She cleared her throat and swallowed. "That saliva helped." She offered a smile. Micah scowled in return. Then she had another idea. "Where are our manners? We haven't even introduced Ravier and Kisa to the baby dragons yet."

"I'm a bit more interested in this deal," Ravier said.

"Nonsense." Taliya patted Starshade's head. "This is Starshade. She had a bit of trouble breathing in Earth's atmosphere but seems to be adjusting now. And over there on Silverspike is Azurrior."

"That tiny little blue thing? That's a dragon?"

"He is the most precious and beautiful dragon to ever live."

"Please tell me he's not the one Javan picked."

"He's not the one Javan picked; he's mine to protect."

"Nice." Ravier squatted in front of Starshade. "She'll grow her scales within the week and gain enough height to be ready to ride a few weeks after that. This will be the easiest collection ever. Usually dragons are released into the wild, but now we have her within our grasp."

"I am aware of that usual practice, being that I am a Dragon Protector. And that's precisely why they will follow the normal procedure and be released into Dusk Territory as soon as they have their scales."

"We're gonna do what with the dragons?" Javan ran his fingers through his hair and left them stuck on his head. "Why would we let them go when we've already started bonding with them?"

"We won't." Ravier didn't raise his voice his voice or show any signs of anger. "That is not going to happen. I have dedicated my life to getting Omri off the throne. I will not have everything I have fought for compromised by some idealistic Protector."

"Too late." The Destroyer stepped forward and nudged Taliya. "Now tell them the rest."

"The rest?" Javan asked. "You mean there's more?"

"Yes, there's more." Taliya wanted to smack the Destroyer. Why did she choose now to be chatty? "As you know, Jane played a critical role in getting us through the portal without being shot at or arrested. Because of that, the Dusk babies are still alive. In return, we will give her what she wants."

"And what is that?" Kenton asked.

"She wants to pit the four Bloodlines against each other to battle for the dragons."

Javan's eyes widened. "Surely you're not saying what I think you're saying."

"Oh, but she is." The Destroyer flashed her white teeth. "With all four Bloodlines competing for the same two dragons at the same time in the same place, this will be the truest, most epic Battle for the Throne in the history of Zandador."

"Don't forget the final part of the deal," Taliya quickly added. "You are not to touch Micah. This Battle makes the contract on his head null and void, and no one is allowed to physically harm another human before, during, or after the Battle. Furthermore, when Javan wins Starshade and I win Azurrior, you join our team and help Javan collect a Midnight Stalker."

"You mean when I win the heads of those two Dusk Stalkers, Javan surrenders his quest for the throne."

"That's crazy!" Javan's eyes practically popped out of their sockets. "I'm not surrendering anything."

"No one is asking you to, Javan." Taliya stopped herself from massaging her forehead to ease her growing headache. She didn't want to rub the healing ointment off that she put on at the river's edge. "What I'm asking is that you do your collecting thing after you give Starshade a chance to acclimate to the land and learn what it feels like to be a dragon. And think about it. How will riding a baby dragon who grew in captivity enhance your skills and confidence as a Collector?"

"That is a valid point," Kenton said. "Javan needs to earn the right to ride Starshade, not expect her to submit because she doesn't know any better."

Happy to have someone on her side, Taliya inched closer to Kenton who stood across from her.

"We set Kisa aside for him," Ravier said. "How would keeping the Dusk Stalker in our care be any different?"

"It's way different." Taliya watched Kisa lick the dirt off her scales. She was that picky about her appearance because she learned how to be her without anyone around dictating who she should be or how she should act. "Kisa had fifteen years of freedom before Javan collected her. She had a chance to live and experience life as a dragon should. All dragons have that right."

"And I have the right to have my deal honored." In one swift move, Jane drew her axe, straddled Starshade, and placed the blade on the weak dragon's neck. "I get my battle, or this dragon dies right now."

Swords flew into the hands of Javan, Micah, Kenton, and Ravier as the men moved into position to surround the Destroyer. Taliya found herself in the middle of the circle alongside Jane. She knew all blades aimed for the Destroyer, but she couldn't help but feel trapped. "Guys, swords down." No one listened.

"Stab me if you want, gentlemen, but this dragon will die with me."

"Javan," Taliya pleaded, looking past the points of his swords and into his glowing green eyes, "don't let her kill Starshade. Please. Agree to the battle."

"We did accept the Destroyer's help to get us through the portal." Kenton sheathed his sword and turned to Javan. "This is your game. You're the Collector vying for the throne. It's ultimately your decision."

"Well?" Taliya bit her lip, held her breath, and waited for Javan to speak.

◊   ◊   ◊

Intentionally avoiding eye contact with Taliya, Javan kept his focus and his swords trained on the Destroyer. He hated the idea of facing her in a battle. He had a hard enough time collecting Kisa when only Micah fought against him. Now he would have to battle three people—one bent on murder—for his dragon? That kind of pressure made him sick to his stomach. "You can take that okty and fly out of here," Javan said. "We'll give you your freedom. Just put the axe down and step away from the dragon."

"I don't want my freedom. I want a battle."

"I like the idea," Kenton said. "The battle will build character."

"My character is fine," Javan said. He wanted to keep Starshade close, bond with her as she grew, and earn her respect so she would choose to let him ride her. That's how he wanted to grow his collection. "My collection is not. I need Starshade in order to win the throne. I can't put her in harm's way."

"She's already in harm's way." The Destroyer lowered her axe so that it touched Starshade's skin. "You have three seconds to decide whether she lives or dies."

"Fine." Javan stepped back, holstered his swords, and motioned for Ravier and Micah to do the same. "You win. You'll get your battle. But you remain our prisoner until it begins."

"Fine." Jane stood, smirked, and surrendered her axe to Micah. "Killing a dragon who isn't strong enough to fight back wouldn't have been much fun. I'll wait until she's grown, but I'll still let you watch me slice her head off."

Javan lunged for the Destroyer, but Taliya stepped in front of him. She latched onto his elbow. "Let's walk and talk."

He reluctantly followed her out into the meadow. When they were away from the prying ears of the crowd around the portal, he jerked free from her touch and halted. "I don't understand you. I thought your job was to protect dragons, not willingly send someone after them who wants to kill them. How could you agree to this insane demand of hers?"

"If I believed for one second that the Destroyer could defeat either one of us, I would never have made this deal with her."

He studied her blue eyes. They were filled with determination and confidence, a lot more determination and confidence than he felt. "It's still a risk. An unnecessary risk."

"Listen, I made this deal for four reasons. One, I know without a doubt that you can collect Starshade before the Destroyer can even get close enough to think about taking her head off. You need to know that about yourself as well."

Javan wasn't so sure about that, but he let Taliya keep talking.

"Two, it was the only way to get her agree to help us get through the portal. If we hadn't come when we did, Starshade would already be dead. And three, you need her to help you collect a Midnight Stalker. I'm not sure if you are aware of this or not, but there is an evil dragon who dominates Midnight Territory. She needs to be eliminated before you can even think about collecting a Midnight Stalker, and the Destroyer specializes in eliminating dragons.

"Aren't you supposed to unite all four Bloodlines, anyway? This is how you do it. You beat the Destroyer in a legitimate battle, get her on your side, and take down Omri with the support of all four Bloodlines."

"Your logic breaks down in one respect: how can we trust the Destroyer? She almost killed Starshade a few minutes ago, and she still won't tell us her name. How do we know she'll keep her end of the bargain and stick with us if I win?"

"Wasn't Micah your enemy not too long ago?"

"Yeah. So?"

"So you already have practice turning your enemies into allies. You'll bring her around to your side."

The prophecy did say he would unite the four Bloodlines. He didn't know any other Destroyers. He might as well work on making this one his friend. "Okay. You make some valid points, and I am a man of my word. But don't expect me to ever agree to any deal again without knowing every detail beforehand."

"That's fair."

She turned to go, but Javan stopped her. "Wait. You said you had four reasons. What's the fourth?"

"Oh. That." She held her head high. "I need to prove to myself that I am a capable Protector. I need to know I can outwit a Destroyer and take a scale from Azurrior's forehead to brand him as Protected before she can get near him."

He saw doubt creep into her eyes. "You will," he said, understanding the importance of needing to prove oneself. "The Destroyer doesn't have a chance."

◊   ◊   ◊

The two old guys wandered off to chat, leaving Micah alone with the Destroyer. Maybe now that she was talking, he could finally learn her name. "I would congratulate you on your ingenious deal...if I knew your name."

225

"A name isn't necessary for you to offer your praise. And by the way, I am indeed done trying to kill you. I don't need a blade to my throat to persuade me to honor my deals."

"How noble of you. But what about the deal you made with my father to assassinate me?"

"Destroying dragons trumps eliminating you. Besides, if I bring the heads of two Dusk Stalkers to Omri, he'll be so grateful that his position on the throne is no longer threatened that he'll overlook the fact that you are still alive."

Micah wanted to tell her that his father didn't overlook anything. You either followed his orders or you died. He didn't much like the Destroyer, but he didn't want her to die. That's why when the battle began, he wouldn't attempt to hunt any dragon. Instead, he would hunt the Destroyer and make sure she didn't succeed in her quest.

CHAPTER 55

Gibbet

The adrenaline that had kept Taliya going for the past few hours began to wane as she and Javan walked back to the portal area. Hunger, fatigue, and fear of the impending battle overwhelmed her. She stumbled, but Javan caught her before she fell. "Thanks."

"You okay? You're looking a bit shaky. Is it because of that cut on your head? The Destroyer didn't do that to you, did she?"

"No. I banged it on the cliff wall, but I'm fine." Using Javan as a prop, she steadied herself. "Just need some food and rest. It's been a long day."

"That it has. I hope warm food and cozy beds are waiting for us wherever Kisa and Ravier popped in from."

"Where do you think that is?" The idea of visiting a new place revived her. "My guess is some cave in the mountains north of here. Where else would he be able to conceal two dragons? Unless he had Kisa take them back to Dusk Territory. They would be safe there, but that would be disappointing because I've already seen that part of Zandador. I'd prefer to explore somewhere I've never been."

"I hope it's not a cave." Javan moaned. "I got used to sleeping in an actual bed while on Earth, and I would like that trend to continue."

"As long as the dragons are safe, I don't care where we sleep."

"I don't think Azurrior is going to be safe much longer." Javan nodded toward Silverspike. The huge dragon was snapping and clawing at the tiny dragon who literally ran in circles around his neck. "I'll go rescue the little guy."

"Please do." She smiled, pleased with the spunk of her dragon. Releasing him into the wild would be good for him but sad for her. "I'll check on Starshade."

Unlike Azurrior, Starshade wasn't moving. She had curled her tail around her body and was sleeping peacefully. "Too bad Azurrior can't share some of his energy with you."

"I wouldn't mind having a dose of that energy myself," Ravier said, joining her. "I haven't slept much since you've been gone."

"Why's that?"

"It took the dragons and I most of the week to get through the mountains. It was only yesterday when we finally reached our destination."

"You got through the mountains? That means you made it to Gibbet." Taliya's heart rate sped up. She had never been that far north before. She had to know what it was like. "Is it true that miniature people live there in elaborate villages in the trees? What kind of food do they eat? I hope it's good. I am pretty hungry. And do the rhinorats really exist? Are they as big and as ugly and as mean as the legend states?"

"I don't know how you say so much so fast. I don't even remember all your questions." He motioned toward Kisa. "How about we have Kisa take us there, and you can find the answers to your questions yourself."

"Gladly!"

"You stay put. I'll gather everyone and bring Kisa over here so we don't have to move Starshade."

"Sounds good." She squatted by Starshade's ear. "Did you hear that, girl? We're going to Gibbet. For once, I won't be the shortest person around!"

Starshade barely opened her eyes and promptly shut them again. "That's all right," Taliya said. "You keep sleeping, and I'll be excited enough for the both of us."

While she waited for the teleportation trip, she commanded her mind to recall everything about Gibbet she had ever heard or read. She wanted to be prepared, but more importantly, she wanted something to think about besides the guilt that ate at her for making that horrible deal with the Destroyer.

◊   ◊   ◊

Certain that Starshade was safely wrapped in Kisa's tail, Javan placed his hand on Kisa's hind leg. "Hands on, people." He waited for everyone to get in position, but before he ordered them to go, he needed to question Kisa. "You sure you can teleport us all at once? I can't even take one other person with me when I teleport."

I could teleport a hundred humans if I needed to, but the little blue dragon is distracting. Nevertheless, I am sure my mind is strong enough to overcome the commotion.

"Then take us to Gibbet." Javan closed his eyes and braced for the tingling sensation this type of travel provided. Seconds later, the sweet aroma of flowers assaulted his nose.

"Wow. This place is amazing!"

The awe in Taliya's voice encouraged Javan to look around. He stood on a soft layer of golden dust among trees whose trunks were wrapped with vines of colorful flowers.

I am going to return for the winged dragons, Kisa said. *When I leave, make sure you glance up.*

Kisa disappeared, and Javan looked up. Tall trees with bushy tops and thick branches surrounded him. But it was what he saw in the trees that took his breath away. An entire city ten feet off the ground lived above him. Swinging bridges connected buildings of all shapes, sizes, and colors to one another. It was hard to tell from his perspective, but the buildings appeared to be made for midgets.

Ravier put two fingers in his mouth and let out a long, shrill whistle. "All is well," he shouted. "We're back, and I have the Collector with me."

Doors and windows creaked open, and little people no more than three or four feet high dressed in clothes that matched the colors of the flowers and tree tops began pouring out of their houses onto the porches and walkways. They were the most adorable group of folks he had ever seen.

"Javan!"

Surprised that someone in the village knew him, he turned to his left and saw a tall, red-haired woman waving at him from a balcony of a round, bright yellow house. Could it be? Was that really who he thought it was?

"Grandmother!" He ran toward her while searching in vain for a ladder. "What's with this place? How do I get up there?" He paused and scanned the bridges.

"I can lead you to a ladder, but it won't help you find your mother," his grandmother Hannah said, seeming to read his mind. "She's not up here."

"Oh." Javan lowered his head and swallowed, too choked up to say anything else.

"That's because I'm right behind you."

He spun around and met the beaming eyes of his mother. "You're alive," he whispered. "I wasn't sure I would ever see you again."

"Nonsense." She was thinner than he remembered and stood with the support of a cane, but she had survived. She hobbled to him. "I missed the first fifteen years of your life. I wasn't about to miss watching you win the throne." She tossed the cane aside and stretched out her arms. Javan smiled and hugged her, thankful to be in the warm embrace of his mother. Then two more arms encircled him.

"This is so touching." Taliya squeezed him and his mother. "Doesn't this feel like a big group hug king of moment? I knew I would be happy if we found you, but I didn't think I would be this happy."

"Thank you, dear." Esmeralda pulled away. "Who exactly are you?"

"Me? Oh. Taliya. Dragon Protector."

"The Dusk Stalkers are alive because of her," Javan said. "She got us through the portal and back."

"Then I must thank you." She shook Taliya's hand. "You look familiar, like someone I know. You must be Hizel's daughter. He was a great, bold man, and a good friend. Then he was assigned to marry your mother. I'm afraid I don't have anything kind to say about her."

"Me, either," Taliya responded. "But I can already tell you are kind and loving. You are a Protector as well, correct? I have so many questions for you. Can we chat? Over lunch? I am quite hungry."

"Hold on, Taliya." Javan gently pushed her away. "She's my mother. I should get to talk to her first."

"No." Micah stepped forward. "I need to talk to her first."

"It's you." His mother shivered and fainted in Javan's arms.

◊   ◊   ◊

Shame cut straight to Micah's heart at the sight of Esmeralda. He remembered every horrible word he said to her and about her while he dragged her around the Land of Zandador in chains. He had slapped her. Kicked her. Whipped her. Yet she never complained. Never fought back. Never ridiculed him. She simply took the abuse she didn't deserve with dignity.

No wonder the sight of him made her faint.

He turned to go, to find anywhere else to be. He certainly didn't earn the right to be in her presence.

"Micah." Javan's voice stopped him. "She wants to talk to you."

He closed his tear-filled eyes and shook his head. "I don't want to cause her any more pain. Let her know I'll stay out of her sight until we leave this place."

"That won't be necessary," Esmeralda said. "It is necessary that we speak."

He slowly turned around and sunk to his knees in front of her. "The things I did to you are unforgivable. Nothing I say or do now can take away the pain I caused, but I am truly sorry. To prove it, I will let you punch and kick me as much as you want, and I promise not to fight back. Please. Make me bleed."

He spread his arms out, lowered his head, and braced for impact.

Soft fingers touched his chin and lifted him up. "Ravier told me you had a change of heart. I see for myself that is true. You are forgiven."

"What? How can you forgive me for the awful things I did to you? I won't let you forgive me." Tears spilled down his cheeks. "I need you to hit me!"

Instead of hitting him, she hugged him. "Perhaps it's time you forgave yourself. Holding on to anger and regret doesn't change the past, but it does prevent you from growing and creating a better future."

He returned the frail woman's embrace and sobbed. With every tear, he let a piece of his past go. And he knew he wouldn't be able to stop crying any time soon. He was going to have to shed a lot more tears to release the dark deeds of his history.

CHAPTER 56

Dragon Assignments

Taliya waved at Myal and Hiara, two of the young girls she had come to know over the past week as she crossed the bridge in front of their house. "Are you all ready for another game of Vine Wars after I take care of the dragons?"

"Yes!" Hiara clapped. "I'll get everyone ready."

"Do you think Javan will play with us, too?" Myal asked. "I want him on my team."

"Hey. What about me?"

"You're good with your slingshot, but he's better at throwing. His team always wins."

"Not today, missy. I'll get him to play, and my team will finally beat Javan's team."

Both girls smiled and scampered off to gather their teams. She had enjoyed teaching them and a handful of other kids how to shoot her slingshot, and they enjoyed teaching her how to play Vine Wars.

The goal of the game was to hit a target with a mini spear while swinging on a vine without getting pelted by a color bomb, which was a berry that grew in abundance here in Gibbet. Thanks to the disturbingly accurate aim of Javan, her team had yet to win a game.

She crossed the long bridge that led to the building where the Dusk Stalkers were living with some of the other animals on the outskirts of the tree village.

Living in the trees was a necessity for the people and smaller animals of Gibbet. Any man-made houses built in the soft ground sunk, but the deep roots of the trees made them strong enough to support buildings and bridges. Also, the main predator in this area was deadly on the ground but couldn't climb trees.

She spotted several of the massive, furry, three-horned rhinorats two days prior and had been glad she was above them rather than facing them on the ground. They were mean, angry creatures that liked to eat people and animals just for fun. The only animal she saw below her at the moment, however, was Mertzer.

"Hey there, big fella. I see you're right on time, but Javan is late."

"I'm here!" Javan dashed across the bridge and joined her on the porch of the barn. His matted hair stuck to his head, his face flushed red from exertion, and his shirt fastened fused to his skin with sweat. "Ravier made me run sprints along these mazes of bridges, and I took a wrong turn on my way here."

"You smell worse than the pigs." One of the pigs oinked as if agreeing with her.

"I've earned this stink." He lifted his arm and smelled his armpit. "That's the smell of a hardworking man. All the pigs do is wander around their square box."

"Whatever." Taliya laughed. "Let's just get Starshade and Azurrior down to Mertzer before they decide to eat their neighbors."

The dragons shared living space with the pigs and sheep. They would easily be able to break the weak barrier separating them from a possible meal if they got too hungry.

It was Mertzer's job to teach them how to hunt. Well before dusk each day, Taliya and Javan lowered the babies to the ground with an elevator made of wood and ropes. Once they ate, Mertzer would bring the babies back to the barn.

Starshade was pacing and stopped when Taliya walked through the door. She had grown to the size of a jaguar although her body and neck were both longer than that big cat. As she stood in the corner and swished her tail, Taliya realized her entire body was covered with brilliant white scales.

"Look, Javan. Starshade has all her scales."

"So does Azurrior. He's not blue anymore."

Taliya didn't recognize Azurrior. His once blue body now sparkled with his dazzling white scales. At half the size of Starshade, he strutted around the room with his long tail pointed up as if to show off his new body.

"You are looking mighty fine with those scales of yours."

"He says 'thank you.'"

"You are welcome." Then the ramifications of what the scales meant hit Taliya. She looked around the small box they were living in and realized it was time to set the dragons free.

The temptation to take a scale from Azurrior's forehead overwhelmed her. The best Protectors took that scale to brand the dragon as protected *before* releasing them into the wild. But she couldn't test her bond with Azurrior and attempt to extract a scale because of that foolish deal she made with the Destroyer.

"It's time," she said, choking back tears. "We need to send them to Dusk Territory."

"You mean right now? Can't we wait another day?"

"They're dragons, Javan. Not farm animals. We've kept them cooped up long enough. I hold my breath every time we send them out with Mertzer, anyway. I always wonder if they'll come back."

"Azurrior is still so small."

"True, but he's fast and smart. Plus he's a fighter. He'll be fine."

Javan paused, then said, "Unfortunately he agrees with you. I'll get Kisa."

He left, and Taliya found herself alone with the two Dusk Stalkers. "I won't be able to go with you to make sure you stay safe, so you'll have to look out for each other. Got it?"

She took their silence to mean they agreed. She sure was going to miss these baby dragons.

◊　◊　◊

"Here's how this is going to play out," Javan said, standing on the soft ground with the big dragons lined up in a semi-circle in front of him. Taliya stood to his side with the Dusk Stalkers on either side of her. Kenton and Ravier stood behind him while Micah watched from the balcony of the prison house where they kept the Destroyer.

Javan cleared the jitters out of his throat and continued in his best authoritative voice. "Every dragon has a job to do. Silverspike, you are to scout out Midnight Territory. I want to know where the other Midnight Stalkers are living and which one would be the best candidate for me to collect. I also need to know which ones I should avoid. Basically, I need a rundown of the threats and opportunities."

"Return within two weeks," Kenton said. "That should be more than enough time to assess the situation."

It will only take one. Silverspike leapt into the air, raining down leaves and branches as he took to the sky.

"Varjiek and Skylark, you are to patrol Dusk Territory. I need to know if Omri has or will be sending any soldiers. Report back here immediately with any sightings of his army."

How long are we to stay separated from you? Varjiek asked.

"Until I come to get you. Take care of yourselves, and look out for each other. Kisa, go ahead and take them, then return for the Dusk Stalkers."

Once the Noon Stalkers disappeared with Kisa, Javan addressed Mertzer. "Micah has authorized you to go, so you are to stay in Dusk Territory. Continue to teach the little ones how to hunt. I'll leave Kisa there as well, and she'll report back to me each week. When you believe the dragons are strong enough to fend for themselves, have Kisa let me know."

Thank my master for offering me this taste of freedom. I didn't think I would ever feel like me again, and I am glad I am no longer the only Dusk Stalker in the land.

"I'll pass on the message." Javan turned to the young Dusk Stalkers. "As for you two, your job is to grow and enjoy life. Listen to Mertzer, and remember that you are the top of the food chain. Act like it. Just please don't eat me when I see you again."

I don't think you would taste very good, Azurrior said. *You're too bony.*

Javan laughed. "I'll be sure to keep the meat off my bones over the next few weeks." He took Azurrior's collar off and did the same for Starshade. "What about you, girl? Are you ever going to let me read your thoughts?"

The Noon Stalkers are set. Kisa popped back in before Starshade had a chance to answer. *I'm ready for the final trip.*

"Return in a week to let me know how the dragons are progressing."

As you wish. I think I would like you to come with me. I didn't like being apart from you when you went to Earth. It was a strange feeling.

"I'll miss you, too, girl." Javan hugged Kisa's snout, then stepped back to stand by Taliya. They watched the tails of the remaining dragons intertwine. Seconds later, they all disappeared.

◊   ◊   ◊

Micah watched his stubby-tailed dragon vanish. Right before he did so, Micah could have sworn his dragon looked up at him and nodded as if to say thanks for letting him go.

"Now that the dragons are gone," the Destroyer called from the open window, "how about you give me my axe back, and let me out of here. I need to have an equal opportunity to prepare for the upcoming battle."

"It's not going to happen. You're stuck in there until we go to Dusk Territory."

"That's not playing fair. You must be worried that I am a better Destroyer than you are a Hunter."

"I'm worried about no such thing."

"Then give me my weapon, and let me train. I have no incentive to run away or hurt you."

"I said no."

"UGH!" She hit the sides of the window, causing the wooden shutters to shake. "How about I give you something in return?"

"You have nothing that I want."

"I have one thing. I know my name. You don't."

Micah took the bait and leaned into the window. With his nose inches from hers, he said, "Tell me."

"My weapon."

"Your name."

"Krystyn. My name is Krystyn."

CHAPTER 57

Silverspike's Report

"You can have the flowers back!" Taliya threw her flower-filled bag at the charging rhinorat and ran in the opposite direction. The bag missed, and the massive, angry animal pursued her. The ugly thing fortunately didn't have anywhere near the speed of a Dusk Stalker, but it was faster than her and getting so close she could feel its spit on her neck.

She thought she would be safe by the lake. After all, she visited here almost every day to gather flowers for medicinal research projects since the dragons left three weeks ago. The only animals she spotted in that time were fish and frogs.

A vine dangled from a branch just ahead. Three more steps. Two. "Ahh!" Too late. Two of the three curved horns from the rhinorat scratched her back as they reached under her shirt and lifted her off the ground. She kicked. Her frantic feet collided with the vine and sent it swinging away from her.

The rhinorat twisted her to the right and to the left. She could hear her shirt begin to rip. If that happened, she would fall, and the animal would stab her flesh with its horns.

The uncooperative vine finally swung into her hands. She latched onto it and pulled herself up and away from the beast, ripping her shirt. Free from the rhinorat, she used the vine to pull herself all the way onto the branch and climbed higher until she was certain she was out of his reach. "You can't get me now," she taunted.

He snorted and snapped his jaws. She put another branch between herself and the rhinorat.

"You know, pal, no one else has had any complaints about the flowers I've picked around here. If I took the ones you were eyeing for your breakfast, I'm sorry. But I have learned how to make lotion with them that will leave your facial skin soft, smooth, and smelling fresh. Your skin sure could use some lotion."

He circled the tree below her. His knotted fur that covered all but his head smelled like he had bathed in manure. His dry, furless forehead creased with wrinkles. The horns that stretched above his oval brown eyes had tatters of her shirt hanging from them that tickled his short, crinkled, ugly black nose.

"If you insist upon waiting me out, I'll have to resort to shooting you with a dart." She took her slingshot off her belt and reached for a dart. That was in her bag. Which she could see fifty feet away on the ground. "Wonderful. Just wonderful."

She leaned back against the tree trunk, chastising herself for wandering this far away from the village by herself. However, she had needed some sort of project to keep her busy. So after joining Javan and Micah on a morning run around the bridges of the villages each day at sunrise, she would explore this area around the lake while they trained with Ravier on sword fighting.

The daily excursions had the added benefit of giving her a chance to practice hitting random targets with rocks flung from her slingshot. She was always back by lunch and spent the rest of the day reading, cooking, experimenting, and observing Krystyn during her controlled training sessions.

The Destroyer was strong, confident, and lethal. Taliya had yet to see her miss a target at which she threw her axe.

The best part of each week, though, was when Kisa teleported in to give her report. And Kisa was due back at any time to give her update. "Yo. Mr. Three Horns. I need to get back to the village, so I'm going to need you to go home. You are going to regret it if you make me miss Kisa!"

As if on cue, a dragon crashed through the bushy trees and sent the rhinorat rushing away. Only it wasn't Kisa. It was the long overdue Silverspike. And his body was a broken, bloody mess.

The most disturbing injury was his wing. The top half of his right wing was folded over and dangling by his side in an unnatural way.

She forgot about her own scrapes from the rhinorat's horns, used her trusty vine to swing out of the tree, and ran toward the hurt dragon.

◊   ◊   ◊

Micah spun to avoid Ravier's blow and lifted his sword to block the next blow. Steel met steel.

"Good," Ravier said. "You're able to adequately defend yourself. You might even be improving. I, however, am still the better swordsman."

"Maybe. For now." Micah wiped the sweat from his forehead. He liked this rapport he and Ravier developed. The man was a tough teacher with high expectations, and working with him during their extended stay here in Gibbet made Micah much stronger. "And I'm still better than him."

Micah pointed to Javan. He stood by Kenton in front of one of the walls of the octagonal house they were using for training. Villagers fought each other to watch the training sessions from the windows.

"The only reason you're better than me is because you're older and have had more practice," Javan said. "I can hold my own in a contest with you."

"You sure you're ready to face me?"

"Bring it on." Javan unsheathed his swords.

"No trickery. None of that invisibility or teleporting stuff."

"Deal." Javan took the scales out of the slots and handed them to Kenton. "Let's go."

The crowd outside began to chant and cheer. Some rooted for Javan. Others rooted for Micah. They were the only ones he paid attention to.

"You know the rules," Ravier said, handing Javan a chest protector. "One point for each stick to the chest. First one to three wins."

Micah and Javan circled one another. Javan was quick with his dual sword action, but Micah was confident with his longer, stronger sword. Still, he wanted to wait for Javan to make the first move.

"Aren't you going to engage?" Micah asked. "If you're trying to wear me out, it won't work. I can do this all day." They circled each other a few more times. "Afraid to attack?"

"Not at all." Javan's eyes darted to a window behind Micah. "Huh. How did Krystyn get over here?"

"What? She escaped?" Micah looked behind him, keeping his sword at his side. That gave Javan the perfect opportunity to stick the tip of his sword in Micah's chest.

"My bad. That wasn't her. But I do get a point."

Frustrated with himself, Micah lifted his sword. Movement at the doorway behind Javan made him pause. "Taliya?" Blood stained her hands, and for some odd reason, she vines of flowers wrapped around her body instead of clothes.

"Yeah, right." Javan kept his swords up and his eyes on Micah. "I'm not falling for that."

"I need everyone to come with me right away," Taliya yelled from the doorway.

Javan still didn't look at her. "Micah and I are in the middle of a contest."

"It can wait," she said. "The dragon can't."

"Is Kisa back?"

"No. It's Silverspike."

Micah sheathed his sword and turned Javan around so he could see Taliya. "I don't know what report Silverspike has from Midnight Territory, but I'm guessing it's not good."

◊   ◊   ◊

239

Dressed in a new pink shirt and black pants and her bag now filled with her healing ointments and cloths, Taliya led the way to the downed Midnight Stalker. It didn't take long. The village was still in sight when the oversized grey figure loomed before them. "Silverspike! I told you not to move. We were coming to you."

He plopped down between some trees and looked at Javan. A moment later, Javan relayed the dragon's thoughts. "He said he flew all the way here with a broken wing, so walking on his perfectly good legs wasn't a problem."

"Perfectly good legs, huh?" She pointed to a long cut on his back leg that oozed blood so dark it appeared purple. "Walking opened up that cut I warned you not to aggravate until I could get some healing ointment on it." Fortunately blood was only trickling from the other surface wounds she had cleaned by giving him a makeshift bath when they were near the lake.

"Give me the healing ointment," Esmeralda said. "Hannah and I will work on his leg while you focus on his wing."

"I hope I have enough." She handed Esmeralda the jar of ointment. "Javan, you keep him talking while we fix him. Kenton, I need you up here with me."

Taliya and Kenton carefully climbed onto the back of Silverspike, careful to avoid his many cuts. She straddled the row of spiked scales along his back and inspected his broken wing. It bent at an awkward angle about a third from the top of the pointed tip. Her ointment wasn't going to heal this kind of injury. "I'm going to need a rod or stick or something to use as a splint."

"We'll find you something," Ravier said from the ground. He and Micah dashed back to the village.

"How did this happen?" Kenton asked, choking on his words. "Silverspike is as tough as they come. How could he have gotten hurt this badly?"

"He challenged Ayzyd," Javan said. "She considers herself the queen of Midnight Territory and decides who gets to live where. She's outnumbered by eleven other Midnight Stalkers, but she has relegated them to the harshest part of Midnight Territory and attacks if they attempt to hunt in her feeding grounds.

"He tried to convince them that if the twelve of them rallied against her, they could reclaim their land. Only two other dragons were brave enough to join him, but the battle did not end well. Ayzyd seemed to know what they were going to do before they did and countered every attack with unrivaled strength and viciousness. They couldn't outsmart or outduel her, and he barely escaped with his life."

Taliya looked at Silverspike's injuries with fresh eyes. Another dragon did this to him, a dragon Javan would inevitably encounter once he collected a Dusk Stalker. Javan was just a little bitty human. What would happen to him when he came face to face with Ayzyd, a dragon who struck fear in other dragons?

CHAPTER 58

Kisa's Report

Javan hoped a walk would shake the dread and doom that gripped his heart after hearing Silverspike's story. Had he come this far only to be denied his final dragon?

Granted, he did still have a Dusk Stalker to collect as well. He already knew her, though. Surely he could talk her into letting him ride her even if she didn't talk back to him. Starshade didn't scare or intimidate him. The thought of going anywhere near Ayzyd, however, sent fear coursing through his veins.

There you are.

Javan halted at the familiar sound of Kisa's voice. He turned and saw his spotless white dragon daintily making her way through the golden sand. She shook each foot after every step as though the sand was the most repulsive object she had ever encountered. "You're looking smashingly clean today."

I'm not as clean as I should be. This golden sand likes to stick between my claws. I already need another bath.

"You can take as many baths as you want after you tell me how Starshade and Azurrior are doing. Please tell me they are ready to ride." He needed to do something active and productive after being cooped up here for the past month. He also craved a distraction to keep his mind off the impending Midnight Stalker problem.

The Dusk Stalkers are becoming feared. They have learned well how to fight, how to utilize their speed, and how to survive. They have definitely established themselves as the top of the food chain.

"Good for those little guys."

They are no longer so little. Starshade is now bigger than Mertzer. She is fierce, and I like to keep my distance even when she's not hungry.

Javan felt a headache coming on. How was he supposed to talk a fierce dragon into letting him ride her when she refused to communicate with him like every other dragon he met? Fortunately his aim with the stun balls was getting better and better. If he couldn't talk his way onto Starshade, he would resort to stunning her into submission. Too bad he couldn't ride Azurrior. At least he talked to Javan. Alas, that dragon was meant for Taliya, and she would want to know how he was doing. "What about Azurrior?"

Kisa averted her gaze and snorted.

"Kisa? What's wrong? What's the matter with Azurrior?"

It's...it's his scales. They are magnificent when he feeds. My scales are spectacular, but even I cannot compete with his beauty.

"You don't need to be jealous." He let out a laugh of relief. "Taliya would kill me if I tried to collect him."

I might have to kill you if you tried to collect him.

"Just because his scales are prettier than yours? That's a bit harsh. One of these days, we're going to have to talk about your obsession with looks. Your character is far more important than the color of your scales."

That sounds wise, but I'm not sure how true that is.

Javan shook his head at the superficial nature of his dragon, thankful to have something to think about besides the danger lurking in Midnight Territory. He would deal with Ayzyd when the time came. Right now, he had to focus on collecting a Dusk Stalker before the Destroyer had a chance to cut off the dragon's head.

◊   ◊   ◊

Micah took his time returning to his room and packing his minimal items once he heard the news that the dragons were grown and able to defend themselves against the four Bloodlines. He didn't want to go. He wanted to stay here.

Aside from the obvious perks of being fed four full meals a day and having a safe, comfortable place to sleep, he felt like he was part of a family. He ate with people. He learned something new every day by working with Ravier and Kenton. He had never worked so hard or had so much fun.

A knock on the door interrupted his thoughts. "Come in."

"Everyone is waiting for you." Ravier walked in. "I see you're packed. You just need this." He handed him his sword, which was leaning against the wall near his bed.

"Thanks." Micah tried to take it from him, but Ravier didn't let go.

"You are good with this sword. Use it for good."

"I may be officially entering this battle as a Dragon Hunter, but I have no intention of using my sword to cut off any dragon tails."

"Promise me that you will do whatever is necessary to keep Javan and the Dusk Stalkers safe."

"I promise."

Ravier nodded and released the sword. He squeezed Micah's shoulder and left the room without another word.

"I'll miss you, too, old man." Micah smiled, threw his bag over his shoulder, and went to find Javan.

◊   ◊   ◊

"There he is!" Taliya waved Micah over to where she, Javan, and Krystyn were standing in front of Kisa. To alleviate her nervousness, she reminded them of the terms of the battle. "Remember the rules. People are off limits. We're battling for dragons, and you can't improve your chances by targeting any of your opponents.

"The first one to conquer a dragon--or in my case mark him as untouchable and mine to protect by taking the scale from between his eyes—wins that dragon. We'll reconvene every five days at noon until the battle is over; the battle ends when both dragons are accounted for."

"This is also an individual battle," Krystyn said. "That means no working together, and no utilizing other dragons to help you win the Dusk Stalkers."

"Agreed."

"I don't agree," Javan said. "Banning teamwork is silly, and we should be able to use all the resources available to us. That includes Varjiek and Kisa for me, and Mertzer for Micah."

"Is that worry in your voice, Collector?" Krystyn smiled a truly evil smile. "If you aren't capable of collecting a Dusk Stalker on your own with nothing more than the resources you can carry, you don't deserve to be king."

"He collected Varjiek on his own," Taliya said, "and he will duplicate that feat with Starshade. Right, Javan?"

"You're right. I've done it once. I can do it again."

"Then we are clear on the terms." Taliya stretched out her arm. "Hands on mine if you agree to hurt no one and work solo during the battle."

"I'm in." Krystyn stacked her hand on Taliya's.

Micah added his hand without a word. He hadn't said anything about the battle since she first mentioned it, and she desperately wanted to ask him what he was thinking. Krystyn seemed to believe Micah was ready and willing to gain control over more dragons if given the chance, but Taliya wanted to believe he had changed.

"I will abide by those terms," Javan said, topping off the stack of hands, "but I don't have to like it."

"Then let the Battle of the Bloodlines commence." Taliya reached out with her free hand and touched Kisa. Seconds later, they found themselves on a hill in a section of Dusk Territory that didn't look at all familiar to Taliya.

A winding river sparkled to the east, open meadows with patches of trees stretched to the west, a mountain range loomed to the north, and a section of Slanted Acres dominated the south.

"According to Kisa," Javan said, "we're in the northeastern section of the Territory. She says both dragons like to stay in and around this area because the landscape here provides the best sources for food and shelter."

"Like I will believe that," Krystyn said.

"Believe what he says or not," said Taliya, "but wherever you choose to go, just be back at this spot in five days to check in."

"I'll see you then," Krystyn said, "and I'll have two dragon heads with me." She sprinted down the hill to the west, leaving the Protector, Collector, and Hunter together.

"I guess I have some hunting to do," Micah said, "but the only one I plan to hunt has two legs instead of four. Good luck to the two of you." He nodded at both of them and followed the Destroyer.

An awkwardness filled the air between her and Javan. Should they shake hands? Hug? Kiss? She shook that last thought away. Of course they shouldn't kiss. They were rivals now. She had to start thinking of him as the enemy. It would be easier if he wasn't so attractive. "Is it true? Do the Dusk Stalkers stick to the northeastern section?"

"That's what Kisa said. I mentioned it because I was sure Krystyn wouldn't believe me and would search for the dragons everywhere but where they are."

"Slick move."

"I have my moments." He flashed her a grin. "You go get Azurrior, and I'll see you back here with Starshade."

"Deal. And Javan?"

"Yeah?"

"Take care of yourself, okay?"

"You, too." Then he was gone without even a handshake.

CHAPTER 59

The Battle for Starshade

Javan spent the next hour and a half cursing himself for not hugging Taliya before they parted ways. But if he touched her, he knew he wouldn't have wanted to let her go. They spent almost every day together for the past few months, and leaving her to collect his dragon just seemed wrong.

She was the only one on his mind as he wandered in and out of trees, through flowery meadows, and over rocky hills. The unexpected sighting of a dragon he hadn't even been looking for surprised him. "Starshade," he said under his breath. What luck!

He hid behind a tree and waited for her to approach. The afternoon sun glistened off her bright white scales as she flicked her tail aimlessly across an open field. Her muscular legs were taller than him, and her long, sleek body made her look like the most athletic dragon he had ever seen.

He tried to connect with her thoughts as she drew closer, but he couldn't hear anything that was going on behind those round, alert eyes. Maybe if he spoke first, she would finally let him in.

Exhaling a deep, nervous breath, he stepped out from behind the tree and into the path of the formidable dragon. "Hello, Starshade. Remember me?"

She halted. Tilted her head. Narrowed her eyes on his.

"I'm Javan. I'm the one who picked out your egg, took you to Earth, and brought you back here. I kinda need you to let me ride you."

She crouched. Pointed her ears up. Snarled.

He took a step back. "What are you thinking, girl? If you let me in, I can answer your questions, address your concerns. I promise I'll take great care of you."

In straining to hear her response, he heard another sound. A bewildering sound. That of an axe whirling through the air.

◊   ◊   ◊

After setting out on her own, Taliya's first order of business was to find a river and build a raft. At least food wasn't an issue. Like everyone else, she traveled with a pack full of food. To set her apart, though, she needed a way to move throughout the territory faster than her competitors and the best chance of finding Azurrior first. Traveling along the rivers the way she did in Keckrick would give her that advantage.

She spotted Javan a few times while hiking north in search of a river but had yet to see Krystyn or Micah. The temptation to follow Javan tugged at her heart. To overcome it, she made herself chop off a branch of a tree with the machete she brought from Gibbet every time her feet tried to follow Javan. As a result, she was now dragging a dozen branches behind her secured in a jumble with some vines.

"This was your stupid idea," she mumbled to herself as she added another branch to her stash. "You had to make a deal with the Destroyer, and now two dragons might die. Stupid, stupid, stupid."

Mumbled words that sounded like they came from Javan's mouth cut into her self-berating session. Who was he talking to? Had he found Starshade already?

She abandoned her pile of sticks and followed Javan's voice. She saw him standing in front of a magnificent dragon she instantly recognized as a grown-up Starshade. Only this dragon wasn't making small talk with the Collector. She was crouching down and poising herself for an attack.

A slight movement to the right forced Taliya to avert her gaze. Krystyn!

The Destroyer waved her axe around and around her head, then flung it at the dragon who was fixated on Javan.

Taliya screamed. "Run, Starshade! Run!"

The dragon startled and took off a second before Krystyn's axe stuck in the tree instead of Starshade's neck.

"Nooo!" Krystyn yelled and stomped toward Taliya. "You. How dare you interfere. Teamwork is not allowed."

"What teamwork?" Taliya stood her ground. "I was doing my job as a Protector by protecting that dragon from your axe."

"You were here with Javan." Krystyn reached Taliya and hovered over her. "You're supposed to be on your own."

"I am. I happened to hear him talking and saw you try to kill Starshade. I yelled for the dragon, not for him. You're just upset because killing a Dusk Stalker isn't as easy as you thought it would be."

"Next time you get in my way," Krystyn said, dragging her finger across Taliya's throat, "don't be surprised if my axe collides with your neck instead of a tree."

The murderous intent in the Destroyer's eyes made Taliya realize just how hazardous Krystyn was to both dragons and to her. This was a life and death battle, and the reality that everyone might not survive made Taliya shiver as the Destroyer walked away.

◇   ◇   ◇

Considering Micah's lifetime of training, he figured hunting Krystyn throughout this battle would be easy. His simple plan was to track her movements and sabotage any attempt she made on the Dusk Stalkers to prevent her from winning. He wasn't technically working with Javan, so he considered himself within the battle guidelines.

He was hunting; he just wasn't hunting dragons.

Unfortunately Krystyn was quicker than he anticipated, and he lost sight of her a few times. When he spotted her again, he noticed her slinging her axe at a dragon. Had Taliya not hollered, Starshade would be dead.

Taliya wasn't always going to be around. That meant he was going to have to step up his skills if he was going to be able to keep Krystyn from killing any dragons.

CHAPTER 60

Caught

Taliya's stomach rumbled as she rowed her raft upstream. Sunset was a few hours away. Soon she would need to stop, set up camp, and eat. She wouldn't be able to eat much. She only had enough food left for one more meal thanks to those hungry hyenas she threw most of her food supply at two days ago in order to get away from them.

The first check-in was tomorrow, and in her four days of searching, she had precisely zero sightings of Azurrior. Now that she was making her way through the northernmost section of the territory, a gut feeling told her that was about to change. Azurrior was close. She could sense it.

Trees rustled to her left. Her heart skipped a beat as she looked to the steep, rocky hill with a scattering of trees. She saw the back of Javan's head instead of the dragon she sought. She desperately wanted to call out to Javan, but she swallowed the words before they could leave through her lips.

She was on her own. He was on his own. That's the way things had to be until they found their respective dragons.

She threw her frustration into her paddling and nearly tipped her raft. As she worked to regain her balance on the water, a high-pitched yelp pierced her ears. Someone or something up ahead was in a lot of pain.

◊   ◊   ◊

Javan collapsed at the top of the steep hill and took a swig of his water. Slightly more than a dollop dripped out. Great. He was going to have to find more water. At least that should be easy. He knew of a freshwater stream not too far away that was a good source of cool, clean water.

Finding dragons was a different story. Those Dusk Stalkers were so stinking fast that they were always gone by the time he got to where he thought he spotted them.

This whole quest was becoming more and more futile without the help of his friends or his dragons.

Knowing that Krystyn was after the dragons kept him searching for them both day and night. He would let himself sleep for one or two hours at a time, then continue searching for any sign of Starshade. The lack of sleep and constant walking through uneven terrain left him feeling exhausted and hopeless.

"Javan?" Micah approached Javan from his left. "Wow, man, you look terrible."

"Gee, thanks." Javan wished he could say the same about Micah, but the Hunter had a vibrant, energized demeanor. "What have you been doing that has you so invigorated? You haven't cut off any dragon's tails, have you?"

"Nah. Nothing like that. I've been following the Destroyer. I love the challenge of keeping up with her. She walks through these woods with a swiftness I have never seen before, and she's setting up brilliantly wicked traps everywhere around here. It's just a matter of time before the dragons get caught."

"Any chance you can tell me where the traps are so I can diffuse them?"

"There are too many. I've gone behind her and undone some of them but haven't been able to get to them all. Your best chance of finding Starshade first is to take to the sky. You need Varjiek."

"I know, but that's against the rules."

"I don't know why you want to follow rules that favor the Destroyer, but I'll do what I can to minimize the damage from the traps. If you don't do something different soon, though, both of those dragons are going to die."

"Hold her off for one more day. We'll reset the rules when we meet tomorrow."

"Javan!"

Javan stared at Micah. "Did you hear that?"

"Yeah. Sounds like Taliya."

"Javan, if you can hear me, come quick!"

"Krystyn's in the area as well," Micah said, "so we can't show up together. You go, and I'll watch from a distance unless I'm needed."

"Thanks." Javan threw his water bottle in his pack and raced in the direction of Taliya's voice.

◊   ◊   ◊

"Javan!" Taliya called for Javan one more time, hoping he was still close enough to her to hear. Then she softened her voice and focused on the growling dragon in front of her. "Hey, Starshade. What seems to be the problem?"

She whirled her long snout around, and Taliya barely dodged a stream of poison. When Starshade tried to turn her entire body toward Taliya, she yelped and spit more poison in the air. That's when Taliya realized Starshade's front foot was stuck in a hole and had been impaled by a spear. Two goats tied to a tree were bleating just out of Starshade's reach.

The hungry dragon had walked right into a trap.

"I can help you. I know you're in a lot of pain, but I can free your foot from that trap."

Starshade snapped at her. Taliya backed away. "How about I go get Javan? I saw him not too far from here."

"Sure," Krystyn said, stepping out of the shadows. "Go get Javan. But it won't matter. Even if you are able to get her out of that trap without her eating you or drenching you with poison, Javan can't ride a dragon with an injured foot."

Irritated that Krystyn was right, Taliya took a dart out of her pouch, dipped it in her paralyzing potion, and loaded it into her slingshot. "It's a good thing he won't need to."

Trusting that the dart was tipped with enough potion to knock the dragon out but not too much to kill her, Taliya shot Starshade.

CHAPTER 61

The Wrong Dragon

Micah rushed down the hill and immediately recognized the area. He didn't need to track Taliya's voice anymore. He knew where she would be. "Yo, Javan!" He caught up with Javan and grabbed his arm. "I think I know where we need to go. This is close to one of Krystyn's traps. Follow me."

He led Javan over a creek and through some brush. Before they reached the clearing where Krystyn left two goats surrounded by holes filled with makeshift spears, he pulled Javan to the ground. From there, they could see that Starshade was stuck on one of the spears. Krystyn was relaxed and laughing out of spitting range of the trapped Starshade while Taliya tried unsuccessfully to get close to the mad, hurt dragon.

"I have to help." Javan started to get up, but Micah yanked him back down.

"You can't ride her," Micah said. "Let Taliya handle this. She'll find a way to protect her."

"What is she doing?"

The guys watched as Taliya loaded a dart into her slingshot.

"She's gonna break the rules," Micah said. "She's gonna shoot Krystyn."

But she didn't aim at the Destroyer.

He blinked, not believing his eyes. Did Taliya really just shoot Starshade with one of her darts?

Starshade screeched, dropped leg by leg to the ground, and collapsed onto her right side. Her front left leg remained stuck in the shallow hole.

As soon as the dragon was down, Taliya ran over, climbed on her back, zipped across her body, crawled up her neck on her hands and knees, and plucked a scale from between her eyes. "Ha!" She yelled to Krystyn. "Starshade is protected. By me. Meaning you cannot kill her. I won."

Micah heard Javan gasp and watched as the Collector's face turned three shades of red.

"Taliya," Javan sprang out of hiding and growled, sounding like he had been caught in one of the Destroyer's traps. "What have you done?"

Taliya stopped smiling while Krystyn's laughter added to the tension. "Nicely done, Miss Dragon Protector." She clapped. "You protected the wrong dragon."

◊   ◊   ◊

"Javan, I can explain." Taliya lowered her hand that held the prized scale and slid to the ground. What *had* she done? How could she have stolen Javan's dragon? "It was the only way I could think of to save her."

"That's not much of an explanation."

"I didn't know what else to do. Starshade's foot was caught, and Krystyn was ready to whack her head off." She talked fast while her feet moved slowly toward Javan. "Even if you made it here sooner, you wouldn't have been able to ride her because she's basically fastened to the ground. You understand why I did what I did, right?"

"You sure *you* didn't kill her?" Javan asked. "She doesn't seem to be breathing."

"She'll be fine. She's just sleeping." She put her hand on Starshade's side to verify. Yup. Breathing. Whew. "The potion should wear off shortly, but I need to free her foot and patch it up before that happens. Will you help me? Please?"

"No, no, no," Krystyn said. "No teamwork allowed."

"That rule only applies when it comes to free dragons." Micah appeared from the other side of Starshade and stopped at her pierced foot. "This one is accounted for, so I don't see any problem with us working together to undo the damage you created."

"Thank you, Micah." Relieved, Taliya wrapped her fingers around Javan's wrist and made him walk with her over to Micah. She could see the tip of the spear poking through the top of the dragon's claw. "I need you two to lift Starshade's leg out of the hole. Once it's free, I'm going to ease the spear out, fill the cut with as much healing ointment as I can, and hope it's enough to block the bleeding."

"How much blood are we talking?" Javan pinched his finger close to his thumb. "A little? I can handle a little. A lot might make me pass out."

"Then you might not want to look until after I get her patched up." She sorted through her bag and traded Starshade's scale for healing ointment.

"Poor girl." Javan stroked her leg, and she moved her head.

"Uh oh," Taliya said. "She's starting to wake up. We need to act fast."

"I'm not touching her if she's awake," Micah said. "Let's do this now."

Positioning themselves on either side of her claw, Micah and Javan reached into the hole, placed their fingers under her claw, and attempted to lift up. Her paw only moved an inch or two. "What's the problem, guys? I need her paw out of there."

"We're trying," Javan said, "but it doesn't want to move."

The dragon's tail slapped the ground. "We better speed up this rescue mission." Taliya jumped onto the paw. "New plan. I'll pull the spear out, then you pull the leg up." She grabbed the spear, twisted it until it loosened a bit, and yanked it out.

Blood oozed out of the gap in the middle of the claw and covered Taliya's hands as she worked to plug the hole. "There. That should take care of the top. Now I need to patch the bottom." She leapt back to the dirt, let the guys lift the leg, and used the last of her ointment to fill the hole in the bottom of the paw.

"Done." Sticky dragon blood dripped from Taliya's hands and soaked her shirt. "I should probably wash off before she wakes up, smells me, and thinks I should be her evening meal. Javan, can you stay and stop her if she tries to walk on that foot? She has those goats over there to eat, and I'll gather some edible plants for her on my way back."

"I can't stay and watch your dragon. I have to get out there and find the dragon you were supposed to protect."

"You can't really be that upset, Javan. You were never able to connect with Starshade anyway."

"I would have gotten through to her eventually, but I guess we'll never know now, will we?"

"Might want to put this conversation on hold," Micah said. "We have company."

He pointed up, and Taliya looked into the fuming nostrils of Azurrior.

◊   ◊   ◊

Javan gaped at the deep blue scales covering Azurrior's neck. The remainder of his scales were still white, and that somehow made the blue scales appear to be even more blue.

Azurrior nudged Starshade. When she didn't respond, he glared at Javan. *What did you do to her?*

Javan stood, keeping his hands in front of him. "We're helping her. She got her foot stuck, and Taliya had to put her to sleep to help her."

He needed to keep Azurrior talking. This dragon was his final chance to collect a Dusk Stalker. Javan couldn't let him get away even if he was at the beginning of his feeding cycle. "She's going to need some food when she wakes up. Is there any particular kind of plant or berry or fruit that she likes we can bring to her?"

"I'll figure that out," Taliya said. "Azurrior, you need to get out of here now. Run!" She picked up a handful of rocks and dirt and threw it at the dragon. He roared, turned, and ran away.

"What is with you?" Javan yelled at Taliya. "First you steal my dragon, then you chase Azurrior away. I won't let you protect him, too. I need that dragon to win the throne, but now he's gone. Why are you sabotaging me?"

"Better gone than dead." She placed her blood-stained finger under his chin and forced him to look up. Krystyn hung from a branch with her axe dangling in the air near where Azurrior's head had been seconds ago.

"Oh." He knew he should apologize and thank Taliya, but he was too mad about losing Starshade to play nice.

"Why are you still standing there?" Taliya shoved him in the direction Azurrior ran. "Go collect Azurrior."

Since he couldn't think of anything else to say or do, he obeyed.

CHAPTER 62

So Much for Rules

Conflicting emotions raged within Taliya as she lost sight of Javan chasing Azurrior. Should she be happy that Starshade was safe? Guilty for protecting the dragon Javan wanted and not protecting the one she wanted? Angry with Krystyn for devising this insane battle?

The sight of Krystyn dropping out of the tree helped her decide on angry. "Did you seriously think you could kill a dragon with me standing right here?"

"That is the second time you have interfered." Krystyn put her axe in its scabbard on her back and marched to Taliya. "This time there are consequences."

"Oh, really?"

"Really." Krystyn punched Taliya in her gut. The shock of the blow caused Taliya to cough and bend over. Before she could breathe normally, Krystyn grabbed her hair, pulled her head back, and slammed her skull into Taliya's nose. Warm blood gushed from her nose, over her lips, and down her chin.

"Krystyn! No! Stop!"

Taliya heard Micah yelling, but Krystyn didn't listen. She threw the dazed Taliya to the ground and kicked her in the ribs. "Next time," she said, kicking her again and again, "keep your mouth closed."

Her self-defense system didn't seem to work, and all she could do was curl herself into a pathetic human ball to ward off the painful blows.

◊　　◊　　◊

Micah watched in helpless horror as Krystyn kicked Taliya. Why couldn't he move?

Because her outburst of cruelty reminded him...of him. How often had he beaten up someone weaker for the tiniest of infractions simply to assert his power? The flashbacks shamed him. But that was then. This was now. Now he could do something to stop a needless beating.

"Enough." His command stopped Krystyn mid-kick.

"She deserved every bruise."

He pulled out his sword. "Leave or fight someone who's ready to fight back."

"Tempting challenge. But there is a Dusk Stalker out there who still has his head. I need to change that before I deal with you for interfering in my lesson." She winked at him and dashed away.

"Taliya." He rushed to her side and gently touched her cheek. "Are you okay?"

She flinched and opened her eyes. "Never better."

"Yeah, right." He smiled and lifted her into a sitting position. "I'm sorry I didn't stop her sooner. It's just that...well..." How could he explain his hesitation?

"You stopped her before she killed me, so that's a plus. Go do the same for Azurrior. Don't let her get to him."

"I can't leave you here like this. You're covered in blood."

"You can and you will. Most of this blood isn't even mine, and there's nothing you can do to fix my bruises. But you can help make sure Javan rides Azurrior."

"It sounds like you're telling me to team up with the Collector. Isn't that against the rules?"

"Krystyn broke the rules when she broke my nose."

"Good point." He stood and sheathed his sword. "Stay safe."

"You, too."

He nodded and took off. He had some serious running to do if he hoped to catch up to Javan.

◊　　◊　　◊

Taliya fought the urge to lay down and bemoan her injuries, injuries which paled in comparison to Starshade's impaled foot and damaged leg. That thought encouraged her to stand and focus on the dragon. Her dragon. The one dragon she had the privilege of looking after for the rest of her life.

"You get to live free," Taliya said, dragging her fingers along the row of spiked scales that lined Starshade's spine starting with her tail. "Your missing scale brands you as a protected dragon. It doesn't make you invincible, though. You're still as susceptible as any other dragon to being beheaded, enslaved, or ridden. But because you are protected by me, no one from another Bloodline can use you to help them claim the throne.

"No Destroyer is permitted to kill you. No Hunter can control you. No Collector can overpower you. You get to run wild, unencumbered by anyone attempting to win the throne.

"But not every Destroyer, Hunter, or Collector wants to win the throne." She paused as she considered the sad reality of what she was about to say. "Sometimes they want to conquer dragons just for sport, and they won't care if you have been branded as protected or not. I am here to make sure that doesn't happen to you, especially since your rarity as a Dusk Stalker may make you a prized target.

"I'll come check on you from time to time and will be sure to watch over you when you shed your scales. Predators you usually hunt will be hunting you when you're vulnerable and without scales. That's another way I help. It's my job to make sure you are protected from such threats."

She traced Starshade's pointy ears and noted her closed eyes. "You are not going to be happy when you wake up. The pain plus hunger is going to put you in a nasty mood. I won't be able to do much for the pain, but I can make sure you have plenty to eat. There's just one thing I want to do before I clean myself up and gather food for you."

She walked around the dragon's long snout and threw her arms as far around Starshade's neck as they would go. She wouldn't ever have another chance to hug her dragon. This would be a moment she would remember forever.

CHAPTER 63

Javan Surprises Taliya

Javan didn't think chasing a Dusk Stalker on foot would do a bit of good, but he ran after Azurrior anyway. The exercise helped him burn his angry energy, and he needed to put some distance between him and Taliya.

After about a mile, he spotted a half blue Azurrior and followed the dragon's trail for another mile. The dense trees on the hilly terrain slowed the speedy dragon down. He also stopped occasionally to eat patches of poison ivy that grew in abundance on and around the trees.

Javan didn't dare approach Azurrior while he was focused on food and hoped he would be able to track him during the duration of his feeding cycle. Then Javan could approach him and attempt to have a rational conversation. That conversation would in theory end with Javan on Azurrior's back.

A twig snapped behind Javan. He glanced back and glimpsed Krystyn. Not good. Maybe he should stop following Azurrior. He didn't want to lead Krystyn straight to the dragon.

"Why did you stop moving?"

Javan instinctively drew his swords and pointed them in the direction of the whispered voice to his right. The points of both swords dug into Micah's shirt. "Dude." Javan let out a deep breath and put his swords away. He kept his voice low to make sure the dragon ahead of him and the Destroyer approaching from behind couldn't hear. "You can't go sneaking around like that. I almost killed you."

"I'm impressed with how fast you drew your swords. Nicely done."

"What are you doing here?"

"I came to help you."

"Well, don't. I have to do this on my own."

"Not anymore. After the stunt Krystyn pulled, all rules are off."

"What stunt?"

"The details aren't important. What is important is that Krystyn spent a lot of time baiting a nasty trap north of here. She's got endless amounts of poison ivy covering a huge nest of red and yellow bugs."

"Azurrior loves poison ivy. He's been eating it all along the way."

"We have to stop him before he bites into that nest. I'm not sure what those bugs are, but I can guarantee they aren't harmless flies."

"No need to rush, fellas." Krystyn walked between them and slapped both on the back as she passed. "Azurrior is too far ahead for you to catch him, and he's too hungry to avoid that tempting ivy. Once he takes that first bite, he's as good as dead."

The dragon slithered out of view. Javan ran after him, yelling at him to stop eating.

◊ ◊ ◊

Taliya added another armful of juicy orb balls to the pile of leaves, nuts, and vines in front of the two goats near Starshade. "There." She brushed the dirt off her arms and wiped at the sweat threatening to sting her eyes. "That should be plenty for you to eat."

Yet Starshade continued to sleep even after receiving the antidote. Had Taliya gotten the dosage wrong? Why wasn't she awake yet?

The one thing that kept Taliya from panicking was the color of Starshade's scales. They continued to change from white to beautiful swirls of green and purple with a few random streaks of blue. That meant she was still alive, but Taliya wanted her to wake up and eat. She wasn't sure what would happen if the dragon woke up past her designated feeding time.

"Come on, girl." She nudged her stomach, not daring to get close to her mouth. "I need you to wake up."

"Good." Javan appeared out of nowhere. "You're still here."

"Whoa." Taliya stumbled into the dragon's body and put her hand over her chest. "Javan. You scared me. I hate it when you pop in on me like that."

"It can't be helped." A concerned look washed over his face as he walked over to her. "What's wrong with your nose?"

"This?" She tenderly touched her sore nose. She had tried snapping the bone back in place when she washed the blood off in a stream but couldn't quite get the leverage she needed to make it move. "This was Krystyn's way of showing her appreciation for my encouraging Azurrior to run from her."

"Are you okay?"

"Other than being a touch tender, yeah." She didn't feel the need to tell him about her bruised ribs. "Why are you here? You should be chasing Azurrior, not talking to me."

"Azurrior's the reason I'm here. I need you to come with me." He stretched out the hand that wasn't holding his teleporting sword. "Please."

The pleading in his pained eyes said more than his words. Something was wrong. Terribly, terribly wrong.

◇　◇　◇

Javan resisted the urge to grab Taliya's hand and teleport her back to that awful scene. But he needed her to stay calm and clear her mind if he had any chance of teleporting them both. "Please," he said again. "Azurrior's in trouble, and he needs your help."

"What kind of trouble?"

"It's easier to show you." She would panic if he told her about the crazed bugs swarming the dragon and wiggled his fingers. "We need to hurry."

"Okay." She placed her hand in his.

"Thank you." He wrapped his fingers around her palm. Closed his eyes. Concentrated on the ledge he had just come from.

"Shouldn't we start walking?"

He looked around and saw they hadn't gone anywhere. "I'm trying to teleport us. Can you close your eyes and clear your mind?"

"I'll try."

"Thanks." He waited for her to close her eyes, then tried teleporting them again. Once again, they went nowhere.

"I'm sorry," she said. "I'm not good at shutting off my mind. I'm worried about Starshade and have no idea what's happening to Azurrior. We should probably start walking."

"There's no time for that!" He could only think of one way to distract her. The hard part would be keeping his own mind focused on where they needed to go.

As she opened her mouth to speak again, he covered her lips with his.

CHAPTER 64

Fire Wings

Micah stepped in front of Krystyn and drew his sword. "You're going to have to get past me before you can get near that dragon."

"No need for such heroics." She shrugged and sat on the ledge of the small cliff. Below them, Azurrior roared and yelped as he battled a swarm of buzzing insects that had yellow bodies and red wings. "I want the dragon to die, not me. I'll wait for the creatures to do their job, which could take a few hours. Then I'll finish the dragon off once he's close to death. I certainly don't want those things crawling on me. They'll kill me a lot faster than they will the dragon."

"How can you be this cold and cruel?"

"I've seen how cold and cruel dragons can be. They don't deserve to live. None of them do."

"What happened to you? Did a dragon kill your parents or something?"

She sat up straighter and pursed her lips, indicating that she was done talking. The Wordless Wonder had returned.

Micah hoped Javan would return as well. He needed to get down there and save that dragon. The fate of the Land of Zandador depended on it.

◊   ◊   ◊

Taliya startled when Javan's lips met hers. She naturally closed her eyes and surrendered to the soft touch. All thoughts of dragons washed out of her mind, and she thought of nothing except the pleasure of being connected to Javan.

In the next instant, she felt herself swirling through the air. The swirling stopped when Javan pulled back. Which left her off balance. And in a different place.

Buzzing and screeching hurt her ears, ruining the moment. "Where are we? What is that noise?"

"Down there." Javan kept his arm around her and pointed at the world below them with his sword. "Do you know what those bugs are and how to get rid of them?"

She gasped at the sight of Azurrior paralyzed by a swarm of yellow and red insects. "Oh, no. Fire wings."

Krystyn clapped beside her. "The girl knows her bugs."

"What are fire wings?" Micah asked.

"They're like ticks with wings. They attach to your skin, suck your blood, and fly away when they get full. Then another one takes its place. They'll burrow under Azurrior's scales and literally suck the life out of him."

"It's a long, slow, painful process," Krystyn said. "And there's nothing you can do to stop it."

"Actually, there is." Taliya turned her back to Krystyn and focused on Javan. "You have to get on him. Ride him north to the marshland. Make him bathe in the swampy mud."

"What good will that do?"

"They use their wings to extract the blood. If their wings can't flap, they can't suck any blood. Drowning them in mud is the only way to save Azurrior."

"Won't those things crawl on me, too?"

"Unfortunately, yes. You just have to make Azurrior run as fast as he can. He has to get you to the mud before the fire wings suck the life out of you."

Taliya watched the fear take over Javan's eyes. He was ready to bolt, and not in the direction that would save Azurrior. What could she say to convince him to put his own life on the line to save the life of the dragon?

◊   ◊   ◊

"This can't be happening." Javan ran his fingers through his hair and tried unsuccessfully to ignore that dreadful buzzing from the blood-sucking bugs. How had his life come to this point? Even if he could save Azurrior, would he be able to get to the mud in time to save himself? "I don't think I can do this."

"Of course you can't," Krystyn said. "Only a suicidal fool would risk jumping on the back of a hungry, hurting dragon and into a swarm of insects eager to drain his blood."

"Of course you *can*." Taliya squeezed his wrist and pulled him away from Krystyn and Micah. "You're the only one who can do this. All you have to do is jump on him from that tree he's standing under and tell him to run like his life depends on it. Because it does.

"This isn't about winning the throne. This is about saving one dragon's life, a dragon who wouldn't even be alive if it wasn't for you. Much to my dismay, you've had a special bond with him before he even hatched. Are you really going to stand here and listen to him die?"

As if on cue, Azurrior let out a wail that tore through Javan's heart.

"I just have to get him to the mud?"

She put her hands on his cheeks. "You just have to get him to the mud."

He took a deep breath, put his hands over hers, and nodded. "Pray for me."

"I will."

"If I fail—"

"Stop that sentence. You're going to succeed." She wrapped her arms around him, squeezed, and pulled back. "You have to go. Now."

"Yes, ma'am." He sighed and took off down the hill, thankful that even if this insane adventure didn't have a happy ending, at least he got his first kiss out of it.

CHAPTER 65

Into the Swarm

"Is he down there yet?" Taliya wondered what was taking Javan so long to get to the tree, but it was a steep hill, and it had only been five minutes. In that time, though, the buzzing from the bugs became louder, and the wailing from Azurrior became more agonized. She needed Javan to hurry. "Why isn't he down there yet?"

"He's got time," Micah said. "Krystyn said it could take hours for those things to kill Azurrior. Javan will get to him way before then."

"That doesn't make me feel any better." She paced along the ledge and kept her eyes on the ground. Most of Azurrior's scales were a deep, translucent blue with a dash of pink here and there. He had to be starving but was too traumatized by the fire wings to eat or move. She wanted to help but knew the best thing she could do was nothing.

"He made it." Micah tapped Taliya's arm. "He's climbing the tree."

Taliya dropped to her knees as Javan did the same. She stayed riveted in one spot as she watched him crawl across the thick branch that dangled over the back of Azurrior. When he looked like he was ready to jump, she closed her eyes and prayed to Javan's God.

◊   ◊   ◊

Javan wobbled over Azurrior on the weakening branch of the oak tree. The dragon was beginning to look more yellow and red than his natural blue thanks to the insects flying on and around him. None of the fire wings noticed Javan yet, but their buzzing was too loud to give him a chance to communicate with Azurrior. Javan was just going to have to pray and jump.

"God," he prayed, looking skyward, "I know this is the stupidest thing I have ever done, but I'd be ever so grateful if You could keep me safe. I'd prefer not to die today." Unsure how God would choose to answer his prayer, Javan launched himself out of the tree and toward Azurrior.

The dragon jerked to the left as Javan fell. He barely managed to catch Azurrior's neck, and he clawed his feet up the dragon's side through the swarm of fire wings. Sharp pinches pricked his skin as he fought to position himself at the base of Azurrior's neck.

Fear gripped the dragon's mind, jumbling his thoughts.

"Run, Azurrior!" Javan spit a bug out of his mouth and yelled again. "Get out of here. Now!"

The dragon didn't respond. Or move.

◊   ◊   ◊

Taliya winced as she watched Javan struggle to secure his seat on top of the dragon. Bugs were swarming over his arms and legs and neck. If those things killed him, it would be her fault. She's the one who convinced him to run right to them.

His screams added to the chorus of buzzing and wailing. What had she done?

No. That was the wrong question. She needed to be asking herself what she could do now. How could she get Azurrior to run?

"I don't really want to watch poor Javan die." Krystyn stood, sending a dusting of pebbles and sand over the edge. "I'm going to take a little nap while those bugs finish their feast. Wake me when he's dead, will you?" She waved and wandered off, but her dusty departure gave Taliya an idea.

"Rocks, Micah. Pick them up and throw them." She picked up a rock half the size of her fist, loaded it into her sling, and aimed it at Azurrior's rear. "We have to startle him enough to get him to move."

"Doubt that will do much good, but it's better than standing here doing nothing."

As Micah hunted for rocks, she released her first shot. It hit its target and caused Azurrior to roar and fling his front legs in the air. He still didn't move, so Taliya shot him again, this time with a bigger rock. "Run, Azurrior. Run or die!"

CHAPTER 66

The Perfect Name

Javan dug his fingers around several of Azurrior's scales and hung on tight as the dragon raised up on his back legs the way his horse Storm used to do. Javan stayed on then, and he stayed on now. What felt like rocks pelted his back, and he heard the dragon grunt when something solid hit his side.

Whatever it was got Azurrior's attention. Rather than merely buck up, he took a few steps forward. "That's it. Keep going. Just move a whole lot faster!"

He stumbled toward the woods to his right. "No. Not that way. Straight ahead. We need to go north."

Hard to move. A coherent thought broke through the confusion. *Pain everywhere.*

"I feel it, too." Another bug pinched the skin behind his ear. "You have to move. Work through the pain. Get us to the marshland. Diving into the swampy mud there is the only way to get these creatures off of us."

They'll come off in the mud?

"Yes."

Without another word or warning, Azurrior launched forward.

◊   ◊   ◊

"That's the wrong way." Taliya screeched when Azurrior dashed to the east and cheered when he corrected course and shot to the north. Once he was out of sight, she breathed a sigh of relief and walked over to Krystyn. True to her word, she had perched herself beside a tree and appeared to be taking a nap.

"You lost." Taliya kicked Krystyn's legs to wake her up. "Azurrior is a warrior. It's in his name. He's on his way to get those despicable insects off of him with a Collector on his back. By the time they reach the swamp, he'll be a part of Javan's collection."

"Yeah," she said, her eyes remaining closed, "I'm not worried about that."

"You should be," Micah said. "Javan is riding Azurrior as we speak. You do understand that's all he needs to do to win the battle."

"He kind of needs to survive as well." Krystyn smiled and finally opened her eyes so that they met Taliya's. "I do believe you've miscalculated the distance to the swamp. It's a good fifty miles from here. Even if the dragon makes it that far—which he might—skinny little Javan never will. Those bugs will have him drained dry before one hair of his touches the mud."

"Fifty miles?" Taliya's chest felt like it had a boa constrictor squeezing it. She thought they were only about ten or twelve miles away from the swamp. That was a tricky but reasonable distance to travel.

Even fifty miles wouldn't be that big of a deal if Azurrior could cover the distance at his top speed, but he wouldn't be able to run fast with hundreds of fire wings sucking his blood with every step. And Javan didn't have nearly as much blood as Azurrior.

In other words, Taliya sent Javan to his death.

◊　　◊　　◊

To keep the fire wings from flying into his mouth, Javan kept his lips sealed. Soon the pain from the bug bites was replaced by an overwhelming weakness. At the same time, Azurrior's sprint turned to a jog. Which turned to a walk. Which slowed to a stop.

Javan leaned his body against Azurrior as the dragon's heart slowed. "Stay with me, buddy," Javan whispered.

Azurrior's head drooped. His front two legs collapsed.

"No. You can't die. You've barely begun to live. Even if I don't make it, you have to keep going. Save yourself. Please."

Javan lost the thumpity-thump feel of the dragon's heartbeat. He wanted to sob, but he was too tired.

A fire wing landed on Azurrior's neck in front of Javan's nose. "At least one of you is going to die with us." Javan crushed it with his fist. That felt so good he crushed another one. And another.

Thumpity-thump. Thumpity-thump.

"Azurrior?"

The dragon stood, lifted his head. *That was strange.* His heart began beating stronger and faster than before. And it was beating in sync with Javan's.

"I think we just bonded."

I'm not sure what just happened, but I feel different. Better. Stronger.

"I'm still feeling pretty weak, so how about you keep running?"

As you wish. Azurrior roared and took off.

The last thing Javan remembered seeing was the azure of the sunset sky set against the azure of Azurrior's scales. "You really do have the perfect name," Javan said. Then smelly mud smothered his face.

CHAPTER 67

United

Taliya lagged behind Micah and Krystyn on the hike back towards Starshade. Images of Javan looped through her mind. The first time she saw him in her humminglo field. The night he learned he could become invisible. The mercy he displayed when he spared Micah's life.

She also recalled the way his bright green eyes danced when he laughed, how he brushed his fingers through his hair whenever he was scared or nervous, and the confidence he exuded every time he spoke to a dragon. The most dominant memory, however, was the most recent. She would never forget the feel of those tender lips on hers as they simultaneously teleported from one spot to another.

"Taliya," Micah said, drawing her back to the present, "I see Starshade up ahead."

"Is she sitting or standing?"

"I can't tell. We'll set up camp here while you go check on her."

"Cool." Taliya worked her way through the moonlit path and entered the clearing. Starshade's scales had returned to white, and she was sitting up. The goats and pile of food Taliya left for her were gone. "I trust you got enough to eat."

The dragon nodded.

"Foot still hurt?"

She nodded again.

"It will take some time to heal. Will you let me check it?"

She jerked her head back and covered her hurt claw with her good one.

"I'll take that as a no. How about this? You let me bring you food every evening until you're able to walk on that leg again. Once you're good, I'll leave you alone."

A hesitation. Then a nod.

Taliya smiled, thankful to be communicating with her dragon. But her happiness was obscured by an emptiness. What good would protecting a dragon do without Javan around? She thought she needed a dragon to protect to serve a purpose. What she really needed was to belong, to be part of a team. More specifically, she needed to be part of Javan's team.

She never should have let him go anywhere near Azurrior and those fire wings. He was dead because of her.

No. He was dead because of Krystyn. She's the one who set the trap. She's the one who needed to be punished.

◊   ◊   ◊

Micah tossed a piece of bread to Krystyn, who was sitting tied to a tree across from him. "Eat up."

"I'll eat after you untie me."

"You're perfectly capable of eating as is, which is why I tied your hands in front of you." He threw more sticks on the fire and began sifting through the food left in his pack. Not that it did much good. He didn't feel much like eating anything after the fire bug attack.

"Listen, there's no point in keeping me with you anymore. Javan's gone, and the battle's over. Let me go."

"Hmmm...no." Keeping her tied up was the only thing giving him the tiniest bit of satisfaction in the wake of Javan's untimely departure.

"I'll tell Omri you're dead. You can go back to Gibbet and live the rest of your life free from a father who wants you gone."

"That's the problem." He zipped up his bag, forgetting about food. "You know about the village in Gibbet. Letting you go would endanger everyone there."

"No, it won't." She grunted. "What will it take to convince you I don't care to see people die. Dragons are the creatures I hate."

"I'm still waiting for you to explain that hatred to me. I also don't understand why you would want to return to Omri and his oppressive ways."

She lifted her tethered hands. "He doesn't tie me to trees."

"I think there's more to it than that. I think he's holding something over you. I want to know what it is."

"I don't care what it is," Taliya stormed into the campsite. "She's responsible for Javan's death and needs to pay. Untie her from that tree, Micah. We're gonna take her to the Zandadorian portal and send her to the Land of No Return."

"Whoa, Taliya." Micah inserted himself between Taliya and Krystyn. "I'm not her biggest fan, either, but isn't the Land of No Return a bit much. She didn't know Javan was going to get caught in her trap."

"That doesn't matter. She should have thought it through. Untie her!" Taliya burst into tears. Micah pulled her into his arms and held her shaking body while she sobbed against his chest.

◊   ◊   ◊

Hours later, Taliya still felt cold despite the warm fire. Micah cooked some soup, but she had only eaten two bites. She simply wasn't hungry. With midnight approaching, she wasn't tired either. "I'm going to find more fire wood."

"Taliya, wait." Micah held up his arms. "Do you hear that?"

"Hear what?" She trained her ears on the woods around her. An owl hooted. Leaves rustled in the wind. Branches snapped. That snapping definitely wasn't a natural sound of the night. "Something's coming."

Micah nodded and drew his sword. She armed her slingshot and prepared to shoot the large animal walking toward them. As it got closer, a rotten odor attacked her nose. "Is that...Azurrior?"

"Looks like it." Micah put his sword away. "He stinks."

"You would too if you took a mud bath in the marshlands. Let's hope Javan's on him."

They carefully approached the dragon who was covered in dried mud. The hope in her heart drowned when she saw he had no rider on his back. "I'm glad you made it, boy." As she choked out the words, she heard a man moan. "Micah, he doesn't smell that bad. There's no need to groan about it."

"That wasn't me."

"It was me." A foul-smelling, muddy Javan sat up in the middle of Azurrior's curled tail. "Meet the newest dragon in my collection."

"Aren't Collectors supposed to ride on their dragon's backs?"

"Typically, yes. But after they've had half their blood sucked out of them by vampire bugs and then nearly suffocated in mud, they find that being dragged along on the tail is a more manageable way to travel."

"Is that so?"

"Yup." He waved her over. When she got close, he said, "I never would have had the courage to collect him without you. He'd be dead, and the Land of Zandador would be stuck with Omri for the next five centuries. Thank you."

"You're welcome." She smiled and hugged him, stinky mud and all. He didn't have the ability to return her embrace, but she didn't mind. He was alive!

"Now where's Krystyn? I need to talk to her. Please tell me she's still with you guys."

"She is." She couldn't wait to hear Javan rip into Krystyn for what she did. "We'll take you to her."

Taliya and Micah helped Javan to his feet. They became human crutches for Javan as they walked to the tree where Krystyn was tied. "How did you survive?" Krystyn asked, her back pressed against the tree.

"By the grace of God," Javan said. "Now before we leave, you will undo every other trap you set so this territory is once again safe for Starshade. Micah will go with you to make sure they are properly taken apart."

"I'll go as well," Taliya said. "I'll want to see for myself that the threats have been diffused."

"That could take a few days," Krystyn said.

"No problem." Javan swayed and readjusted his grip on Taliya's shoulders. "It will take me a few days to regain my strength, anyway. Then the four of us will head to Midnight Territory with our dragons as well as Kenton and Ravier. What I need to know now is this: what kind of traps can you come up with when you have a team helping?"

"They'll have to be much more sophisticated than anything I put together here. Ayzyd is centuries old and highly intelligent. Luring her into any kind of trap will not be easy."

"Nothing about this entire process has been easy. Just tell us what you need, and we'll make it happen." Javan kept his right arm on Taliya's shoulders and stretched his left hand to Krystyn. "Welcome to the team."

"Joining you isn't exactly my big dream in life, but you did win, and a deal's a deal." She shook Javan's hand with both of hers. "You're my new boss."

"Hands in, everyone," Javan said. "Let's take a moment to celebrate the unification of the four Dragon Stalker Bloodlines."

"I never thought this day would come." Micah placed his hand on top of Javan's and Krystyn's. "But I'm glad I'm a part of it."

"Same." Taliya added her hand to the pile, but she felt more apprehension than enthusiasm.

Krystyn winked at her. "Guess we'll have to postpone that trip to the Land of No Return."

"Guess so." Taliya did not wink back or smile. She stared into the Destroyer's wicked eyes, wondering what kind of trouble she would cause in the final stage of the Battle of the Throne.

EPILOGUE

Krystyn kept a smile pasted on her face as she squeezed Javan's hand. She wasn't thrilled that he had survived, but she could make this development work in her favor. She would honor her agreement with the Collector. And she would slay every Midnight Stalker they came across.

Every. Last. One.

Her job was to ensure Omri remained on the throne. What better way to do that than to sabotage the only one who could take it from him?

She would make sure Javan failed and thus earn the power Omri promised her as the Queen of Tirza.

NOVELS BY D.K. DRAKE

The Dragon Stalker Bloodlines Saga

BOOK 1: **The Dragon Collector**
BOOK 2: **The Dragon Hunter**
BOOK 3: **The Dragon Protector**
BOOK 4: **The Dragon Destroyer** *(coming soon)*

ABOUT THE AUTHOR

D.K. Drake brings you entertaining, engaging, wholesome adventures too packed with action to leave room for eye-rolling sappiness or mind-numbing fluff.

She is a Christian, a foster parent, and an avid runner. One of her goals is to run some sort of race in every state and (almost) every continent (no thanks, ice-covered Antarctica!).

She lives with two of her sisters in the great state of North Carolina and encourages you to trust God, believe in yourself, and fight for your dreams.

Get Exclusive Access to More {FREE} Stories Today!

Want to know a secret? Then come a little closer. That's it. Now lean in. Listen closely with your eyes because I'm typing these words with a whisper...

D.K. Drake doesn't exist.

I made her up. Just like I make up the characters in my books. In other words, D.K. Drake is my pen name. Why did I choose to write under this pen name? What do the "D" and "K" stand for? What is my true identity?

I answer all those questions and more for those who want to be email buddies.

When you become one of my email buddies, you get FREE access to the D.K. Drake starter library that includes the short story "Cops, Robbers...and Dragons?" (This is the story that sparked the idea for the entire Saga!)

You'll also get notified about new books and deals, have a chance to join the Advanced Reader Team, and keep up with my real-life adventures as an author, a runner, and a foster parent. All you have to do is visit www.AuthorDKDrake.com and sign up to the Insiders mailing list for FREE today.

A PERSONAL STORY
FROM THE AUTHOR

I love making up stories and living in the world of my imagination. But the story I most enjoy sharing is the true story of the day I accepted Jesus Christ as my Savior. So I want to share that story with you now...

As I listened to my mother read the Bible to me and my three older sisters before bed that night, I realized something important: I was a sinner.

I may have only been four years old, but I knew right from wrong. I knew it was a lot easier to choose to do the wrong thing than to do the right thing. I knew when I did something wrong, I got in trouble.

I knew my natural tendency was to tell lies to cover my mistakes. I knew my natural tendency was to be impolite to those in authority over me. I knew my natural tendency was to be selfish rather than look out for others.

So when I heard that "all have sinned and fall short of the glory of God (Romans 3:23)," I knew that verse was talking about me. I had sinned. That meant I had fallen short of God's glory.

When I heard that "the wages of sin is death, but the gift of God is eternal life in Christ Jesus our Lord (Romans 6:23)," I knew I was deserving of death but wanted God's gift of eternal life.

When I heard that Jesus said, "I am the way, the truth and the life. No one comes to the Father except through Me (John 14:6)," I understood that believing in Jesus was the only way to experience that eternal life and see the kingdom of God.

So when my mother finished reading the Bible that night, I asked her what I needed to do to be saved.

She sent my sisters to bed and sat down with me with her Bible open. She made sure I understood I was a sinner in need of God's forgiving grace. She made sure I understood that salvation comes by grace through faith, not by anything I do.

I told her I understood and wanted to ask God to save me. We thus knelt side by side along the couch, and she prayed with me as I asked God to forgive me and save me.

Then something wonderful happened: God saved me! The instant I asked for salvation, I felt His presence wash over me. I felt different. Renewed. Alive. I didn't quite understand it at the time, but now I realize that presence I felt was the Holy Spirit. He came to reside in my soul at that moment, and He has never and will never   leave.

I was still a sinner, but now I was a sinner saved by grace. My sin nature still lived in me, but now so did God in the person of the Holy Spirit. Now I was equipped to fight my sin nature, and the battle between my fleshly desires and my Godly desires is a battle that will rage within me until the day I die.

As I fight that battle, I have learned to structure my life in such a way that allows me to stand strong in Christ. I do that by making seeking Him, serving Him, and sharing Him my number one priority in life.

I find great comfort, joy, and delight in living for God and obeying His commandments. I am far from perfect and still get derailed from time to time. I have made more mistakes in my life than I care to admit and have disappointed my God in ways that break my heart to recall.

But I serve a gracious, forgiving, loving God. He made me. He saved me. And he gave me gifts to use, dreams to pursue, and people to love along the way.

That's what makes life fun. Seeking God. Serving God. Sharing God. And loving others.

If you haven't experienced the kind of fun, peace, and joy that comes from knowing God, I encourage you to open your Bible and seek Him today.

Don't have a Bible or aren't sure how to seek God? Then contact me by sending an email to dk@authordkdrake.com. I would love to hear from you!

AUTHORDKDRAKE.COM

www.ingramcontent.com/pod-product-compliance
Lightning Source LLC
Chambersburg PA
CBHW030035180626
46810CB00001B/382